DEATH AT HORSEY MERE

ROSS GREENWOOD

B

Boldwood

First published in Great Britain in 2025 by Boldwood Books Ltd.

Copyright © Ross Greenwood, 2025

Cover Design by Head Design Ltd

Cover Images: Alamy and iStock

The moral right of Ross Greenwood to be identified as the author of this work has been asserted in accordance with the Copyright, Designs and Patents Act 1988.

Every effort has been made to obtain the necessary permissions with reference to copyright material, both illustrative and quoted. We apologise for any omissions in this respect and will be pleased to make the appropriate acknowledgements in any future edition.

A CIP catalogue record for this book is available from the British Library.

Paperback ISBN 978-1-80549-731-8

Large Print ISBN 978-1-80549-732-5

Hardback ISBN 978-1-80549-729-5

Ebook ISBN 978-1-80549-733-2

Kindle ISBN 978-1-80549-734-9

Audio CD ISBN 978-1-80549-725-7

MP3 CD ISBN 978-1-80549-726-4

Digital audio download ISBN 978-1-80549-727-1

This book is printed on certified sustainable paper. Boldwood Books is dedicated to putting sustainability at the heart of our business. For more information please visit https://www.boldwoodbooks.com/about-us/sustainability/

Boldwood Books Ltd, 23 Bowerdean Street, London, SW6 3TN

www.boldwoodbooks.com

For Breakers Café
Gone but not forgotten.

NORFOLK MAJOR INVESTIGATION TEAM STRUCTURE

Detective Superintendent
Zara Grave

Detective Chief Inspector
Vince Kettle

Detective Inspector
Ashley Knight

Detective Sergeants
Jan Pederson – Emma Stones – Bhavini Kotecha (Maternity)

Sergeant
Hector Fade

Detective Constables
Barry Hooper – Sal Freitas – Morgan Golding – Zelda Cartwright

Family Liaison Officer
Scott Gorton

Twinned Detective Team Sergeant
Ally Williamson (Suspended)

Forensic Pathologist
Michelle Ma Yun

When the sun comes up, I couldn't tell where heaven stopped and the earth began.

— FORREST GUMP

Sometimes it's hard to tell the difference between gods and monsters.

— HECTOR FADE

1

For the past few months, the wings of a giant, trapped butterfly had been beating against the inside of Akari's chest. A fluttering that was most active at night. How could she sleep or even relax when life was finally about to begin? Her best friend, Camille, must have felt Akari's eyes on her because she looked across. They gazed at each other and shared huge toothy grins. Camille was ready, too.

Camille indicated right and turned her red Fiat 500 convertible down Newmarket Road, top down even though the air still had a nip to it. Akari's concern about catching a cold had been met with Camille's laughter, a playful punch, and a holler.

'We're young!'

The nippy car raced through the last of the blossom, blowing it around them, giving the sensation of driving through pink snowflakes. Like a scene from the movies.

Akari forced herself to focus on the moment. Her mother constantly reminded her of just how fortunate she was. Cruising along a tree-lined avenue on a beautiful late-May Sunday afternoon in a brand-new electric car, with Oxford University on the horizon, meant Akari knew it was hard to disagree.

She punched the air. 'Young and in love!'

'Oh my God, Akari, I'm sorry,' said Camille. 'You were telling me about Damian, and I went off on a rant about my idiot boyfriend. Ex-boyfriend.'

'That's okay.'

'So, why hasn't Damian decided on taking a year out?'

Akari thought of Damian and almost pinched herself. He'd already been the most popular boy at school when her family had arrived in Norwich a few months after senior school had started. She'd spoken to him only a few times over the following years, but when they'd begun their A-levels, she'd found herself sitting next to him in Biology and Chemistry. Their shared dream of becoming doctors had fuelled a spark.

Last summer, Camille had dyed her hair black, and Akari had changed her dark hair to blonde. Camille had reckoned she resembled a sickly Goth and had been blonde again four days later, but Akari loved her new golden locks. The contrast with her brown eyes and sandy skin immediately caught many an appreciative eye.

During that holiday period, the girls had also convinced their parents to pay for a make-up course run by a woman in Norwich who had worked in Hollywood. When Akari had returned to their private school for her final year, she'd had armour.

The response from her desk buddy, Damian, had been instant, even though he'd resisted until just before Easter. His girlfriend of four years, poor thing, had fought a valiant but doomed battle, and Akari had emerged victorious.

Akari's face flushed as she recalled her and Damian's last

night together. She pushed the heady memories away and thought of what he wanted.

'He said nine months away from me is too much, and I should take a year off and go with him.'

'Right. Backpacking around Australia and working on farms is such a boy thing. You could always meet him for a holiday in Sydney at Christmas.'

'That's what I said, but he's worried I'll meet someone else at uni and break his heart forever.'

'Yuck! We know what he's after.'

'Camille!'

'I've got a *great* idea for what to give him as a little going-away present.'

'What?'

'A large slice of your cherry pie!'

'Camille!'

Akari protested, but her heart and head had been screaming for months she was ready. Times were changing. Being a bright girl, and having read plenty of Shakespeare, she understood love was a shifting tide with no guarantees, but the moment had come with Damian, and she'd taken it.

'My mum tried to talk to me about having sex,' she said.

Camille's nose wrinkled. 'Double yuck, although it would have been worse coming from your dad.'

Akari laughed. 'It would take my father a thousand years to navigate around that topic. What about you and Barney? Are you really over?'

Camille sneered. 'Yup. There's no way I was allowing Mr Bonehead to deflower me. He'd probably want the football team to cheer him on during his performance. I know it's old-fashioned, but I like the idea of waiting until your wedding night.'

'I'm struggling to wait until prom night.'

They giggled together as Camille stopped just past the entrance to Akari's house. Camille rested a hand on her best friend's leg.

'I'll pick you up for the cinema from here tomorrow. I love your mum, but if I go down the drive, the gravel will give me away, and I'll never escape.'

The street was empty. Most of the houses had triple garages, so nobody parked on the road. It gave the area a prestigious feel. Akari's father often commented on their green and peaceful neighbourhood.

'Shall we stick to weights at the gym tomorrow morning?' asked Akari. 'I could do with a few Pilates-free days.'

'Defo. I'll see you tomorrow, then. What time are you seeing Damian tonight?'

'Five. I'm driving to his, then we're going for a meal. Apparently, he's got something to tell me.'

'Uh-oh. Wedding proposal!'

Akari stuck her tongue out, then got out of the car and walked around to Camille's side. Guilt gnawed at her for not telling her friend she'd had sex. It was probably the only secret she'd kept from Camille, but just her and Damian knowing somehow made it more special. Perhaps she'd let the news slip in a few days.

A van zipped by and screeched to a halt right in front of Camille's Fiat. The driver leapt out with a clipboard.

'Akari Kato?' he asked Akari, guessing the shorter girl with the blonde hair was the one he was after.

'Yes.'

'I've got a special delivery.'

Akari glanced across at Camille, who was enthralled. The man had opened his rear door by then and pulled out a huge fluffy bear. The driver smiled, but Akari's gut twisted with unease.

'This is for you,' he said.

Akari shook her head. Damian was as likely to buy her something like that as she would purchase him a trip to the opera.

'It's got to be a joke from Damian,' said Camille. 'Or maybe it's a secret admirer,' she teasingly added.

The man looked past them both, then threw the bear into the air and over the windscreen so it landed on Camille's lap. Akari heard heavy footsteps from behind, but the driver had lunged at her. A bright blue crackle of electricity sparkled in his hand. Time slowed. A scream formed but froze in her mouth when pain ripped through her chest. Warm liquid filled her underwear as someone picked her up as though she were an empty cardboard box.

She was carried into the van and rested on her side, then she felt a slight prick in her neck. A squeak of protest or pain came from Camille, while a damp cloth was pressed over Akari's mouth. She held her breath and tried to struggle, but her arms and legs wouldn't respond. After a few seconds, the van tipped to one side as a dead weight thumped next to her. Akari was forced to inhale through the fabric and was surprised it merely smelled sweet instead of toxic.

Behind her, Camille released the beginnings of a shriek, but it was quickly muzzled. There was a groan from her friend and then silence.

The chill of the van's wooden floor seeped through Akari's thin gym clothes. She looked behind out of her watering right eye and could make out a middle-aged man's face, streaked with cruelty. He stared back. Her eyelids quivered, then closed.

The van door closed, plunging the interior into darkness, but

Akari was already unconscious. The final image that had registered was the expression on her abductor's face.

It was one of pure evil.

2

Since her promotion at the start of the year, DI Ashley Knight usually arrived first in the office at the Operation and Communications Centre (OCC) in Wymondham on a Monday morning. She enjoyed the peace and the opportunity to focus on the week ahead.

Her routine comprised making a cup of coffee, then having a head-to-head with her boss, DCI Vince Kettle, at eight. Their discussions were proving essential to keeping on top of the Vampires, a criminal organisation that had dominated the entire period. Even though she'd worked in the department for a decade, her spell as inspector had been a baptism of fire.

There were ten minutes until their meeting, so she checked her personal emails and found one from Rightmove about a property she might be interested in. After a flick through the photos, she stared out of the window of the police headquarters, lost in thought.

'Money problems, or relationship worries?' asked a gentle voice next to her.

I fed your suggestion up the chain and the bosses liked it. The NCA loved it.'

Kettle let his words sink in. The National Crime Agency had been taking a bigger interest in the Vampire investigation as the incidents piled up. What was at first sight thought to be mostly a Norfolk problem had spilled over to Suffolk and beyond.

Kettle twizzled his pen as he stared at her.

'There have been a few serious issues over the weekend, which I need to tell you about. Then I'll introduce you to Sebastian, and you can give him the lowdown.'

'That doesn't sound good.'

'No. Did you hear about Esra and Mercedes, who went missing from Ipswich a week ago?'

Ashley nodded. 'Yes, sir. I've been kept informed. They were assumed to be a young couple running away.'

'It didn't seem a big deal, but Mercedes' mother insisted she'd never do a flit at her age, especially seeing as she and Esra hadn't been dating long. He's from a traveller family who'd settled in Ipswich.'

Romany Gypsy and Irish Traveller people were vastly over-represented within prisons. They only made up 0.1 per cent of the population, but 5 per cent of prisoners identified as belonging to that community. Their prevalence was a cliché for a reason, but the stats also meant the vast majority of the community were law-abiding.

'Does the boyfriend have any previous?'

Kettle shook his head.

'Nope. CID suspected they had eloped and would resurface soon enough. CCTV showed his car being driven away from her house, although the view of the driver was unclear.'

'Have they reappeared?'

'His vehicle has turned up next to a field beside Herringfleet Windmill.'

'Where's that?'

'Near Lowestoft. He was dead in the driver's seat with a plastic bag over his head.'

Ashley grimaced. 'That doesn't bode well for the girl.'

'My concern precisely. Did Esra take her, do something stupid, then decide he couldn't live with the consequences?'

'Do you want me to head over?'

'No, I'm just making you aware. Suffolk MIT is at the scene. They've asked if Michelle can do the PM. Their guys have their hands full with the findings at the pop-up brothel discovered this Saturday.'

Pop-up brothels were exactly that. Houses, caravans, and even vans, were swiftly set up to sell prostitution, then quickly shut down, with the authorities often behind the curve. Airbnbs were also being used for some of the high-end trade.

'Another one?'

'I'm afraid so. I was hoping all the arrests over the last few months would have the finds tapering off. Anyway, the other important thing I have to tell you is Holland have made a breakthrough.'

'Excellent.'

The Dutch had started having serious problems not long after the Montenegrins flushed their people smugglers out of the country.

'Yes, the Amsterdam area is where many of the traffickers fled to. I've got another meeting with the NCA this afternoon, so I'll catch you later about that.'

Kettle kept his gaze on her. There was more. 'The journalist needs to hear it all.'

'Okay. Will there be a press officer with us?'

'Not this time.'

'Right.'

'The final bit of news is your former colleague will be pleading guilty to misconduct in public office at Cambridge Crown Court this morning.'

'Ally?'

'Yes.'

'Interesting.' Ashley thought of her conversation with Sebastian. 'Should I mention anything about that to this reporter?'

'I think he'd prefer the term investigative journalist, but no. Steer clear. Give him the background and where the current investigation is heading, but no names.' Kettle scratched his chin. 'Funnily enough, it was the public who exposed the ring in Holland after a *Crimewatch*-type programme, by flooding a helpline with what they'd seen in their own communities. So you were spot on with your idea of getting these details into the newspapers. Well done.'

'I assume Sebastian's work will be checked before it's released.'

Kettle chuckled.

'Of course, but he comes recommended. An NCA lawyer's eyes will see his article before any publication does.'

Ashley rose from her seat and strolled to the door. She stopped and glanced back.

'Will Ally get a custodial?'

'I suspect there'll be an adjournment for a probation report before sentencing on Thursday. A year is likely.'

Ashley gave him a knowing smile. 'I see.'

Kettle mimed zipping his mouth shut because both he and Ashley knew Ally had been working undercover when he was feeding intel to criminals. He'd been arrested and charged, which kept up the pretence.

Later that week, an innocent man would be sent to prison, meaning his covert work was far from over.

3

Ashley headed to Reception, where she found the journalist. It would have been hard to miss him. He towered over Ashley as he stood and shook her hand. Sebastian looked similar to DS Jan Pederson, one of her team who had been promoted to sergeant. Jan was a rangy type who lived quietly and healthily, with many hours spent on golf courses and tennis courts. He was typically Danish. Serious and steady, with good manners. The guy before her had bright eyes, which scanned her face with a hint of mischief.

She returned his smile and extended her hand.

'I'm DI Ashley Knight. Thank you for coming in.'

'Sebastian Elias.'

Ashley almost laughed. She was not expecting such a thick Norfolk accent.

'Have you been here before?'

'Not for a while.'

'I'll give you the penny tour, and then we can chat in one of the offices.'

'Perfect.'

She showed him around the still-fairly-quiet state-of-the-art building with pride. It was a far cry from some of the shabby buildings she'd worked from in the past. When they reached the incident room, Ashley paused.

Sebastian placed his hand on the door handle.

'They said I'd have access.'

'The victims' details are on the walls, and there are a lot of them. Let me bring you up to speed before we go in. What you've heard so far won't have scratched the surface.'

'I've been told the trafficking organisation spreads all across Europe, with multiple homicides in numerous countries.'

'Yes, that's true.'

The playful expression on Sebastian's face slipped away for the first time, replaced by a focused intensity.

'They said it was my scoop alone, and nothing would be off limits.'

Ashley smiled at him. 'Who are "they"?'

'My contacts.'

Ashley knew it would be the NCA, but it seemed Sebastian wouldn't confirm that.

'I suspect nobody gets to know everything, but *they* will check your work, and *they* are not people to upset, so you'll hear it all apart from the specifics. Do you fancy a coffee first?'

'No need, I'm local and had one before I left.'

'Wymondham?'

'Yep.'

Ashley grinned at him. Wymondham was a pretty town with decent shops, lovely restaurants, trendy cafés and relaxing pubs. It hosted many events, such as the popular Wymondham Music Festival. It was also the location of the office where they were standing. Sebastian had probably walked to see her.

'That's fortunate for you, and very handy for today.'

'Lucky for my parents. I live at their place. Let's crack on. I'm intrigued.'

Ashley escorted him to a meeting room, where he took out a voice recorder and a pad from his briefcase. Ashley didn't need notes. She'd been living the case for the last year.

'Okay,' she said, taking her glasses off. 'Give me a summary of what you know.'

'There were two criminal enterprises operating in Norfolk and edging into Suffolk. The Romans were nullified, but the Vampires went to ground. They are the ones causing you problems.'

'Correct.'

'Their area of expertise is people smuggling for any business where they can make a large profit. Sexual exploitation, domestic servitude, criminal behaviour, forced labour, but not the organ trade.'

'Not yet at least.'

'There are obvious issues with the UK's borders, particularly in the summer months, so there are immigrants everywhere. They can be easily taken advantage of due to their fear of the authorities. Most have had a long, hard journey, and will do almost anything to avoid being deported.'

'That's one element of it.'

Sebastian nodded. His hair was shaven to what Ashley guessed was a grade two. Up close, she noticed numerous small scars on his face and within his hairline. The lobe of his right ear was missing. He absently touched it when he next spoke.

'There is also forced trafficking. It's the dark side of an already dark moon. The recruitment, exploitation and trans-portation of innocent people. I've published articles before about the young men and women who are promised jobs and homes in rich cities in America and find themselves in trouble.'

'Right. Criminals then exploit those youngsters into shoplifting, pickpocketing, sham marriages, benefit fraud, begging, drug cultivation and dealing, you name it, but the organisation we're pursuing has a major focus.'

'The Vampires' business is prostitution.'

Ashley nodded. He was well informed.

'Yes, but the Vampires are only the English tentacle of the serpent. Has Typhon been explained to you?'

'No, they said to ask you what it is.'

Ashley took a deep breath.

'We don't know whether Typhon is a person or an organisation, but the Slovenians believe it is an overarching power, which was initially based in their country. It spread from there.'

'Wasn't Typhon some type of Greek super-god?'

'I have a friend who can give you a better explanation if needed, but yes. He was the biggest and most terrible monster. As with all Greek mythology, nothing's particularly clear to me, but, from what I understand, Typhon was created after Zeus slew the Titans.'

'Slew?'

'It's a word. Okay, he defeated them. Typhon later mated with an equally unpleasant type, who then gave birth to some of the most famous beasts in history. Care to guess at a few of them?'

'It's been a while since I watched *Jason and the Argonauts*.'

'The ones I'm aware of are Cerberus, Sphinx, Scylla, Chimera, Hydra and Ladon. The Typhon organisation kept this structure. We suspect six leaders operated under these names in six geographical regions. So far, Sphinx, Scylla, Chimera and Ladon have been captured. Killed actually. The other two's whereabouts are unknown, although they were rumoured to be in Holland.'

'So, they were like call signs. Wasn't Cerberus a three-headed dog and Hydra a nine-headed dragon?'

'That's correct.'

'Wouldn't they be simple to catch, even in Norfolk?'

Sebastian smiled impishly, which Ashley reciprocated.

'You'd have thought so. To sum up, we don't know whether there's a Mr or Mrs Typhon running the show, but even though the group was deeply embedded all over Eastern Europe, we have them on the run. I'd even go as far as to say they are in a panicked retreat.'

'Your idea is my article continues to flush them out because it will encourage people to inform on them, like with the cartels.'

'Yes, that's the hope. Norfolk people tend to know their communities. Strangers are noticed, especially out of season. Norwich is trickier because it's a much bigger urban centre. Including the greater area of the city, there's well over a quarter of a million people, but we should still get decent intel through the helpline from across the whole county.'

Sebastian rubbed his temples for a few seconds. The mischievous expression had returned.

'Surely a helpline isn't something to rely on.'

'Maybe so. The truth of the matter is we think it's almost over, but people are still dying. Every angle needs to be worked. The quicker we end it, the better it will be for all of Europe, us included. We don't want this Cerberus or Hydra slipping away, only to start again in the future.'

'Understood.'

'The NCA has picked up increased chatter on the dark web as the organisation falls apart. Their soldiers, workers, whatever you want to call them, are fleeing, mixed in with refugees, many of whom are from Ukraine.'

'I suppose it's easy to be anonymous when five million people are on the move.'

'Exactly, but they're not just running. They're disposing of any evidence before they leave.'

Sebastian frowned. 'Which includes people?'

'Yes. This is the most important piece of what I'm going to tell you. We believe Typhon is responsible for hundreds of deaths.'

'Hundreds?'

'Yes. Maybe more. Their whorehouses are little better than factory farms. Once an individual's use is over, a business decision is taken.'

'Like with battery hens.'

'Exactly.'

'I see why the NCA is so desperate to crush it out of existence.'

'Yes, and remember, only the living can talk. It might be worse than hundreds. Six hundred thousand people go missing in Europe every year. The criminals have been at it for a long time. They run an efficient and ruthless ship. Humans are a freely available asset and always have been.'

'But this Typhon gang is disintegrating.'

'Yes, the intel says they moved through Northern Europe, with the security services whittling them down as they went. Poland and Belgium had plenty of success. My boss has a meeting with the Dutch today, who have also made excellent progress. We'll hear more later in the week, which I assume you'll be party to.'

Sebastian frowned.

'If you excuse the phrase, isn't this a little international for a provincial force like yours in England? Surely the NCA or MI5 would deal with all this.'

'That's rather insulting. Are you implying Norfolk's Major Investigation Team is unsophisticated, inexperienced or narrow-minded?'

Sebastian grinned. 'You know what I'm saying.'

'The intelligence services are dealing with the international aspect, but the Vampires were already in Norfolk and now Suffolk. They've scattered throughout both counties and are setting up pop-up brothels and safe houses, then dismantling them a month later, or even sooner. Norfolk has tens of thousands of migrants, especially through the picking season. With so many undocumented individuals around, it's like whack-a-mole.'

Sebastian leaned back in his seat.

'I get it. You want an exposé-type article in as many forms of publication as possible. Ordinary people hate this sort of thing. It's inhumane.'

'Yes, the issue is incredibly emotive.'

'Norfolk and Suffolk are vast counties, though, with thousands of holiday lets, caravans, guest houses, abandoned buildings, farms, ruins, and so on. By the time you're aware of the criminal enterprise's location, it's often too late. You're hoping the public will notice faster.'

Ashley gestured for him to continue.

'CCTV is scarce compared to heavily populated cities, but there is something here those places don't have. Gossips.'

'I prefer the term caring members of a neighbourhood community.'

'They can spot a stranger a mile off. You want a county of informants.'

'Exactly. We'll have a special landline with experienced staff. There are numerous undercover operatives in various positions, but resources are stretched. The NCA simply doesn't possess the workforce for an area so huge, so they're forced to use locals. They're using MIT.'

'This case is serious stuff.'

Ashley's expression hardened.

'This is our chance to destroy Typhon, before more of Europe's youngsters are murdered.'

4

They walked into the bustling incident room. Sebastian strolled around and nodded at the others present, who were tapping away on computers or deep in discussion. He went to the window and stared out thoughtfully. He was obviously an experienced writer who kept abreast of recent events, but she suspected it was more than that. She wandered over to him.

'Have you reported on this topic a lot?'

Sebastian shifted his gaze to hers and held it.

'You've been honest with me, so I'll return the favour. I've worked all over the world, covering stories like these. After school, I joined the Royal Navy, then moved into more specialist roles. I saw investigative journalists in various countries during my tours, with their camera guys, doing brave and exciting things, and I fancied a piece of it. So, when I left the forces, that was the direction I took. Afghanistan, Darfur, Ukraine, there's always somewhere new. People trust me to tell their stories fairly.'

'What if your article is smothered? I thought you hacks felt strongly about freedom of speech.'

'That's why they trust me. I've seen things, fought for things. Sometimes, the greater good requires silence. I understand that.'

Ashley nodded at him respectfully. She guessed he'd been in the Royal Marines.

'Okay, let me introduce you to a few of my team. They'll give you more background. We can meet for lunch and have a chat this afternoon, to answer any remaining queries you may have.'

Ashley escorted him to their office. The only person present was DS Emma Stones. At six feet tall with a large frame, she dominated a room. Emma pumped Sebastian's hand enthusiastically.

'I'll leave him with you until early afternoon, if that's all right,' said Ashley.

Emma's eyes widened.

'It's okay,' said Sebastian. 'I've got notes to write up, but it'd be great if I could ask you both some questions as and when.'

'Of course.'

Ashley returned to her desk and dived into her emails. Her stomach had begun to rumble when an email pinged in from Kettle.

Come to my office immediately.

Ashley shut her laptop and strode towards his room. She walked straight in to find Kettle frowning at his screen.

'Close the door, please.'

Ashley did, then sat down.

'Something concerning has happened. It could be nothing, or it might be everything.'

'Fire away.'

'Yesterday afternoon, two young women, both seventeen-year-old schoolchildren, were reported missing.'

Ashley swallowed deeply. 'Oh.'

'One of them is the only daughter of Hanzo Kato.'

Kettle tutted when Ashley failed to comment.

'There were rumours he wanted to buy Norwich City Football Club.'

She shrugged.

'He owns CyberOne Semiconductors.'

'Nope.'

'Hanzo is rich and influential within the city, but, unusually for someone so wealthy, he's a genuine guy.'

Ashley wondered who Hanzo had influence with.

'I assume CID is dealing?'

'They're only getting involved now. The parents rang in last night, frantic, but there were no suspicious circumstances apart from phones were going unanswered. Kids go awol all the time. These two are nearly eighteen. How often do the mothers and fathers state their child would never do something so careless? Then the youngsters return the next day looking sheepish. The parents were told missing people generally reappear within forty-eight hours, but they should ring back in the morning if they hadn't heard from them.'

'And Hanzo did.'

'Correct. He'd contacted everyone he could think of throughout the night, and nobody knew anything. Both their Apple mobiles were still turned off, which hasn't been the case with his daughter, Akari, since she was about nine years old.'

Ashley considered the information – iPhones could be turned off without the passcode. She supposed the kids could have done it themselves, but for what reason? The batteries might have gone flat, but that was unlikely for both phones. Youngsters were so reliant on their phones nowadays that they tended to keep them charged up.

There was the possibility of a significant accident, resulting in a fireball, water immersion, or going down an embankment, but they were usually reported swiftly.

'Were the girls out in a car?'

'Yes, a brand-new convertible.'

'Which has now been spotted on CCTV and that's why you're concerned?'

'Yes, both families live on Newmarket Road. The girls attended a Pilates class, which has been confirmed, drove home together, which was caught by council CCTV. The vehicle turns into Newmarket Road for little more than five minutes, then it returns the way it came, but with only a driver inside.'

'Which girl was driving?'

'Neither. The recording showed a dark-haired man in a baseball cap.'

Ashley made the link straight away. 'Same MO as the Ipswich couple who went missing after they were believed to have eloped in his car. Cameras nearby picked up his vehicle and he might not have been the driver.'

'Yes, but that CCTV was grainy. This image is crystal clear. There are other similarities. Road cameras caught both vehicles heading towards business parks. This time it was the Vulcan Road Industrial Estate. I can't recall the Suffolk one.'

'Was the car they found the lad in registered to him?'

'Yes.'

Ashley rubbed her neck while she thought. 'There are a few differences, then. Two rich students and a couple from a housing estate.'

'I might not have connected the cases if I hadn't been to the meeting that just finished.'

Ashley's sense of impending doom heightened.

'The Dutch meeting?'

'Yes. Without being disrespectful, the police and security services in Eastern Europe aren't what they are in the west. Record-keeping is improving, but it's still not great. In rural areas, it's downright poor. They don't have access to the latest technology. Understaffed but motivated at best, corrupt and lazy at worst. The Dutch police, however, are rated as the finest in the world. They've been communicating with all the other countries and pulling all the stats together to compile a report which should sum up the scale of the problem. Experts have recognised a new pattern of abductions. They also made a breakthrough yesterday which confirms their darkest suspicions.'

Ashley wasn't sure where he was going.

'Are you referring to them recruiting youngsters with false adverts and then exploiting them?'

'No, sorry, the Dutch think they located one of the main leaders early this morning. They had him hemmed in on the roof of a building, but he jumped off the side rather than be caught. A guy who was there, who didn't jump, has talked a little, but he's insisting on being given a new identity. He said the man who tried to fly off the sixth floor was Cerberus.'

'One of Typhon's remaining children.'

'Yes. The NCA have heard on one of the organisation's Telegram messaging services that Cerberus was compromised. As more players fall, we're learning more and more, enabling us to move faster. They're on the run and in disarray.'

'What are the Dutch so concerned about?'

'The villains are getting more ruthless. Multiple bodies were found in the flat where Cerberus had been hiding out. As the men involved get more desperate, so do their crimes.'

A cold dread settled over Ashley.

'It sounds like the functioning remainder of Typhon is operating as if it's the end of their days.'

5

Ashley swiftly joined the dots.

'The trend they've noticed was the victims were being taken off the streets. Not trafficked, abducted.'

Kettle bobbed his head.

'Exactly, but in the other countries where it has occurred, it seems to have stopped and there haven't been any recent cases. The informant who talked this morning said he and Cerberus had been on the move for six months. The guy reckoned Cerberus duped him into getting involved, then threatened him with violence when he tried to leave. He and Cerberus planned to escape from Holland in a few days. Everyone else had already gone.'

'Don't tell me he'll be given a new identity.'

'I'm not sure. Rules are being broken. Risks are being taken. There's a chance to finish this right now. There might only be one leader left. Hydra.'

Again, Ashley saw what was ahead.

'They're fleeing to Britain.'

'Well done. What's one of the methods used in the past to move their victims?'

'Container ships.'

'And where's the busiest container port in the UK? One that's the perfect gateway to Europe.'

Felixstowe in nearby Suffolk. The unspoken answer hung heavy in the air.

She tutted.

'If their chatty guy is right and he and Cerberus were the last due to leave Holland, then the others would have already arrived. Won't they already have dispersed throughout the rest of the UK?'

'That was mentioned at the meeting, but, remember, Norfolk and Suffolk were the places where the Vampires already operated. This is familiar territory. They control a network here. They do have a big problem, though. The European police have confiscated and frozen the assets of those they've caught.'

'So, the ones who fled here could be running low on funds.'

'Right. They'll need easy, fast money. Forced prostitution fits the bill perfectly. The business is secretive by nature and there's always demand.'

'You're right, that is concerning. I take it the NCA are sending people here.'

'Mostly just to Suffolk. There simply aren't enough staff to cover both counties. They don't know Norfolk like we do, so it's a case of us continuing to do our best and seeing how the investigation progresses. Your idea was a good one. If the public are on side to look out for anything unusual, we might get lucky.'

'It's not luck if we plan for it. The men involved are liable to make mistakes if they're desperate.'

Ashley slumped back in her seat. It had become clear just

how much danger the youngsters of Norfolk were in. Sebastian's article couldn't come soon enough.

'Any good news?' she asked with a smile.

'Michelle will do the PM this afternoon of the lad assumed suffocated by a plastic bag. His body doesn't seem to have been abused beforehand, and it doesn't appear to be a staged suicide. You visit the parents of the missing children in Norwich. We'll arrange a TV crew to record a plea for help this evening. I'll attend and make a statement.'

Ashley pursed her lips.

'I assume the parents of the poor missing kids from Ipswich also received an inspector call less than twenty-four hours after they went missing, then had an appearance on mainstream news channels with a DCI.'

Kettle raised his eyebrows.

'I hope you're not implying we treat the children of wealthy people differently.'

Ashley rolled her eyes. 'Not at all.'

'I almost forgot. I do have some interesting information for you. The NCA has borrowed some resources from the Met. They're setting up a data-collection room here at Wymondham due to us having the newest facilities. There's a tonne of information which needs collating. We'll try to link the data to the Dutch finds. Some of the police's brightest talents will be here tomorrow, in particular one who has already proved himself by creating an algorithm to track social media accounts. That will be all for the moment.'

Ashley's heart skipped a beat. 'Hector?'

'The one and only.'

Ashley left Kettle's office with a huge grin on her face. She hadn't seen Hector since he'd left to work in a new team for the Met. That was six months ago.

When she arrived at the office, only Emma and Barry were present. Sebastian was typing away in a corner.

'Where's everyone else?' she asked Emma.

'Zelda's father's been rushed to hospital, and Jan is at the dentist.'

'Shit. Is he going to be okay?'

'I think it's just a filling.'

'Emma!'

'Yes, she just texted that her dad's going to be fine. Morgan and Sal have just gone to a possible murder in Blofield.'

'You're kidding. When did that happen?'

'No need to panic there, either. Reading between the lines, they're probably natural deaths. Both deceased are in their late eighties. The PC who attended the scene used to be on Control. She always was overenthusiastic.'

Ashley smiled. It had to be Jenny, who had become a constable because Ashley had inspired her. She updated Barry and Emma about Kettle's news.

Barry made a scoffing sound. 'Bloody typical. Rich gits calling the shots.'

'Yes, I thought you'd say that, so I'll visit them with Emma, knowing you wouldn't be able to zip your mouth. Barry, arrange a press conference, please.'

Barry scratched his head. Ashley huffed.

'If you ring Gabriella, she'll sort it for you. Then you can go back to solving the meaning of life or whatever else you were up to. Try not to upset the journalist while we're gone.'

As they were leaving the office, Ashley chuckled.

'What's amusing you?' asked Emma.

'I was checking out our matching clothes. We look like we should be starring in *Men in Black*.'

Emma glanced at Ashley's near identical black suit and white blouse with smart shoes.

'More like ladies from Next.'

Emma booked a car out and they set off. 'Where are we heading, exactly?'

'Newmarket Road.'

'Ooh, nice.'

'I don't know that area of Norwich particularly well. Obviously, Ally's team tended to deal with the city, but don't you live near Newmarket Road?'

'Close, but not close enough,' said Emma. 'It always reminds me of Notting Hill.'

'I thought the term Golden Triangle meant the place was full of drug dealers when I first heard it. Why is it called that?'

'Estate agents coined the term because of the golden price tag of the properties. It's a friendly place, where they have summer events.'

'How golden are the prices?'

'Some parts of it aren't too bad, but you can't get much for less than half a million.'

'Too golden for my liking. Both missing girls live on Newmarket Road.'

'You could probably triple the price tag for that street.'

'Wow.'

'Don't worry. We'll be chief superintendents soon. Then we can move there and be neighbours.'

Ashley smiled at her friend and colleague.

'You know what? You've blossomed since you made sergeant. I have your six-month performance review to do soon, but it's going to be a breeze.'

'I do feel different. Being big has meant I haven't always felt confident. Not without six vodkas inside me anyway, but being promoted has really helped. I feel strong and capable. I could snap Barry like a twig.'

Some of Emma's transformation had come after throwing her husband out, but he'd returned with a new attitude.

'Home life still good?' asked Ashley.

'Yeah.' Emma paused, as though considering whether to say anything. 'It probably makes me a bad person, but part of me was looking forward to dating again. But we've got back into the old routine. Mine is to wake the kids, do their packed lunches, maybe some ironing and washing, shag husband once a week while thinking about all the packed lunches, ironing and washing that needs to be done. I know I shouldn't complain. The children are happy and stable. Our finances are solid. I suppose nobody has everything.'

'You could have nothing like me.'

Ashley was only half joking.

'Rubbish,' barked Emma. 'You're the fresh catch of the day. Fit, pretty, debt-free. Homeowner! Get your ass on Bumble. Take your pick.'

'Sorting through edited and ancient photographs of divorced men is about as appealing as looking for dead pigeons in the loft.'

Emma nodded enthusiastically.

'A friend of mine joined Tinder. She had a date with this one guy which went great guns. He took her somewhere expensive, insisted on paying, and chatted intelligently about various topics. The only issue was him being a little overkeen.'

'A stalker would not improve my life.'

'He wasn't quite Pepé Le Pew, but flowers arrived the next day. Then he sent her a picture of him holding a spade beside a big hole he'd dug.'

'Perfect.'

Emma laughed out loud. 'It was fine. He's a builder, and they were the foundations for an extension to his massive house. Anyway, she saw him again and the last I knew, he was taking her away for a quiet weekend in the middle of nowhere. I've not heard from her for a while, so it must be going well.'

'Emma!'

'I'm kidding. She can't believe how lucky she's been.'

Ashley's phone rang, saving her from commenting further. It was the pathologist, Michelle Ma Yun.

'Hi, Ashley. I've started the initial observations for the post-mortem on this possible suicide. What are your plans for today?'

'We've got two missing girls. I'm heading to their houses to speak with the parents.'

'Missing, presumed dead?'

'It's a long story. Let's call it a PR exercise for now, but it could be important. Why do you ask?'

'You need to head here afterwards.'

6

Emma turned into Newmarket Road and drove past the grand homes along it. She checked the numbers, then indicated right and swung between a pair of open gates with imposing stone pillars. The house beyond was no less impressive. They trundled through the thick gravel around a circular hedge and parked next to an Audi SQ8. Even Ashley knew you'd receive little change from a hundred grand from buying one of those.

Emma switched off the engine, her gaze fixed on the property.

'Early twentieth-century in the tradition of the flourishing arts and crafts movement which was popular at that time. Prime location, south-west of Norwich city centre. Built of plain stone and Norfolk red brick, the property is perfectly symmetrical and retains its stunning period detail.' She sighed. 'I'm a failed estate agent. It was all I wanted to do.'

'What happened?'

'The financial crisis in 2008. I lost my perfect job. The market froze and my dream was over. I ended up unemployed and back in my old bedroom. The police were looking for women, so I applied through desperation.'

'Their loss, our gain.'

'I was fortunate. I reckon I just failed the bleep test, but I beat most of the blokes at the strength challenge, and they slipped me through. It's weird that I probably wouldn't be doing this if there hadn't been a recession.' Emma stared at the ornate front door, which then slowly swung open. A thin woman, arms crossed and huddled into an oversized cardigan, gazed at them with dark eyes. Mascara had streaked down both cheeks. For a moment, her expression flitted to optimism from dread. Emma growled, 'Lucky me.'

Ashley nodded. This was a rotten part of the job. They weren't delivering a death message, but it had been twenty-four hours now since the girls went missing and the odds would soon tip that way.

'Come on. Let's hear what they have to say.'

Ashley and Emma strode to the door, introduced themselves, and showed their warrant cards.

The lady studied their IDs. 'I'm Victoria Kato. Akari's mother. Her father is in the kitchen. Waiting.'

Victoria, voice strained, resembled nearly every parent Ashley had met who was hoping for a positive update on their missing children. Face a ghastly grey. A wraith, even after such a short time, almost as if she had never been alive.

The detectives followed Victoria inside to a vast kitchen. A large table had three people seated around it. The only woman in the group rose and rushed over.

'I'm Aveline. Camille's mother. Do you have anything?'

Aveline had a slight accent. Probably French.

'I'm DI Knight and this is DS Stones, and I'm sorry to say we have no further news yet. Our Criminal Investigation Department has a lot of experience, and their team will soon be here. I can assure you we're taking this very seriously.'

Ashley walked over to the men, who both stood. She shook hands with them.

'Stefan Dupont. Camille's father.'

'Hanzo Kato.'

'Please take a seat,' said Ashley. 'All of you.'

Emma opened her notebook and sat at the end of the table. Ashley remained standing. She glanced around the spacious room. Her entire downstairs could fit into this kitchen. Floor-to-ceiling windows revealed an established garden full of blossom, trellises, statues and flowers. It was enchanting.

Inside was far from that. Ashley often felt like an intruder when she visited homes for this purpose. The air was already heavy with sorrow and regret. These parents would have entered a twilight world. Until the children were found, minutes would stretch to eternity, while days vanished in seconds.

Both men stared vacantly ahead, haunted eyes sunken in their heads. They would probably be typical of most males in this predicament and would turn themselves off, knowing if the news was dire, they would be forced to step up.

Information and descriptions were often best sought from the mothers. While there was still hope, they would continue to function.

She turned to Victoria, then nodded at Aveline.

'What I need is a recent photograph of both the girls and some background on them.'

Aveline picked up two brown cardboard folders from the kitchen table.

'Here. We've prepared these. One for each child. We printed off pictures, described their natures, social media addresses, email, everything we could think of. I couldn't sleep. None of us have. Our children would not leave voluntarily.'

'Are you French?' asked Ashley.

'Yes, sorry, my accent comes out when I'm stressed. Stefan and I met in Paris and came to Norwich to work for CyberOne Semiconductors twenty years ago.'

Ashley opened the folders and slipped out the photographs. The girls looked a little like sisters. Blonde locks, slim, freckles. Small features. They closely resembled their mothers, as though the women had provided most of the DNA.

Ashley glanced at Stefan, who appeared over six feet tall with a solid heavy jaw and a bald head. Hanzo's hair was a striking jet black, and his eyes held a quiet intensity. Ashley noticed some subtle features hinting at Japanese ancestry, but, overall, he seemed unique, unlike anyone she'd met before.

Victoria attempted a smile.

'Akari's hair is actually dark brown, but she dyed it blonde a year ago and loved it.'

Ashley knew the officers from CID would take down the nitty-gritty when they arrived, but her gut was already fearing the worst.

'I'll need you to truthfully answer some tough questions. One of the most likely reasons for young women to go missing is boyfriends. Or drugs and alcohol.'

'No,' said Hanzo, vehemently. 'They are good girls, diligent students, into fitness, sport, hobbies, study, and they're not interested in boys.'

Ashley's eyes wandered to Stefan, but he was staring stoically into the garden.

'Camille and Akari have had the odd flirtations with boys, but nothing serious,' said Aveline. 'They talk to us about everything. We joke they have two homes, two families, two sets of parents. Their phones are never off. Someone has taken them both.'

Ashley was inclined to agree. The other common trigger for girls to leave home was conflict with their parents so she had to ask.

'Any big rows with you guys? You know, are they flexing their wings, hormones?'

Hanzo glanced at Victoria.

'No,' she said. 'They are happy.'

'Do either currently have a boyfriend?'

'I don't believe so,' said Aveline.

'No boyfriend, just friends who are boys,' said Hanzo.

Ashley looked over at his wife, Victoria, who swallowed deeply.

'Akari has been getting friendlier with a young lad.'

A doorbell jangled, disturbing the stillness. Victoria rose from her seat.

'That could be him now.'

Ashley and Emma waited while Victoria answered the door. The young man she returned with appeared cut from the same cloth as the girls. His clothes and trainers were understated, but even Ashley recognised the labels. He had shoulder-length hair, through which he kept running his fingers after tipping his head. She noticed Hanzo staring at the lad intently.

'This is Damian. He lives in the neighbourhood,' said Victoria.

Damian strode over and shook Ashley's hand firmly. Up close, she could see he'd been crying. He didn't appear a likely suspect for a kidnapping or a double homicide, but there was something in his demeanour that indicated guilt. Ashley asked him to take a seat.

'How do you know Akari and Camille?'

'We attend the same private school. I've known them both since the first year of seniors, but it's only lately we've become close.'

'Close to both, or close to Akari?'

'Being near to Akari means being near to Camille. We've only been seeing each other a little while, though.'

'Is it serious?'

Damian looked as if he was stopping himself from glancing at Akari's father.

'Getting there. You know how it is.'

'Sadly, it's been a while since I was young and in love. Remind me, please.'

'Kind of crazy. I didn't really notice her before this year. I'm into sport, she likes arts, then one day we clicked.'

'And her disappearing is out of character?'

'Of course. They're both square bears. I'm the type who gets into trouble.'

Ashley raised an eyebrow. Damian's reply was stammered.

'Being late, missing class, kids' stuff.'

'When did you last see her?'

The boy's face rapidly reddened. 'Friday afternoon.'

'Was it just the two of you?'

He swallowed. 'My parents are away for a long weekend.'

Hanzo leapt to his feet and Emma rose half a second later to stand next to Damian. She dominated the space.

Hanzo snarled at Damian.

'What have you done with my daughter?'

'Nothing. I'd never hurt her.'

Ashley needed to nip this in the bud, unless it was true.

'Have you got an alibi for yesterday, Damian?' asked Ashley.

'I was chilling at home. Watching films, listening to podcasts, playing PlayStation. Akari had plans with her parents on Saturday and Camille on Sunday. We were due to meet tonight. Honestly.'

Hanzo slumped back onto his chair while Stefan still stared

out of the window. Both women's gazes were fixed on Damian. Ashley wasn't sure what to think.

'Are there security cameras outside this house?'

Stefan finally contributed.

'Yes, Hanzo and I have scoured the footage. We observed Camille roll up the drive and pick Akari up, but the car didn't reappear later.'

Ashley frowned. She didn't know how much had been explained to the parents.

'So, Camille's Fiat wasn't caught by those cameras after Pilates?'

'No. The girls don't always enter the gates if they're dropping off because the stones can flick up if you accelerate too fast over them,' said Victoria, who then sobbed, probably remembering an incident where she chastised the girls for doing that and longing to have the chance now.

'Are the details of the vehicle in her folder?'

'Yes. Akari's, too, but that never left the garage. They prefer Camille's little runaround.'

There was a firm knock at the front door. Aveline disappeared, then reappeared with two women who Ashley knew were missing persons specialists from CID. Ashley introduced everyone. Then she beckoned one of the officers, Janice, out to the hall.

'This doesn't look good, Janice.'

'No, I read the file on the way over. I'm local and their private school keeps their kids on a tight leash. Even without that, they're rich with little to run away from.'

'The boyfriend's a possible angle, but you've heard about the missing teenagers from Ipswich.'

'Yeah, I was involved there. That case was similar but it has differences too. Apparently, Esra had been planning to sell his motor, so we thought for a bit he'd sold it. The car hadn't been insured for months, yet others at the hostel said he was driving it around, so we wanted to talk to him about that anyway. You obviously know a member of the public found his body, but there's still no sign of his partner. It's been a week now.'

Ashley didn't need to mention her concerns for the girl to someone as experienced as Janice. She decided to let her get on with her job.

'I'm going to the mortuary to hear the results of her boyfriend's post-mortem. Do we have a next of kin for Esra?'

'No, he was in the traveller community, but he had left it behind.'

'He ran away to leave the circus?'

Janice smiled. 'Something like that. To be honest, we haven't gathered much background for him. The Sanctuary was providing a room.'

Ashley nodded. The Sanctuary offered housing and support services to youngsters. In particular, care leavers and those with addiction issues.

'What did they say?'

'We went to the place he was staying and it looked like he'd left some stuff, but that's not unusual. He lived quietly. Didn't chat to too many people. His closest friends moved to Brighton a week before they went missing but we couldn't locate them. The hostel staff reckoned he might have followed them, but it seems Esra was a bit of an exaggerator.'

Ashley thought of previous cases where identification hadn't been thorough enough, and there had been serious consequences.

'Did the victim have ID?'

'Nope, but it's got to be him. We're checking fingerprints and DNA from his room, but it'd help if someone ID'd the body.'

'Perhaps from Mercedes' family?'

'There's just her mother. She has other kids, most of whom are well under eighteen.' Janice frowned. 'I'm hoping Esra killed himself and left her somewhere alive.'

Ashley nodded, even though she suspected that was unlikely.

'I'll ring you after the post-mortem.'

'Thanks. What's your gut feeling here?' asked Janice. 'One of ours, or one of yours?'

Ashley gave her a sad smile. 'This will end up ours.'

8

Ashley and Emma stepped outside the house into the late spring air and returned to their car. Ashley glanced around the front garden. Sunlight streamed through the trees, birds, chirping with joy, flitted through the branches. For a moment, she envied their carefree existence, a stark contrast to the ticking clock her team faced.

She rang Kettle back at OCC and gave him an update as Emma drove them to the hospital. Janice would gather all the details he needed for his statement, but the post-mortem results might point the investigation in another direction. Ashley called Barry next to ask him to investigate the most important angle. Find out how the women were transported.

'Okay,' he replied. 'I'm on it. It's going to be a van, or possibly a truck. There can't be too many in the right location considering we have a tight window of time. Give me an hour.'

Ashley thought back to the devastated parents as Emma parked and they strode to the mortuary. A crew would arrive and film them begging for the safe return of their children.

Press conferences with grieving families were morally

exploitative, but a necessary evil. Nothing else could achieve a similar impact. Life at its rawest, hearts flayed, desperate pleas. The morbid fascination of a glimpse into hell. Viewers experienced a deep-down, almost guilty relief that it was someone else's misery, but people couldn't forget. The whole country would want to help.

One of the mortuary staff let them in and they went straight to Michelle's office. She jumped out of her seat when they appeared and kissed them both on the cheeks, which was unusually affectionate for her.

'Afternoon, guys.'

'Hi, Michelle,' said Ashley. 'You're in good spirits.'

'I guess so. Grab a pew.'

'I take it you have something concerning?'

'More confusing than concerning. Hang on and I'll get the images up.'

Emma and Ashley sat opposite her. Emma picked up the cup on Michelle's desk. It said, *What's a pathologist's favourite type of entertainment club? Open Mike night.*

Michelle's lips curved upward, hinting at amusement.

'Scott bought me that. He's got such a quirky sense of humour.'

She pointed over at a vase filled with fresh flowers. The roses bloomed in an uncommon shade of peach, their petals a delicate blend of pink and orange. Surrounded by stunning blue hyacinths, and some Barbie-pink blooms, which Ashley didn't recognise, it was quite a display and wouldn't have been cheap.

Some women thought flowers conveyed the deepest feelings. Barry had come over with a box of Roses once, but he'd eaten all the good ones while Ashley was cooking him a meal, which he then couldn't eat because he was too full. She experienced a twinge of jealousy and the sinking feeling of a missed opportunity.

Michelle's half-smile turned into a beam.

'Scott had those delivered. This is the first time a man has sent me a bouquet for no reason. I spent five minutes after they arrived hunting in the packaging for an apology for what he'd done. Funny thing is, I've never had such nice flowers here, and they've really lifted my mood.'

Ashley forced herself to smile at Michelle. She wanted to be happy for her. Michelle had been a cool character when they'd first worked together. Reserved, taciturn and all-business, but after a few drunken sessions and some enjoyable team meals, the women from those evenings had forged a close bond, especially Emma, Michelle and Ashley.

'Right,' said Michelle. 'The findings from the post-mortem were pretty much what you'd expect from a nineteen-year-old boy. Healthy, fit and strong. All organs in perfect condition. The only signs of damage were to his teeth.'

'Fighting?' asked Emma.

'No, absent dental hygiene. He's had a few fillings, but there's obvious decay. I'd be surprised if he hadn't been in pain, or at the least struggling with sensitivity.'

'That fits if he's from a poor community, although I doubt it drove him to end his own life.'

'No, but with his arms free, at first look, it does appear a suicide. As you know, it doesn't take long with suffocation. Consciousness is lost within seconds of the brain being starved of oxygen. After a few minutes, irreversible damage occurs to the brain. We'll look further into that, but seeing as he was found with a bag taped around his head, we can make a confident assumption about the cause of death.'

'It always surprises me people don't pull the bag off,' said Emma. 'There must be a rising panic.'

'This is the item. It's thick plastic.' Michelle brought up a picture of a substantial clear bag. 'It's not the type of material in which you could quickly poke an air hole, but people's minds are often set when they reach this point.'

'Might someone have tied the bag around his head and staged it?' asked Ashley.

'That's possible, but pathologists use the circumstances of how bodies are found as much as the condition of them to make their judgements. It seems unlikely he'd be driven somewhere relatively public to be killed in this manner. What would there be to gain?'

Ashley scratched her head.

'True. Why risk getting caught when you could drive him to an isolated wood or empty house?'

'Unless this place means something to the person who did it,' said Emma. 'It's picturesque there. Although I suppose it's more likely the location was special to Esra. Maybe it was where he used to take Mercedes.'

'And it's definitely Esra?' asked Ashley.

'Yes,' said Michelle. 'He's easily identifiable. Part of his description was his nose cartilage was severely damaged. He had broken knuckles too at some point. In conjunction, I'd say they were fighting wounds instead of something like a car accident. They're common injuries together for a certain type of person.'

'Bare knuckle as opposed to amateur stuff?'

'That would be my guess.'

'So, troubled background, travelling community, maybe substance abuse.'

Michelle nodded, then brought up another image.

'This is my concern. There are fading bruises on his body.

Nothing too drastic, but something relatively serious must have happened for me to still be able to make them out a week later.'

'Sounds like he could have resisted or fought if he was taken?'

'Yes. There are no marks around his neck though, so he didn't try to scratch off the bag. He's been missing for a while, so where was he? There are no other wounds.'

Emma tutted.

'Perhaps he is responsible and got the injuries kidnapping Mercedes. Maybe they had a row and she told him it was over. He could have snapped. That's got to be the best explanation. He's taken her somewhere, out of his mind, and ended up killing her. Wracked with guilt, with life in prison ahead of him, he decided to end it.'

'Exactly what I thought,' said Michelle. 'Until I found this.'

Michelle located a photo of a hairy wrist. She zoomed in.

'Look at the hairs.'

Ashley and Emma stared blankly at the photograph.

'Sorry,' said Ashley. 'I presume this is Esra. What am I looking for?'

'Some of the follicles are missing. Both wrists are the same.'

'I wouldn't have noticed,' said Emma.

'That's why I'm amazing,' said Michelle with a grin. 'I popped a sample under the microscope. Some patches of the epidermis are uneven.'

Ashley took a moment to join the dots. 'He was bound?'

'I'm saying he might have been, but not in the usual way. Criminals nowadays use cable ties, which are perfect for the job. Quick to apply, cheap, easy to cut and release, but almost impossible to remove by the victim. They always leave obvious marks.'

'Which means?'

'Perhaps he was restrained, but with something softer. A bed sheet or tea towel, perhaps secured by tape.'

'Wouldn't he be able to struggle out of something like that?' asked Emma.

'Yes, that's my explanation. Those binds could have kept him in one position, so he didn't thrash around, but they weren't stopping him from fleeing.'

Ashley got what she was implying.

'They were preventing escape by a different method, like locking him in a room.'

'That's plausible.' Michelle paused. 'The approach used could be important.'

'And those marks could be more recent?'

'Yes, I'd say so. Last few days.'

'And his body hasn't been interfered with or damaged otherwise?'

'No.'

'He could have had a gun pointed at him,' said Emma.

Ashley nodded in agreement. 'He was too frightened to escape.'

9

Mercedes awoke with blurred vision. For a moment, thinking she was in her own bedroom, she reached her hand out to check for her sister in the darkness, but numb fingers grasped at cold air. Mercedes shot upright, and it all flooded back.

A sharp pain came from her bladder, but she lay still and contemplated. Asking for the toilet was an opportunity to talk with her captors. Only one of them ever replied, but that was better than nothing. He always said not to worry. Esra was okay. It gave her hope to cling to, when everything else had been stripped away.

Mercedes took a few deep breaths. What a crazy situation. She understood not to run or cry out, recalling they'd told her the consequences of either would be terrible.

As her eyes adapted to the gloom, she noticed her food tray had gone. When they'd first been taken, she couldn't eat, but eventually the room had become like any other, and her appetite had got the better of her. She'd eaten both packs of sandwiches, the apple, a bag of crisps and a KitKat. Afterwards, remorse had washed over her, but she needed her strength. Maybe there'd be a chance for them both to escape.

An image of Esra laughing in their local pub a few weeks ago surfaced. He was an unusual lad, but they'd connected. In some ways, she'd found the other half of her. He loved to watch her out of the corner of his eye, and she loved to catch him doing so. He couldn't wait to tell the people they met how lucky he was, and how pretty she was. How happy they were.

Her mother had been the only negative. Mercedes heard her voice.

'Please be careful. Don't leap into anything. You're young and beautiful, so don't sell yourself cheap. Stick to modelling. This boy is troubled. You'll meet wealthy guys. Hold out for a life of luxury.'

Like a stuck record.

Mercedes almost chuckled at her mother's naivety. She had met many rich people, quite a few of whom had wanted to immediately fuck her, even when she was underage. One guy had, even after she'd declined participation. She'd never told her mum. So going to bed with Esra hadn't been a big deal, at least not on account of her virginity.

The experience with him had been fine, though. He'd been more nervous than her, and it had been over quickly. Eventually, they'd got the hang of it, and now they were often intimate. She was even close to having an orgasm on the last occasion. The future had been rosy, until it wasn't.

It was hard to believe what had happened to them. One minute laughing in the car, then an arm shooting through her open window, a jolt of electricity, a wet rag rammed over her mouth and nostrils, then a prick in the neck. She woke in this room. They explained Esra was nearby, but she had not heard his voice. She suspected he understood to be quiet, too, but had he also guessed their promises were lies?

Clumping feet approached her door. It creaked ajar and a large man with a flat nose and thick beard entered. He carried a bowl of water in his hands and a small towel over his arm, which he set down. A bar of soap sat in the grey liquid. He dropped a toothbrush on the floor.

'Breakfast soon. Then wash self. Clean teeth.'

Mercedes stood and tried to give him her sweetest smile. The one that got her second place in the Miss Ipswich competition.

'I need the toilet, please.'

'After eating.'

'Can I talk to Esra today?'

Her visitor took a hairbrush out of his pocket.

'Brush hair.'

'I'd like to see Esra, please.'

When the man stared at her, his eyes seemed to shine in the dark. His grin was cold. He chuckled, slowly, deeply.

'Yes, maybe.'

Mercedes waited for him to close the door. He didn't bother locking it. She knew not to leave. Mercedes looked over at the bowl and shrugged. There was nothing else to do. After cleaning her face and teeth, she set about brushing her long blonde hair. Anything but consider what came next.

There'd been a few visits from strange men over the first few days, but she hadn't been mistreated. She thought about the person with the evil eyes when he came. He'd been easy-going, but then his questions had warped. She'd refused to answer. He'd soon put an end to that. His voice in her ear a dry whisper.

'There are many ways to open your mouth.'

She'd told him everything.

Mercedes had been worried about rape. She fluffed her hair,

then slowly ran the brush through it and attempted to focus solely on the action. The evil man never concealed his face. She would recognise him again in a heartbeat.

Life had forced Mercedes to grow up fast. She saw the world as it was, understood its harsh lessons. It was clear her number was up.

10

Ashley and Emma left the mortuary and headed back to the car. Ashley took out her bobble and ran her hands through her hair.

'Fancy a trip to Suffolk, Ems?'

Emma rolled her eyes. 'Shouldn't Ipswich family liaison do it?'

Ashley nodded. 'I'll contact them and ask if they can meet us there, but I want a word with Mercedes' mother. See how things are at home. It doesn't seem like Suffolk MIT have made much progress with this case. The couple appeared like young runaways, you know, star-crossed lovers, making rash choices. Instead, they were taken.'

Ashley rang Janice back at Newmarket Road first and told her what Michelle had implied.

'Shit,' she replied. 'We'll look bad for not taking their disappearance seriously, but you know how stretched we are.'

The last statistic Ashley had seen was someone went missing and was officially recorded every ninety seconds in the UK. Who knew what the unofficial figures were? Most police forces had around twenty people disappear each day, so

Janice's team constantly fought an uphill battle with too few resources.

There was no point in Ashley commenting on that fact. It was a case of carrying on and doing their best. That seemed to apply to everything nowadays. From schools to hospitals, GP surgeries and ambulances.

'Okay, Janice. Let me know if anything changes. I'm heading to Ipswich.'

'Of course I will, and do the same for me.'

'How are you getting on with the press conference?'

'Starts at five. I've spoken to that numpty, Barry, and he assured me DCI Kettle will be here by then to sit with the parents. Kettle can do his bit, then just the mothers will talk to the cameras. As is always the case with these situations, I'm in awe of the poor women.'

Ashley finished the call and rang Barry at OCC. He answered straight away.

'Barry. Any progress with the car these girls went missing in or any suspicious vehicles nearby?'

'Yes, I've hit the jackpot. There was a white Vauxhall Vivaro van in the area right around the time they disappeared. Nothing particularly shady about that, but I ran the plates. They're for a five-door Honda Jazz hatchback. I found the van on the same camera that we found the Fiat 500 heading towards the industrial estate.'

'That has got to be how they moved the girls.'

'Yeah. They must have been taken from the Fiat, then lobbed in the rear of the van. One of the abductors then drove their car. Simple. It's a big estate, but that's where we have to begin searching. I'll grab Kettle and ask him to call in the necessary before he leaves for the press thing. We need as many people there as possible looking for that Vivaro.'

Ashley gave him an update from her end. Barry cursed.

'This Mercedes looks like a goner.'

'Nicely put, Barry.'

'Just saying it how it is.'

'Emma and I expect to be late back, so give me a ring if any updates come through. Let the team know there'll be a meeting at ten in the morning.'

'Will do.'

Ashley hoped they'd have some news by then. She rang Ipswich MIT and spoke to a DI Rashford there, who advised her a family liaison officer (FLO) had been assigned to the case, but they weren't going around to see Mercedes' mother, Donna, until the next day. Donna hadn't yet been told a deceased male had been discovered. Again, it struck Ashley that Mercedes' family were experiencing a different service from that which the Norwich parents had received. Ashley explained what she and Emma wanted to do and Rashford agreed it was a decent idea and to report in with him afterwards.

Ashley pulled her laptop out for the rest of the journey and read up on the Ipswich disappearances. Ipswich CID had investigated after two days and, to be fair, they'd been fairly thorough. The couple running off together had seemed the most likely explanation. With both victims over eighteen as well, no access to phone records or bank accounts was possible, unlike with missing children, unless the police had significant cause for concern. One worried mum was not enough, especially when that mother had also admitted the pair were head over heels.

Ashley studied a photograph of Mercedes. She had an all-American look. Big white teeth, curling blonde hair, and a drop-dead slim figure. Ashley made a connection.

'All these girls look a little similar.'

'Young and pretty?'

'Yeah, young, beautiful and blonde, but they all appear super healthy. Like they spent their upbringings riding horses, playing tennis and taking their summers in the Dordogne.'

Emma knew Ipswich well with having grandparents living there.

'I'm reasonably sure Mercedes wasn't summering abroad.'

'No, but that's how she appears.'

Emma turned into Kingston Road and resumed her estate-agent-style commentary.

'We're now moving into more budget-friendly territory. There are three-bedroom doer-uppers here where you might get change from two hundred thousand pounds. Some social housing. Some criminality, but band A for affordable bills. In our opinion, an up-and-coming area. This property comes with nearly all double-glazing and most roof tiles are in place. Toilet may need upgrading.'

Ashley chuckled. The area differed greatly from Newmarket Road. She stared down the long terrace. It wasn't that dissimilar to where she lived. Narrow houses, small front gardens, on-street parking, but most people had made the best of what they could afford. She noted most of the cars were newer than the one she owned.

Emma pulled up outside Mercedes' property. 'Why am I not surprised?'

Ashley looked at the house. The paint on the door was a faded pink, and the windows dirty. Rubbish had accumulated in the small, concreted-over front garden. The wall had needed a fresh coat of render quite some time ago and the house had the honour of being the most dishevelled in the street.

'I'm sure it's lovely inside.'

Ashley got out and knocked. The woman who answered the door had a harried expression.

'What?'

'DS Emma Stones and DI Ashley Knight. Are you Mrs Donna Keeble?'

The officers showed their warrant cards. The woman blinked as though grit were in her eyes. Ashley noted the baggy misshapen T-shirt and the large hole at the knee of her leggings.

'Yes, I'm Donna. Is this about my Mercedes? Oh, God. No.'

She slumped to the floor before Ashley or Emma could step forward. Ashley crouched and rested a hand on Donna's shoulder.

'It's not about Mercedes. We need to talk to you about Esra. There's no news regarding your daughter.'

Emma helped Donna up and practically carried her inside. The lounge was small and messy. A young lad of about ten was sitting on the stained carpet, finishing a jigsaw that had only nine large pieces.

Donna tousled his hair as she walked past him and slumped on the sofa.

'Sorry, it's a mess. I've kind of gone to pot with Mercedes disappearing. We managed together over the years since Wayne died, so it's tough without her.'

Ashley grinned at the boy.

'Wayne?'

'My husband. He dropped dead at fifty-five.'

'How many children do you have?'

'Four. Ferrari and Portia are twins. They're both thirteen and in their third year at seniors. Connor here is twelve. He goes to a school for people like him, but he's not wanted to go since Mercedes left.' She reached over and ruffled his hair again. 'Looking after your mam, aren't ya?'

Connor gave her a vacant smile. Donna returned it, then her face fell.

'I saw on the news a man's body had been found. Was it Esra?'

'Yes, I'm afraid so.'

Donna's chin trembled. 'And no sign of my girl?'

Emma walked over and perched next to her. She placed a hand on Donna's shoulder.

'No, but we're looking hard. We've got leads now.'

Donna had leaned in to Emma, but she abruptly sat forwards and shook her head.

'I appreciate your words, but you were too late for Esra, and that don't look good for my Mercedes. We may be poor, but we aren't daft. I told 'em a week ago she wouldn't have run out on us.'

'I got the impression they were madly in love,' said Ashley.

'Yeah, they was besotted, but she still won't have cleared off without saying. She's a special girl. A godsend. My Wayne left us with nothing but bills. Please, bring her home.'

'We're doing our best,' said Emma.

'Are ya?' Donna squinted at her. She rubbed her eyes, which revealed ragged nails and raw fingers. 'Esra had nobody else, poor boy. I'll go and see him.'

'Thank you.'

'I stuck the news on to check if there was anything new. Apparently two young girls have been grabbed from Norwich. I saw their folks are on TV later. How's about my fucking press conference?'

'It's different when they're under eighteen,' said Ashley softly.

'Well, it shouldn't be.' Donna scowled, but she had no energy left for anger. 'How did Esra die?'

'He suffocated. Possibly suicide.'

Donna leaned away and grimaced as though she'd drunk vinegar. 'I knew it'd end in tears.'

'Why was that?' asked Emma.

'My kids haven't had much, but they've learned right from wrong. We're a family. They weren't going to be dragged up.' Donna looked from Ashley to Emma. 'I can tell those who were raised like I was. It changes you. Life don't treat you fair. My Mercedes had options. Coulda found a guy who wasn't on the edge. The world is against poor kids who get together. She could have done better than Esra. Look!'

Donna leaped out of her seat and grabbed a large folder resting against the wall. She opened it, flicked through some paperwork, then showed the officers an A4 picture of Mercedes all made up in evening wear. What might have been a diamond necklace sparkled on her elegant neck.

'See. Everyone fell in love with her. All the men wanted her.'

Ashley nodded grimly. That had been her downfall.

11

It was nearly seven when Emma dropped Ashley back at Wymondham. Barry, the only one left in the office, filled her in.

'Uniform are at Vulcan industrial estate. They spotted a white van that is similar to the one on the footage near Newmarket Road. It's parked in a lay-by.'

'Are the plates the same?'

'Different. They're chasing the owner.'

'I suppose there are a lot of white vans.'

Barry grinned at her.

'Nah, this looks dodgy. It was good old police gut feeling from that wily sergeant, Frank Levine. He crouched down and noticed residue, presumably from sticking tape on the number plates.'

'Ah, well done, that man,' she said. 'Can't we pick the lock, or use force for that matter?'

Kettle wandered into the room and stood next to her as Barry shook his head.

'Levine was single-crewed, so we were double-checking while another two units headed over. They've just arrived. Who knows what might be in there?'

Kettle's mobile rang. He listened for a moment, then spoke calmly.

'Jemmy the rear doors. I'll wait on the line.' Kettle strode over to a spare desk and took a seat. A minute passed. 'Yes, I'm still here.' He listened again. 'Seal it off. Get CSI.'

'That doesn't sound good,' said Ashley after he'd finished the call.

'The vehicle was a bit battered, but it was clean and functional. Levine suspects it was sold recently, and the plates switched. He found a hair clip and strawberry lip balm in the back.'

'Had they rolled into the sides?'

'No, that's the worrying part. The items had been left in view.'

Ashley shook her head. If this was the van used to abduct the girls the signs weren't good. The van had been dumped, and those responsible hadn't been careful. There was little else they could do except wait while Uniform continued their searches.

Ashley rang Ipswich MIT and told them what Mercedes' mother had said. She updated the file with her notes and decided she'd had enough for the day.

It was unlikely anything would change until the morning. She was walking out with Barry when Kettle passed them. He said to watch *BBC Look East* at ten thirty that evening. Most news outlets would mention the incident, but the full interview with the girls' mothers from Newmarket Road would be on TV.

Ashley sat in her car and texted the rest of the team the information. She reached home a little before nine thirty and stared at her house as she got out. Mill Road was a safe place, but her home felt empty and dark when she entered, as it often did. She considering calling on Arthur next door, then remembered the press conference. Her phone beeped with an incoming message. It was from Hector.

> You probably won't be able to sleep tonight, such is your joy.

Ashley smiled and replied.

> That's true. I love a geek-fest.

> I'll have you know we're information experts.

> Debatable.

She relented and finished her text with the words:

> Can't wait.

Hector's help would be important, and not only with establishing the connections between the recently missing people. His findings could link all the other Vampire investigations together and hopefully to Typhon abroad. Anything his team found might give them that tiny edge they often needed.

Ashley grabbed a tin of Lidl baked beans and sausages, emptied the contents into a bowl, and put it in the microwave. She sent Hector a photograph of the tin while she waited for the toaster. That would stop him from sleeping.

She took a tray through to the front lounge and ate in silence with her mind churning. After washing up that day's dishes, she grabbed a Twix bar and turned on the telly just in time. After an introduction, *Look East* switched to the kitchen at Akari's parents' house in Norwich. DCI Kettle sat at one end of the long table. He introduced himself and gave the background, keeping it brief.

The people who would make an impact were the women beside him.

Victoria Kato was steely faced. Her eyes bored into Ashley's lounge.

'My daughter's name is Akari Kato. She is seventeen years old. Akari likes Pilates and tennis. She loves her best friend, Camille, and she has so much to live for. My plea is to the people of Norfolk. You know your cities and towns, your friends and your neighbours. Be on the lookout for our girls. Find them for us, for me. For yourselves. Don't let them be a tragic footnote in our county's history. Ring the helpline for anything, anything at all, and bring our babies home. Thank you.'

The camera gradually moved in for a close-up of Victoria. She blinked slowly, then nodded firmly, but her chin trembled. The focus moved to Aveline Dupont, whose gaze had been on her friend. She stared at the table for a moment. Her chest rose as she pulled in a desperate breath. When she looked up again, tears bled down her face.

'My daughter's name is Camille. She is eighteen in two weeks. I know Camille wouldn't have run away. It is clear she has been taken. Please, return her. Bring them both back. Our lives would be over if anything happened to them. Drop them anywhere safe. I beg you. Just...'

Aveline's eyes scrunched closed. Her mouth formed an ugly line. She held her head and gasped. Then she straightened her shoulders and gritted her teeth. Her eyes bulged as she concentrated.

'Ma vie. Mon âme. Mon tout!' A huge sob engulfed her. She tried to smile, but her expression was tortured. 'Whoever has her. Please, don't hurt her. Let them go. End this now. I forgive you.'

Ashley had taken a mouthful of her chocolate biscuit and

had to force herself to chew. She leaned back in her seat as the camera stayed on Aveline's distraught face, then panned out to include Victoria. Ashley typed the French words into Google as the women on the screen gripped hands.

Aveline's words translated as my life, my soul, my everything.

Such strong women. Such unforgettably powerful performances.

But would they be enough to bring their daughters home?

12

Ashley woke tired the next morning. Her sleep had been disturbed by thoughts of the young women from Norwich. At the door to leave the house, she ruefully eyed her jogging shoes. Exercise had slipped off the agenda again since she'd been promoted, and she wasn't exactly sure why. Her muffin top had come out of hibernation and Ashley was currently in the unenviable position of being too thin for her fat clothes and too fat for the thin stuff.

She grabbed her trainers and placed them on the sofa, where she would actually have to move them later that evening to sit and watch TV. Surely that would do the trick.

It was an hour's drive into OCC. Time she usually used to get her head straight and allow details of current investigations to trickle through her mind. She hadn't been called, nor received any emails, so there had been no more progress since the van find. Ashley disliked missing persons cases because of the continuous dead ends. In some instances, the people were never seen again, and the investigation died a slow death, but she suspected this would be different.

The first officer she saw when she reached work was Hector. He was waiting for the kettle to boil in the small kitchen and she couldn't help a huge grin forming. She'd half expected him to have changed, but he still looked like a tall Eddie Redmayne in a tailored suit.

Hector was one of the last officers admitted on the Fast Track programme. He'd spent six months learning the ropes with Ashley's Major Investigation Team. After a combative few months, which was partly down to his upper-class upbringing and lack of real-life experience, he'd fitted in well. The fact he'd been brought in at his young age to run the data team for a case this serious spoke volumes.

When he turned and saw her, he raised an eyebrow.

'Were you checking me out?'

'I was focusing on your receding hairline.'

'It is not.' But his hand rose to his forehead.

'Twenty-five is a challenging time for men. Denial won't help you cope with the changes.'

Hector's face broke into a smile. His long stride had him next to her in seconds, and he gave her a hug. Ashley looked up into his eyes.

'Oh, we're huggers now, are we?'

'It's a London ting.'

'You say that so naturally.'

'I will admit, it doesn't roll off my tongue.'

'You're here early.'

'Yeah. I'm meeting a guy from the NCA here. I'm not sure of his exact position. A Mr Beckett.'

'Not on first-name terms?'

'I've only met him once before, but I found him formidable.'

'A "knock you out with a flick of his hand" kind of fella?'

'Not quite.'

'Shame, I was hoping to introduce him to Barry.'

Hector cocked his head to one side. 'This investigation has the potential to send shock waves across Europe. Reputations will be tarnished, careers shattered.'

'I haven't seen any specific stats on the emerging patterns for this case yet. These missing women are worrying enough.'

'I've already found some concerning trends, but I'll need today to firm up on them. Data is coming in from all over now. The NCA reached an information-sharing agreement with Brussels regarding Typhon.'

Ashley took a moment to process Hector's language.

'Do you think there's a Mr or Mrs Typhon, or just regional leaders such as Cerberus and the others?'

'I haven't had time to look at any of the dark-web chats, but Mr Beckett said Typhon has never been referred to in the first person, like Hydra, for example.'

'What is Beckett's first name?'

'Mister. You'll understand when you meet him.'

'So, these children of Typhon. How many were there?'

'In mythology or now?'

'Both.'

'There's no exact consensus with either. Scholars disagree historically, but it seems we've caught the main ones apart from this Hydra. Mr Beckett wants everyone here for a presentation at 5 p.m., so make sure your team is back. I'll link in with you regularly. Keep me up to date with all the latest.'

Ashley saluted. 'Yes, Drill Sergeant!'

'Cute.'

Ashley gestured to the journalist, Sebastian, who had arrived. 'Are you having anything to do with him?'

'Who is he?'

Ashley explained.

'Maybe. I've heard him mentioned. It's Mr Beckett who has oversight of what Sebastian publishes.'

Ashley smiled. So, it was Beckett who was checking Sebastian's work.

'Okay. I'd better get on. Do you have any thoughts about these missing girls?'

Hector shook his head. 'I just pray the Vampires didn't take them. My team of three will be here at nine. Kettle's given us the conference room, so we can spread out.'

'Any idea how long you'll be here?'

'As long as it takes.'

Ashley felt like a mother, desperately asking as many questions as possible while their child was in a talkative mood.

'Come for tea tonight. I'll cook.'

Hector scratched his chin. 'Not tempting after that photo you sent me.'

'Takeaway from the Bann Thai?'

'Deal.'

Ashley left him to make his drink and returned to her office as the rest of her team filtered in. Kettle had allocated her another two new starters after Jan Pederson and Emma Stones were promoted to DS, but neither of them had been released from CID yet.

Emma ensured the incident room had all the details for Akari, Camille and Mercedes, then went to gather the troops for the meeting.

Ashley headed there early and rang Control to see if there had been any further developments, but there hadn't. Kettle arrived and stood at the back as Barry, Zelda, Morgan, Jan and Sal came in with Emma.

'Okay, guys,' said Ashley. 'You should have read your emails by now and be familiar with Esra and Mercedes, as well as Akari and Camille. Our focus is on the Norfolk girls for the remainder of the week, Suffolk has Mercedes, but she could be in either county. If we haven't found any of the missing women by then, there's a chance they have been moved further away, or we could be too late. Did everyone watch *Look East*?'

All those present nodded.

'I want you out in threes today. Start where the white van was located. Be careful. Remember, Akari and Camille's abductors are liable to be ruthless and violent, and likely desperate. Jan and Emma will head a team each. Let's work our way through the industrial estate.'

'There's not much CCTV around there,' said Barry. 'I checked last night for possible routes in and out of that location if a driver wanted to avoid being recorded. There is one, so they could have got away scot-free, but it's not straightforward. The encouraging news is traffic was fairly light on the footage I observed, so there shouldn't be thousands of registrations to verify.'

'I'll ask another team to study the council's cameras,' said Kettle. 'I've also agreed with the head of CID that his missing persons team will tackle the softer angles to this case for a few days for us. Talk to the victims' friends, relatives and neighbours, and check social media. The families are allowing access to both girls' laptops and phone records.'

Ashley remembered the incident Morgan and Sal went to the previous day.

'Anything from your call yesterday?'

Sal grimaced. 'One of them had been dead a while. I reckon the other didn't report it, then died of natural causes. Both bodies gone for autopsy.'

'I gave that back to CID,' said Kettle. 'I'll allocate a family liaison officer to head over this afternoon to Newmarket Road. Any other angles or thoughts?'

'If both mobiles are still off, then it looks bad for those girls,' said Sal.

Ashley patted Sal's arm. He had a daughter of a similar age. 'It's possible this is going to lead to a ransom demand.'

'The parents are wealthy,' said Kettle. 'Or at least two of them are.'

Barry huffed. 'That'd be about right. Those with money get saved.'

'I saw Hector entering the conference room,' said Emma. 'Has he anything to add?'

Kettle bunched his jaw. 'No, but he's concerned.'

'I was away yesterday,' said Zelda. 'What exactly are we saying here?'

'Sorry, Zelda,' said Ashley. 'I'll sum up for everyone. Looking at what we know, we believe this Typhon organisation has been pushed out of Eastern and Northern Europe to their last bolthole. Here. We're closing in on them, but too slowly.'

'And these missing women?'

'To put it succinctly, they don't bother with the recruitment and exploitation of their victims any more. They're just plucking young people off the street, then transporting them like cattle.'

Barry gave Zelda a hard smile.

'So, if these girls aren't found soon, they'll be off to market.'

13

The team dispersed, and those who were leaving the building for the industrial estate did so shortly afterwards. Kettle checked in with Ashley numerous times throughout the day, but she never had anything new to tell him. From where Ashley was sitting, the search had been a washout. She ordered the two teams back in for four thirty and they caught up in the same meeting room as earlier.

'I can see by your faces it's been a long day,' said Ashley.

'Sure has,' said Emma. 'The Vulcan estate is pretty big, with quite a few units which are either unused or appeared that way. Sometimes nobody came when we knocked, even at units that seemed to be in use. There are vehicles parked everywhere. We checked the registrations as we passed them. Nearly all had insurance. Some were registered as off-road, even though they were left at the side of the road. It's obviously not strictly legal, but Eastern European kidnappers aren't likely to be filling in statutory notices. We have kept a record of those.'

'In conclusion?'

'We got nothing.'

'Jan?'

'Same. We could have walked past the unit they were operating from and not known. Some of the guys running firms tried to be helpful, others blanked us. I know we didn't have a wasted day, but it feels like it. Anything from CCTV?'

'No, there are so many routes out of the estate the team checking them found themselves with a big job. They spotted two recently registered cars which were uninsured. Uniform are attending the home addresses, but one was a Mini, which doesn't seem likely.'

'No ransom demands while we were away?' asked Sal.

'Nope. Both girls' social media accounts are completely open to their friends, so a pal kindly went over and showed the parents everything. Scott Gorton attended as FLO. Their laptops are full of what you'd expect from a seventeen-year-old schoolgirl's computer. Like us, Scott fears the worst.'

'Any luck in Ipswich?' asked Jan.

'No, the same. They suspected they were waiting to find Mercedes' body, but now they share our concern she's going to be put to work somehow with Camille and Akari. These girls could be the tip of a horrifying iceberg.'

'That hardly bears thinking about,' said Emma.

'Yep, but we know it happens. Abductions for prostitution were rare in this country, but with so much legal and illegal migration, it's becoming more common.'

'Our women aren't illegals though,' said Barry.

'No, but could the Vampires be a bunch of men under the leadership of this Hydra? The infrastructure of their operation is still intact in England. In a way, it's clever. Just take the girls and disappear. If they escape detection, then the victims can be moved and exploited in rented homes and disused motels and warehouses.'

'The kids may be hooked on heroin by the weekend,' said Morgan.

Drugs were often used to control the women. It didn't need mentioning that forced prostitution tended to be a short career with the evidence burnt or buried afterwards.

'Did the plea from the parents help?' asked Emma.

'Nothing obvious from the helpline. A few leads are being looked into, but I'm not hopeful with what we've had so far. The girls really do appear to have vanished into thin air. We have to accept it was a professional job. Anything else?'

The officers were deep in thought. Ashley could sense their frustration.

'Okay, Hector's taking a meeting in the main conference room at five. Take a break and I'll see you there.'

Ashley spent the time catching up on her emails before setting off. The conference room had a large table with seating for twenty around it. When Ashley's team arrived, those seats were all taken with people already standing behind them, so they were forced to stand at the back of the room. This was okay for most of her guys, but Ashley wasn't much over five feet, so she pulled rank and edged through the throng. She smiled when she spotted Hector at the front, next to a balding, bespectacled man in a sensible suit. Was he *the* Mr Beckett? When DCI Kettle arrived, he strode to the front and stood beside them.

The guy with the glasses cleared his throat.

'Thank you for coming. My name is Mr Beckett. I'm a director at the NCA. I will assume you've all heard of the investigation into a people-trafficking organisation spreading across Europe. I'm here to tell you we're reasonably certain the perpetrators are here in Norfolk.'

Beckett glanced around the room. His glasses were slightly opaque, so it was hard to ascertain exactly who his gaze was fixing on. His voice was soft, but it had an aura of power. Ashley suspected Beckett commanded respect wherever he went. He continued.

'Yes, in your county, and in Suffolk, too. I know you work closely with MIT there. They'll hear this presentation tomorrow morning. Both counties are in the top ten by area in the United Kingdom, but not in the top twenty by population. Much of the land is farms, holiday homes, woods and beaches. Transport from the ports means the roads are often busy with trailers and containers. Tourism is the fifth biggest employer.'

Beckett checked his notes.

'Our task is to end this operation once and for all. To round up the ringleaders and place them in jail for the next thirty years. Any questions at this point?'

'Is it just this Typhon or are the Vampires part of it?' asked one of the other detective inspectors present.

'The Vampires and the Romans, who you eradicated, were both smaller heads of a bigger serpent, Typhon. That's our focus. Our intel suggests the UK branch of Typhon is based in your two counties and was commanded by a man called Hydra, or the Hydra. We believe he ran the operation from elsewhere, but an informer told us he fled here. The Dutch police service cracked Typhon's communication channels, and they suspect Hydra is the last boss left to catch. Their sources revealed Felixstowe was regularly used as an entry point to the UK.'

Again, Beckett studied the sheet of paper in front of him.

'The Port of Felixstowe in Suffolk is the United Kingdom's largest container port. It deals with nearly half of Britain's containerised cargo. Four million containers per year. A figure which clearly makes our job difficult. NCA agents are dealing with that angle. Tourism and farming lead to a huge movement of holidaymakers and workers, which also makes our task harder. You struggled to pin down the Vampires before for precisely those reasons. We believe the remainder of Typhon have infiltrated their network, becoming one and the same. Anything to add, Chief?'

Kettle nodded.

'I reckoned we'd caught most of the Vampires' crew, but it does appear their ranks have been bolstered. We must finish the job. I accept we don't have many leads at the moment, so think outside the box. Seb has been working with us for two days and has compiled a report that will appear on various websites tonight and in all the newspapers tomorrow. In it are some worrying trends, which Hector will reveal to you now.'

Hector took a step forward. He appeared every inch the confident professional.

'I spent this morning studying the stats of those who have gone missing across Europe. As you know, the lost are legion. I've stripped it down further, looking at only young people, many of whom were trafficked. This afternoon, I conversed with a counterpart in Amsterdam who has been collating the statistics for his country. To be concise, we suspect there has been a widespread campaign of murder.'

There was a bit of a hubbub as those present digested the news. Hector spoke over them, and everyone quietened.

'There are clear trends. Once the trafficked have served their purpose, they are quietly and brutally disposed of. The Romans weren't that ruthless, but we never knew exactly what happened to the Vampires' victims. They may have always done this in the UK, or it's possibly a recent tactic. Regardless, it definitely occurred in Europe. Any questions?'

'How do they know the victims of trafficking are being murdered if nobody misses the individuals or has a clue where they went?' asked Emma.

'The answer to that is becoming shockingly clear. The countries weren't talking to each other. Remains found in one country were not reported internationally. Connections weren't made. Victims were simply recorded as John or Jane Doe. What's brought the information together is the work done by the officers in Holland. It seems the traffickers started taking Dutch girls without bothering to fool them with jobs abroad, or cheap routes into the UK.' Hector folded his arms. 'What is Amsterdam notorious for?'

'Tulips?' asked Barry, looking sweet-faced.

Hector shook his head. 'The criminals took prostitutes. Undeniably an intelligent move.'

'Ah, I get it,' said Barry. 'It's like fantasy football. They're picking experienced players.'

'Interesting analogy, but yes. At least those women would understand the trade. Reports of them missing might not have been taken seriously either. As worrying is that they also selected females going about their normal lives and collected them off the street. Abducted them. Many were never heard from again. The reason we know this is because some were found dead. A few of them shortly after the people responsible took them. We're getting more information on this angle, cause of death, et cetera, but it happened in other countries too, although the reports remained in the originating country in most instances.'

'Why would you take someone to kill them soon after?' asked Ashley.

'We don't know. I'm checking for ransom demands. Perhaps they weren't paid. Maybe the victims fought or tried to escape. Accidents happen. Men in these types of professions aren't gentle. Drownings are common in trafficking across water. I hope to have more on that over the next few days. In the meantime, we need to crack on and work with what we have.'

Ashley focused to get her head around what he was saying. This was gruesome news. People stolen to order. She cleared her throat.

'Were the women in Holland all blondes?'

Hector grabbed a file from the table and flicked through it. He took his time, even though an entire room waited on him.

'That's a good spot, Ashley. To be clear for those present who haven't seen their photographs, the three women still missing in Norwich and Ipswich had blonde hair, as did nearly all those in Holland. I'm not sure what that means, if anything. Sometimes rich men from Arab nations request working girls who are blonde or fair-skinned. That could be a factor.'

'I think I speak for everyone by saying we're desperate to get going, but we need more direction.'

Hector gave Ashley a knowing look.

'I can help with that because you've brought us nicely to the final connection we've made, and the oddest one. In Holland, the victims were discovered near places of natural beauty. What else is Holland famous for?'

'Windmills,' shouted Sal.

'Yes. There were windmills near where the bodies were dumped. It's a definite pattern. Where was the man found yesterday in Ipswich?'

'Herringfleet Windmill,' said Ashley.

More mutterings filtered throughout the room. Hector waited for silence.

'Holland has over a thousand windmills. Those types of buildings are scattered throughout all of Europe. Norfolk and Suffolk probably have around a hundred.'

Ashley had seen them all over the county. 'I suppose there

may already be remains near one. In the bushes, or thrown off cliffs, or sunk if they're near water. I'm thinking of Mercedes Keeble in particular, but why would a killer go to the bother of dumping them in such specific locations?'

Hector shrugged. Beckett removed his glasses and looked at the sea of faces. He had dark eyes, which settled on Ashley. They gave him a sad and pensive air, as though life had forced him to make some terrible decisions.

As their gazes connected, Beckett went from being someone in a room you'd never remember, to a person in a crowd you'd never forget.

'There might be nothing special about the location,' he said. 'After all, those places tend to be rural and devoid of visitors at night. Drop-off and escape would be fairly simple.'

Ashley wasn't happy with that explanation.

'Yes, but some are busy tourist locations during the day. At least, they are out of winter. The bodies were found at Herringfleet and in Holland, too, so it's not as if the criminals have worked hard attempting to conceal them.'

Beckett put his glasses back on.

'A valid point. That disregard is something I find extremely concerning.'

14

Beckett ended the meeting and Ashley found herself filtering out of the room with Sebastian.

'Can I have a quick word?' he asked.

Ashley followed him to his desk in the corner, where he'd been working.

'Sure, Sebastian, although it seems people who know you well use Seb.'

He dipped his chin. 'You may call me Seb.'

'Maybe I will. What's up?'

'What was he implying by saying bodies left near windmills were extremely worrying?'

Ashley paused, considering her words carefully. 'It's possible the locations were simply convenient,' she began, 'but if there's a reason behind it...' She trailed off.

Sebastian's eyes widened. 'Like the killers wanted them found?'

'Maybe, or the locations might point to the deaths being ritualistic.'

'Do you mean the killer is psychotic or demented?'

'It could be a satanic cult.'

'Right, I have been in countries where they're more common.'

'You've clearly been around,' she said with a hint of a smile.

'Only in the nicest possible way. I've met people in a lot of places where the only life they value is their own.'

'Luckily, we don't meet too many people like that in Norfolk.'

'It only takes one.'

'True, but I think what concerned Kettle more than devil worshippers was the fact the bodies weren't well concealed.'

'Surely that helps the police.'

'In a way, yes, but why aren't the killers being more careful?'

Sebastian pursed his lips as he thought.

'Idiocy, complacency, or overconfidence.'

'Perhaps all of them, but remember, these guys operate in the shadows. Typhon has evaded the authorities for decades. The Vampires seem to vanish at will. With their years of experience, they'll have developed methods and tactics to escape detection. They're probably prepared to sacrifice members underneath them to keep themselves hidden. Maybe the people actually dumping the bodies have no idea who's behind it all. They're just following orders, keeping their heads down. The real mastermind is so far removed, they think they're untouchable. That's why they're so brazen – they don't think anyone can connect the dots back to them.'

'It's difficult to hunt or capture someone who doesn't exist.'

'Exactly. A myth or a legend, or even just a rumour, is hard to pin down. Perhaps it's not overconfidence.'

Sebastian frowned. 'That's not encouraging. In fact, it's pretty scary if you consider what's been going on.'

Ashley gave him a small smile. 'Lost the faith already?'

He chuckled. 'Never!'

'Good man.'

'Are you off home now?'

'I am.'

'Fancy coming out for a bite to eat, or you look like you could rustle up a delicious meal.'

'I hope your reporting skills are better than your detective skills if you think that. Won't Sebby's mummy wummy have dindins on the table for her special boy?'

Sebastian leaned back and stretched in his chair. 'Takeaway?'

'I already have a date tonight.'

At that moment, Hector marched past.

'Ashley, the earliest I can get to yours is about nine. Is that okay?'

'You're pushing it, but I'll have the food ready.'

Hector strode away, leaving Sebastian and Ashley looking at each other. He crossed his arms.

'I can't compete with the golden one.'

'Funny you chose that phrase. Barry used to call him that.'

'Hector's impressive for his age.'

Ashley was about to make a retort then stopped herself. Why had she slipped into flirting? This guy was not boyfriend material.

'Will you be in tomorrow?'

'Yes, all week. Kettle warned me there's likely to be more unwelcome news. Rain check?'

Ashley couldn't help herself as her stomach gave a flirtatious quiver. 'Sure.'

She drove home in a good mood, until she remembered Bann Thai wasn't open on a Tuesday. Cromer had a new Vietnamese restaurant, though, so at eight o'clock she strolled there and ordered a variety of dishes. The staff were super friendly. Even so, she wouldn't tell Hector where his dinner had come from. He might not be impressed with food from the Yumy Yumy House.

At nine fifteen, Hector knocked on her door. She opened it to see him running one hand through his hair and undoing his tie with the other. Ashley stepped back to let him in.

'Any later and I'd be in my nightgown heading up the stairs with a candle.'

'Apologies. Another link emerged, which complicates things a little.'

Ashley took his jacket off him and hung it up. She reheated the dishes and brought them through, still in their plastic containers, and placed them on the coffee table. Hector chuckled when she dropped a plate and cutlery in his lap.

'Glass of wine?' she asked.

'No, tomorrow's looking busy.'

'Come on, spit it out. What have you found?'

'It's not just near windmills that the bodies have been discovered. It's also lighthouses.'

'Well, we have quite a few of them, too, but not loads.'

'There was a body located in Holland near Giethoorn. The area is nicknamed the Venice of the Netherlands. It's a bit like the Norfolk Broads.'

'A bit?'

'The buildings are more like the cover of a chocolate box.'

'Sounds lovely.'

'Actually, Holland has other similar famous places. There are incredible working windmills at Zaanse Schans, and Kinderdijk has nineteen of them, many in a row. Breathtaking. Have you been?'

'I went to Holland once on a school trip, but I had a special cookie early in the day and the rest of my visit was sort of a blur.'

'You're a class act.'

'Total blur, actually. I assume there weren't any remains found at those nineteen windmills?'

'No.'

'Perhaps they're too famous.'

'Yes, maybe there are too many people about, even at night.'

'Hector, it's late. As much as I'm enjoying your Dutch windmill presentation, what are you suggesting? That we search all the lighthouses and windmills in the county?'

Hector's jaw clenched. A flicker of desperation flashed across his face.

'It might come to that.'

'You said there were around a hundred windmills and now you want to add lighthouses?'

'I need to have another look at it tomorrow. Maybe I can narrow it down. There's something else linking them, though. I can feel it.'

15

A sigh escaped Ashley at the prospect of the immense task, but she'd long stopped ignoring hunches. Hector had closed his eyes. She wondered if something else was on his mind. A slurp of spicy noodles caught his attention.

'Slob.'

'What's bothering you?'

Hector lowered his fork.

'I reckon Kettle is concerned where responsibility is going to lie when all of this unravels.'

Ashley pondered that for a moment.

'That's because Kettle's been around the block. If we solve the case, the NCA will take the credit. If there's a cock-up, we'll carry the can, but that's for him to worry about. Let's not talk business all night. What have you been doing? How come you haven't been back, especially to see the woman of your dreams?'

Most of the single men at OCC, as well as some of the married ones, wanted to date the classy Gabriella, who was the team's admin manager, but her parents were elderly and frail, which took up a lot of her time. She had long ginger hair, which had led to Barry nicknaming her Gingerpuss as opposed to Glamourpuss. Hector hated the nickname, even though she didn't appear to mind. He'd been out with her a few times, as friends, but that was it as far as Ashley knew.

'Did you keep in touch with Gabriella?'

'I tried to, but I was overkeen.'

'Hot like a dog, not cool like a cat?'

'Very much so. You know, overly long emails, replying immediately to every text with a question, so she felt the need to reply.'

'Classic stalker tactics.'

'Yes, I scared myself. Her father died a few months ago, and her mum has advanced Parkinson's and had to go into a home.'

'I'm sorry to hear that.'

'I've only had one or two texts from her since.'

'She'll be grieving. Well, I'm sure you'll bump into her at work. Try to be chilled but interested in how she's doing.'

'Yeah.'

'Talking of cool cats, I must say you were composed up there today. You've gained in confidence.'

Hector tried not to beam but failed.

'Thanks. Going to the Met was stressful and daunting, but after a few weeks I realised the few colleagues who were attempting to make my life difficult were just bigheads and bullies. I knew I was the best person for the job. It's what I'm good at. I called a few of them out after I'd proved myself and they folded, as bullies typically do. Dealing with the NCA when they began asking for help was like operating on another level, but we were busy, so I got on with it. Returning here has felt like coming home, so my confidence came easy.'

'Good for you. Obviously, the kudos is mine. Taught you all I know.'

'Clearly.'

They ate in companionable silence, but Ashley's mind had slipped to the case and in particular the windmill link.

'You said some of the kidnap victims were found murdered shortly after they were taken?'

'Yes, not many men, but a couple of females in Holland. There were more women who died quickly elsewhere.'

'And those females were all attractive?'

'From the images I've seen, most were what you'd describe as stunning, but others were simply fresh-faced and glowing with the beauty of youth.'

'So, age might be a factor, but killing so quickly doesn't make sense. Surely the idea is to work the girls, if that's the reason they were taken. They're not like the poor blokes in Russian penal battalions.'

Hector frowned. 'Eh?'

'Single-use soldiers.'

'Ashley!'

She smiled at him before continuing.

'I can understand the odd accident or bout of rage. The men responsible are scum, after all, but that doesn't account for so many girls dying just after being taken. It's a waste of time and effort, and a loss of their resources if the gang need money.'

'That's Mr Beckett's big concern,' replied Hector. 'Maybe they are single use. There's a condition called erotophonophilia, where the individual gets sexually aroused by the thought of murdering someone during a sexual act.'

'I've seen cases of throttling, gagging and ligaturing where the participants have died by accident, which were mostly linked to a kick from the loss of oxygen, but none were deliberate killings. Snuff movies were reputedly around in the eighties, but, if you can believe it, that was even before my time.'

'Well, it's a rare and controversial sex disorder with an obvious lack of empathy or fear of consequence. People with erotophonophilia are sometimes called lust murderers. They usually have mental health issues like antisocial personality disorder, psychopathy or narcissism.'

'Brilliant.'

'It's a type of paraphilia, the same category as necrophilia and cannibalism, where the chances of successful treatment are minimal to zero for chronic cases.'

'Jeez, those poor girls.'

'Yes, it's a big worry. Typhon as a collective has proved itself cunning, disciplined and well above average intelligence. It's possible these deaths stem from the sale of an extremely specific service to incredibly rich people with twisted urgings.'

Ashley briefly wondered where he'd got his information from to make the connection, but the clever little git probably knew of the condition already. This theory certainly sounded feasible.

'And the Typhon organisation is desperate for money. Prostitution pays well, but finding a stunning woman for a sick wealthy type might pay thousands.'

'I'd say much more, and any risk is minimised due to only a single event taking place.'

'Clinically put, Hector. Although, it's not the sort of thing you could advertise.'

'No, but the data indicates these killings have been occurring for years. Typhon may have a client list. People who are interested in this kind of pleasure are ill. Without treatment, they would remain sick, reoffend repeatedly, and perhaps escalate.'

'Their customer database never becomes inactive because their customers are never cured.'

'Right, and the more often they did business together, the more trusting the clients would become.'

'They might fly in for the service and be gone hours later.'

'Yes. Erotophonophilia is almost entirely a male hobby. Maybe this Hydra is into that sort of thing himself. We've never come close to catching him. It's hard to profile men who are both psychotic and emotionally disordered, but they tend to be rich and successful.'

Ashley was too tired for this level of concentration, but it would save going through it again in the morning.

'No wonder Beckett's concerned. What about the boy who died?'

'Esra? No idea at this point. Perhaps they only wanted Mercedes, but it was easier to take them together.'

'When the couple were probably distracted by each other?'

'Yes, then they simply disposed of him.'

'Whatever is going on, it's chilling.'

'Barbaric,' Hector said, a tremor in his voice as he pushed his half-eaten plate away. 'Such disregard for human life.'

'I know.'

Hector wasn't finished.

'The architects of these crimes, the filth who carry them out, are nothing but monsters.'

16

Prakash Gutta loved the serenity after dawn had broken at Horsey Mere. The deserted car park, the hushed roads, the windpump standing sentinel. He whistled as he slowly pushed his bicycle along the path. This was his place. An unspoiled, ageless landscape where nothing much mattered. Like the weightless, wispy clouds above him, life's burdens melted away.

Bitterns skimmed the surface of the river, swans paraded in pairs, and herons glided by. The gentle, caressing breeze seemed full of melodic birdsong. Prakash drew in the fragrant air; wildflowers mixed with the earthy scents of the marshes. There had been nothing remotely like this in his arid homeland of Rajasthan. Perhaps that was why he loved it and came so often.

Prakash knew it wasn't for the angling. He certainly didn't catch much. Pretending to fish was an excuse to wave at the sailors as their boats and barges cruised by. He enjoyed the fleeting connection with the outside world, but today he sought solace under the vast expanse of the azure sky.

He often imagined his wife, Aparna, gazing down on him. Twenty years she'd been in heaven. He understood that was part of the reason he returned to Horsey Mere. They used to visit often. Sometimes, he felt as if he could almost reach up and cup her face, as he used to do.

He left the track and took one of the minor waterways. A bead of sweat dripped off his forehead, even though the morning sun lacked strength. The extra weight in the panniers and a backpack on his shoulders used to be no bother. Now it hinted at the passing of time. He found a nice, secluded spot, and left his bike leaning against a stubby tree. There were few extravagances of late, but he had a big grin as he got out his efficient flask and erected his excellent folding chair.

After a few minutes, he'd emptied the panniers and laid out his blanket. He chuckled to himself. The forecast had been good, and he'd brought a picnic. Maybe he could get cosy under his coat and have a nap. The reeds rustled next to him as he sat, and the gentle water lapped against the bank. He admired the translucent clouds as they drifted by.

He'd enjoyed a peaceful minute like that, basking within nature's rich tapestry, when he remembered the Hobnobs he had packed to have with his drink. Even being immersed in such a soothing symphony was better with a decent biscuit.

Prakash was relishing his first bite when he noticed movement at the edge of his vision. A lily pad had detached itself from a group and drifted in front of him. It wobbled as though something was caught under it. Huge pike lurked in the river, although he was yet to catch one, but whatever it was seemed larger than that.

Prakash stepped into the stream. He cursed as deceptively deep water slopped over the rims of his wellies and soaked his socks. After edging out a few metres, he paused. Treacherous mud and slimy stones shifted ominously underfoot. He dared not go out much further. His eyes squinted into the water. There was something there.

Prakash reached out, but his hand hovered in the air. He almost grinned at being silly, knowing nothing in the water could hurt him, but a smile wouldn't come. The lily pad moved. At first he thought he could see a large plastic bag, then he leaned back in disbelief and blinked.

The lily pad edged away, seemingly taking its quarry with it, but there was no mistaking the horrifying sight.

Suspended, not far under the water, eyes wide with the finality of death, fair hair fanning out around her perfect features, was a beautiful girl.

17

Ashley was almost at work the next morning when her phone rang. While pulling over, the engine spluttered, reminding her it was time to get a new car. Perhaps one with a proper hands-free and fewer dints. She suspected her mobile had voice-control activation, but God only knew where. Maybe Hector could explain how to set it up. Although she'd feel like a geriatric asking him.

'DI Ashley Knight.'

'Good morning, ma'am. We've had notification of a potential body sighted at Horsey Mere.'

Ashley knew the location reasonably well. Her next-door neighbour's son, Oliver, had done a school project about the mere's history and Ashley had helped him with research on the Internet. The mere was a tranquil expanse owned by the National Trust and nestled in the northern Broads. Horsey stood for Horse Island, which used to be a poor grazing area surrounded by marshes.

Her brow furrowed at Control's choice of words. 'Sighted?'

'A fisherman saw a body floating past.'

The image of the windpump, a stark silhouette against the landscape, flashed through Ashley's mind. She remembered reading about the windpump, how it helped transform the marshy land into fertile farmland. Now, it had perhaps been a silent witness to a terrible crime. Over the years, as the water-ways developed, the area had become a place of natural beauty. She wasn't completely sure what the difference was between a windpump and a windmill, but a murderer was unlikely to make any distinction.

'Any more details?' said Ashley, her voice clipped with urgency.

'Blonde hair. Youngish. Female.'

Ashley thought of Akari and Camille, but grim intuition told her it was more likely Mercedes, who'd been missing for longer. Gathering the body wouldn't be too hard. Being only a mile from the coast, the weather could still be wild, with flooding a risk when ferocious gales whipped off the North Sea, but in late spring, it would be a tranquil place.

'Okay, it's tidal there, so the RNLI from Cart Gap might be able to help with recovery.'

'I'll contact them.'

'If they don't have a boat available, I'll find a local craft. The river folk all muck in at times like these. We shouldn't need the fire brigade if the victim is floating.'

Ashley had seen a couple of casualties recovered from reeds with a boat hook.

'Understood.'

'What time did he spot the woman?'

'A bit before eight.'

'Do you know when high tide is?'

After fifteen seconds of tapping, Control replied.

'Nine thirty.'

'Right, so she might have drifted downstream, and will possibly be on her way back towards the sea if we aren't quick. The current can run reasonably fast through Horsey Mere, so she may have moved a fair distance. There's a car park at the windpump. I'll meet everyone there.'

'Do you want CSI now, and what's your ETA?'

Ashley needed a crime scene first, but it was only a matter of time. They'd need to check the bank to see if they could find where the body went in. Unfortunately, that bank ran for over a hundred lock-free miles.

'One CSI van for the moment. I'll need as many people as possible for searching. DCI Kettle will arrange that.'

Ashley tapped her free hand on the steering wheel. She'd driven past North Walsham, so she wasn't far.

'My ETA is thirty minutes. Let's inform the family liaison officers who have been dealing with the missing girls that they'll be needed today, and I'll be in contact after nine.'

Scott Gorton would have to talk to the parents in Newmarket Road, even if it was just to inform them the missing girl from Ipswich had been found. They couldn't let them hear the news without warning them beforehand. The Ipswich FLO would have a grimmer task.

'That's confirmed, although the Ipswich FLO isn't on duty today. I'll tell Scott Gorton you'll contact him after nine.'

Ashley had a sinking feeling the task of visiting Mercedes' mum would fall to her.

When they located the corpse, the first things they'd need would be to have the victim identified and a doctor to certify life extinct. The quicker the better, so they could get the full post-mortem started.

'I'll be in contact as soon as the body is recovered. Have a GP forewarned and please let the mortuary at the Norfolk and

Norwich know we'll be needing an urgent PM. Ask DS Jan Pederson to meet me at the car park with whoever is on call for MIT this morning.'

'Yea, ma'am. DC Barry Hooper is already en route.'

Ashley cut the call knowing Control would organise everyone else who needed to be there. She made swift progress to Horsey Mere even though her ageing motor groaned at times in protest. Two marked estate vehicles had parked up. Four police officers were talking to an elderly Asian man. She glanced at the parking charges, where it seemed inflation had run rampant. There was a café, which didn't look open.

The officers cast her a guilty look, with nobody having put a barrier at the entrance yet. She walked over, stood next to them and waited.

'We've just arrived, ma'am,' said one. 'Setting up an outer cordon now.'

'Excellent,' she said with a drip of sarcasm. 'Anyone familiar with this place?'

The men shook their heads, while the old man raised his arm. Ashley held out her hand, which he shook.

'Detective Inspector Ashley Knight.'

'Prakash Gutta.'

Ashley checked her watch. Eight thirty. She asked one of the officers to stay. 'Take some notes for me.' Turning to Prakash, she touched her fingers to his arm. 'Hi, Mr Gutta. Sounds like you've had quite a morning. Can you tell me about it, please?'

'I come here two or three times a week. Usually the same place. I like a little tributary not far from here. It's quiet. Too shallow for boats. I fish at the main lake during the season, but I'm happy to sit and watch nature.'

'But you saw something different today?'

'Yes, a child floated past with the incoming tide.'

'A child or a woman?'

Prakash shrugged as though at his age it was hard to tell, but his eyes fixed on the mere as though searching for her.

'Maybe a teenager?'

'Was she out of reach?'

'Yes, just, but I saw her face clearly. Young with light hair. Pretty.'

'What was she wearing?'

'I'm not sure. The water's about a metre and half deep there. She was mostly submerged. I'd guess at something white, maybe see-through.'

'Does the river run quick there, perhaps when the tide turns?'

'Not on that part. I suspect she'll still be nearby.'

Barry arrived and one of the officers stationed at the cordoned-off car park granted him entry. Ashley heard a puttering motor behind her and spotted a small RIB (Rigid Inflatable Boat) in RNLI colours appear further up the river. Ashley turned back to Prakash as Barry marched over.

'It's quiet here. Is that normal?'

'Only first thing in the morning. That's why I like it. The area will be busier later. You can leave your vehicle here and walk to the seal colony, but the café and windmill don't open until ten.'

'Windmill or windpump?'

'Sorry, I got into the habit of saying windmill when I arrived seventy years ago, but its purpose was to pump water, not mill grain.'

'Right. How far is the spot you were at this morning?'

'Fifteen-minute walk.' He smiled. 'At my slow pace.'

'Thank you, Mr Gutta, we really appreciate your help.'

He gave her a nod and turned away. Ashley puffed out her cheeks.

'Barry. You direct operations here. Have Uniform keep the public out until we're finished. Tell visitors to go home because we'll probably be here all day. If we find a crime scene, I don't want it trampled. CSI will arrive soon. We'll need a tent to cover the deceased.'

Ashley had a word with the RNLI inshore RIB pilot, who introduced himself as Mervyn and his partner as Georgie. He said if Ashley and Prakash walked, they'd follow on the water.

Ten minutes later, Prakash directed her along a branch off the main river. He stopped where he'd left his seat and bicycle.

'I couldn't get a signal here, so I rushed back before I rang 999. It took me a little while on foot, but I don't like cycling on the grass.'

'No problem. You did well.' Ashley stared out across the water. Nothing stirred. A dragonfly hovered near her face, then vanished. 'This was the location you noticed her?'

'Yes, she was about two metres from the bank.'

The RIB reached them. They had a better vantage point than her.

'The tide hasn't turned,' shouted Georgie. 'The body will probably have drifted further in, not out. There are plenty of weeds, so I'm confident we'll find her soon.'

The revs of the engine lifted slightly, and the boat edged forwards. Ashley glanced around her. The location was so serene. So much greenery. But that peace was about to be broken by an incident that broke any sane person's core beliefs about how life should unfold.

The distant windpump, a looming presence, seemed to watch them. She turned to Prakash.

'Is there any other access to this offshoot, or would you need to stop at the car park?'

'You'd drive or cycle along Horsey Road, then park up.'

'Do you think she went into the water where you were sitting?'

'Probably not. The body was drifting from the right. I guess she might have come from anywhere up or down the river. The tide moves things around.'

Ashley huffed out a breath. They could spend weeks there looking for evidence that didn't exist.

'What's it like here at night, or before dawn?'

Prakash gave her a funny look. 'Dark.'

Ashley chuckled.

'Yes, I suppose it would be. I meant, could someone come here unnoticed?'

Prakash scowled. 'The body's going to be one of those girls that went missing, isn't it?'

Ashley saw no point in lying. She nodded.

'Yes,' he said. 'You could easily sneak here.'

They stood together. The sun had risen high enough to burn the last of the low-hanging mist away, and it cast the landscape in what should have been a comforting glow. A blackbird sang its morning song nearby, oblivious to the tragedy unfolding. Fresh foliage overhead and a riot of flowers below ought to have given Ashley the sensation of looking into a storybook, not a crime scene.

As the breeze whispered through the trees, there came a fateful cry.

'She's here!'

The idyllic scene shattered. The nightmare had begun.

18

It was a short walk along the bank to the gruesome discovery. Mervyn, at the back of the RIB, feathered the throttle to maintain their position. Georgie was perched at the front, as if mesmerised by the swirling current. At a metre and a half, the bottom would be visible.

'She's here,' Georgie called out again, her voice tinged with sadness. 'Caught by the weeds, but she's about to break free.'

Normally they'd leave the victim in situ if they were stationary, but there was no point in letting the body drift and bump the bottom or hit debris. Forensics would prefer the body left in the river, but the ticking clock of the investigation gave Ashley a quandary. A few hours could mean another death. Ashley needed to know who it was, and how long the body had been in the water. An internal temperature was the best indicator of the latter. Urgency laced Ashley's voice.

'Can you get her out?'

Georgie used a pole to check the depth.

'Yes, I'll lift her, and Mervyn will do the rest. Shall I bring her to the bank?'

There was no reason for that just to move her again later. 'No, take her back to the stream up to the car park. A tent should be ready.'

Ashley supposed it might be a different girl. The odd suicide occurred along the Broads, and swimmers or kids messing around got into trouble with the main river's depth being up to four metres. The water would be extremely cold, with strong currents. Ashley watched Georgie slip from the RIB into the water. She took a deep breath and vanished for a few seconds, then reappeared cradling the victim. After steadying herself, she raised her burden up. Mervyn hooked his hands under the small body's armpits. While Georgie held the boat in place, he hauled the woman on board.

Ashley couldn't see the face clearly. The skin there and on the hands was the colour of alabaster, but the figure seemed to be that of a young, slim person.

'I'll meet you back at the car park,' she shouted.

Mervyn nodded and began the journey with his sad cargo. Ashley turned to the old guy next to her, who'd taken his cap off.

'Prakash, we'll need you to make a statement. I want to thank you for your help, too. Your quick thinking saved us a lot of time and effort by ringing this in. We'll be able to let the family know now.'

'I suspect they'd take worrying over hearing about this,' he said, trudging past her.

The car park was busy when they returned, mostly full of marked police vehicles. Barry and Jan were talking to the hunched grey-haired lead from CSI, whom Barry had once nick-named Dracula when he used to dye his hair black. Ashley walked over to them.

'Barry, can you take a statement from Prakash? Gerald, nice to see you.'

'Ashley,' Gerald replied, a weary smile on his face. 'Seems we keep crossing paths under the most unfortunate circumstances.'

'Tell me about it.' Ashley sighed. 'I assume you've worked the Broads many times, so you'll know what a large area it is.'

'Not as often as you'd imagine. I think the tranquil nature of the place makes people behave. Barry said it's likely one of the missing girls I read about in the paper. Am I looking for a weapon?'

Ashley gestured to the two unfortunate officers hauling the body off the boat. It was uncivilised for the deceased and an unpleasant task for the living.

'I haven't seen her. Give me a minute.'

A tent had been set up, and the victim was placed inside. The doctor had also arrived and was beginning his job. Ashley entered the tent and stood beside him. The girl had a snug, thin white hoodie on, collar zipped to the chin, and some tight black leggings. De rigueur wear for most teens. The trainers were muddy, perhaps from dragging along the riverbed, but they appeared new.

Michelle would need an internal temperature reading taken, but Ashley wanted to see if there was an obvious cause of death first. She still hadn't identified which girl it was with the straggly hair over her face. While the doctor rummaged in his bag, Ashley put on a glove and gently moved the wet strands from her forehead and cheeks. The grey skin was cold and stiff and she spied a small mole next to the victim's nose. Ashley now knew who had gone to a watery grave.

'Can you check if there are obvious injuries, then I'll leave you to it?'

The doctor crouched and manipulated the arms and legs, then he unzipped the hoodie. He checked her torso, then rose without saying anything. Ashley knelt. The red marks on either side of her throat weren't glaring, but they were there. He rolled the body slightly and she noticed more at the back of the neck. Michelle always said the dead bruised like the living, so the colouration would come out more in time if she was strangled recently.

'Thank you,' said Ashley, and left the tent.

She returned to Gerald, who had been chatting to the RNLI crew.

'No obvious weapon has been used,' she said. 'No puncture wounds. Possible strangulation. Perhaps held under until she drowned. I shall leave the scene in your capable hands. Barry and Jan will be here for a while.'

'Okay, we'll shut the car park and windpump for the day. Georgie explained about the body drifting in the water, so we've got a busy day searching for an entry point. I'll call a full team in and spend today here, but without further intel it'll probably be a wasted effort. The girl could also have been killed elsewhere, then thrown into the river. That may be anywhere within a thirty miles radius if it was done a few days ago.'

The GP interrupted them.

'The body temp is nowhere near ambient. Considering how much warmer she is than the water, I'd say that she's not been in there for long. Your pathologist might be more precise, but I reckon around four hours.'

'Make that just a few miles,' said Gerald.

Ashley scratched her head. 'Police divers?'

'Yes, definitely. I'll have them start at the branch of the river where she ended up. Who's to say there aren't other bodies out here?'

Ashley frowned. 'Yeah, that would certainly ruin my day. Keep me posted, and I'll do the same if anything pertinent comes up.'

Ashley walked over to Barry and Jan. Ashley could tell them what to do, but Jan was a sergeant now. He'd said in his appraisal he'd like to progress further, so she asked him what his plan was.

Jan gave her a firm nod.

'Sergeant Levine's arrived. I'll ask him to organise his people to interview whoever's about. There are a few cruisers and canal boats parked up.'

'I think the term is moored.'

Jan chuckled.

'Oh, yeah. Maybe they heard something. I'll talk to Kettle so he can arrange a press conference. Which girl was it?'

Ashley told him and he shook his head.

'Poor thing. First, I'll notify the FLO to inform the parents, then I will ring Michelle at the hospital and give her the details, and Hector will need to know. A death like this should help him confirm what he suspects.'

'Good, what else?'

'I know Horsey village a bit. You recommended Horsey Gap to me for seal watching at the end of last year and it was excellent. There must have been two-hundred seals on that stretch of beach, although it was extremely smelly. There's only one proper route through that area, Horsey Road, so I can get Sal to look for CCTV. The village only has about forty houses, but there will probably be some Ring doorbells.'

'I'll drive through on the way back,' said Barry. 'If it's that small, I can soon check for security cameras.'

Ashley gave him a nod. Then she realised they'd overlooked something.

'What are we missing about access, guys?'

'Shit!' said Barry. 'The river. They could have bought a dinghy, hired a boat or stolen one and got out at any point in a hundred miles of waterway.'

'That's true, but we can only work with what we have,' said Jan. 'Emma has dealt with the Broads Authority plenty of times before. They'll give us some advice. The speed limit is only between three and six miles per hour, so even in four hours, they wouldn't get far.'

'Yes, because murderers always obey the speed limits,' scoffed Barry.

'Let's hope they did speed,' said Jan. 'It's extremely obvious to other river users and pisses them off. They'd remember.'

Ashley gave him a smile.

'Excellent work, guys. Sounds as if you have everything covered. Text me with the time Michelle says she'll have the post-mortem done by. There's no reason to keep the girl here, so get her picked up and taken to the mortuary asap. We simply don't have the resources to do much more than a cursory check to the rest of a huge body of water like this unless we get further intel. The specialists will advise. When you're speaking to river users, ramblers and dog walkers, remind them to be extra vigilant for the next few weeks. To be safe, and perhaps they might come across evidence. I'll ring Kettle though and see if he wants to consider organising a huge search.'

'Is calling in hundreds of officers above your pay grade?' asked Barry.

'Yeah, thank God. Even with that many, Gerald's right, we'd need to be lucky to find anything.' Ashley had another thought about who was best placed to deliver the terrible message from their find. She blew out her breath. 'Hang on, guys.'

Ashley took her phone out and rang FLO Scott Gorton, who answered on the second ring. She talked him through the morning's events. He was quiet for a moment, the lull a loaded silence.

'Are you coming to break the news with me?' he asked.

'I should,' she replied, her voice tight. 'I've met all the parents. Are you available now? We'll get it done.'

'Yes, we'll need to do it pronto. I'm not far from the Suffolk border on another case, but I'll be free fairly soon.'

'I'll meet you there. Let's say eleven thirty. This won't get to the press that quickly.'

'See you then, give or take a few minutes.'

Ashley finished the call. Jan and Barry had been listening.

'I assume you heard that?'

'Rather you than me,' said Barry. A feeble attempt at lightening the mood.

Ashley exhaled deeply. She would have time to prepare in the car. Both with what she would say and to get herself in the right frame of mind.

'I'm going to ring Kettle from my car. I'll be out of touch for half an hour while I deliver the news.'

Ashley returned to her vehicle and called her boss.

He listened quietly while she updated him.

'Tragic, but not unexpected.'

'What's your call on searching the Horsey Mere area?'

'The crime scene teams will do what they can today. I'd like fingertip searches, but our resources have been pulled all over. Many officers are helping at an unrelated incident in Ipswich, but your helpline also received a tip-off last night about a brothel out near Thetford.'

'My helpline?'

'It was your idea. The brothel was a small one. Two females in a mid-terrace. One in her thirties from Thetford. One seventeen-year-old Eastern European. The English girl gave her mother's address, being NFA otherwise, so that's what Scott was doing, taking her there so he could do a bit of devious questioning as to how she got into the business in general, and how she wound up in that particular place.'

'Do you mean was she abducted?'

'Exactly.'

'So, you think it's connected to everything else?'

'I'm not sure. The detective I spoke to said the foreign guy overseeing the property didn't seem to know much about what was going on inside. He was just an enormous bit of muscle in case the punters got feisty, but he came quietly. The women workers argued with the police when they turned up. Explained they were busy.'

Ashley chuckled. 'I'm not picturing blonde-haired innocents.'

'Quite the opposite, by the sounds of it. I'm sure Scott will update you when you've delivered your message. What's your plan afterwards?'

'I'll return to OCC via the mortuary, if Michelle's cracking on with the PM.'

Kettle sniffed on the other end.

'I don't fancy our chances of finding the other two girls alive.'

'Me neither, but I want to hear what Michelle has to say. It looks like our victim was strangled in the early hours of the morning. It's possible she was drowned by being forced under or thrown in while still conscious, but what I want Michelle to tell me is what else happened to her before she died.'

'We can guess what happened.'

'I suppose so. Let's hope her investigation says otherwise. Okay, I need to leave.'

Ashley hung up and turned on the engine, put the car in gear, then accelerated to her difficult meeting with Scott, at Newmarket Road.

19

Ashley didn't forewarn the parents at Newmarket Road. She knew she didn't need to. When a child was missing, a parent stayed in the house in case they returned or rang the landline. She supposed it was a little different nowadays with mobile phones, but even if they had both gone out separately, she knew one parent wouldn't be far away from home. If Ashley called, she couldn't inform them of the death over the phone, but they would know something was wrong. The agonised anticipation of her arrival beyond torture.

As the lone parent of Mercedes and other children, Donna had few options. She'd want to trawl the streets, desperately searching for her eldest daughter, but commitments would keep her at home. At least for her, at the moment, there was still hope.

The Kato house was before the Dupont property on the street. Ashley slowed and stopped at the entrance and recognised the same cars on the drive. She noticed Scott had arrived behind her, his usual reliable timekeeping a grim comfort at that dark moment. Would it be better to tell them all together? She parked up. Scott pulled alongside her and wound down his window.

'I think both sets of parents are here,' she said, her voice little more than a murmur.

'Okay, let's get on with it,' replied Scott, his tone resolute.

That was one of the reasons she liked Scott. She could always draw strength from his composure. Barry would have said 'let's get it over with'. There was quite a difference. The thing was, she'd found delivering death messages got easier. Not easy, but accepting someone had to do them helped. Experience also assisted her in detaching herself from the raw emotion. The job needed focus and professionalism. Nothing you said would lessen death's sting, but you could give the grieving family support, guidance and, hopefully, justice.

Even so, as she and Scott stepped across the chunky gravel stones on the driveway they seemed to crack and crumble, like treading on eggshells.

Scott knocked. 'You okay to lead?'

Ashley had got her head in the right place on the drive over.

'Of course.'

Victoria Kato answered the door. For a split second, she forgot their likely purpose, but her fleeting smile quickly dissolved into terror. Her hand shot to her mouth.

'I'm sorry to say we have some news,' said Ashley. 'Are the Duponts here as well?'

All Victoria could manage was a nod.

'Is everyone still in the kitchen?'

Victoria turned and lurched away. A cry came from her. Ashley sensed the tension in the house, the air heavy with fear. The other parents were gaunt-faced spectres, hunched around the dining table. Two-dimensional shadows of the humans they used to be. Victoria slid into a seat next to Aveline. Four faces shifted to Ashley, four sets of eyes like shattered ice.

Scott sat quietly on a chair next to Victoria. Ashley stood in front of the table. In the still room, nothing moved, her voice tinny in the deathly silence.

'We've found one female body so I can talk to her parents first. There's still no sign of the other child.'

'No,' barked Aveline, her voice cutting through the room like a razor. 'Tell us together.' She glared around the table, bobbed her head once. With flared nostrils, both rows of teeth appeared as her face twisted into a gruesome, rictus grin. 'Tell us now!'

'I'm sorry, Aveline. Camille was found at Horsey Mere.'

Aveline's eyes widened, her mouth dropped open. Her hands raised and flexed. A short scream cut through the quiet. Then another shriek cracked the air, long and high. Her back arched as if a fiery demon had surged from the scorched depths of the darkest pit, thrust his flaming fist into her chest, and torn out her heart. She collapsed in her seat as though it were her own life that had been cruelly taken.

There was a gap of a few seconds, then Aveline cried out again. A sound that seemed to last forever until Victoria pulled Aveline to her. Hanzo resembled a waxwork model of his former self. Stefan stumbled from his chair and staggered across the room like a toddler swaying over his first steps. He gasped repeatedly as if Ashley's news had emptied the oxygen from the kitchen. At the French doors, he stopped and looked back. His eyes burned with imagined horror, tormented by pain, fists clenched, his whole face seized in a silent howl.

Stefan heaved the doors open, then stepped through. He turned and closed them. His expression, as he stared into the room, was of a man who needed a pistol to shoot, or a tall building from which to jump.

Like Ashley, Scott had been there many times before. He went after Stefan. Ashley took the seat next to Victoria, who held Aveline tight to her chest. Hanzo finally moved. His head swivelled towards Ashley like the gun turret on a tank.

'Was it definitely Camille?' His voice barely a whisper.

'Yes, the mole near her nose was clearly visible.'

'Where's my daughter?'

Ashley didn't have a clue. All she had was empty platitudes, but she tried.

'We're doing all we can to find her.'

A bellow of rage from outside bounced off the windows. Testament to the fact the police had fallen short. Hanzo rested his forehead on the glass table, shoulders shaking with silent sobs. Victoria began to weep. Aveline released another strange high-pitched wail, not a banshee heralding a death, but a mother, keening for her child.

For the first time in her life, Ashley felt a pang of gratitude that she wasn't a mother.

20

Ashley ended up staying an hour. She decided to leave when Jan texted her that Michelle would shortly begin a preliminary inspection of Camille. Michelle preferred the parents to have confirmed a child's identity before the full invasive process began.

Stefan had returned to the kitchen after ten minutes of bellowing at the sky, as she'd known he would. He'd demanded explanations, details. Victoria had taken Aveline to the lounge when he'd started shouting again. Victoria squeezed Ashley's shoulder as she'd walked past, as if to say, I know you're doing your best.

When the women had gone, Hanzo had not been so forgiving. Ashley had struggled with scant answers for him. He'd left the room as well when Stefan had demanded to hear exactly how his daughter had died. Ashley had expected that, too.

Scott needed to stay for longer. People had walked into the traffic after hearing their child had been murdered. It would also be handy having someone at the house, with the possibility Akari might appear near where Camille had been found. Scott could arrange for a viewing of the body as well. It was much safer if he drove the parents to the hospital. Ashley said she would ring him when they were ready.

When she arrived at N&N's mortuary, Michelle was in the middle of the examination, so Ashley pulled on scrubs and joined her. She left her humanity in the changing room and stepped into her detective role to stare at the body.

'Hi, Ash. This is interesting.'

'How so?'

'I've been keeping up with current events, so I anticipated Camille having been abused in a variety of ways.'

'And she hasn't been?'

'No. She's obviously been killed, this isn't a natural death, but, apart from that, her skin below the neck is flawless.'

'No sexual abuse?'

'That's what I'm saying. There's no bleeding, bruising or tearing in the areas I was expecting there to be. The hymen has gone, but this girl is muscular and toned, so it could easily have been broken by sport, for example. Everything is normal. No red marks around either opening.'

'What about consensual sex, although it's unlikely in the circumstances?'

'Intercourse is a mechanical process, often with varying amounts of lubrication. Even gentle sex causes blotches and chafes. I'll be able to tell more when I take samples, but I'm confident she hasn't had sex in the last forty-eight hours, and she certainly wasn't forcibly raped.'

'Anything inside, anywhere?'

'Nothing obvious. I'll test for fluids, both human and from other sources.'

'Did she drown or was she throttled?'

'Very much the latter. I put a camera down her throat, and

there was a little water in the lungs, but not enough to be fatal. The method used to kill her is intriguing. Manual strangulation, with discoid bruises here.'

Ashley followed where Michelle was pointing at the back of the neck. 'Fingertip bruises?'

'Yes, and these at the front are probably thumb marks to compress the jugular veins. Whoever throttled this woman did it while facing her. They were strong, too. The hyoid bone has been broken. That occurs in around twenty-five per cent of hangings and half of strangulations. It's quite hard to damage it otherwise because it is so well protected by the structure of the jaw and throat. A bouncing cricket ball might do it, but it's most commonly done during car accidents and strangulation.'

'The neck didn't feel broken.'

'Unless the world's strongest man was having a dark day in Norfolk, you'd be unlikely to tell. The spine is surrounded by muscle. Damage is usually caused by dramatic impacts, like falls. I know Hollywood loves a neck-twist dispatch method, but it's only possible for the most powerful of people. I've had a peek in the throat, but the internal inspection of that region is one of the final stages of the post-mortem examination after the chest organs and the brain have been removed. Once I've drained the neck area of blood, I'd expect to find extensive injuries to the larynx and the trachea. Deep bruising will also be present.'

'How strong exactly would you need to be to cause these injuries?'

'Reasonably, to crush her neck in this case, but not very to kill. A moderate person's weight pushing down would be enough to compress the airwaves and cause death.'

'I expected her to have been raped.'

'So did I, but maybe whoever was responsible just liked murdering, or perhaps he stroked them beforehand. Got off on the terror. He could have licked or massaged them, or enjoyed the thrill of the chase. When did she go missing?'

'Sunday.'

Michelle returned her gaze to Camille's body, checked her eyes and prodded the skin.

'I'd say she's well hydrated, but I'll need the microscope to be sure. That means she was given drinks in captivity. The stomach's contents or large intestine will tell us if she was fed. As for how long she was in the water, judging by the mottling and her temperature, I'd estimate she went in around 4 a.m., shortly after she died. You know how hard it is to ascertain the time of death in these circumstances. I could be out by hours either way.'

'The doc at the scene said similar.'

Michelle had crouched to stare at a mark on Camille's midriff. 'There's a red mark here. I missed it earlier. Might be nothing, or it could be a burn. Cigarette or something. I'll check that, too.'

They stripped off their PPE, dumping it in the bin provided, and returned to the office. Michelle sat behind her desk.

'The parents can come in later this afternoon, or first thing in the morning, then I'll crack on.'

Ashley noticed a box of Milk Tray next to Michelle's computer. Michelle shoved them over.

'Sorry, I've eaten my favourites.'

Ashley glanced at the box expecting to find a few creams remaining, but it was the soft chocolates that had gone. She selected a hazelnut swirl with glee.

'You've left all the best ones.'

'I swear he's trying to fatten me up.'

'Going well with Scott, then?'

Michelle beamed. 'It'll be six months soon.'

'Ooh, the point where you decide if you're in it for the long haul or not.'

'Yes.'

'Are you?'

'Yeah, I think so. We've not really talked too much about our future plans. He was married before, so he might not want to do that again.'

'Do you want to get hitched?'

Michelle cocked her head to one side.

'It'd be lovely if he wanted to, but I can understand why he wouldn't. That's the cold clinician in me. I get paid a lot more than him, so I don't need the security.'

Ashley smiled at her friend. She looked content.

'Must be nice.'

'Which bit?'

'Decent bloke. Future together. Planning. Sharing.'

'It is. Are you dating?'

'No, I'm still hoping to steal Arthur away from Joan.'

Michelle chuckled. Arthur was Ashley's neighbour who was well into his seventies.

'All the good ones are taken, eh?'

A twinge of jealousy surfaced, but it was her fault for not making a move on Scott, or at least flirting better, so he had made one. She refocused on the case with the brief chat giving her time to deal with what she'd just seen.

'It's so strange that Camille was virtually unblemished.'

'Her tox screen might help, but it will be a while before we get that back.'

'You think she was drugged?'

'It's likely to have been done to keep the victims from thrashing around, but any injection marks would have healed by now.'

'I wonder if she tried to escape.'

'There are no visible bruises or scratches, so if she did, she didn't get far. Marks could still come up but remember the fingernails.'

Ashley recalled Camille's perfect pink false nails. 'You're right. They pop off typing, never mind fighting. Perhaps they drugged her and she was unconscious.'

'That would make sense because otherwise her attacker strangled her face to face. They'd have been looking at each other. With the bruises on the back of her neck and at the front being similar in hue, I wouldn't be surprised if he was powerful enough to kill her standing up.'

Ashley bared her teeth. 'She barely struggled at all. Why?'

'Perhaps she was simply petrified when the monster attacked her.'

21

Ashley returned to OCC and spent the rest of the day dreading unwelcome updates concerning Akari or Mercedes, but they never came. Although, there was no good news either. Kettle appeared on TV again late afternoon, gravely giving the sombre details of that morning's find. He urged vigilance on the Broads and reiterated the helpline number.

Barry found no helpful CCTV at Horsey, and Sal told her the closest traffic cameras were too far away from the scene and were situated on busy roads. They'd be useless without a narrower description of any vehicles involved in the crime. Ashley was contemplating going home when Kettle summoned her to visit his office. Sebastian, seated outside, gave her a smile when she arrived. She knocked and went inside. Hector and Beckett were sitting opposite her boss.

'You need to hear this, Ashley,' said Kettle.

Hector turned his laptop around to show Ashley an Excel spreadsheet.

'What am I looking at?'

'Solved and unsolved deaths from the countries who have reported back, which may link to our trafficking gang.'

Ashley scanned the list and whistled. 'So many.'

'Yes, almost two thousand over a ten-year period. There are probably many, many more and the pattern is something we should have noticed before.'

Ashley glanced over at Beckett, who nodded. 'I'm afraid so.'

'How many bodies were found near windmills?'

'That's what we've been working on this afternoon. Approximately a hundred confirmed murders at various beauty spots. Mostly windmills, then lighthouses, but also windpumps. Some at lakes and castles.'

'How many are for young females?'

'From these figures, around fifty. Older women and men feature too, but another stat stands out. A significant number of those fifty don't appear to have been prostitutes at any point. They were trafficked, but they didn't get far.'

Ashley's mouth went dry.

'How many were strangled?'

'Over twenty.'

'Michelle and I were saying how odd it was for Camille to be unmarked other than strangulation injuries. Do you have toxicology reports?'

'A few deaths led to thorough investigations, but not many. Some of the strangulations have a similar MO to Camille's demise, being found submerged in water. A few victims had ketamine and chloroform in their systems. We're doing more research, asking for further information, but it will all take time.'

'Does this get us any closer to finding Mercedes and Akari?'

'I think it's reasonable to assume that if Mercedes was taken for the same reason, and seeing as her abduction occurred before Camille's, she's likely dead. We just haven't discovered the body.'

Ashley could see where this was going. 'I got the impression there were too many locations for us to search.'

'Remember I said I had a sense of there being a connection? Well, I assembled a photograph of each scene and watched them in a reel. There is a pattern.'

Ashley guessed. 'They're beauty spots?'

'Almost. The windmills and lighthouses all appear in working order or are being used for other things. Many have been converted to residential accommodation, for example.'

Ashley didn't get it.

'How does that help?'

Kettle shouted for Sebastian to come in.

'Seb knows Norfolk and has been helping us out with some research. What have you found?'

'There are five well-known lighthouses on the coast, maybe seventy windmills. Suffolk has four lighthouses, and over thirty windmills, although only half have working machinery. We're going to whittle the total down to a manageable number.'

Now Ashley understood. 'Right. I've seen quite a few around the county in total disrepair or standing lonely and unloved in fields. Does that mean we're ruling those out and going to search the rest?'

Beckett nodded. 'Whoever we can spare from both counties MIT teams will walk around the sites Hector and Seb select, starting in the morning. Detective Superintendent Graves called me this afternoon. Pressure from politicians, I expect, but she also wants a one-mile radius from the spot where Camille was found searched tomorrow. That will be Uniform's task.'

'One person at each site won't have the time or capability to be thorough,' said Ashley.

'True, but at the least we'll have first-hand experience of the terrain if another incident occurs.'

Ashley was thinking hard. 'Whoever dumped Camille in the river didn't try too hard to hide her.'

Sebastian nodded. 'Exactly. It makes me wonder if they actually want their crimes on the news. I mentioned the kill sites, or perhaps just dump sites, in my article, but we can release another piece saying we're considering areas of natural or architectural beauty. The public will be able to help by keeping an eye out.'

'Could that cause panic?' asked Hector.

Beckett almost chuckled. 'It might be that time.'

Ashley considered the names of Typhon's leaders as Hector slowly closed his laptop. 'Typhon and Cerberus.' She waited until she had all their attention. 'Greek mythology. Gods.'

Hector smiled at her. 'I've been wondering about whether we're in the realm of sacrifices, although, historically, they usually involve blood being spilled. Blood was seen as the sacred life force. The Greeks and Romans did perform sacrifices but traditionally with animals.'

Ashley rubbed her temples. Such a terrible waste of life made no sense.

'I suppose human sacrifice is as believable an explanation as any. Right, let's allocate areas. I'll do Cromer. It'll be too dark for me to look around the lighthouse when I get home, but Happy Valley is as beautiful a spot as any in the county. Should we be searching in pairs in case anyone bumps into a gang of Eastern European body snatchers?'

'Yes,' said Beckett. 'That's sound thinking. Hector's final list will go out this evening. We'll send two officers to each area, even if we have to allocate them more than one spot. We'll regroup here later. We've also got NPAS flying over the Broads in the morning. Then it will need to refuel. Let's take stock at that point. We can direct the helicopter wherever we like in the afternoon.'

Ashley casually glanced around the room. She detected a distinct lack of energy, which wasn't surprising considering all that had happened and the task ahead of them. At times such as these, it was easy to pray for a moment of luck or one of genius, but everyone present would know methodical police work usually won the day.

She folded her arms. 'The net has been cast, and at least nobody else has been taken. I'll have the team fired up tomorrow.'

'If it's okay, I'll go with Ashley,' said Sebastian, looking at her. 'I wanted to talk about your career and job. Perhaps I should write a piece on you.'

'I doubt my life's interesting enough for that,' replied Ashley. She rose from her seat. 'Anything else, or I'll brief my team now?'

'Surely that's enough for one day,' said Kettle.

Beckett appeared deep in thought, but she caught Hector grinning as she left. Sebastian followed her outside the room.

'Maybe you can cook me breakfast afterwards.'

'You're so presumptuous. Perhaps you should bring breakfast with you.'

'Deal. We could watch the sunrise.'

'You better not knock on my door at 5 a.m., but meeting at mine is fine. I'll message you my address, then we'll walk up.'

Seb's banter was forefront in her mind as she returned to her desk, but an idea crept in.

Perhaps Mad Geoffrey could help.

22

Ashley drove home via the petrol station, where she filled the car first, then her belly, after selecting a sandwich deal, which came with crisps and a chocolate bar. It was no wonder the pounds were sneaking back on. Although, in this instance, there was method to the madness. East Runton had a fish and chip shop, Will's Plaice, and it would still be open. Being hungry near that spot was dangerous.

When she reached the village, she took a left after The Fishing Boat public house on the main through road, parked on Felbrigg Road, then returned to the pub. She could hear Geoffrey cackling from outside. A local legend, he'd fished the waters for over half a century and frequented the pubs most nights for as long. He was semi-retired now. Ashley suspected he'd ridden the grey line between honesty and illegality since he was a child.

Ashley pushed open the door and stepped inside. Geoffrey, standing at over six feet tall, saw her first.

'It's a raid, everyone,' he shouted. 'Empty your pockets...' he paused for dramatic effect '...and spread 'em.'

The woman next to him at the bar, who must have been well into her eighties, nudged him with her elbow.

'I'm not falling for that again.'

Geoffrey's booming laugh echoed through the pub.

Behind the bar were what Barry called a mother-daughter combo. Landlady, Sue, and her daughter Lucy. They resembled each other in both looks and easy smiles.

'Long time no see,' said Sue, serving the man beside Geoffrey.

'I was here in March,' replied Ashley.

'Exactly.'

'Usual?' asked Lucy.

'Yeah, but just a half.'

Ashley smiled at the young woman as she poured her drink.

'You'll have no space left soon, Lucy.'

'For what?'

'More tattoos.'

Ashley paid the chuckling girl and leaned against the bar. Nearly thirty years she'd been going to this pub. Traditional boozers were a dying breed, but The Fishing Boat's pool and darts teams still ran. They served decent food at a reasonable price, kept good ale, and cleaned the toilets. Even on a midweek night, the place was reasonably full.

Jane and Regan were bringing steaming plates of pasta out. Ashley tried not to look at them, but, despite her petrol-station snack, her stomach growled treacherously. She felt Geoffrey's presence next to her.

'Don't see much of you around town now, Ashley.'

'I'm too busy sitting at home in the lotus position, chugging carrot smoothies or almond milk.'

'Nothing to do with your promotion?'

Ashley stared up into his weathered face. 'You don't miss much, do you?'

He tapped his nose. 'It pays to be in the know.'

'Well, it's funny you mention being in the know. That's why I'm here.'

'Hey, no thumbscrews on darts night.'

'That was yesterday.'

Geoffrey rolled his eyes. 'Who's the one who doesn't miss much?' He grabbed his drink and beckoned to a table in the corner. Ashley followed him over.

'What is it?' he growled.

Ashley made sure nobody could overhear, then whispered one word to him.

'Prostitution.'

Geoffrey held his hands up. 'Guilty as charged, but I was skint and needed the money.'

'Very amusing. There are a few women around who provide a service to you horny old sailors when your wives have cried enough.'

'And an invaluable service it is, too.'

'Have there been any changes lately? New operations moving in?'

'How would I know? I don't pay for it. I'm knackered these days fighting off the desperate birds who want to shag me.'

'I'm talking about young girls. Too young for this line of work.'

Ashley detected a flutter in his eyes. He knew something.

'Come on, Geoffrey? Tell your favourite piglet.'

Geoffrey's smile faded. He drank half his pint in one slurp and grimaced. 'Underage?'

'About eighteen.'

He took a deep breath. 'No names.'

'I need names. These are children.'

'You said they were eighteen.'

'Some were younger.'

Geoffrey squinted, then shook his head. 'Nah, I gotta live here.'

Ashley bared her teeth, but she understood. 'If you can't give me names, give me places.'

He rested both of his big hands on the table and leaned into her.

'I got this from a guy who knows a guy. Take it how you want.'

Ashley waited.

'This bloke regularly used a whorehouse in Thetford. Or thereabouts. Went there for years. Had a favourite who was a tough bird, but she looked after the old-timers like him. Easy money for her. He was never there long.'

'Not the details I'm after.'

'Anyway, he gets offered a prettier bird. Younger. Angelic.'

Geoffrey finished his drink with a large gulp. He waved the glass at her.

'I'll buy you another in a minute.'

'So, even though it's quite a bit more expensive, the dirty old git is tempted, but it's not his scene at all. Finds himself in the middle of nowhere. The guys aren't smiling when he arrives, so he pays his cash, but he really wants out. It's a grim set-up. Rear of a trailer.'

'Whereabouts?'

'He didn't say. The girl was pretty, but she weren't no pro. He guessed that straight away. She seemed dead-eyed, and younger than his daughter, so he backed out. They got arsey, thinking he wanted his money back, but he told 'em he couldn't get it up. They let him go.'

'What do you mean, they let him go?'

'The old guy used to be hard as nails in his time, big too, but he was proper scared. Stalled his car in the rush to leave.'

Ashley folded her arms. 'Did it teach Ernie a lesson?'

Geoffrey scowled. 'Shit. How did you guess?'

'Tell me the location, or I'll be scaring Ernie myself. Didn't he move to Diss?'

'Yeah, his missus chucked him out. Probably cos of the women.'

'Jesus. Is he in a caravan?'

'Maybe.'

'Where?'

'Look, I'll find out.'

'I want the exact address of where that trailer was, and find out what he means by trailer. Rinse everything out of him, and I mean everything. If he spills his guts, I might not look too hard into finding him. That girl could have been seventeen, or younger.'

Geoffrey had a sheen of sweat on his forehead. He ran his hand across it. Ashley laid a five-pound note on the table. He stared down but left it where it was.

'For your beer. Ring me tomorrow morning by eleven. Have you still got my number?'

'Yeah, yeah, I'll do what I can.'

She kept quiet as Lucy collected their glasses.

'Having another, Ashley?'

'Geoffrey is, but sadly I have to go.'

'You should visit us on Sunday. There's a live band.'

'I'll see.'

'Feel free to bring that tall posh lad again.'

'Would he survive the night?'

Lucy giggled, then blushed. 'Probably not.'

After the barmaid had gone, Ashley rose from her seat and glared down.

'Someone's nicking people's children, pimping them out, then killing them. That comes before any friendship.' She switched from her work demeanour and gave him a reassuring nod. 'You'll do what's right, Geoffrey, because you're a good man. Imagine if it was one of your own who'd gone missing.'

His head lifted, her words sinking in. He met her gaze and nodded.

23

Ashley woke before dawn the next morning and couldn't get back to sleep. She tried to doze but found herself looking forward to seeing Sebastian. It had been a while since she'd had company up on the clifftop. At six, she rolled out of bed and opened the curtains. It was a bright day. She took a shower and got ready. After making a cafetière of coffee, she took a mug to the front door. The sun rose behind her property, but she loved how it painted the rooftops of terraced houses over the road in a radiant glow.

A lone seagull soared gracefully overhead, catching the early morning breeze as Ashley's lungs filled with the salty tang of the sea, which was only a ten-minute walk away. Her shoulders drooped as her eyes threatened to close.

She heard the door to her neighbour's house open.

'Greetings, Ashley.'

'Arthur. I've not seen you for a while. Been hiding from me, or from Joan?'

'Nothing like that.'

The way he spoke had her analysing his face. She noticed

with concern he appeared tired. Ashley never used to say more than hello to Arthur until the Cromer Beach investigation, but they'd become friends. His partner, Joan, was a plain-talking Scottish paramedic in her sixties who'd met Arthur after a bonding session during that case. They were a good match.

'I've been looking after Joan.'

'Is she poorly?'

'Her back. She attended a scene outside a late bar in Norwich. There'd been a drunken fight, which kicked off again when she turned up. She got pushed over the stretcher and wrenched some nerves. You can imagine how Joan likes being laid up in bed.'

Ashley smiled with relief it wasn't something worse, knowing Joan wouldn't be a great patient. She was usually a ball of energy.

'Anything I can do?'

'No, you know how back injuries are. Affects your entire day, so it's just a matter of time. She'll hopefully be able to return to work soon.'

'Send her my best, will you? I'll get a card later taking the piss out of her. I saw one with that Frankie Boyle joke about Scotland being a negative place.'

'Go on.'

'If Kanye was born in Glasgow, he would have been called No You Cannae.'

Arthur chuckled, but he and Joan had become a tight unit who savoured their unexpected late-life connection. Her injury was clearly playing on his mind. 'She'll like that. I'll pass on your best.'

A car pulled up opposite, and Sebastian drew his long frame from it. He strode over, lifting his sunglasses when he was in the shade. She turned to introduce Arthur, but he'd gone back inside. Sebastian leaned on her gate.

'Lovely day, Ashley.'

She checked her watch.

'Sebastian. I was expecting you in an hour. Trying to catch me in my nightie?'

'I took you for more of a negligee lady.'

'Nope. Nightdress, to be precise. Neck to ankle, shoulder to wrist, thick grey nylon.'

'Sounds hot.'

'Roasting.'

Sebastian chuckled. 'Do you have those funny high slippers with the zip up the middle?'

'Of course, in green.'

'Foxy.'

'I see you haven't brought breakfast.'

'No, that's why I'm early. I was planning to get a coffee and order some bagels, but everywhere's shut.'

'That's NFN. Normal for Norfolk! Nobody gets going until eight. Why don't we have a wander around the lighthouse? I'll take you for a fry-up in town after.'

'Deal.'

Sebastian was wearing shorts, sandals and a Firetrap T-shirt. She felt overdressed in her white blouse, black trousers and sensible shoes. He checked out her footwear.

'Do I need to put walking boots on?'

'No, I'm going to OCC afterwards, remember? Kettle has some stuffy rules about his officers arriving in beachwear.'

'I thought the lighthouse was on a clifftop.'

'I take it you don't know Cromer well?'

'No, my mum's family all came from Great Yarmouth, so we usually went there for our holidays.'

'Okay, come on. I'll tell you about the area while we walk.'

'I'm all ears.'

Ashley grabbed her phone and handbag and they set off up the street.

'The North Sea of Cromer is notorious, even more so nowadays, with oil rigs, gas platforms and wind farms, but sand banks have been the main problem for shipping. Because of that, we've had a lighthouse for nearly four hundred years.'

'I assume not the same building.'

'No, the sea and weather pound away here relentlessly, although the current lighthouse is still about two hundred years old. It was about half a mile from the beach when it was first built, but it's much closer now.'

Ashley guided Sebastian over the road and stopped at the entrance to Kings Chalet Park. She pointed to the wooded area on the right.

'You can walk through the trees in Happy Valley to get to the lighthouse, or there's a drivable route next to the golf course. We'll go this way past the chalets. People could also approach via the clifftops from Overstrand, or the other direction from Cromer town centre, or even through Warren Wood.'

'Sounds like a great place to sneak in and out of.'

Ashley nodded. 'Yeah, it's perfect for that. The lighthouse is operational, so you can't go inside. Locals come for magnificent views over the cliffs and to walk their pooches, but it's never that busy here.'

'So, there are employees all year around looking out over the area.'

'No, the lighthouse is automated now.'

She pushed open the gate to the field popular with dog walkers.

'There it is.'

She pointed at the stubby white tower with the revolving optics.

'Oh, it's not a bad building, but I've seen better.'

'Cheeky, but yeah, I agree. The red-striped Happisburgh Lighthouse is more impressive. This one is only eighteen metres high, but its position on the cliff makes it over eighty metres above sea level, so the light can be observed for more than twenty miles.'

They walked past the swings and zip wire.

'Fancy a go?' asked Sebastian.

'Maybe another time.'

A stocky brown Labrador rushed over and bumped Ashley's hand with its nose. She looked down into his big eyes and couldn't resist stroking him.

'You're a handsome boy. Where are your owners?'

Ashley glanced around and spotted a man walking out of a copse towards them. She recognised him straight away.

'Morning,' he said.

Ashley recovered fast.

'Morning, Ally. How are things?'

'Good.'

Ashley detected tension in the air, but it wasn't between her and the suspended DS Ally Williamson.

'This is Sebastian.'

Ally smiled at him but didn't shake his hand. Sebastian didn't offer his. She decided to avoid the topic of Ally's upcoming sentencing later that day.

'What are you doing here?' said Ashley.

'My mother moved to a bungalow on Cliff Road a few years ago. She's eighty and frail and wanted to end her days at the seaside. I have time on my hands, so I've been walking Buster here for her. We both need the exercise. Mum had started the breakfast when I left, so I'd better head off. Nice to see you again.'

With that, Ally nodded once at Sebastian, then walked to the chalet park exit without looking back. Buster appeared confused, then bounded off after him. Ashley had seen the direction Ally had approached them from, which was through the woods from Overstrand Road. No wonder the pooch was puzzled. His walk had been cut short. Ashley turned to Sebastian, who gave her an unconvincing smile. Ashley filed the information away.

After walking through the last of the trees, they threaded their way between the banks of shining green ferns. The combination of smells from sea and wood usually intoxicated Ashley, but she was focused on the reason they were there.

They trudged up a steep track in between the clifftop and the lighthouse. Sebastian moved easily and offered her a hand at one point. She shook her head with a wry smile, but still took it.

At the top, she guided him to the cliff edge, where they stood together and gazed out over the sea.

'This is what people come for.'

Sebastian breathed in deeply through his nose and smiled. Then he scanned the shoreline towards Overstrand. Wooden groynes framed the sand and stone beach perfectly. Cawing birds flitted past accompanied by the rhythmic crash of the waves. He looked the other way where the end of Cromer pier jutted out, then stared above him at the crystalline sky.

He beamed at her. 'Lovely.'

'Take a seat,' she said, breaking their gaze and leading them over to one of the many memorial benches that dotted the area. Sebastian read the plaque before he sat.

'"Lydia Wainwright, 1932–2018".'

'I wouldn't mind one of these after I die.'

'Yeah? Why?'

'The idea of leaving a seat for others to relax on and admire their surroundings appeals to me. This spot is incredible. Feels like heaven.'

Sebastian slipped his sunglasses back and stared at the small cumulous clouds as they wandered lazily across the blue canvas above them like fluffy sheep. Ashley could already feel the heat on her bare arms.

Sebastian draped an arm across the back of the bench. 'Would you want yours to be here?'

'I suppose that depends on whether we find any dead bodies.'

24

Ashley had walked this spot countless times, yet the dense foliage and deep gullies served as stark reminders of how easily objects could be out of view. Someone could get pushed off the cliffs into the gorse and not be seen for months. She suspected the other search sites would be similarly challenging. After an hour, they went down the hidden path to the beach and strolled to the shoreline.

Ashley pointed back at the cliff face, which was covered with bushes and stubby trees. Sebastian frowned.

'Even a helicopter wouldn't see them in all that.'

'I was just thinking that, but if anyone dumped a body in the open, we'd know soon enough. The smell would be off the scale in a few days with this mild weather.'

'Unless they wrapped the victim in plastic.'

'Good point, although they didn't bother doing that at Horsey Mere.'

They had a cursory check at the bottom of the cliffs, but time was pressing on, so they headed back up the steep wooden steps.

Both were puffing when they reached the top. Ashley led the way along the top path, which dipped towards town.

Cromer, in all its glory, lit by sunshine, came into view.

'Another wow,' said Sebastian. 'I'd forgotten what a sight that is.'

The sea sparkled next to the impressive pier with the high church spire towering over the pretty, colourful buildings. Ashley felt pride in her home town. She was glad they hadn't found anything.

They were soon at Breakers Café, which was always one of the first in town to open. Ashley tended to share her custom around in Cromer. All the cafés and restaurants had a little something different to offer, like the Doggie Diner, or the sea views at Rocket House and Whitewater cafés. Breakers simply did the best breakfast.

Even though it was in the centre of Cromer, it had a family-run, community vibe, especially out of high season. The owners, Nikki and Martin, were both behind the counter.

'Morning, Ashley,' said Nikki. 'We've missed you lately. You want your usual?'

'Yeah, two, please. I've been trying to eat more of them funny green things people keep talking about.'

'Ah, so that explains your absence. It's a slippery slope,' said Martin. 'Next you'll be biting crunchy red things.'

Sebastian and Ashley grabbed a seat at the window and relaxed in the friendly atmosphere. Various locals popped in and engaged in good-natured ribbing. Sebastian leaned over and whispered.

'It's like breakfast at the Waltons'.'

When their plates arrived, Sebastian rubbed his hands. He enthusiastically bit into his fried bread. Ashley grinned. She'd brought Hector here once, and he'd stared at the greasy slice as if it were plutonium.

'So, Sebastian, I find it strange that as a journalist you have so much access to this investigation.'

'You guys wanted an article to gain wider awareness. My work is sought after, and the top brass knew I'd get it published widely.'

'That doesn't ring true. It's against protocol to provide you with this kind of information about an ongoing investigation, unless you aren't who you say you are.'

Sebastian had made himself a bacon and sausage sandwich with his toast. He paused mid-dunk over his egg.

'And who do you think I am?'

'You mentioned being in the Royal Navy. Judging by the scars on your head and the missing ear lobe, I would guess you weren't working scrubbing pans in the galley. My bet is the Royal Marines.'

Sebastian slowly munched on his sandwich. 'Kettle mentioned you were bright and that I could trust you.'

'So why not tell me the truth straight away?'

'He also said you'd work it out.'

'Care to explain?'

Sebastian sipped his tea.

'Look, you understand how these things operate. It's better if as few people as possible are in any loop. People slip, or get drunk, or make mistakes.'

'Ah, like you?'

'Pardon?'

'This morning, we met Ally. He's generally polite. Shakes people's hands when he meets them. It was obvious you two knew each other. I can't imagine a reason why you'd have met or even heard of him if it wasn't connected to all this, which means you're also aware he's probably heading to prison soon. Do I get told what's going on there, or do I need to suss it out in my own time?'

'Impressive.'

'I'm guessing you work for the NCA now, but a front as a reporter gets you access to places which the powers that be find handy.'

Sebastian coughed. He'd finished his meal faster than she had. He took another sip of his drink. 'We're much alike.'

'Oh, really?'

'Yes, we have a career we love, even though we sacrifice certain things.'

'Such as?'

'A home life.'

'Haven't you ever been married?'

Seb's eyes narrowed for a moment.

'Once. When I left the marines, I thought I could be a nine-to-five man. Bagged a job at the *Telegraph* writing articles on wars around the globe. Commuted to work. Wanted a baby.'

'What happened?'

'I was stood at Clapham Common Tube station one summer day, sweating in the fug, surrounded by suits, heading to an office to breathe air-conditioned air and lean over a keyboard, with the prospect of endless similar days stretching out ahead of me.'

'You had an epiphany.'

'Sure did. Then I self-destructed my life.'

Ashley wasn't certain how to respond, so she finished her drink. 'Sorry to hear that.'

Ashley suspected he'd now probe her relationship history, but he didn't. 'Tell me something interesting about yourself. What's the most thrilling thing you've ever done?'

Ashley chuckled. 'A bungee jump. A long time ago.'

'Bungee?'

'Yeah, I'd done a tandem skydive before, but this was different. Adrenaline pumped through me all morning beforehand. Then I was standing on the edge. My whole body screamed don't leap. The band around my ankles didn't register strongly enough to my eyes and brain that I wasn't going to die.'

'Did you scream?'

'More a long *argh* sound, but yes, and I was still tripping from it five hours later. Like I'd survived. Life felt good. Real.'

'Food tastes great. Love seems stronger. Friendships closer.'

'Yeah, I suppose.'

'That's why we do what we do. We need drama. Excitement.'

'True, but I don't want that when I get home.'

'Are you sure?'

Ashley playfully shook her head.

'Come on, Sebastian. Time to go.'

'I think you can call me Seb now.'

'Oh, we're friends now, are we?'

'Seeing as you felt confident enough to order for me, and the fact you read me like a cheap paperback.'

Ashley held the door for him. 'I did, didn't I, Seb?'

He gave her another of his impish looks as he passed her.

'I find having friends has benefits.'

Ashley followed him out and tried not to laugh.

'I bet you do.'

25

Ashley and Sebastian strode back to Mill Road and drove separately to OCC. The office filled with energy as everyone returned from where they'd been, but any enthusiasm dwindled when nobody reported anything fishy in Norfolk. Suffolk MIT appeared empty-handed, too. The helicopter had hovered for two hours over the area around Horsey Mere and hadn't seen anything untoward. Neither had the multitude of uniformed officers who had gone to search in the vicinity.

Ashley was at her desk when Scott arrived.

'Trying day yesterday,' he said.

'Yeah. I assume identifying the body didn't improve yours.'

'No, that proved to be extremely unsettling. The mother, Aveline, gently shook Camille, as though she was asleep. It was heartbreaking. Have you made any progress with finding the other girl?'

'Do you mean girls?'

A touch of colour rose on Scott's face. 'Sorry, any sign of Akari or Mercedes?'

'Nope.'

'Michelle said she'd have the tox reports back by eleven thirty.'

'Okay, I've got a chat with Kettle then, so I'll give her a go now.'

She was tempted to ask him how things were going with Michelle, but managed to just say, 'Catch you later.'

Ashley scowled when she remembered Geoffrey had promised to ring her by eleven. She had a mobile number for him. Her frown deepened when she discovered it was out of service. Michelle answered her phone straight away.

'Morning, Ash. PM's finished. As we suspected, no internal wounds and no recent drugs or alcohol.'

Ashley explained about the other finds with ketamine and chloroform.

'That's the problem. I suspect they were knocked out with drugs like those, but then the body will expunge them in a few days. It will show in the hair tests, but as I said, those take longer to come back.'

'Okay, we can look into ketamine dealers, although the drug is everywhere. What else?'

'I found considerable damage to the throat area, but I've seen much worse. It wasn't a wild, passionate kill.'

'What the hell does that make it? Some kind of efficient execution?'

'It's possible a woman did the strangling.'

Ashley huffed out a breath. 'What about that red mark?'

'It's a burn, but not from something as hot as a cigarette. Could be a taser.'

'From the prongs?'

'Actually, no, they leave obvious marks. A stun gun. Perhaps they used it to shock her, then bundled her into a van. Smothered her face and injected a tranquilliser.'

'That sounds plausible. Efficient, too. Okay, thanks for bumping her up your schedule.'

'No problem. Ash, we haven't been out as a group since Hector's leaving do at The Grove. We should do that again. It was fun.'

Ashley did not fancy another night watching Michelle and Scott share oxygen.

'Yeah, I'll try to sort something out.'

'Great. See you soon!'

Ashley checked her mobile phone for a missed call from Mad Geoffrey, but there wasn't one. He'd be Dead Geoffrey when she saw him next. She walked towards Kettle's office for her meeting, but he stepped outside before she got there and directed her to the boardroom. Hector, Beckett, and Sebastian were all there waiting for them.

Kettle took a seat, as did the others, except Beckett. It was clearly his show.

'Take a pew, please,' said Beckett. 'I hear we've been rumbled.'

Ashley gave him a tight smile but remained quiet.

'Right, Ashley. I'm sure you understand we need your discretion, but seeing how you're close, I'll take you the whole way. As you will be aware, NCA staff have Quad powers. We're constables, immigration officers, customs officers and general customs officials. We deal in trafficking, immigration, cross-border crimes and international child abuse. Matters of national security. We've been involved in the search for this Typhon organisation for over a year. It's not been easy.'

'Nor for us.'

'Of course. My full name is Irwin Beckett. DCI Kettle's grade is similar to mine. The NCA has its own staff shortages just as you do. We're considerably stretched through Northern Europe with this, not to mention trying to investigate in the UK at the same time. We haven't had much to go on either.'

'I would have expected you to call the reserves.'

Beckett chuckled.

'We brought Seb. You were right about him. He is currently contracted to the NCA as an advisor and assists in a variety of ways, but he is a journalist. We have him this week. The important thing you aren't fully aware of is that through the Dutch force's capture of one of Typhon's team, we've managed to get access to what was an encrypted Telegram communication group. Through that, we infiltrated another. It is now evidently clear the Typhon organisation has almost disintegrated. We're almost there, but not quite. Apart from the chatty criminal who the Dutch got to break ranks, nobody else has talked, but we now have a flood of top-notch intel, and it's given us an idea. Explain, Hector.'

Hector gave her a little nod, as if it were the first time he'd met her.

'We've got at least eight members of the Vampires in jail. All appear low-level minions, but the guy we arrested in Thetford for aiding and abetting illegal activity, notably bouncing for a brothel, Filip Bosko, doesn't seem to be affiliated with them. He could work for Typhon.'

'Didn't you say he was small fry?' said Ashley.

'That's what we deduced, but we're challenging those assumptions in light of new intel.'

'Do you think he's Hydra?'

'Probably not, but he may be close to him, or her.'

Ashley felt everyone's eyes on her. 'I'm not so sure. My contact from Norfolk, a fellow called Geoffrey, said the older woman at the Thetford brothel was experienced. Geoffrey's a bit of a rough diamond, but I trust him with something like this. If she was abducted and forced into her roles, it happened a long time ago. So let's keep an open eye on the Hydra angle for the moment.'

'His intel matches with what the prostitutes said, but Bosko gave nothing at all except his name. What we have learned is when a group from the same organisation end up in prison together, they talk. It's hard to maintain focus all day, every day, and tongues loosen.'

Ashley took a moment and realised where this was heading. 'What happened to Ally this morning?'

'Twelve months custody, so he'll serve half.'

She crossed her arms. 'You can't send Ally to jail and hope he learns something inside. That won't work. He'll be killed at HMP Norwich. He must have arrested half of the inmates at one point or another.'

Beckett smiled, but it didn't reach his eyes.

'Yes, we were conscious of that, which was why he was sentenced at Cambridge. He'd never have gone to Norwich. HMP Peterborough is his destination. We'll house him on the induction landing, then send the Thetford guy, Bosko, to court tomorrow morning and do the same to him. They'll be wing buddies. There are other assets at that location as well.'

Ashley wondered what other assets meant. 'Won't this Bosko be suspicious at being sent to a different nick?'

'Not at all. Norwich jail is vastly overpopulated. They're shipping new arrivals out all the time, mostly to Peterborough. Quite a few of the men we caught at the other brothels are already there. As soon as Bosko gets on the wing, other prisoners will tell him they were shipped there, too. The prisoners who are moved always moan about the extra distance from home, because many of their relatives won't visit if the journey is long or expensive.'

Kettle cleared his throat.

'We've had a call from a DCI Barton in Peterborough. Their major crimes unit discovered a pop-up brothel in Millfield, which is a culturally diverse area in the north of the city. Neighbours said it was a new operation. I've got a telephone meeting with Barton today, but it's a similar MO to what's been going on in Norfolk and Suffolk.'

Ashley smiled. 'So, the people connected to that will end up on the same wing as well.'

Beckett nodded. 'Yes, and anyone else we nick from now on. We'll have a range of surveillance measures in place, which, as you can imagine, in a place like that, needed high-level sign off. This is an extremely serious case concerning, not only our nation's safety, but European security, too.'

Ashley suspected what they were doing in the prison was on the edge of legality. There'd be covert surveillance, listening devices, and multiple undercover officers. Beckett continued.

'Peterborough CID also investigated a suicide they had in the woods next to Sacrewell Farm, not far from the city.'

'A woman?'

'No, their victim was found in his car with a plastic bag over his head. An almost identical end to Esra's.'

'Sounds as if what's left of the operation could be scattering into Cambridgeshire if we don't nip it in the bud.'

'Yes, which would be concerning. We're trying everything to get this finished. Just one break might be all we need.'

Ashley could see Typhon behaved like a virulent cancer, moving from place to place, infecting and killing.

Hector beckoned her over to the map on the wall. He was showing her where they believed Typhon had been operating in Europe when Gabriella knocked on the door. She caught Hector's eye and smiled, but her gaze stopped on Kettle.

'Apologies for the interruption, but I have an important message for DI Knight.'

'Deliver it, Gabriella.'

She looked at Ashley.

'A guy rang the switchboard asking for you. The man, who would only leave his telephone number, insisted the information was urgent, and that you were to be told immediately.'

'What did he say?'

'He wouldn't give any specifics. What he said was, "I have the location."'

26

Ashley grabbed her mobile from her pocket and rang the number from the piece of paper Gabriella placed in front of her.

A gruff voice answered. 'Yeah?'

'Is that you, Geoffrey?'

'Don't give me any grief about ringing late. I've been trying to get hold of ya, but I forgot your details were on an old phone.'

'No problem. I appreciate your efforts. Now, what's the location?'

'Well, it's not an exact spot.'

Ashley maintained her composure. 'Tell me what you know.'

'Right. As I said, a dodgy friend heard of a terrific opportunity. Beautiful women. All he had to do was ring this number, and they'd give him the address. He rang it, was asked what make his car was, and got told to wait opposite The Foundry Arms.'

'In Northrepps?'

'Yeah. So, he drove there, and a bloke was waiting. Said to follow him. Took him through some strange twists and turns for twenty minutes. You know the type of countryside out there. Narrow roads, no streetlights. Black as coal if the moon ain't out. The geezer finally stopped at the edge of some common land. There was a big campervan and a trailer parked there.'

'Do you mean the detachable bit of a lorry?'

'His words were a metal box on a flat bed.'

'Was it a container, like from a container port?'

'Look, he didn't say, but that sounds right. Inside had been made into two narrow bedrooms with single beds. He was taken to the end one.'

Ashley's blood ran cold. This was exploitation on another scale.

'Then what happened?'

'An aggressive bloke took his money. Two hundred pounds. Explained he had ten minutes.'

'But he didn't do it.'

'When he got in the compartment, he thought she looked like a schoolgirl and had red eyes an' all.'

'Did he say she was drugged or upset?'

She heard Geoffrey swallowing deeply.

'He didn't know. She said to him, "It's okay." That stopped him in his tracks.'

'What about her description?'

'Small pretty thing with blonde hair.'

Ashley wracked her brains. 'When was this?'

'Last Tuesday night.'

'Did he spot anyone else there?'

'Nah, just the guy outside. Nasty-looking fella. Murderous evil expression. Definitely not the type to mess with.'

'No other girls?'

'The door for the second room was shut, and it was quiet.'

'Where is Ernie now?'

'I didn't say it was him, and even if it was, I heard he moved away. My battery's dying. I better go.'

Ashley wasn't fooled. Geoffrey wouldn't answer this number again, and it'd be a while until he was in The Fishing Boat.

'Wait. Let me sum up. It sounds like they're driving this trailer around. Stopping in places. Touting for business through known users of sex services. Then they leave and go elsewhere to do the same thing. It's a mobile operation.'

'I reckon that's right.'

'Did he see any weapons?'

'Nah, he said the fella outside didn't need a gun. Reckoned he could eat concrete.'

'Anything about the container, lorry or campervan, which would help us recognise it?'

'No, it was pitch black. So, all he saw was by torchlight. The girl's room was dim. He didn't want to stare at her too hard. The trailer was battered and light-coloured. Had a couple of letters on the back-door bit. He also said something about seeing a satellite dish. That's it. Nothing more. My phone beeped, so I'll catch you later.'

'Cheers, Geoffrey.'

Ashley ended the call and relayed everything she'd heard. Hector had been taking notes as he'd listened and added to them.

Beckett nodded.

'Good, good. The people who use prostitutes don't talk. Especially ones who are ambivalent about the age of the women, so this is a real coup. The container modus operandi is something that's been reported abroad. They've been found on fire not long after the police first sniff around. Any evidence is gone. They probably use the same containers to move the women through Europe.'

'They'd have to keep the operation going for a while to earn back their investment,' said Hector.

'Exactly, which means we have a chance of locating it. They might be in the vicinity, but not the same spot.'

Ashley was still shocked by the clinical nature of those responsible, while feeling repulsed by what the women must go through.

'Did they find remains in the burned containers?'

'No, but the Europeans have never found anyone who said they were forced to work in one, either.'

Beckett didn't need to state the obvious about the women's fate after their usefulness had ended.

'Camille can't have been in this situation,' said Ashley. 'She was virtually unmarked below the neck and there was no sign of sexual activity.'

'Let's deal with what we have,' said Kettle. 'We can return to Camille afterwards.'

'The area is complex,' said Hector. 'Lots of small roads, criss-crossing lanes, huge trees to hide under, even old warehouses or barns.'

'Use the helicopter,' said Ashley. 'You've got it this afternoon. Start at The Foundry Arms and circle out. How many container lorries are going to be parked next to a campervan in the middle of nowhere?'

'That's a great idea,' said Kettle. 'They'd stick out from a distance, too, so NPAS could swiftly cover a large area.'

Ashley nodded. Mounted to the nose of every National Police Air Service helicopter was an HD colour video camera, a stills camera, and an infrared thermal imaging camera. Powerful lenses could give them over a hundred times magnification, which meant they could see objects clearly from several miles away.

'NPAS should keep the bird out of sight and sound as much as possible,' said Sebastian. 'Otherwise, we could spook them.'

'Yes, there is that,' said Beckett. 'Right. I need a strategy. We might have time to put NPAS up twice if we're quick. I'll arrange for a tactical unit to be on standby in case we get a sighting. They'll go in tonight if we find the location. What's the weather forecast?'

Sebastian checked his phone.

'It's perfect. Only a bit of cloud. The pilot will be able to stay pretty high with decent visibility. There'll be less noise, too. Helicopters and planes are always flying overhead around here, so, as long as they don't get too close, I doubt the criminals would notice.'

Beckett folded his arms and stared around the room.

'Spare a thought to what's happening on your doorsteps. Every minute that passes by means more people suffering, so let's focus. There are likely two girls experiencing hell on earth right this very minute. Let's get them home.'

27

An hour later, Kettle, Beckett, Hector and Ashley had put a plan together and spoken to NPAS. There had been no time to set up a visual link to the helicopter's camera, so they sat around the table listening to a radio on speaker as the commentary from one of the air observers came through. An audible high-pitched whine could be heard in the background from the engine.

'Hotel Nine Nine reporting five hundred metres over The Foundry Arms in Northrepps. As agreed, circling and moving out, searching for prior and current location of the lorry and campervan.'

Beckett spoke next.

'Ground commander. Sorry to reiterate this but try not to spook them. If a place appears possible, mark the spot. We'll have tactical units check later.'

'Understood. Nine Nine out.'

For the following five minutes, they sat in silence, almost expecting NPAS to find the container straight away, but there was no more contact with the helicopter. Beckett and Kettle left instructions to ring Kettle if the situation changed, and they both departed for a meeting. They didn't say whether they were going to the same one.

Hector smiled over at Ashley.

'Dream team back again.'

'I'm wondering how you came to be part of this operation. Did you know Ally was undercover before?'

'No, of course not. I only found out about this investigation a month ago. Kettle recommended me to Beckett, who pulled some strings and got me taken off the social media project. If I'm honest, it had gone quiet. Beckett's guys have been working solely on this ever since the demise of the Romans' organisation. It appears this Typhon has been the scourge of Europe for the best part of a decade, and nobody realised.'

'It's mad the countries involved didn't communicate.'

'Cross-border trends are always difficult to spot.'

'I suppose that's not so hard to believe seeing as the UK has struggled in the past with just cross-county investigations.'

One of Hector's team knocked on the door and he shouted for her to enter. She spoke quickly.

'I've emailed you the latest stats we've pulled together. The trend you noticed is becoming clearer. Young women are definitely being killed instead of being worked, and another cohort of mostly older females appears to have been murdered after being worked. There are also men of all ages who were taken at the same time as the women who have been dispatched by similar methods. Cut throat, ligatures, gunshot to the temple. Some could be suicides, but we're thinking they're more likely staged.'

'Thank you. Keep going.'

When she'd gone, Hector clicked his fingers.

'They take the youngsters in pairs, then use the other person to control them.'

Ashley grimly agreed. 'Like with the sisters in the Romans' investigation.'

'Yes. Those captured are told to behave, comply, or they'll kill their girlfriend/best friend/daughter/partner immediately.'

'That doesn't explain why some are swiftly murdered. Although it seems only the younger ones are killed in that way. Maybe we were right, and it is some sort of sacrifice.'

'Yes, but a sacrifice to what? I find it hard to believe a secret society in thrall to the devil is responsible for all this.'

They kept the radio on in the background while they worked for another hour, but no sightings came. Ashley had a thought spring into her head.

'You said the ancient Greeks sacrificed mostly animals?'

'Yes.'

'How about the Incas or Aztecs?'

'Interesting. You could ask Seb about them. He told me he's heading to South America next.'

'I suppose they would have used the names of Aztec gods.'

'True.' Hector paused. 'I must say, you and Seb work well together.'

Ashley detected a note of humour in his comment but was saved by the radio springing to life.

'Hotel Nine Nine. As expected, there are plenty of spots where large vehicles appear to have turned or stayed. The most promising one was on Nut Lane, but we've not seen any lorries or containers that match our parameters. There are campervans everywhere. Search continuing with about thirty minutes of fuel. Over.'

'Received, over,' said Hector.

'Have you spoken to Gabriella since you got back?' asked Ashley.

'Yes, we had a phone chat last night and caught up.'

Hector's rueful expression indicated she hadn't told him anything he wanted to hear.

'You should date other people.'

'That's what she said.'

'There you are. Embrace the generation Z dating world. Swipe left or go to alcohol-free hook-up nights where you can bond over slagging off my generation for ruining the housing market, the economy, the environment and the climate.'

'I see how that would be fun, but I don't need to attend dating evenings to do that.'

'I reckon you're too clingy. Women find it off-putting. Tell her you plan to see other women. In fact, say you have a date, even if you haven't. If she cares, it'll annoy her. If she isn't bothered, then you weren't in with a chance, anyway.'

Hector pulled a face at her and turned his focus to his laptop.

Ashley drummed her fingers on the table. 'You do know you're missing out on man's last true quest.'

She grinned as Hector fought a losing battle with his intrigue. Eventually, he raised his eyes from the screen. 'This better be worth it.'

'I was reading an article by Petronella Wyatt in *The Daily Telegraph*.'

'Now that does sound like fiction.'

'Hey, I'm well read. Admittedly, someone had left this particular newspaper in the canteen.'

'You're losing me.'

'She argues that becoming civilised has cheapened every experience. We watch life through TV screens and even war is like a video game. There's no holding a bunch of roses and waiting for a steam train to pull in, not knowing if the person you're waiting for is on board. No chasing after woolly mammoths with a flint spear.'

'Are you comparing Gabriella to a huge hairy beast and me to a caveman?'

'Shut it and listen.' Ashley airily waved a hand. 'Wyatt was saying love is the only remaining true adventure. At least, I think she was. Even in this day and age, love is still dramatic. Unpredictable women who enthral, even torment, without whom life is dull and flat.'

'And this is linked somehow to a night out at a Norwich nightclub?'

'Stop being facetious.'

'Nice word, and it does fit, although perhaps more by luck than judgement.'

Ashley blew a raspberry.

'I'm saying you're depriving yourself of the heady excitement and danger of exposing yourself to exotic highs by not diving in head first.'

'That sounds as if it might be fine concerning matters of the heart but terribly worrying at a public swimming pool.'

Ashley rolled her eyes. 'You deserve to be on your own.'

'No, I get it. I'm missing out on the most exciting journey there is.'

Ashley glanced over to check if he was being flippant again, but he was staring pensively into space. She went back to checking her emails.

Kettle and Beckett returned when the helicopter was almost out of fuel. Beckett picked up the radio.

'Ground commander to Hotel Nine Nine. Any luck?'

'Hotel Nine Nine about to return to base, but we may have something. Clouds have lowered, so we needed to get a little closer.'

'What's your location?'

'I've taken grid references, but the closest place is Banningham.'

'Tell me what you see.'

'Light grey container on the back of a blue lorry cab. Parked on what looks like waste land next to a ploughed field. There's a campervan beside it.'

'Any markings on the van or container?'

'Bear with me. Yes. The rear of it has ICS painted in big letters.'

'ICS is an international Dutch shipping company. How certain of that are you?'

'It's clear as day. We've captured the registrations of the vehicles. Peeling away now, but we spotted a small satellite dish on the campervan.'

Ashley and Hector shared a look. They had their quarry.

28

Irwin Beckett rubbed his hands together.

'Now we're in business.'

Kettle checked the clock on the wall behind him. It was 4 p.m.

'Irwin and I have been talking with people in case we needed to arrange a tactical infiltration, but we must move quickly. It needs to be this evening at the latest, or we risk them moving on, or hurting the women in that container. Irwin, you have more experience of this than me. What are you thinking?'

'With everything I've heard, let's aim for ten thirty. Not long after dusk. Bright glaring torches on the end of rifles tend to grab people's attention, and we'll make sure the helicopter has FLIR. Even with my mandate, this paperwork will take a while to be approved, so Kettle and I will operate from here. Ashley, if you'd like to organise things with your people. We don't know what we're going to find, but you've been involved from the beginning. If one of those girls is there, it'll help to have a female present. Especially if I can't get specialist officers to attend at such short notice. I'll know about that shortly.'

Ashley folded her arms.

'Will I be issued a snub-nosed pistol and a black flak jacket with MIT in big yellow letters across my back? I'll be the hero running in a few seconds after the officer with the Enforcer.'

Beckett smiled.

'You'll be given a crackly police radio, and you'll get to wait about a mile away until the tactical firearms unit has made the scene safe.'

'Understood, sir.'

'Irwin's fine.'

Ashley smiled and nodded. Hector would love hearing her call him by his first name.

'Thank you, Irwin.'

Ashley returned to her office and called a meeting to update her team. By the time they'd gathered, Beckett confirmed he was unable to secure any officers trained in dealing with trafficked women or children until the next morning. DS Emma Stones would have been perfect, but she had a prior commitment at one of her kids' school play, so Ashley asked DC Zelda Cartwright to come with her. Ashley then rang Norfolk social services, who had a location where female victims from these situations could be taken at any time for support and treatment.

Barry and Jan were coming to have first-hand experience of what they discovered, so the team would be on the ball much faster in the morning if it affected the direction of their investigation.

At 10 p.m., Ashley drove down Colby Road and stopped on the verge outside St Botolph's in Banningham. It was a stunning flint church for such a small village.

Zelda whistled.

'Sal was telling me Norfolk has the greatest concentration of medieval churches in the world.'

'I can believe that.'

'I don't get it. This place is tiny. Who the hell paid for a massive building like that?'

'I believe a lot of the churches were something to do with the wealthy wool merchants.'

'Men showing off?'

'I should think so.'

'They're so pretty. The stones and all that.'

'Apparently, the round flint was broken open to reveal a dark blue face, which the craftsman used to form the outside surface of the wall.'

'Into churches, are ya?'

Ashley smiled at her.

'No, I heard it from Sal, when we were out together on a night like tonight.'

Ashley had done a performance appraisal with Zelda, who had joined her team after Ally's was disbanded, but she hadn't revealed much. She was a laid-back woman in her early thirties with a gothic vibe. Ashley knew little about her personal life. Barry suspected she was a lesbian, although that was after he asked her out and she just ignored him.

She noticed Barry's car turning and parking behind them. Ashley yawned and grabbed the flask she'd made earlier. Zelda brought out two KitKats, and they munched and sipped companionably for a few minutes.

'Zelda's an unusual name,' said Ashley. 'I like it.'

'Thank you.'

'How are you getting on with the guys?'

'Sweet. Love them all.'

'Even Barry?'

'Especially Barry. I'm a single child, so he's the irritating brother I never had. The type that steps in if you get bullied. I feel a bit sorry for him. He isn't sure who he is or what he wants.'

Ashley nodded at her perception.

'Got any life plans?'

'Are you asking if I'm dating, or whether I want your job?'

'Either's fine.'

'MIT is cool. I'm learning all the time. It's only been two years since I moved over from CID. I'm into poetry and reading groups. That's my thing. My career is a nice contrast. Promotions will happen or they won't.'

'Like a bonus but not a focus. I get you. It's great you have a healthy way of coping with the pressures of this kind of work.'

'Blokes will come along too, or not. Funnily enough, I had a tasty meal with my previous boyfriend at The Crown over there. Last meal, actually. It's lovely inside. Like pubs you see on old TV programmes.'

Ashley's eyes widened.

'Why was it your final meal?'

Zelda grinned.

'He told me after we'd finished eating that we were through. Said it wasn't working out. Must have been chewing with my mouth open or something.'

Ashley coughed. 'How long had you been together?'

'Two years.'

'Brutal. I hope you made him pay.'

Zelda turned to Ashley and tilted her head to one side.

'To be fair, it wasn't a terrible break-up. He wanted to settle and make plans. I didn't. He loved me, so he tried to end it nicely. I reckon he hoped I'd beg him to give it another go and say let's have kids, but I thanked him and walked home. I only live in Aylsham, which, by the way, means I know this area well.'

Ashley couldn't help herself. 'What's it like round there, then?'

'It's a maze of tight roads, many of which are no good for a lorry. These guys must have someone local helping them.'

There was a knock at the window. Barry crouched when Ashley wound it down.

'Any news?' he asked.

'No, Kettle said he'd be on the radio as soon as the helicopter was two minutes away. The firearms unit should already be in place. Infrared will let them work out who's about, then they'll head in.'

'We'll hear the gunfire from here.'

'Let's hope not, eh?'

A burst of static came from the radio. Kettle's voice boomed out.

'Ground commander to all units. Hotel Nine Nine is approaching the location. Are you receiving, Hotel Nine Nine?'

The helicopter's flight officer responded.

'Yes, we're two minutes out. Visual on the vehicles. You might want to hold fire. A car has pulled into the patch of ground they're parked on. Plate is HK04DDU. Driver has exited the vehicle and is talking to a man outside the campervan.'

Sal had run the number plates for the van and truck. The first had come back as unknown, and the second was registered to a car that had been scrapped. Kettle's voice returned.

'Ground commander. Keep your distance for a minute. It's probably a customer.'

'That's a negative. He's now leaving.' Hotel Nine Nine paused. 'Interesting. He's driving away in a different car.'

29

Kettle didn't respond straight away.

Ashley pressed the talk button on her radio.

'Tango Two Six. Which direction is he headed?'

'Towards Banningham village. He'll be at your location in a minute.'

Ashley pointed at Barry.

'Get back in your car and keep your heads down.'

Ashley nodded at Zelda, who had been briefed what she had to do.

The air observer warned them. 'Twenty seconds.'

Ashley and Zelda leaned towards each other, feigning a kiss as the grey BMW saloon cruised past.

Ashley had a burning desire to chase it, but the main prize was ahead. 'Tango Two Six. Vehicle has passed. Single male driver.'

Kettle responded. 'Ground commander. Leave the BMW. The plate's reported as scrapped, but the registration of the vehicle he arrived in belongs to a Maksim Wozniak in Norwich. We'll check it later. The BMW's details are going into ANPR. Foxtrot Five Four, ready?'

That was the call sign for the tactical firearms unit.

'Confirmed. We are in position.'

'Hotel Nine Nine. How's it looking?'

'One heat signature in the trailer, one in the campervan. Two at the far edge of the area concealed within trees near the road. Sending grid coordinates for Five Four.'

The line was quiet for a moment.

'Foxtrot Five Four. That's all received. We're ready to go in. Spotlight assistance on the two figures at contact. Over.'

'Ground commander. You have permission.'

Ashley stepped out of her vehicle. She imagined the team from Tactical filtering through the trees. Ashley looked back at the picturesque pub. A slinky animal of some kind scampered across the road. An owl hooted in the distance, then the peace was shattered by what could only be automatic gunfire.

It was a short burst. Ashley returned to her car. They waited a further three minutes before the next person spoke over the net.

'Foxtrot Five Four. Situation calm. Two targets in the woods neutralised. Both were armed with knives. One male suspect in custody from the campervan. Tango Two Six needed for the female we found in the second room.'

'Ground controller. Tango Two Six head in. Your other unit, pursue the BMW. Details en route. An ARV team is on standby to assist them.'

Barry came on the radio. Never one for call signs, he simply said, 'Received.'

Ashley put the engine into gear and set off. Zelda had a map on her phone but gave directions without taking too much notice of it.

The road was wide enough for a lorry, but it would make passing extremely tricky. They were soon at a cut towards a flat patch of scrub next to some farmland. A figure in black fatigues, rifle in hand, emerged and waved them down. The helicopter's searchlight above and behind meant she was cast in shadow. Ashley got out and showed her warrant card. Zelda did the same. The woman nodded.

'I'm Sergeant Mariner. Come with me, please.'

Mariner escorted them to the rear of the trailer, where both the metal doors had been opened. Her chin raised slightly. She had a thousand-yard stare. Ashley briefly wondered if she'd had it for years, if it arrived after what her team did to the men with weapons, or if it appeared on seeing inside the container.

'The girl is in the furthest room.'

'Okay.'

'She wouldn't come out. Perhaps it was the uniform.'

Ashley gave her a thumbs up as more vehicles arrived. A marked estate car with its doors open was parked on the other side of the trailer. There were three people sitting on the back seat. Two officers and a man between them. Ashley guessed the middle one would be the survivor from the campervan.

An ambulance parked behind Ashley's car and Ashley turned to Zelda.

'Ask the paramedic for a blanket. It's better if we get whoever it is checked out here, but she may be too traumatised.'

Ashley wasn't sure who *she* was going to be, and traumatised could mean many things. The woman might not be anyone they knew, but she'd seen crimes like this before; humans treated worse than vermin. Maybe for Akari and Mercedes, they were already too late, and this was someone new.

She pushed those thoughts away and stepped up onto the back of the trailer. The rotors above were blasting the air around, but Ashley still got a strong whiff of something unpleasant. It reminded her of entering a crack den when she'd been in uniform many years beforehand. They'd been too late then.

Ashley had brought a torch and she shone it down the tight corridor. There were two doors in what appeared to be balsa-wood walls. They were both open. She tapped the material as she advanced. It sounded thicker than she'd thought. The nause-ating smell intensified.

At the first door, she kept her torch low, then gently lifted it to illuminate the bed where a figure lay. Empty, unblinking eyes stared upwards. Ashley shone the light on the woman's face, hoping for movement, but the firearms officers would have been thorough with their checks. She was dead. Ashley didn't recog-nise her. Using a gloved finger, Ashley pulled the door closed.

She carried on to the second room. There was a dim bulb in the wall, which filled the room with an orange glow. A girl, blonde hair hanging loose over half her face, had backed into the far corner in a tight gap between the bed and the wall. She wore a lacy bra and knickers. Both ill-fitting. One foot was bare, the other had a high heel loosely dangling off it.

The visible eye followed Ashley as she stepped inside. Ashley quickly glanced around. Beside the single bed stood a cheap wooden seat with a couple of plastic bottles on it and a packet of condoms. On the floor in the right corner sat a large fluffy brown teddy bear, grotesque in the half-light.

Ashley painted her most reassuring smile on her face.

'My name's Ashley. I'm a police officer. It's going to be okay. Let's get you out of here.'

The girl tried to retreat further into the wall. Ashley held out her hand.

'You can trust me, Mercedes.'

30

Mercedes slumped backwards, her eye narrowing. Ashley looked for some clothes. There was a thin dressing gown half under the bed. She picked it up, then returned her gaze to Mercedes. The young woman shook her head. Ashley took a step away.

'No,' said Mercedes, her voice barely audible. 'Not that.'

Ashley stayed at the door.

'I recognise you from a photograph your mum, Donna, showed me. She's been so worried. You're safe now. Will you walk out with me?'

Mercedes stared at her. Unmoving.

'There's an ambulance outside. Lots of police. The bad guys have gone. I'll get a blanket for you.'

Ashley turned to fetch it.

'No!' Mercedes jumped off the floor. 'Don't leave me.'

Ashley held out her hand again, which the girl grabbed. The passageway was too narrow to walk side by side, so Ashley took the lead. Mercedes shuffled slowly behind her.

Zelda was almost shining under the stark beam outside. She bellowed something to the firearms officer next to her. The woman nodded and shouted into her radio. A few seconds later, the beating blades of the helicopter and its punishing spotlight receded into the night sky.

Zelda passed the blanket to Ashley, who swiftly wrapped it around Mercedes' shoulders. Ashley climbed down from the back of the lorry but Mercedes paused in the doorway, expressionless, white-faced. She scanned the area as though looking for threats, then sat on the edge of the container. After a few seconds, she placed her hands on Ashley's shoulders and Ashley lifted her off. She weighed so little. Mercedes stood unsteadily so Ashley kept a hold on the girl's waist.

'Can you sit in the ambulance for them to check you over?'

Mercedes' hands instantly clenched harder on her shoulders. 'No!'

'We need to make certain you're okay.' Ashley paused. There was no easy way to say what she had to. 'We'd also like to collect evidence from you.'

Mercedes gritted her teeth. Eyes flashed wildly. Her voice was half snarl and half sob as she whispered into Ashley's ear.

'I'm barely hanging on. I will scream the fucking place down if just one more person touches me.'

Ashley held the fragile girl close.

A small whimper escaped from Mercedes. 'I want my mum.'

Ashley and Kettle had discussed taking the girl to a safe house, but it was clear Mercedes' mental health needs would be best served by being with her mother.

'Let's get in my car. I'll drive you home now.'

Mercedes stiffened in Ashley's arms. She cast a glance across. 'Esra?'

Ashley had considered how she would answer that.

'I'm so sorry, Mercedes. He didn't make it.'

The girl closed her eyes. 'That's okay. It wasn't your fault.'

Ashley and Zelda helped the barefoot woman over the road and placed her in the rear of their vehicle. Ashley slid in the back beside her. Before Zelda could shut the car door, Ashley put her hand out.

'Fetch another blanket, please.'

'Sure.'

'You drive. Ring Kettle first and give him an update. Explain to Mariner, too. I'll call Kettle as soon as we've returned Mercedes to her mother in Ipswich.'

'Understood.'

'Kettle earlier organised a female officer to attend Mercedes' house if we needed one, but he said it might take a little while for her to arrive. We'll stay until she does.'

Zelda gently closed the door and strode over to the sergeant. She had a quick conversation, then took her mobile from her pocket.

The marked car with the arrested man in it had gone, as had the helicopter. Ipswich was over ninety minutes away from Banningham, even at that time of night, but Mercedes was functioning and calm now. It would be nice if she returned to her mum in the same state.

Ashley stared over at the container and the campervan. For a few seconds, complete fury rushed through her system. She gasped and unclenched her fists. Mercedes shivered beside her. Ashley rested an arm across her shoulder and pulled her in. She controlled her breathing and boxed the rage away.

It would smoulder there, and Ashley wouldn't rest until justice was done.

31

Mercedes drifted into a half-sleep punctuated by shouts and groans. An oppressive air built in the vehicle as if her trauma was seeping out and demanding to be acknowledged. Ashley clung to the hope that, if she could get the girl home in one piece, she would be okay, even though her head said that was unlikely. The journey became the longest drive of Ashley's life, and she'd once driven to Scotland.

They didn't want to wake Mercedes, so Zelda and Ashley couldn't chat to ease the tension or pass the time. Zelda whispered whether they should ring ahead, but it was better that Mercedes rested, and they were only sixty minutes away by then.

Ashley attempted to tune into the constant hum of tyres on tarmac and the reassuring rhythmic plink of the indicators. She felt Mercedes stir slightly. The girl moved closer, like a rescued puppy, desperate for some warmth and contact. Ashley hugged her in tight.

The miles rolled by. Ashley caught Zelda yawning numerous times. Ashley would need to drive on the way back, so she tried to doze. It was brilliant news they'd found Mercedes alive. Even though she'd been in captivity for a relatively short amount of time, anything could have been done to her. It was a wonder anyone got over such things, but Ashley knew they could eventually, so there was hope. People pulled the power from somewhere.

Zelda turned into the street Mercedes lived on and parked outside the girl's house. It was gone one in the morning, but a light was on. Ashley had suspected there would be. The waiting hours stretched into oblivion at night. She imagined Donna staring at a blank TV, her heart breaking, while her brain searched for solutions that no longer existed. For many, as time ticked by, that hope would wane. A gnawing ache would take its place. One that would never leave.

'Knock, please,' said Ashley.

Zelda got out and shut the door. She strode up the short path to the property. Ashley watched the front door open before she arrived and a hunched figure peered out into the night. It took a few seconds for the woman to realise her relentless cycle of whispered prayers had been answered.

A trembling hand rose and seized the door jamb. Ashley lip-read her reply.

'Where?'

Zelda pointed back at their pool vehicle. The incredulous mother pushed past Zelda and raced towards the car. She frantically wiped the condensation from the back window. Donna's gaze lasered in. Mad, disbelieving, praying. Mercedes' head was still resting on Ashley's shoulder with her face out of sight, but her mother's eyes locked on her golden hair.

Donna's face contorted with scepticism. Zelda steadied her as she opened the door. Donna lifted a hand to her throat, words failing her. She stretched out to touch the blanket.

'Mercedes,' she whispered.

The girl tensed next to Ashley, then relaxed. She pushed the blankets off her and clambered out. Robotic. For a microsecond, Donna's eyes widened at the underwear, then she reached forward with a mother's strength, and hauled her daughter into a fierce embrace.

'Oh my God, oh my God, oh my God.'

As Donna held her vice-like, Mercedes peeked up at her face in disbelief. They stared into each other's eyes, both lost for words. Zelda took an arm and helped Donna escort her daughter inside. Ashley followed. She stopped at the front door as they laid Mercedes on the sofa. Donna pulled the throw off the back and rested it over her.

Ashley beckoned Zelda out of the room.

'Donna. We'll leave you to be together, but we'll wait in our car until a uniformed officer arrives. Do you need anything?'

Donna managed to tear her gaze away.

'Just thank you, thank you. We'll be fine. I won't ever let her out of my sight again.'

'We'll need the clothing, when you get her changed.'

'Okay.'

'We'd like to do tests, so maybe not showering.'

Donna's grin turned into a protective stare, which Ashley had been half expecting, so Ashley doused the flames.

'Someone will be here first thing to talk to you about all of that.'

Donna's smile returned as she hugged her daughter.

'Whatever.' She glanced up at Ashley, face earnest. 'We're together now.'

Ashley also smiled, then slipped her business card onto the arm of a chair. She knew for Donna, at that moment, nothing else mattered than being with Mercedes. The long road ahead at least existed. A few hours ago, there had been only a rapidly approaching dead end.

'If you have any questions, about anything, please ring. Or chat to the officers who'll wait outside. Family liaison should arrive around nine.'

'Do we have to speak to them?' said Donna. 'She needs rest.'

'I'm afraid it's procedure. We don't know what we're dealing with here. Mercedes' safety is paramount.'

Donna looked back again, this time with worry in her eyes. Then she scoffed, and her face formed a snarl that displayed a feral promise to rip apart any threat that dared cross her threshold.

Ashley glanced at her watch when she got outside. It would take two hours to return to Cromer, and that was after they were relieved, but she didn't mind one bit.

32

Ashley got back in the car and puffed out her cheeks. Their job became extremely difficult when the victim was also the evidence. Mercedes couldn't be more vulnerable at this point. Even though she wasn't a mother herself, Ashley instinctively knew that Mercedes being with Donna at home was the best place for her.

'Only a stupid person would try to go in there.'

'Protective mum, uh?'

'Yep, a ferocious tiger. Right, I'd better chase Ipswich for those uniforms.'

'They just rang to say they're on their way.'

'Good job. How are you feeling?'

'Exhausted, but also kind of energetic. I don't think I could sleep even if I was at home.'

'No, I feel the same. I'll ring Kettle.'

Ashley put him on speaker. He didn't sound tired either.

'Ashley.'

'Morning, sir. You're on speaker. Zelda and I are outside Mercedes' house.'

'How is the girl?'

'She's been so strong. I'm guessing the breakdown is in the post. It'll hit her shortly, and then some.'

'Did she talk on the way back?'

'No, not a sausage, but she tucked into me. You know how some scream and scream and won't let anyone near them? She was the opposite.'

Kettle remained quiet and Ashley imagined his brain whirring. Mercedes had the key to much of the puzzle. Even though she was over eighteen, Ashley had been thinking of her as a child. Getting answers out of victims was fraught with danger. Specialist officers would be available, but Mercedes might need time and space before she could revisit what had happened to her.

Kettle obviously had the same thoughts going through his mind.

'We'll discuss it later. There are other things I want to talk to you about.'

'Okay.'

'The man the tactical unit caught in the campervan didn't have time to use his phone, or dispose of it, so we should be able to get into that. He's here at OCC now but has said less than Mercedes.'

'Did he ask for a solicitor?'

'Nope. Lay in the holding cell and closed his eyes.'

'Well, at least we have him. Did Barry catch up with the bloke who drove off before we arrived?'

'That's the other thing. Barry headed after the vehicle. ANPR located the plate on the A140. That's towards the registered home of the car the man arrived in, so Barry carried on to that address in Norwich. If this guy is a punter, then he could be helpful, but the changing of his car suggests he's an employee.

Either way, we want him nicked asap. If he is a customer, we'll uncover more details about how he heard about the girls.'

'Yeah, he might provide more of an idea about the network. Perhaps give us a different angle to attack the organisation from. Either way, at least it's another link in their business out of play.'

'Right, but the number plate was later identified by ANPR near Blofield.'

Ashley understood straight away the vehicle wasn't going to its registered address.

'So, he took the A47.'

'Yes.'

Ashley pictured the map in her head.

'Where's he driving to? Great Yarmouth?'

'Hector and Irwin are here. We're pulling an all-nighter and have been discussing it. Hector has the strongest concerns. Let's see if you're on the same page. What's near Great Yarmouth?'

'The Sea Life centre?'

Kettle chuckled. 'I'll help you out. Gorleston is three miles further along the coast.'

Gorleston was famous for its incredible sandy beach, which sat below a grand promenade. It also had another feature overlooking the entrance to the River Yare.

'There's a lighthouse.'

'Yep. Now, he could be going to any number of places. Tunstall Dyke has a windmill, which isn't particularly striking, but the one at Freethorpe is more promising. It's isolated, as is the one at Berney Arms. That also looks a possibility.'

'Are you wondering if this is the guy who strangles the girls?'

'Yes, and he may well be about to do just that, or to dispose of a body.'

'Would a wealthy or powerful person be involved in driving to the middle of nowhere and changing cars?'

'Probably not.'

'Perhaps he's disposing of the remains of someone who was killed earlier.'

'Or he could be the delivery guy.'

Ashley swallowed.

'Yeah, there is that. Unfortunately, we have no idea how many women started off in that container. At this point, we don't know how the person we found in there died.'

'No, but let's focus on this guy. As you said, he may be en route to a multitude of locations, so we're operating on educated guesswork. It's the early hours of the morning, through country roads with few traffic cameras, and even fewer uniformed police.'

'Succinctly put.'

Ashley imagined the map again. 'He might even be heading as far as Felixstowe. To the port itself.'

'Yes, maybe to collect more victims. We know Typhon uses containers, so we decided to keep our options open and wait for him to trigger the next camera along the A47, but he didn't drive that way.'

'Where is the next camera?'

'Just after Acle.'

'Right, so we have to assume he went into Acle, but didn't leave via the A47, which means he's either stopped or turned off. If he took a turn, we guess again.'

'Yes, he could have gone north or south.'

'Where do those roads lead?'

'That's the thing. There are bloody windmills all over the place in that part of the county, but Hector's gut feeling is he prefers being near the sea.'

Ashley exhaled deeply. 'What is it with windmills and lighthouses?'

Hector's voice came on.

'The more research I've been doing, the more I realise how much people love them. Some have incredible histories reaching back centuries, outstanding architecture and are at breathtaking locations. You should see the photos of the Rubjerg Knude Lighthouse in Denmark or The Maiden's Tower in Istanbul. Stunning.'

'I'll take your word for it. Basically, we're going to have to gamble. It's like roulette where you can't cover every number. We can cover areas and make a few single bets.'

'Agreed,' said Kettle. 'The River Yare is south, so, if it's a lighthouse he's after, there'd be no point in turning off at Acle for Gorleston. He'd simply head towards Yarmouth, then turn south.'

'So, he's probably gone north, unless he suspects he's being followed?'

'If he does suspect and keeps to the quiet roads, we'll lose him, but, as you said, we're forced to gamble. The road northeast leads to a number of villages.'

'I don't know that area well.'

'First is Billockby, then Fleggburgh, but a turn-off heads to Martham, with a multitude of windmills and windpumps in the vicinity.'

'Shit. He could be returning to Horsey.'

Hector's voice was next.

'From what I've deduced, only one body has been found at each location, so it's unlikely he'd use the same place twice. What if he headed to the coast straight across?'

Ashley knew that location much better.

'Winterton, and another lighthouse.'

Ashley was quiet while she ran it through her mind. 'That's got to be your favourite.'

'Agreed, and your casino analogy was a good one. We'll spread whatever resources we have over the different lighthouses and the biggest windmills, but our money's also on Winterton.'

'Do you still have the helicopter on standby?' asked Ashley.

'Nope. The pilots worked from first thing this morning to late. Safety regulations dictate flying time, and maintenance needed to check the bird over as well. Seeing as all of this is guesswork, we can't commandeer one from London.'

'You'll have to send Barry to save the day,' said Ashley, half jokingly.

She heard Hector cough, but the next voice was Beckett's.

'Barry and Jan stopped for food and drink at a twenty-four-hour petrol station. They're waiting in a lay-by just after Martham now, before the Winterton turn-off. I've sent the armed response vehicle that was going to meet them at Mile Cross to Filby. Seeing as they're in an obvious, powerful black SUV, we had them wait on the less likely route to the lighthouse.'

'An ARV should be enough for a single man.'

Kettle's voice sounded next.

'Remember, the suspect is in a car. We need two vehicles to be sure of blocking him in. There also might be a living hostage inside the vehicle. It's a far from ideal situation.'

'What can Zelda and I do?'

'We want you to head over to their location now. Leave Zelda behind if your relief hasn't arrived.'

Zelda's face fell, but Ashley understood. They wanted a woman present again, just in case there was a captive in the BMW. Headlights blinded Ashley as she was about to reply. A marked car pulled in opposite them and she blew out a breath.

'The cavalry have arrived here, so we're on our way.'

'Thanks, Ashley. It's been a long day, so drive carefully.

Michelle said the Horsey Mere girl was probably killed as the sun rose. Hector thinks that could be part of the ritual.'

'What time is that? We don't want to be five minutes late.' Hector replied.

'At 4 a.m., so you've got time to get there. I've checked the weather.' There was a slight pause from Hector. 'The sky is clear.'

He didn't need to state the obvious. This was north Norfolk. It would be a beautiful dawn.

Ashley understood there were more than a few assumptions going on, but the car had been seen leaving a horrific scene. It was as good a supposition as any, and they had nothing better to go on.

'Okay, I'll ring when we've reached Acle.'

'Fine. Hang on a minute.'

Ashley could hear the three men talking in the background. There had been a shift in the urgency of their voices. Kettle's voice returned.

'The messenger services the Dutch and we have been tracking sprang into life a little while ago. Irwin has been notified that if the chatter from it is to be believed, the man we captured in the campervan near Banningham was the Hydra.'

33

Ashley smiled as Zelda shook a clenched fist.

'Did he have a driving licence confirming that?' asked Ashley to Kettle.

'One titled Mr T Hydra? No, but the Dutch had a loose description of him. Stocky, strong, ginger hair, stark features, slight limp. They all match.'

'Excellent. I'll speak to you soon.'

Ashley hung up and offered to take the wheel.

'No, it's okay,' replied Zelda, her voice unwavering. 'I'll carry on. Talk to me, though, so I don't fall asleep.'

'That's reassuring.'

Zelda's expression didn't change. She turned on the engine and pulled out. 'I've got a few questions for you. Call it on-the-job training.'

'Fire away.'

'I've had virtually no dealings with the NCA. People say they're Britain's answer to the FBI, but I assume that's not right.'

'Fewer windcheaters, baseball caps and Glocks. More beer bellies, glasses and cheap shoes.'

'And not like MI5?'

Ashley shook her head.

'The NCA deal with the type of crime we're tackling now. Trafficking, gun smuggling, cybercrime, laundering, national and international corruption. The type of thing local forces aren't set up to do.'

'Such as the scene at Banningham.'

Ashley nodded.

'I suppose Kettle could've called a tactical unit or an ARV. Whether or not he'd have got either so fast is another point, but we would struggle with the follow up if an investigation moves across multiple counties and countries, or, like in this case, is Europe-wide. The NCA tend to take over cases and that's the last we see of them. The fact we're assisting them just goes to show how thoroughly Typhon has infiltrated the criminal network of our country and abroad. The NCA's resources are overstretched, which has kept us involved.'

'And MI5?'

'They're the Security Service. So, terrorism, espionage, Martinis, industrial sabotage, and shagging.'

Zelda didn't smile. She seemed troubled for a moment.

'I heard Ally got sent to prison.'

'Yeah, that's true.'

Zelda wouldn't be aware of his undercover work, so it would be a challenge for her to deal with being let down so badly.

'I still can't believe it. He was so good to me.'

'I know, but let's change the subject and talk about that another time. Do you know why your mum called you Zelda?'

'Are you wondering if she got it from the lady from the Terrahawks?'

Ashley chuckled. 'No.'

'Funnily enough, my gran was the spitting image of that

puppet before she died, but the reason I was named Zelda was because my mother liked Nintendo when she was a teenager.'

Ashley shot her a surprised look. 'Are you saying you were named after the hero in *The Legend of Zelda*?'

'Yep. I'm not sure it goes with Cartwright, which is the kind of surname a farrier has.'

'Well, all the best people are conundrums.'

They chatted loosely about holidays to keep themselves alert, but Zelda brought the conversation back to work as they neared Acle.

'The NCA do seem a bit like the FBI, though. Imagine the paperwork we'd need to complete for all this surveillance. Would we even get it authorised?'

'I've found the higher up you are, the more you can fill it in retrospectively. They probably have a big red stamp which says National Security.'

'I'm half hoping this is a wild goose chase. One dead girl per shift is my limit.'

'Ditto.'

Ashley rang Kettle.

'Yes, Ashley.'

She immediately noticed he was keyed up. 'We're not far now.'

'Good, because we've had a break. The BMW has driven past Barry's position and turned towards Winterton Lighthouse. He must have stopped elsewhere to wait for dawn.'

A wave of adrenaline washed over Ashley. 'What's the plan?'

'We've been working on it. The ARV is heading over to Barry. FYI, they are Officers Khan and Cash.'

'Okay, I've worked with them before.'

'We have authority to engage.'

Ashley didn't keep her driving qualifications up to date, nor did Barry, Jan or Zelda. Only Sal on her team kept current.

'Barry's not cleared for that kind of engagement. Neither am I.'

Beckett's voice came on.

'We're aware of that, Ashley, but the first duty of a police officer is the preservation of life. The Yanks say it best. We have a job to do.'

Ashley thought of the terror of anyone who might be in the back of the BMW. Barry had done the tactical pursuit and containment course, but it was some time ago. Ashley had at least worked in Traffic for years. She'd chased joyriders through the steep streets of inner-city Sheffield. She should be able to block in a car on Norfolk's tight country lanes.

'Okay, we're fifteen minutes away. What do you want us to do?'

'Drive to Winterton but stay on the line. We'll be adjusting as we engage.'

'You're going in now?'

'Yes. Every minute that ticks by could be crucial. Hopefully, the ARV can complete the task on its own if the road is narrow, but Barry and Jan will likely be needed. The men at the container weren't armed with firearms, so it seems unlikely this guy is. The lighthouse is decommissioned and now a holiday let, so there shouldn't be anyone around outside at this hour.'

'Okay. We'll head straight towards the lighthouse.'

'Good. If the driver somehow evades the others, you'll be our last hope. Other units are redirecting, but they're too far away. If the suspect leaves his vehicle when we don't have eyes on him, we're looking at a manhunt with limited resources. We'll probably lose him in the dark.'

Ashley cut the call and asked Zelda to pull over. She got out of the car, walked around and opened the driver's side door.

'My turn to drive.'

34

Barry blinked in an attempt to clear the sandy feeling from his eyes, but he was buzzing too much to feel fatigued. He missed the sharper end of policing. Not enough to return to uniform, but enough to relish opportunities like this, even though it was dangerous. That said, he hadn't been himself of late.

It had been nearly six months since Ashley had called time on whatever it was they were having together. Barry had convinced himself then that he wasn't bothered, but as the weeks went by, he missed spending time with her. Sex had been great, as if they had been made to fit with each other. She'd given him space. Not cared about his past and asked for nothing.

When she had wanted something, a little commitment, he'd moved the conversation elsewhere. He'd told himself she was too old and one day he would want children, but he doubted he had a paternal bone in his body. He wasn't sure what to do with these thoughts, which were unusual for him.

'You okay?' asked Jan, staring out of the windscreen.

'Yeah, I'm fine. Bit tired.'

'I didn't mean it like that. You've been quiet for weeks. Less piss-taking.'

Barry frowned. He hadn't bonded with the tall Dane. He liked golf and fishing, which Barry didn't consider real sports. The Ashley distraction must be obvious, though, if he'd noticed. He considered opening up to Jan, then shut his mouth swiftly. He just couldn't.

'I'm good.'

'I suspected maybe you had piles.'

'Your jokes are about as welcome as them.'

Jan turned to him.

'Are you fine with me and Emma getting promoted? It surprised me you didn't get one of the positions.'

Barry had to admit to being annoyed, but if he was honest with himself, which wasn't easy, he'd thought he had it in the bag. Now his pride was bruised, but he had only himself to blame for not taking work more seriously. He ruefully wondered if he was finally growing up.

Barry was saved from any more distressing inner analysis by the ARV pulling alongside their vehicle. The officer in the passenger seat, Khan, gave him a thumbs up. His voice came over the radio. He spoke calmly.

'Follow us thirty seconds behind. Low gear, low revs. Slow. No lights. We want the driver unaware of our presence for as long as possible. When our lights come on, that's the sign. Be prepared to swiftly catch up. Ground command believe he'll be in the seafront car park. Beach Road is pretty narrow. Not much, if any, passing room. Grey BMW.'

'Haven't you got a stinger?'

'We do, but if we burst the tyres, he'll probably still try to evade us. As you know, they often lose control and crash shortly after. We don't know who else is in the car and whether they're belted in.'

Barry nodded. 'What if the driver jumps out and runs? Will you open fire?'

'No, Barry. At this point, he's not Jesse James. We'll chase after him. Grab your torch. We hunt in pairs. You're with me. I'm a marathon runner. If he can't do one in under three hours, he's mine.'

'And if he's armed.'

'Then we'll shoot him.'

Barry almost said, 'Unless he shoots you first,' but managed to hold back. 'Okay, we're ready.'

The ARV set off through East Somerton. Thirty seconds seemed a long time for them to wait, but they couldn't have been doing more than fifteen miles an hour, so they were still in sight. Barry followed and resisted the urge to move closer. They reached Winterton and drove along Black Street past Winterton Fish Bar. Barry remembered telling Ashley how great Winterton's beach was, and that he'd take her. He never had.

The car in front slowed further at the turning to Beach Road and its rear lights went out. Barry turned his own off and relied on the streetlights to show him the way. After the village hall, the road sank into the gloom, but it wasn't pitch black. The night was yielding to the faintest of glows on the horizon.

Barry licked his lips. He found himself catching the ARV up.

'Check your speed,' said Jan.

'It's them. They're slowing.'

Khan's orderly voice echoed out of the radio.

'There's a curve ahead. The car park is around the corner. It should be locked, which means if he's here, we'll be on him as soon as we round the bend.'

Barry dropped into second gear but kept the clutch down. 'Understood. We're set.'

'Do not let him past. We are full beam and move in three, two, one. Go!'

Barry flicked on his headlights, lifted the clutch, and pressed hard on the accelerator. The Vauxhall Insignia was built for comfort, not speed, and it took a few seconds to respond. The headlights from the 4 x 4 lit up the toilet block on the right. Barry couldn't see another vehicle. The ARV wasn't stopping, though. It veered right.

Barry spotted the grey car. It must have been parked behind the toilets. The ARV's brake lights flashed on, but it slid through the sand. The two cars were going to collide, then the ARV's tyres caught, and it stopped dead. The BMW squeezed by. Barry realised the ARV hadn't wanted to hit the other car without knowing who was inside.

The BMW came speeding along Beach Road towards Barry and Jan. The section they were driving down had thick posts on one side and a marram grass-covered bank on the other.

'Do it,' growled Jan.

Barry braked and yanked on the steering wheel. His car pulled to a forty-five-degree angle. There was no way past. He saw the ARV turn and chase the BMW, which hurtled directly towards him and Jan.

Barry's breath caught in his throat. Time slowed. His life didn't flash before his eyes. Instead, he had tunnel vision of the growing threat. The roaring engine sound switched to screeching brakes. Instinctively, Barry raised his hands. A couple of seconds later, after a tiny bump, he let them fall. The vehicles were bonnet to bonnet. The other driver, a man with a thick beard and full head of black hair, sat behind the wheel, eyes bulging with shock.

Khan sprinted to the driver-side window.

'Armed police! Hands off the wheel, or I will shoot.'

The man's hands were out of sight. Barry watched anger rise on his face. The other ARV officer, Cash, appeared. Another pistol was pointed at the passenger window of the BMW.

'Raise your arms. Now!'

With a final defiant tilt of his head, the suspect raised his arms, and Barry breathed again.

35

Ashley and Zelda strained to hear the commentary from the ARV's radio. It sounded as though it wasn't going well until she heard one of the officers shouting for the driver to get out of the vehicle, then to place his hands behind his back.

Ashley reached Winterton. She cruised through the village and headed to the beach, where she saw Barry's car ahead. When she pulled up and got out, he was handcuffing a bearded man against a grey BMW while Khan and Cash kept their guns trained on him.

She got out to hear the man complaining.

'Hey, what is this? I do nothing.'

'I'm arresting you on suspicion of...' said Barry. He looked towards Ashley.

'Dangerous driving,' she said.

The ARV officers holstered their pistols while Barry cautioned the suspect. Cash shone his torch through the window at the back seats of the BMW. He shook his head.

'What's your name?' asked Ashley, stepping past Barry, who still had the suspect pressed against the side of his car.

'Maksim Wozniak.'

'Why did you try to drive off?'

'I was scared. Who knew who you are?'

Ashley walked to the rear of the vehicle where Jan was standing. Behind him, the first tip of a rising orange globe had appeared. A soft luminescence covered the dunes leading to the beach and the rhythmic lull of the waves provided a strange background to the tension that filled the air. If any seabirds were awake, they were elsewhere.

Ashley gently rested a hand on the boot.

'What's in here, Maksim?'

'I do not know. I'm the driver. I drive here. Must wait until four in the morning, then leave.'

'Can you open it, Jan?'

'I took his keys out of the ignition, and it works in this lock, but it won't lift.'

'What do you think's in there, Maksim?'

He shrugged and attempted a smile. 'Picnic?'

'Does the boot open?'

'Yes, needs technique. I show you.'

'Don't move until I say,' growled Barry.

If Barry had cuffed him correctly, the only weapon Maksim had was his head. The look on Jan's and Barry's faces meant that, given the chance, they would split it. The guy didn't appear to be too concerned, though, which made no sense. Maybe they'd made a mistake, or, more distressing, the man was some kind of decoy. Leaving the scene in a different car had pulled their attention and resources away from the real action.

'Walk,' said Barry. He held one elbow and Khan the other.

Maksim shuffled around his car. Dressed in a faded Superdry T-shirt and loose jeans, he reminded Ashley of a carpenter who'd installed shelves for her years ago. If she had to guess his mental state, she'd say worried, but not frantic.

Maksim appeared to lean away from the boot when he was next to it, as though something wild might leap from inside.

'Turn key, push hard above lock.'

Ashley did, but nothing happened.

'Harder. Bounce.'

Ashley turned the key again and used all her weight. The lock clicked open, and the boot rose a few centimetres. Ashley took a step back, then gingerly lifted it. The lid of the boot moved swiftly to its full extension. Jan pointed his torch inside.

Ashley stared down. The colour rapidly draining from her face.

'Fuck,' said Barry, slowly.

Maksim echoed the word.

Curled into the bottom of the car, like a marble cherub found on a child's grave, was an ashen teenager with striking, long, blonde hair.

36

Ashley noticed Barry turn to Maksim with anger rising on his face. She rested her hand on Barry's shoulder but caught a flicker of movement in her peripheral vision.

Barry noticed, too. 'Her fingers moved.'

Everyone stared inside the boot. The girl was still again, then her head twitched. She seemed to be sleeping, or perhaps drugged.

Ashley twisted Barry around so he was facing her. 'Calm down.'

Cash beckoned her a small distance from the BMW. He had an earpiece in.

'Ground commander is up to speed, ma'am. They'll need an update on the girl's condition. All other units including medical are en route.'

'Okay. Stick Maksim in the back of your vehicle before he gets hurt. I expect Kettle will send a van to take him to OCC.'

Ashley stared over at Maksim. He held her gaze. His mouth opened and closed, then he blew out a breath. The beard gave the impression he was bigger than he actually was, but his forearms were well muscled. She walked over to him with Khan and Cash.

'Maksim Wozniak. I'm arresting you on suspicion of kidnapping.'

By the time she finished cautioning him, his head had dropped. He made no comment as Khan and Cash took him away.

'Right, Zelda. Let's lift her out of the boot. Jan, move our cars to the side, so the ambulance can pass through. Push Maksim's BMW out of the way if you can, so you don't have to get inside it.'

Jan pulled on plastic gloves, then his head jerked. Ashley heard it too. A car rapidly approaching the narrow road's entrance, too soon to be other responders. The engine quietened, headlights stopped moving, then the motor roared to life as the vehicle reversed away.

'Shit,' said Ashley. 'Barry. Ask the approaching units to record the registrations of every vehicle they pass. I didn't get a make. Jan?'

'No. Dark blue or black maybe, that's all.'

'And tell them to stop anything of that colour.'

The sun was winning its battle with the night as Ashley perched herself on the lip of the BMW's boot. A few birds had arrived. Two seagulls squabbled overhead. Even the sea sounded louder, the waves crashing longer, as though stretching itself for the day ahead. Ashley reached over and gently shook the girl's hand. Ashley was pretty certain who it was, and that was confirmed when she opened her eyes.

'Hello, Akari. My name's Ashley. I'm a police officer.'

Akari lay there. She blinked a couple of times, and her mouth began to form a smile. Then she crossed her arms in front of her. Akari appeared to be clothed in the sportswear she'd been taken in. There were no visible marks on her face.

'We'll get you out of here. How do you feel?'

Akari moistened her lips. Her voice came out as a croak. 'Where am I?'

'You're safe now. Shuffle over to me, and I'll help you.'

Akari took her hand and eased herself over. Zelda helped Ashley lift her from the boot. The girl shivered. Supported on both sides, Akari stumbled towards their car but slipped inside with no trouble. Ashley rested one of the blankets that had been used to warm Mercedes over her.

'An ambulance is on its way. We'll have you checked out, then drive you straight home.'

'I'm fine. They didn't hurt me.' Akari sniffed. 'Where's Camille?'

Ashley got in next to her and gestured for Zelda to sit in the front. They closed the doors.

'We're looking into that now.'

'I want to go home.'

'Yes. Give us a few minutes.'

Akari's shoulders trembled and a huge gulping sob came out. 'Please. I want my mum.'

They were only half an hour from Newmarket Road. Just like with Mercedes, the trauma of what had happened to Akari would soon hit her. Many kidnap victims turned themselves off to get through the ordeal. They functioned, but didn't think. When Akari's mind began to process her experience, being with both her parents would be a major help in getting through it. Ashley made a quick decision. She squeezed Akari's hand.

'Zelda, start the engine and turn the heater on. I'll be back in a minute.'

Ashley stepped from the car and strode towards Jan. Half of the sun had swiftly risen, seemingly from the depths of the sea. It cast everyone in pastels of pink and yellow. Barry and Jan seemed to shimmer in the early morning light, but up close, with the adrenaline leaching from their veins, their faces were grey.

'Is she okay?' asked Jan.

'We're going to take her home. She seems physically fine. Even said they didn't touch her. So, you two can hand over the scene, then head off yourselves. We all need to sleep. I'll head back to mine after Zelda and I have been to Newmarket Road.'

'Do you get the feeling something horrible was going to happen here?'

'I don't think it was a ransom handover.' Ashley blinked her eyes. She thought of the boy with the nine-piece jigsaw and suspected she'd currently struggle with one of them. 'We've nicked the driver and we have Hydra in the cells. Let's hope this is the end of it.'

Jan usually gave the impression of healthy clean living, but huge bags had formed under his red eyes, and his shoulders drooped. He appeared closer to fifty than thirty.

Ashley suspected she looked sixty.

'Tell Kettle I suggested a 1 p.m. meeting tomorrow. We'll go through all of this and interview Maksim and Hydra afterwards. Someone can talk to Mercedes and Akari in the late afternoon or evening, too, but nobody can function without rest.'

'At least the two girls are safe.'

Ashley had nothing else to say. She trudged back to the car and found Zelda had got in beside Akari. The inside was warming nicely. She reversed out of where Jan had parked the vehicle and drove swiftly down Beach Road. She slowed and stopped for a marked car that had driven past the village hall. The driver and she wound down their windows. The driver appeared vaguely familiar, but she couldn't drag up a name.

'Morning, ma'am.'

'Morning. DS Jan Pederson has the scene. You can head straight on up. Situation is under control.'

'Thank you, ma'am.'

Ashley drove in silence for a quarter of an hour, then Akari piped up.

'How could this happen?' she blurted out. 'They took us in daylight. What did we do?'

'It wasn't your fault,' said Zelda. 'It was bad men doing bad things.'

'I don't understand. Camille and I have never upset anyone.'

'It's them, not you.'

Akari shook her head as if to clear it. 'Why was I at the beach?'

'We're not sure yet.'

'Was Camille there, too?'

Ashley glanced in the rear-view mirror. Akari seemed in control. They had to ask what happened to her at some point. She might have something important to tell them. Perhaps it was better to do that now.

'Were you with Camille?'

'At the beginning. They kept us in the lounge of a house. Left us to watch TV. After a day, they took her away. I was asked loads of questions. Sexual stuff. I thought they were going to rape me. I didn't reply at first, but an ugly man came in with terrible breath. He told me to answer immediately and honestly, or he would bring me one of Camille's eyes.'

Ashley cursed under her breath.

'Is it okay if Zelda takes some notes, Akari? We need to know as much as possible, so this doesn't happen to anyone else.'

Akari sniffed, then wiped her nose with the blanket. 'Of course.'

'Ugly?' asked Zelda.

'Gaunt – is that the right word? – features. A kind of lined face, but the room was gloomy. Maybe I was scared and imagining things. I answered everything after that.'

'What sort of questions were they?' asked Zelda.

'Are my parents wealthy? About my sex life. If I had a boyfriend. Then they asked the same questions about Camille. Whether she was having sex, or if her parents were rich. They said if I kept quiet and caused no trouble, neither of us would be harmed. Our parents would just need to pay the ransom.'

Ashley noted Akari's speech speeding up.

'Try to keep calm, Akari.'

'No. We have to find Camille.'

'Didn't you see her again after they removed her from that room?'

'They never brought her back. It got really quiet. I only ever saw two men. They told me not to look at them, so I can't describe them well. One had brown hair but always wore sunglasses, but he was quite old. The guy with the craggy face had reddish hair.'

'And they treated you okay?'

'Yes, even though I kept saying I wanted to go home. When I cried, the ginger one just said not to worry. The money would be paid soon.'

Ashley caught Zelda's frown at the second mention of a ransom. Had their captors demanded one but the parents not told them, or had they been using it as a means of keeping the girls calm?

To give them hope, when perhaps there was none.

37

Ashley cruised through Norwich's deserted streets catching glimpses of the cathedral spires. By the time she reached Newmarket Road, daylight had fully arrived, leaving the sky a vibrant blue. Akari had stopped answering any questions and withdrawn into herself. Zelda had offered a hand for her to hold, which she'd seized. She'd shuffled over to lean against her in the same way Mercedes had with Ashley.

Ashley kept her window a smidge open to help keep herself awake. She stared out of it when she arrived at the Kato residence. There were lights on in every room downstairs despite it being daylight, testament to a sleepless night. The gravel churning under the car's wheels jarred in the peaceful quiet of the large plot as she trundled up the drive.

Ashley had placed only one foot out of the vehicle when the front door opened.

Hanzo appeared. He wore the same clothes as when Ashley last saw him. She couldn't remember when that was, which was further proof she needed rest. Hanzo's face asked a thousand questions, when there was only one he desired the answer to.

Ashley smiled at Hanzo and nodded. He flew down the steps and stamped over the stones. Ashley opened the back door of the car for him. He eased himself inside and gently smothered his daughter. He laughed and cried at the same time. Akari's arms were pressed around him, fingernails dug in. Zelda got out of the other side.

A cry came from behind them. Victoria stood frozen in the doorway, lit by a chandelier behind, arms raised. After a few seconds, she lurched forward, staggering into a run past Zelda, and plunged into the vehicle. She released a high shriek, then joined the desperate huddle.

Ashley and Zelda had moved away to give them some privacy when Stefan Dupont appeared at the door. He must have stayed to support as Akari still wasn't found.

Stefan spoke quietly and without emotion.

'Is it Akari?'

'Yes.'

'Is she okay?'

Ashley nodded. 'Yes, she seems unharmed.'

'That's good.'

'How are you holding up?'

Stefan shrugged. 'I'm not sure.'

'Is Aveline here?'

'No, she's been in bed ever since. Not eating, not sleeping.'

'Did you ask your family liaison officer for some support?'

'No. She's like a mute.'

'I'll have him get in touch.'

'Thank you, but I know experts in most fields. There's no cure, is there?'

Ashley wasn't sure how to reply. Telling someone at this moment that time would help would be stupid and insulting.

'I'm so sorry for your loss.'

Stefan took a few steps towards her. His voice was louder.

'I'd like to rip the person responsible to pieces with my bare hands.'

Ashley nodded. She understood that.

The Katos clambered from the car. Hanzo and Victoria gabbling as if they'd won the lottery and couldn't believe it. They clung to Akari, who wobbled precariously, her face so pale she resembled a doll. She noticed Stefan, who had stepped to the side to allow them to pass.

Akari came to a halt.

'If you pay the money, Stefan, Camille will be fine. They didn't hurt me.'

Stefan walked over to the intact family. He held eye contact with Akari.

'No ransom was sought for either of you.'

He squeezed Hanzo's arm and then Victoria's.

'I'm so happy for you both.' To Akari, he said, 'Sadly, it's too late for Camille. She is dead.'

Stefan marched robotically down the drive. Ashley closed her eyes as Akari's screams filled the air.

38

Ashley awoke later that morning, in exactly the same position as she'd fallen asleep, disorientated by the unusual alarm sound. She recalled setting two to make sure she got up. This was the second one waking her at 11 a.m. She forced herself to rise and take a shower. There was a strange taste in her mouth, which she realised was the sausage and egg McMuffin she'd had on the way home.

After a huge glass of orange juice and a bowl of bite-sized Shredded Wheat, she grabbed an apple, a banana and a bottle of water and set off for the office. The roads were busy and slow, with vehicles aplenty, so it was 1 p.m. by the time she got in. She went straight to Kettle's office but he wasn't there, so she headed to the conference room.

Hector, Kettle, and Beckett were sitting around the table and they all looked as bleary-eyed as she felt. She suspected she'd had the most sleep. Kettle pulled himself out of his seat.

'Afternoon, Ashley. We're pushing the discussion back until five. There's too much paperwork to complete first. HOLMES needs all the latest information to function. I'd like you to do a summary at the end of the meeting.'

'What's going on with the interviews from our arrests?'

'You can ask your guys who weren't involved yesterday to do them.'

'Okay, Sal and Emma will do an excellent job. Have the suspects been offered representation?'

'Maksim has asked for a London solicitor. He says it's a friend of a friend. They seem legit. Eastern European focused. Someone's on their way. The craggy-faced guy refused to give a name until we said we couldn't ring his solicitor without one. He told us it's Vladimir Nikolayev.'

Hector chuckled.

'Morning, Ashley. Impressive work yesterday. A quick Internet search will tell you Vladimir Nikolayev is a famous murderer, so we can take the name with a pinch of salt. Not in the league of famous Russian serial killers Andrei Chikatilo and Alexander Pichushkin, but the press nicknamed Nikolayev The Cannibal, and The Ogre. The courts sentenced him to death, later commuted to life without parole.'

Ashley thought back to Hector's theory that the deaths they were dealing with might be human sacrifices.

'I assume you've checked whether Vladimir's escaped from prison. Maybe the Russians let him go to fight in Ukraine.'

Beckett cleared his throat.

'He's messing with us. Even the Russians aren't daft enough to let people like him out. Besides, there's no resemblance between them.'

'Plastic surgery?'

'I suppose anything is possible, but Nikolayev is at the Black Dolphin Prison, which nobody has ever broken out of. They live in cages. Despite the conflict, there are avenues of communication, so we will check. The telephone number he provided was for a firm of solicitors in Norwich, which checks out. A man there said he would attend.'

'What's happening with the girls?'

'I've spoken to the head of child services about Akari Kato, but she's nearly eighteen, so they aren't that interested. Of course, they'll offer support and direction, but the parents are loving and close to Akari, so they are inclined to let them care for her. To save time, Scott will be FLO for her case and Mercedes'. He's planning to visit the Katos today. I wanted to check if you had the time. You have a lot on your plate, but you might be the best person to attend with him.'

Ashley appreciated him asking but it was obviously a sensible idea.

'Agreed. Akari said some unusual things before we dropped her off. She mentioned ransoms. Stefan said they never received a request. After he left, Hanzo swore to the same thing. Did we get any evidence of a sum being asked for?'

'No, nothing.'

'I'm wondering whether one was offered, or even paid, and we never knew. We've had a parent pay before, then deny any knowledge.'

Beckett squinted while he thought.

'Could the Katos have paid one, but the Duponts didn't?'

'It's a possibility. Perhaps the criminals took the money and carried on regardless.'

Kettle rubbed his eyes. Ashley suspected these three hadn't gone home.

'Okay, I'll go with Scott to both parents' places when he's ready. We need to talk to the girls while their memories are fresh. It's anyone's guess whether they will talk or shut down as a coping mechanism.'

'Thank you,' said Kettle, 'and well done from me and Irwin with this case. Staunch work yesterday.'

'Team effort, sir.'

Ashley went back to her desk and spent the afternoon updating various computer databases. Jan and Barry arrived at two. Zelda at three.

'Sorry,' she said. 'Slept straight through the alarm.'

With her dark make-up, Zelda's red eyes appeared almost demonic.

'No worries, get on with your paperwork, then go home.'

Once Maksim and Vladimir's solicitors had arrived, Ashley prepared Sal and Emma for the interviews. If there were any guilty pleas, they would likely be offered at the first interview, but Ashley's hopes weren't high.

She made a call to Scott just before 5 p.m. and agreed a time to meet. The whole of MIT and various other OCC personnel filtered into the large meeting room at five. Beckett took a seat at the front with Kettle. When asked, various departments gave their most recent updates, but there was no fresh intel.

When they were finished, Kettle waited for everyone's attention.

'Okay. We've made a lot of progress this week, but it's not all been plain sailing. I'm hoping we're entering the final phase. DI Knight will give you a summary of our next steps.'

Ashley walked to the front of the room.

'Right. Both suspects have kept quiet and calm since they arrived, but their solicitors are here, and we'll see how the interviews unfold. We're under the impression Maksim doesn't know how much trouble he's in. He may be our best chance of information. We'll refer to the other guy as Vladimir, even though it's likely not his name.'

Ashley checked her notes.

'I'm heading to the mortuary after this meeting to find out how the woman in the container died. Afterwards, FLO Scott Gorton and I are heading to Newmarket Road to talk with Akari. She gave us some information last night, which is on the file. Then Scott and I are off to Ipswich to see Mercedes. Bosko, the muscle at the Thetford property, was remanded in prison today. He's going to be there some time while this unravels. Both Maksim and Vladimir will be heading the same way. Long sentences await them.'

'Is that all of the bosses caught?' asked Gabriella.

'If Vladimir is Hydra, then it appears that way. The organisation may well disintegrate without leadership. Let's hope no more girls go missing. We certainly haven't caught all the underlings, though. We spotted a car that might have been heading to meet Maksim in the early hours of this morning, but we didn't get a plate for it. We need to continue being focused and remain vigilant. There could be many more victims in the UK who still need rescuing from whatever servitude this organisation has forced them into. Has anyone got anything to ask or add?'

Nobody did. The burning question was whether they'd won a battle or ended the war.

Only time would tell.

39

Thirty minutes later, Ashley arrived at the mortuary and went to Michelle Ma Yun's office. Ashley sat opposite her desk as the pathologist massaged her temples.

'Long day?' she asked.

'Aren't they all lately?'

'Seems that way.'

Michelle stretched.

'It's not just that. Dead bodies don't normally faze me, but so many young ones close together is having an effect.'

Michelle usually had glowing skin and vibrant eyes, but both were dulled. Ashley dreaded to consider what she herself looked like in the mirror. Probably not much better than those in Michelle's cabinets.

It was probably a hugging moment. Michelle and she got on well, but Ashley had never been much of a hugger. She reached over and squeezed Michelle's hand instead.

'I believe we're close to the end now.'

Michelle gave her a wistful look. 'I've been doing this long enough to know the end is when I'm busiest.'

'Keep going. You're doing an excellent job.'

'Right! Jane Doe from yesterday. I assume she hasn't been ID'd?'

'She has distinctive features and is above average height, but nobody on the misper list matches up.'

'I suspect that's because she's foreign. We'll do DNA to confirm her heritage, but the bone structure is likely Eastern European.'

'She'll be one of the exploited migrants. We'll cross-check with the other countries' lists.'

'It's awful, isn't it?' Michelle frowned as she brought her screen to life. 'Imagine losing contact with a child. Then your local police inform you the authorities in another country, thousands of miles away, have discovered them in a container and needed to use DNA for identification. It's hard to imagine the type of people who could do this to an innocent girl.'

Ashley didn't need to imagine them. There was at least one of them in custody at OCC.

'Their ruthlessness and disloyalty to each other are often their downfall. A man from their organisation in Holland has revealed a lot about their operation, and we have two surviving women who will hopefully provide more.'

'Are they all right?'

'It's difficult to say. They've probably been lucky, considering their predicament. Psychologically, I'd be concerned though.'

'Right. Okay, I can't give you too many hard facts regarding the latest woman, so I'll surmise. Dead less than eight hours. Pale skin on her face from blood pooling. Rigor mortis only just beginning. Body was still cooling. Tox screen not back, but there are track marks on the right arm. I suspect the habit is relatively recent because the injections have only been done in one area. No obvious major injuries. I've had a quick look with a camera down her throat and the airways seem clear and the stomach empty.'

Michelle looked up and shrugged. 'At present, the cause of death is unknown.'

Ashley tutted, but bodies often kept their secrets. 'I suppose an overdose is likely?'

'Yes, if I had to make a guess, that would be it, because otherwise there's nothing obvious. She has early signs of malnutrition. The nails are painted, but in bad condition. Her skin is dehydrated. It's unusual to have a completely empty stomach, but her intestines will tell me when she last ate.'

Ashley suspected the full post-mortem was likely to unpeel an extra layer of horror from the poor girl's final few days.

'Any estimate of how long she's been mistreated?'

'I'm guessing they gave her heroin, or possibly ketamine, to make her compliant or unaware of what was happening. The track marks on her arm would suggest a few weeks to a month.'

'Thanks. That's helpful. I'm meeting Scott at Newmarket Road.'

'Ah, so it was you he dumped me for?'

Ashley raised an eyebrow.

'We were going out to the cinema tonight, but he cancelled because of work.'

'Sorry, and we've got to head to Ipswich again afterwards, so we won't be back until tennish.'

'Tell him I said hi, then. We're not getting much time together lately, and I want to have a chat with him.'

'Sounds ominous.'

'After speaking to you about not being bothered about getting married, I realised that even though I'm not, I should know if it's off the cards.'

'That's fair. It has been six months.'

'The baby thing also needs addressing.'

Ashley wondered if she was the right person to be having this conversation with her. 'Do you want kids?'

'Maybe. I'm not, like, super-focused on it, but I need to get my head around that if he is a solid no. He might not want to start again.'

'Would that be okay? You're only in your mid-thirties.'

'I wouldn't say it's a deal-breaker.'

Ashley felt uneasy giving advice, seeing as part of her wanted to growl, *Dump him, then he can be all mine!* Michelle and Scott were both friends, and Michelle had confided in Ashley before that she didn't have many.

'Do you remember me telling you about Scott's bogey eating?'

Michelle grinned. 'I do, although I haven't seen him munching on any yet. Perhaps he hauls them out while I'm not looking.'

'Then he keeps them in a special tin until you go to sleep.'

'Yuck.'

'Back then, you joked that wasn't a deal-breaker. Now no kids may not be one either, *and* you've also said not getting married wouldn't bother you.'

Ashley left it there. Michelle's grin fell away. She drummed her fingers on the desk.

'I get where you're coming from. Relationships should be about compromise.'

'Yes, but don't think you understand what's going on in Scott's head, or what his plans are. He is a man. He's probably pondering whether a beaver could beat an aardvark in an arm wrestle.'

Michelle's smile returned. 'Aardvark all the way. Thanks, Ash. As always, good advice.'

Ashley was a little unsettled as she drove to Newmarket Road, but her conscience felt clear, so she directed her attention to the case. What had Akari been doing since yesterday? It was human nature for her to have asked her parents what happened to Camille. The next logical step would be her looking on the Internet, where the gruesome details were everywhere. It would bring home just how fortunate she'd been, but she wouldn't feel that way.

Scott's car was parked in the street, so Ashley pulled in behind him. He got out as she did.

'Evening, Ash. I hate to leap straight to business, but this isn't going to be simple.'

'Great.'

'I rang Akari's and Mercedes' parents this afternoon to explain when we were coming and ask if there was anything they needed. Donna began telling me not to bother. I was explaining it was necessary for us to understand exactly what happened, when Mercedes took the phone off her and stated she will talk to me once, so I'd better get it right the first time, and only if you were present.'

'That's promising.'

'Maybe. Her voice was emotionless. I spoke to Hanzo earlier, and he replied that while we were welcome to come, only he would speak to us, and not for long.'

'Did you explain to him his daughter is old enough to be interviewed without him and it wasn't his call?'

'No. I got the distinct impression the family would simply become uncooperative, perhaps they wouldn't even answer the door.'

'I suppose his response is understandable.'

'Yes, but possibly not extremely helpful to our investigation. You have a connection with the girls, so I'll take notes. Let's see if we can persuade him to allow a brief discussion with his daughter, otherwise we'll need to arrange a future date. Playing hardball won't get us anywhere.'

They trudged up the drive. With no vehicles in view and only one light on, the place appeared deserted. Hanzo took a full minute to answer the door, offering a weak smile that didn't reach his dark eyes and hollowed cheeks. His crumpled clothes betrayed his emotional state. In the kitchen, he offered them a drink. They declined, so he could sit down straight away.

He lifted the glass tumbler in front of him, which contained a clear liquid, had a sip, then grimaced.

'Thank you for coming, but I fear your journey was wasted.'

Ashley noticed the white of his knuckles as he held his drink. Grey stubble showed on his face.

'It's no trouble,' said Ashley. 'How is Akari?'

'Not good. She asked how Camille died. What could we say?'

'It's a hard thing to explain.'

'We were vague, but my girl is too sharp. Akari announced she needed to lie down. I knew Akari had lost her phone, but instead of resting, she went on her laptop. About fifteen minutes later, she screamed again. We couldn't settle her. A friend came, a doctor. He was going to sedate her, but she was so tired, she fell asleep.'

'Where is she now?'

'A colleague has a lodge in the middle of nowhere. He offered, so my wife has taken her there. It's quiet, surrounded by nature, no traffic, a place to heal. There's even a lake. Perhaps she'll finally let me take her fishing. I will join them after you've left.'

Ashley knew she had only minutes remaining.

'Thank you for waiting for us. It's natural you've put your

daughter's well-being first, but we still have a lot of questions we'd like to ask. Her answers might be the difference in putting an end to this organisation or merely wounding it.'

'I understand.'

Hanzo took a business card out of his top pocket and slid it across the kitchen table towards her.

'You may contact me via email. If you have questions, I will consider whether to ask her them. I can't promise anything.'

Scott stood and shook Hanzo's hand. He gave him his card.

'Please call if you need any help, or if Akari wants to talk about what she went through. Like Ashley said, one little recollection may be of significant value to us. We don't want any other women to be at risk. Use me as your point of reference. You'll probably have your own questions as you process everything. I don't mind when you ring me.'

At the door, Ashley shook Hanzo's hand too.

'I'm sorry this happened to your family.'

'Me, too. Akari kept saying she was sorry. I said it wasn't her fault. She wept, then told me she lied to them, and she'd lied to us.'

'Do you know what about?'

'No. She broke down again, so I didn't push it.'

Ashley kept her questions in. 'Okay, thank you for seeing us.'

Hanzo gave them a quick, stiff bow, then shut the door.

She and Scott returned to their vehicles.

'Your car or mine?' asked Scott, poking the rust that was appearing on her wheel arch.

'Don't touch that. The whole thing will disintegrate.'

They set off in his Toyota.

'Is this new?'

'Yes, you know I get one with the job.'

'Lucky you.'

Scott was quiet as he drove. After a few minutes, he turned to her when they were stopped at traffic lights.

'What do you make of Akari's comment about lying?'

Ashley had been considering the same thing. 'I think I know what it was.'

40

When the light turned green, Scott pulled away, lost in thought.

'No,' he finally said, shaking his head. 'I still don't see it.'

'Akari said the men who took her asked weird questions about her sex life. It's obvious they were finding out if she was a virgin.'

'Why would they want to know that?'

'Why do you think?'

'If they were forcing them to be prostitutes, were they concerned they'd have no experience?'

'I reckon the reverse is true. There are men willing to pay big bucks for purity.'

Scott was an experienced officer, but revulsion still flashed across his face.

'Let's pray there aren't too many of them in Norfolk.'

'Who knows where the customers are coming from?'

'But why kill the girls when they were finished?'

'Maybe they paid enough to not conceal their faces, and Typhon disposed of the body afterwards.'

'I hope you're wrong.'

'Camille may not even have been molested. We don't know why she was killed.'

They both sat in glum silence as Scott's car ate up the miles, but, as often happened when they spent time together, they broke into banter.

'Are you dating?' he asked.

'Why is everyone interested in my love life?'

'Seems a shame if you're not. You're a catch.'

'Hot, stylish and happening?'

'I was thinking solvent, employed and relatively clean.'

Ashley nudged him with her elbow. 'Cheeky.'

'I have got some news.'

'News or gossip?'

'Actually, I have both. Which would you like first?'

'Gossip, gossip!'

Scott chuckled. 'Okay, the goss is Gabriella went out on a date with Mark from Custody.'

'No-o-o!'

'Yep.'

'They were spotted walking through Norwich Lanes.'

'Perhaps they're just pals.'

'Kissing pals?'

Ashley decided not to mention Hector. 'Ooh, juicy. Barry will be devastated.'

'Didn't Hector like her?'

She smiled. 'Yeah, he did. Quite a bit, in fact. I don't envy you telling him.'

'Not tempting. Seems to me that's an inspector-grade job.'

Ashley grimaced at the prospect. 'What's the news?'

'My daughter's pregnant.'

'No way. Isn't she fourteen?'

'Try twenty-three.'

'Wow. A grandpa, and before you're sixty.'

Scott, who was only a couple of years older than Ashley, looked over at her and laughed. 'Now who's being cheeky?'

They continued the journey chatting about how life could turn on a sixpence, but they both naturally quietened as they approached Mercedes' home. She answered the door with her head down and immediately stepped outside. The officers could hear young children shouting in the background.

Mercedes slammed the door shut behind her with finality.

'Let's go to the pub.'

41

Mercedes had dressed in black jeans and a slouchy hoodie. Her hair was drawn back into a tight ponytail.

Ashley got a glimpse of tired eyes, before an oversized pair of sunglasses were lowered.

'We should do this at the station.'

'We do it at my local. Now or never.'

'Wouldn't you rather talk to us somewhere quiet?'

'Oh, it will be quiet. Come on, the place isn't far.'

Mercedes strode off and they followed. She didn't speak for the two minutes it took them to arrive. Ashley was no stranger to rough pubs. This one was at the end of its tether. It smelled of smoke, despite the smoking ban being in force since 2007. The person responsible had to be the thin, hard-faced woman behind the bar because, except for a guy who appeared to be asleep in the corner, there was nobody else to blame.

Mercedes strode to the bar. The barmaid looked up and smiled.

'You okay, girl?'

'Yeah, Viv. Trade still tough?'

'A big game's on and we ain't got Sky no more.'

'Can you afford to repair the TV?'

'Nope. Look, I 'eard what happened. Sorry, luv, but you'll get over it.'

'Thank you.'

'Usual?'

'Yeah. This pair are paying.'

Viv cast an eye over them as if they'd crawled in naked and covered in jam.

'What you 'avin?'

'Sparkling mineral water, please,' said Scott with a smile.

'Same,' said Ashley.

The woman plonked a pint of flat lager on a beer mat and placed two tumblers of clear liquid next to them.

'Five quid for the Stella. Tap water's free. Shout if you need anything, Mercedes.'

Ashley paid with a forced smile. The girl grabbed her glass and moved to the far corner of the pub. The table appeared unstable when she rested her drink on it and Ashley's chair creaked when she sat down. Scott, being the heaviest, lowered himself down carefully. This was the type of boozer that the neighbourhood would complain about when it closed, even though too few used it when it was open.

Mercedes took off her sunglasses. The light above the dartboard shone down on her heavy make-up. She seemed ageless at that moment. Neither twenty nor forty. She'd raised a barrier against the world. To heal behind. She hadn't been offered a quiet lodge or been visited by a friendly doctor.

'Thank you for talking to us, Mercedes. We know this can't be easy. This is Scott Gorton. He's a family liaison officer.'

'Are you the investigators for this case?'

'I am, but Scott is here to provide support.'

Mercedes barked out a laugh, but her expression didn't change.

'My mum told me how Esra died.'

'I'll drive you to see him at the mortuary,' said Scott. 'Assist with the funeral arrangements.'

'I doubt he had the money for one.'

'No, but the council will help. I'll give you advice if the press contact you.'

'We had a few reporters around earlier.'

'What did you say?' asked Ashley.

'They left sharpish. My mum was three sheets to the wind by then. She's pretty terrifying like that.'

Ashley nodded. 'It's okay if you'd like your mother here.'

'She's unconscious. That's how she copes. Sometimes I envy her.'

Mercedes picked up her pint and took the tiniest sip. She placed it back and shook her head.

'But it wouldn't help me. I've still got a chance. I need to be strong, or my life won't be worth shit.'

'I can direct you to counselling. Make referrals,' said Scott.

'They'll want to talk about it. That's not for me. I need to forget.'

'Counsellors know what they're doing.'

Mercedes pulled a face.

Ashley decided to be straight with her.

'We need to ask you what happened to prevent anyone else from going through the same thing. Based on what you've just implied, remembering might be tough for you. I'd prefer to talk in a nicer environment. We can have an outreach worker with us. Whatever you think is best.'

Mercedes moved her drink to the other side of the table.

'You have ten minutes. Ask anything you want, but I won't

speak to you again, and I can't see the benefit in telling the world.'

Ashley glanced at Scott, who took out his notebook. She turned back to the blank-faced girl, who bobbed her head once.

'Okay. What happened to you?'

Mercedes spoke in a monotone.

'Some men approached our car looking for directions.'

'Can you describe them?'

'Not really. It was so quick. They had caps, big coats and sunglasses. I don't believe I saw them again.'

'Did they have beards or moustaches?'

'No, sorry. They seemed organised.'

'Okay, what happened next?'

'We were snatched, bundled into a van, driven to a house somewhere, then separated. I was told if I didn't cooperate, Esra would be seriously hurt. They fed me, but told me to shut up if I tried to talk. I was moved to a campervan after a few days and driven elsewhere. The curtains were always drawn.'

Ashley thought of the women in the Bacton Wood case being trafficked through Eastern Europe. It was the same modus operandi. Organised crime at its very worst, but this had occurred in England, and Mercedes and Esra hadn't been coerced or fooled. They'd simply been taken.

Mercedes' face twisted, reminding Ashley of her mother's search for strength.

'They told me what I had to do, and I did it.'

'I'm so sorry, Mercedes.'

'It was obviously horrible, but not as bad as you'd think. I could never see how women did that sort of thing, but I can now. Nobody took long. Weirdly, most of the men were gentle. One apologised, another said he couldn't when he saw my face, even though I think he probably could.'

When she reached the part where Ashley had looked in at her in the trailer, a tear ran down her face. One she didn't wipe away.

'I thought I was seeing things when you arrived, and they'd hidden something in my food.'

'Did they try to give you drugs?'

'They offered them, but I refused. I wanted to be ready to go if the opportunity arose. Esra's friends were criminals. Some of the men who came to the campervan reminded me of them. It's not like the movies. They're drunk and careless and so I hoped someone would make a mistake and leave a door open or something. The other girl took the heroin. Her English was poor, but she'd been there for at least a couple of weeks. Maybe I'd have taken that option after a while.'

Mercedes sniffed. 'I take it she was dead?'

'I'm afraid so.'

'Yeah.' The word came out in a dry sob. Then her face reformed the hard mask. 'We used to nod and smile when they let us out to stretch our legs, and occasionally whispered to each other when it was quiet. The walls were thin, and they threatened to hit us if they heard.'

Ashley considered how to phrase the next question, then ploughed on, as the clock was ticking.

'It's hard for me to ask this, or word it correctly, but they seemed to make sure your visitors didn't hurt you.'

'Yes. One of them was clever. The evil-looking guy. They fed us, let us shower, gave us clean clothes and underwear. I guess he looked after us for a reason.'

Ashley blew out a breath. 'You were so brave.'

A flash of anger flashed in Mercedes' eyes.

'I wasn't brave. I endured. My brothers and sisters need me. Mum tries most of the time, but she won't make old bones.

When my chance came, I was going to run.' She shook her head. 'It never did. The man in charge was careful. Always watching.'

'Did they ask you about being a virgin?'

Mercedes folded her arms. 'Yes.'

'Why do you think that was?'

She shrugged. 'The ugly one was focused on my reply. Perhaps innocence was what he liked.'

'What did you tell him?'

'That I was far from one.'

'Do you think he was the person who kidnapped you?'

'I don't know.'

'Can you tell us exactly what happened when you and Esra were being abducted?'

'We were sitting in his car with the windows open, outside my house. A bag was placed over my head, so I didn't see anyone. The only thing I remember is catching a dude looking at me funny a few days beforehand.'

'Can you describe him?'

'Not really. I saw him from a distance. I just got a weird feeling when I glanced over at him. It was kind of creepy. Short brown hair. Sunglasses. Slim and fairly tall.'

They asked a few more questions, but Mercedes had little more to say. She abruptly stood with her pint virtually untouched.

'I'm going.'

Ashley got out of her seat.

'I can see how this is hard for you, but we need a full signed statement. One giving us as much description as possible of all the men you saw.'

Mercedes finally smiled.

'You've had enough from me. I'll walk home on my own.'

Ashley's mind whirred for how they were going to get this

necessary information. Mercedes didn't have to provide a state-ment, but she would have to go to court if asked, although Ashley knew no judge would prosecute a woman who refused to talk about an experience like Mercedes'.

Scott handed Mercedes his business card. She stared at it for a moment, slipped it in her pocket, then wandered out.

Scott went to take a sip of his water, then thought better of it.

'That was hard to hear.'

'Yes, but it's made me more confident around my thoughts about Akari. What do girls lie to their parents about?'

'Everything?'

'Okay, what topic would they most likely never discuss with them? Especially their fathers.'

Scott gave her a grim smile. 'Sex.'

'Yes. She comes from a nice family. Education is important. Her folks would have been worried about her relationship with her boyfriend. She deceived them, too.'

Ashley recalled Damian's face when he'd arrived at the Kato property. Young love was all-consuming. They might well have had sex for the first time on that Friday afternoon when his parents were out.

'If I'm right, Maksim drove her to the beach to be raped and killed, or just killed. Whether he would do it, or if she was to be handed over to someone else, I don't know.'

'Whereas Mercedes was used goods, so they put her to work.'

Ashley nodded and stood up to leave.

'If you think about it, Mercedes got abducted before Camille. Not being a virgin saved her life.'

42

Ashley headed to work early the following morning and was first in the office at seven thirty. She made a coffee and borrowed a couple of digestives from a packet someone had foolishly left on the fridge. Sebastian surprised her by being next in, seeing as it was a Saturday. He wandered over in what looked like Levi's, with a smart but loose white shirt, and perched on the edge of her desk.

'My last day,' he said.

The mouthful of biscuit she'd just eaten suddenly felt difficult to swallow.

'That's a shame. I've kind of been expecting some James Bond antics from you to save the world.'

'I'm happy to come over to yours and show you some 007 action.'

Ashley coughed and crumbs sprayed onto her laptop.

'I bet you are,' she said, collecting the bits with her fingers. 'Thank you, by the way. Your article was brilliant. The public really helped with this case.'

'You talk as if it's finished.'

'Hmmm.'

'I might be available for consultancy.'

With that, he offered her his business card in much the same manner Scott had the previous night to Mercedes.

Ashley took it. 'Aren't you shortly going to be crawling through the Amazon swamps with a Bowie knife between your teeth?'

'I'll be chatting to retired cartel members in dingy Mexican bars with my laptop open if that does it for you. Back to reporting, but I'll probably end up helping the NCA again in the future.'

'No wrestling with crocodiles?'

'Feeding the caimans?'

Ashley removed a card from her top pocket and slid it across the table to him.

'If you survive, ring me when you get back.'

She was saved from his riposte when Kettle came out of his office and called her in. She'd messaged him the previous night to say there was nothing that couldn't wait until the next day.

He listened with a scowl while she updated him.

'Poor girls. Unfortunately, we didn't have a lot of success after you left yesterday. Barry and Morgan went to Maksim's house, but there was no answer. Barry had a word with the neighbours. One side rarely spoke to either side. The other said Maksim's wife, Jolanta Wozniak, had gone away and would return today. She talks to him about gardening. He'd seen nothing of Maksim lately and wondered if they'd split up, but he was too polite to ask.'

'That needs following up as a priority. Did he say when she'd be back?'

'He thought early afternoon because she had asked him to look out for a Royal Mail delivery.'

'Okay. I'll get someone on it for an early evening call. We won't ring her beforehand.'

'Good idea.'

'Any related drama elsewhere in Norfolk or Suffolk?'

'Quiet as the grave. I checked with the NCA first thing. The communication channel we've been monitoring traffic on was dead. The Dutch raided a property yesterday, but it was long abandoned. They think it's over in Holland. Irwin is talking with them this morning because they've offered to help here.'

'Damn. I was hoping Telegram would be full of chatter about Hydra being captured. Maybe they've rumbled that the channel isn't secure.'

'Perhaps.'

'And neither of our new arrivals spilled a bean in the interview room?'

'No, both spent hours with their briefs, but said no comment to us. Custody rang me five minutes ago, though. Sounds like Maksim is the type who stews overnight. He wants to talk.'

Ashley jerked a thumb back at the empty office. 'We should do it immediately, before he changes his mind. Are you ready to go?'

Kettle chuckled. 'I'm a bit out of practice, but Hector's in the conference room. I've just emailed him to say he has an interview to do with you.'

'Cool. Nothing from the other guy, Vladimir?'

'Zip.'

'I'll see if he'll open up afterwards. Even if there's no response, I may get a feeling from him, especially if I let slip others are talking.'

Ashley grabbed the phone on Kettle's desk and rang Custody.

'Custody, Sergeant Mark Smith speaking!'

Ashley smiled. It was no wonder he sounded upbeat.

'Hi, Mark. Ashley here. Bring Maksim to interview room one at eight, please. Hector and I will speak to him in there. Any reports from last night?'

'Yeah, funny you should say that. I started at six and checked the log. We had a drunken brawl in town, so the cells were full, even the isolation suite. Maksim and Vladimir were at opposite ends of the custody unit. They began shouting to each other. The officer on duty went to tell them to shut it, but quietly stood outside their cells for a moment, to see if he could hear what they were saying. They mostly spoke in their own language, although he could recognise it as an argument. Then it got really aggressive. Nasty even. We moved Maksim to the quiet cell.'

Ashley tapped the desk appreciatively. Not all the night officers were fastidious about filling in the observations book, especially if they were busy.

'Excellent. Tell the staff I owe them cakes.'

'Will do.'

'Did they guess the language?'

'Perhaps Polish.'

'Who was the aggressor?'

'Definitely Vladimir. He went on a major rant at the end. The officer had to tell him to keep it down long after Maksim had gone.'

Custody had a draining job. Sometimes the drunks or the furious would rage for hours. There wasn't much to threaten them with nowadays, seeing as they were already under arrest and banged up. The days of a cell visit by the largest man on duty were long gone.

Ashley finished the call. Kettle gave her an appreciative nod and returned to his screen. Ashley made her way to the conference room, where Hector was staring at the map of Europe.

There were so many pinned flags, it resembled a colourful hedgehog. He tipped his head to the side.

'I should have got smaller pins.'

'Or a bigger map. I assume it still makes sense to you.'

'Of course. Are we doing the interview now?'

'Yes, with Maksim Wozniak. His solicitor has been in, which is unusual at this sort of time. I suspect Maksim wants to talk.'

'Who's leading?'

'Me. The guy is mid-forties, so I may have common ground with him. He may be after a deal, but we'll see.'

'Perhaps he'll want to unburden himself of his terrible guilt and shame.'

'That would be a nice surprise.'

At five past eight, Mark brought Maksim to interview room one, where they were waiting. He was alone. His clothes had been taken as evidence, so he was in baggy blue tracksuit bottoms and an ill-fitting T-shirt. As he sat, Ashley noticed the muscles in his arms flex. With his bushy beard and full head of hair, he reminded Ashley of a shorter Gerard Butler in the film *300*.

Hector cautioned him and confirmed he wanted to talk without a solicitor present.

Maksim nodded.

'I'll tell the truth. No need solicitor.'

He nodded again when Hector explained the conversation was being recorded. He leaned forwards, hands open on the table.

'This getting very crazy.'

'How can I help you?' asked Ashley.

'I want to explain my side. This shit is deep.'

'You're right. It doesn't get much deeper.'

'I'm only a driver.'

'Tell me about your job.'

'That's it. I've been struggling with bills since last year. The factory gave us less hours. I got offered driving work from a friend of a friend at Polish club. Easy money. Drive package to different place in UK. One hundred pounds cash. I do at weekends. No problem.'

'And the package was a person in your boot?'

Maksim's eyes rounded. He lifted his hands. 'Holy shit. No way. I never see such a thing. A box. It was always a sealed cardboard box. At the beginning.'

'The job changed.'

'Yes. After a little while, the money got better. I drive my car to place, swap car, then drive to another place, change car, return to my car, go home. Two hundred pounds. I quit factory. Ridiculously hard work. Give me big muscles but sore back.'

'Go on.'

'Then they ask me drive to Europe. I go. Have fun. Feel part of something. More money. Still driving cars. No funny business.'

Ashley suspected what he was trying to do. A classic defence was minimising the suspect's involvement.

'You don't seem daft, so you must have known what you were doing was illegal,' said Hector.

'What is daft?'

'Dim or stupid. In fact, you seem an intelligent man.'

Maksim chuckled.

'Of course, I know dodgy. They say is money or gems to Europe. Hidden in car chassis. Not stolen. Issues with taxation and permits. I state no to drugs. Too heavy penalty. Occasionally, I bring a person back with me. No package, no gems.'

'Girls?' asked Ashley.

'No, men. Workers like me. With passports and papers. No problem. Sometimes I worry about drugs, but when I mention, they become angry with me. I take a bit of cocaine for tiredness. What's your phrase? Slippery slope cannot get off.'

'Did you tell them you wanted to quit?'

Maksim shifted in his seat. 'I worry about it a lot. My wife cross. We are not close anymore. I no want prison. I'm not stupid.'

'You admit your part as a courier of trafficked victims.'

'No, not victims. Guys have ID. Workmen.' Maksim moistened his lips. 'Just things as courier.'

'Did you see any females?'

'Sometimes at various places. I don't talk to them. I was feeling very bad. I have a daughter.'

'How old is she?'

'Twenty-two. Just finishing university.'

'Was the routine at the campervan and lorry a regular thing?'

Maksim exhaled. 'No, first time there. I will go to prison for this?'

'Yes.'

'How long? Two years?'

'Much, much longer.'

Maksim's mouth dropped wide open. 'What? For being driver?'

'Not knowing your cargo isn't much of a defence. You're clearly part of a huge operation. The offence of trafficking carries a heavy sentence of around ten years, except if it's committed using kidnapping or false imprisonment. If that's the case, there is a maximum sentence of life.'

Maksim stared off into a corner, whispering what Ashley guessed were swear words in his own language.

'My wife. Can I see her? She does not answer her mobile. We fall out. She says I changed.'

'Your wife will be able to visit you in prison.'

Maksim's expression was pained.

Ashley decided now was the right time.

'There is a way to appeal to the judge when he eventually sentences you.'

'What you mean?'

'Do you want the judge to go easy on you?'

Maksim's swift reply showed his desperation.

'Of course. How I do that?'

'You must tell us everything.'

43

Maksim shrugged. He leaned back and placed his hands flat on the table.

'I told you everything.'

'We'll need specifics,' Ashley pressed. 'Times, dates, people, numbers, descriptions, locations.'

His eyes darted from side to side. 'To snitch,' he whispered.

'Yes. What is your relationship to the man in the cells with you? Who is he?'

Maksim's hands retracted as though he'd touched something burning hot.

'I cannot.'

'You need to focus on yourself now, or you'll be away from your family for a long time.'

Maksim closed his eyes. When they opened, any energy had drained from him.

'I have made a big mistake, but I could make worse one. Let me think.'

Ashley called Mark and had Maksim collected. She said to bring Vladimir next.

'What do you reckon?' asked Ashley while they waited.

'He's obviously aware of how ruthless the gang are.'

'Yes. What kind of a man with a family is going to inform on this kind of criminal organisation?'

Hector tutted. 'That's why they've got away with it for so long. It's strange, though, isn't it?'

'What?'

'The mentality of criminals. Their lack of reasoning and common sense. How many gang set-ups persist in perpetuity nowadays?'

Ashley frowned at him. 'Does that mean last forever?'

'It does. With the rapid progress in crime scene analysis, plus increased CCTV and now AI, it's only a matter of time before their chosen careers end in long sentences or death.'

'Bingo! I'm glad you understand.'

Hector wore a sharp suit, and, with his legs crossed, he appeared more than a little camp when he cocked his head and asked, 'Are you being condescending?'

'Not at all. Discovering why those involved in each case are offending can be the single most important key to solving an investigation. Some criminals are just stupid or desperate. Like Bosko, they're henchmen. Perhaps they believe they'll never get caught. Many simply don't consider the consequences, which is why longer sentences aren't much of a deterrent. They enjoy being bad men. There's access to women, drugs and excitement, or, more often, it's money. There are few plotters and planners out there, and even fewer masterminds.'

'They're the truly dangerous ones.'

'Yes, and that's the reason people like Irwin Beckett are allowed to bend some of the rules to catch those people. The benefit for society makes that acceptable.'

'Doesn't it make us as bad as them?'

'Not even close.'

Vladimir arrived at that point. Ashley could see why he had been described as ugly, but his features were more striking than repellent. He reminded her of Calibos from the film *Clash of the Titans*. In the same strange way, he was handsome but incredibly cruel-looking.

Hector cautioned him and explained they wanted to give him the opportunity to ask any questions after time to mull things over. He also offered him the assistance of the duty solicitor on arrival, which Vladimir declined. That was strange. What had he and Maksim said to each other last night? The detectives wouldn't look a gift horse in the mouth.

Vladimir stared at Ashley and didn't even glance at Hector. There was intelligence in his green eyes. She wasn't expecting his voice to be calm.

'There's no saving me, is there?'

'Saving you from what?' she replied.

'Prison for the rest of my days.'

Ashley guessed him to be around fifty years old.

'Perhaps if you help us.'

Vladimir rolled his shoulders theatrically and smiled, but they weren't the actions of a madman.

'We both know that's not true. You can all relax now. It's over. As far as I'm aware, there's only one more functioning whore-house left and a few men scattered throughout your country. We've been like soldiers fleeing the battlefield. You've been cutting us down as we ran.'

'Is that so?'

'We lost. You win.'

'Retreating isn't surrender,' said Hector.

Vladimir glanced over at him and tipped his head in agreement. Ashley doubted she could hoodwink this guy, so she asked what she wanted to know.

'The location of the last place would be helpful. That would be a start in you and I building a relationship.'

Vladimir's gaze flicked back to Ashley. 'If I do, will you explain how you found me?'

'Maybe.'

'I need more than a maybe.' He grinned, which made the lines in his face deeper. 'You can't trust anyone these days.'

'You aren't in a strong negotiating position.'

'It's in an industrial estate.'

'There are many.'

'Tell me who betrayed me. Either that, or I'll give it up for a steak supper.'

'You're not in *The Matrix*.'

'Sometimes it feels like it.'

'Is that how you can do what you've done?'

Vladimir leaned forward in his seat. 'The truth is, I enjoyed it. The power. The status. I'll spend the remainder of my life in a cell, but I'll have some excellent memories to keep me company.'

'That might be more than thirty years,' said Ashley. 'Would it be worth that?'

Vladimir glanced down for a few seconds. When he looked up, his eyes were glazed, and he didn't comment. Only a crazy man wouldn't be terrified of that future.

Ashley detected something else in his expression. Perhaps there was regret amongst the fear. Her moment had come.

'Are you the person known as Hydra?'

Vladimir frowned, then let out a small snort. He shook his head, his chin jutted out.

'I'm nobody.'

Ashley didn't believe him.

44

Ashley and Hector went straight to Kettle's office afterwards, but he wasn't there. She pulled out her phone, which had been set to silent, and found a message from him telling her to go to the conference room.

When they arrived, they found Beckett and Kettle deep in discussion. She and Hector took a seat. Ashley glanced around at all the photographs, maps and stacked files. It would be a relief when they were all gone, and they could move on to something new and local. Yet crime was changing. There would be more similar cases. So many people were desperate. Living costs were rising. Homelessness was increasing. Hundreds of thousands of migrants were arriving. Some taking extreme risks. Technology was changing, which helped in some ways and hindered in others. Meanwhile, the prisons were so full they were letting inmates out early.

'How did it go?' asked Kettle, who'd come to stand next to Ashley.

'If he's to be believed, Maksim is no more than a driver.'

'That's his defence.'

'Yes, but it seems credible. He fears what he's done, and what he's become complicit in. Whether that's buyer's regret or something else, I don't know.'

'Did he give you anything concrete? Something that helps nail their operation down? If people are paying to kill youngsters, I want them named and found.'

'He clammed up when I told him what we'd need if he wanted his cooperation to be taken into account. Said he'd think about it.'

'Did Vladimir speak to you?'

'A little. I think we have our man.'

Kettle grinned. He turned to Beckett, who took off his glasses and smiled.

'Well done,' they said in unison.

'Him being the big boss is believable. He came across as intelligent, with excellent English.'

A small frown appeared on Beckett's face. 'Why did he talk after refusing to yesterday?'

Ashley nodded at him. Beckett was always on the money.

'That's what's troubling me. He didn't seem a talker, even after time locked up. Him and Maksim argued last night, shouting to each other's cells. I suppose they could have realised the futility of their situation and given up. They could hardly have been caught more red-handed. Not only that, Vladimir matches quite an unusual description.'

'Did he seem resigned to his fate?'

'Yes, but not desperate. Maksim, on the other hand, might completely crack. He wants to see his wife when he gets to prison. We should swiftly facilitate that if we believe she's likely to tell him to come clean. Vladimir said it was all over. Nearly everyone and everything has gone except for one operation in an industrial estate.'

'Did he say which one?'

'Not yet. Vladimir understands there'll be no deal that keeps him out of jail for decades, but he wanted to understand how we caught him.'

'Perhaps he wants revenge if someone informed on him,' said Kettle.

'That's possible. He might just be curious. He said we could have the location of the last brothel for a decent steak.'

Beckett chuckled. 'Well, that means we've saved ourselves the price of a sirloin, then, thanks to you and Seb.'

Ashley grinned at him. 'You know where it is?'

'A man who moved house fairly recently to near one of the entrances to Hadleigh Road Industrial Estate read Seb's article. He'd been following the cases in the news, anyway. He walks his dog at dusk, so in the winter that's pretty early, but it's much later now. You know what those industrial places are like outside working hours.'

'Dead.'

'Yes. Since he's been there, he's noticed a steady stream of cars going in each night. He's obviously been reading too many crime novels because he sat in his bedroom for a whole evening and counted them in and out. There were twenty. Said quite a few of them appeared shifty, or not the type to be entering a business park in the evening. He rang 999 this morning not long after you went in with Maksim.'

Ashley nodded. 'What's the plan? Surveillance?'

'We considered that, but the media has got hold of this container find somehow. I don't know where that's come from, but leaks happen when there are busy operations. Mercedes or her mother might have talked. Sold their story.'

Ashley doubted that, but it wasn't important at that point. 'Are we going in now?'

'We looked at our options,' said Kettle. 'A press release tonight being one. The logic of that being simple. If they have an eye on the news, they would make an obvious choice.'

'Get out of Dodge.'

'Right, and we'd be waiting. It's a hell of a lot easier to grab them fleeing than us entering a building which potentially contains armed men. That's a high-risk play. Stray bullets. Hidden explosives, you name it. Obviously, there are also victims inside.'

Ashley scowled. 'Disposable victims.'

'Precisely. Therein lies our problem. If the people running the operation in there got a whiff we're onto them, they may simply shoot all the girls in the back of the head.'

'Do I need to get my Uzi 9mm and flak jacket out again?'

Kettle almost smiled.

'Not this time. NCA London is handling it. They're heading in now.'

45

Branislav Stanković peeled his eyes open. He lay there staring at the gently swinging bare bulb above him. The mystery of the draught that caused it to gyrate had never been solved. He suspected the roof was the cause, but his days of clambering around in loft spaces were over. The cot bed creaked under him as he struggled to his feet. He detected a ripping fabric sound underneath him. He shrugged. It had to be ten years old, and he could afford a new one.

'Christ,' he said to himself. 'Time flies when you're having fun.'

A grin crept across his face despite the agony from his big toe and the shooting pain from his sciatica. He squirted water into his throat from an old Evian bottle with a sports cap, then brushed his teeth. The small mirror he'd glued to the office wall displayed his blotchy, veiny skin. He spat into a wastepaper bin.

His old leather-strapped watch told him it was late morning. The previous night had been annoying. A punter, blitzed on cocaine, had beaten seven bells out of their newest acquisition.

Gregor had knocked twenty-seven bells out of the bloke, but it meant there would be aggravation when the others woke.

Branislav stepped out of the office onto a high railing and stared at the storage units below. Once, all twelve of them held girls. He'd been sent a steady stream of workers for years, but the numbers had dwindled and were now little more than a trickle. The good times never lasted, though. If his life had taught him anything, it was that. You should enjoy your pleasures while you could.

There were only four women now. Perhaps three after last night. They'd want showers and food. Or heroin. You had to let them clean and feed themselves, or quite a few gave up and died. The game was to keep them ticking over. Allow them to talk with each other. Build relationships. Survive. Those who still resisted the drugs needed to believe in hope.

Every now and again, he used to release one from the front door to a big fanfare. Give her an envelope with some money. They loved that. Gregor would be waiting around the corner. He'd take the cash back and deliver the girl to those who were more depraved than even Branislav was.

He made his way along the corridor and down the steps. The familiar, dank smell met him as he approached the first unit. He pulled the keys from his pocket. Like a jailer, he went along the row opening doors one after another, then strode back and stood at the bottom of the stairs. A redhead stumbled out of her room. She was still pretty, if heroin chic appealed. Empty, unseeing eyes fell upon him. She tapped the crook of her elbow.

'Need.'

'Clean yourself. Eat.'

'Not need that type of food.'

She walked towards him and rested a hand on his shoulder. 'Please.'

'Ten minutes. Take a shower.'

There was a little dining room for the women and a single shower stall in the toilet next to it. Branislav hadn't seen her in either for weeks, but that didn't bother most of the punters, or him.

He returned upstairs and grinned at the mirror. His teeth had been strong and white. They had been his pride and joy. It was why he'd rarely smoked, but even they were yellowing now. In fact, his entire body appeared poisoned. By his lifestyle, from what he'd seen, and by what he'd done.

He didn't regret anything though, not one bit, but when it was time to sleep, even he dared not stare into the abyss. The memories came at night. They circled within his dreams like snarling phantoms. The heavy drinking had started after he began waking in the twilight hours with a shriek in the back of his throat. He had taken up a new diet to prevent those spectres calling, one of straight spirits from a filthy glass, which had led to increased sexual violence. Both had whittled him away to a dark shadow of his former self.

The morning sun glanced off the blinds into his eyes, so he went over to close them. Before he had a chance to do so, an unusual truck drove by the front of the building. Branislav had seen similar before. Riot police often arrived in them during the uprisings. He rubbed his temples.

The demise of their operation had been in the news. He'd even read an article in the newspaper about it. His mate, Bosko, had messaged him saying it was all tumbling down and they should flee, but he and Bosko were the same. Men like them never saved money. They both gambled. In England nowadays, addicts had no chance. The glossy betting shops and the twinkling, flashing, buzzing, beeping terminals in them were more enticing even than the women. Bosko and he had often sat at a machine beside each other, feeding in notes, laughing, and vaping when the manager wasn't looking. He smiled. More good times.

Bosko had been caught by the police. The others had gone quiet, too. Jailed, fled, or dead. Branislav frowned. Imagine decades in prison. Endless long nights in jail without any of his sleeping medicine would probably be worse than hell itself.

It was unlikely the blocky van had arrived for another business. Only the boy, Gregor, a slack-jawed fool who thought he was Bruce Lee, was at the premises with Branislav. To be fair, Gregor looked mean when he swung his nunchucks. They would be in his drawer at the reception desk. Two sticks connected by a chain. Better hope for his sake he didn't touch them. He was still young enough to have a life after his sentence finished.

Below, a succession of men in fatigues and helmets filtered past the side of the building, silent in their approach. The leader lugged a big metal shield. The final person carried a red battering ram. Branislav opened the cabinet drawer and pulled out a Heckler & Koch MP5 machine gun. He walked back to the bottom of the stairs.

The sounds of splintering wood echoed along the corridor from the entrance. He recognised Gregor's shout, which was cut off after a popping sound. A silencer or a low velocity round. It was clear these guys weren't coming to negotiate.

Branislav knew what would go through his mind when the time came, and it wouldn't be his children, whose faces he could barely picture. A wife once, who he'd liked quite a bit until he had changed. Had Branislav been forged in the furnace of those days, or was his true self merely released by the chaos?

Images of the death squad he had operated within filtered into his mind. Their atrocities had been off the scale, but they'd been a tight team. He still missed the camaraderie. Strange to call what they'd done exciting. He supposed there were no rules in war. The Geneva Convention had been easily ignored. He thought of his closest friends from back then. Emil, who couldn't handle it any more, and Zoltan who didn't want to stop.

Branislav was a boy once, though. A lad who liked kites. And a girl he loved at school. She said he was kind. Did those children exist, or was it all just a dream, a wish, and he'd always been broken? Perhaps once, he had been capable of pure thoughts.

The image that seared itself into his brain as he took a step into the passageway, still holding his gun, was of the face of the sergeant of the death squad. A man so strong, focused, heartless and devious that even the huge Zoltan was wary of him. A genius, too. His tactical thinking and forward planning had got them through the wars.

Branislav's MP5 was a futile gesture. It was used to strike terror in those who stared down its barrel. Without ammo, he would have to use it as a club. A flood of armed men poured into the building. His hand twitched. It was the final voluntary movement his body would make.

A hollow-point bullet zipped into the centre of his forehead. Made to deform upon contact because of a collapsible space within the tip of the projectile, bullets like these lessened the possibility of a ricochet injuring innocent parties nearby. The metal caused massive damage as it expanded and spread through the area of impact.

Branislav's final thought, as the dark curtain fell on his evil life, was of that sergeant's name. Vladimir Davidović. The man who had become the Hydra.

46

Ashley strolled to her desk and checked her emails. It was hard to concentrate, knowing what was occurring, but it wasn't long until Kettle rang and asked her to head to his office. Beckett and Hector were waiting.

'How did it go?' she asked Beckett.

'The warehouse is secure. It was a small self-storage unit. Sal quickly verified its background for me while they went in. There are business records and tax returns going back twenty years. A new owner took over the business ten years ago. It's called Branston's Storage.'

Ashley frowned.

'Surely it hasn't been used as a brothel for a decade?'

'It looks like it. Sal's continuing to look into its history.'

Ashley assumed, by their lack of emotion, that not all the news was good.

'Four girls were saved,' said Beckett. 'One of whom was in a critical condition. It'll take a while to find out exactly what went on in there, but our intel was sound.'

'Any suspects for us to question?'

'No. Some kind of martial artist was at Reception, and an older guy pulled a machine gun out. Both were killed.'

Ashley had half expected the unit to be empty. She felt some pressure easing.

'Maybe that place really was the final one,' she said.

'Perhaps. We could do with either of the two men we have in Custody fully cooperating, or maybe the suspect from the Thetford raid.'

Ashley considered the prisoners. Bosko, Maksim and Hydra. It didn't appear likely they'd give up everything. Talking at interview was one thing. Being completely honest was another. 'Are any of the crews we captured at the other brothels liable to break rank?'

Kettle blew out a breath.

'A team of four Romanians all gave Ion as their surname, despite clearly not being related. Their set-up appeared to have been more consensual. The working girls knew what they were doing. None of the men claim to speak English. Two Bulgarians who got caught with a female in the back of their van said the same as Maksim. They were paid to drive her to a meeting place. The woman said she wasn't forced. Those two blokes are at court today for pleas. Doubt they'll talk.'

'Okay. Maksim is our best shot. I'll take one of my team and visit his wife this afternoon. She should be back by then.'

Beckett had something else to say. He cleared his throat. Ashley suspected they'd made a decision before she arrived.

'As I mentioned before, we have some assets at HMP Peterborough, so we're going to charge Maksim and Vladimir, then send them to Norwich magistrates' court next week. They'll go straight to the remand wing at Peterborough, where the Romanians are. You'll get one more chance to turn either man tomorrow. See if they name the others we're missing.'

Ashley gave them a smile full of confidence she didn't feel.

'They'll run out of men if we keep killing them. Those left will soon get the message that Norfolk is too dangerous a place to do business.'

'Yes, I just get the sense that, if we were playing Jenga, the tower isn't yet splattered on the floor. Even though I'm ready to return to London and forget about your not-so-peaceful part of the country, I don't want another girl to be abducted to be given proof I need to stay. We must keep the pressure on. Prisoners talk. If we got confirmation others are out there, even if we don't hear names, that would help.'

Ashley left the room and headed back to the office. All her team were there, no doubt in the hope they'd be putting the investigation to bed. She pulled them into a meeting room and gave them the latest.

'Is that it?' asked Barry. 'We caught Hydra, and that was the last whorehouse?'

'Duh,' said Sal. 'He might have been lying to us.'

'Beckett doesn't feel this is over, and neither do I, but I'm not sure why,' said Ashley. 'Let's wait until we hear from the officers at the industrial estate. Get your paperwork up to date. Morgan, you're coming with me to see Maksim's wife later.'

At 3 p.m., she booked out a car, and they began the drive to Maksim's house. Mile Cross boasted the fifth highest crime stats in the city and was only about ten miles from OCC. Morgan drove the Vauxhall Astra hard with a slight smile. Ashley glanced over.

'Hoping to get home in time for dinner?'

Morgan grinned. 'Sorry, I like to put every car through its paces.'

'I saw you in a Fiesta earlier this week. What happened to the Mustang?'

'I was concerned the diff had gone, but I dropped her, and it's probably bearings.'

'Any chance of that in English?'

'I took the Mustang to pieces and didn't have time to reassemble it. Hence me being in the wife's car.'

'Ah, right. Well, that brings me nicely onto us having a chat. I confessed to Zelda I haven't spent as much time as I'd like with you two after your move from Ally's team. Usually, we'd bond after a big case has closed, but this Typhon investigation has been dragging on for a long time. It's like a beast that's eaten my leisure time, too. I must say, you always look pretty chilled.'

'I'm a car buff. Have been since I was a kid. I did grow an afro when I was twenty, so I was cool for a couple of months, but it kept getting in the way under the bonnets, so I shaved it off and accepted my lot as a petrol-head.'

'Sounds like you have a healthy pastime to de-stress yourself.'

'Yeah. Working on and driving motors is my escapism. The smell, the sounds, the handling of the vehicle. I love it all.'

'Ally spoke highly of you.'

'Detectives and mechanics possess similar skill-sets.'

'I suppose Barry's big end is often blowing.'

Morgan raised his top lip.

'Unfortunately, I'm able to confirm that's correct, but what I meant is they're both about solving puzzles. Look at the evidence, narrow down the possibilities, test your theories, rule stuff out, until there can only be one answer.'

'I guess that's true.'

'You're spot on, though. We all need time for ourselves. Some activity or place where our soul heals. My wife walks for an hour each morning, her and the dog, before the kids get up. She'd have strangled me by now otherwise.'

Ashley raised an eyebrow. Morgan chuckled.

'Yeah, that's probably not the best joke during this case.'

'You know, I've stopped running regularly, and that was my thing. I only live a ten-minute stroll from the beach, but I can't even recall the last time I took my shoes off and strolled in the sand. Felt the gentle waves tickle my toes. This weather brings it home. Today should be a day spent outside. The sun is shining. Clouds floating by. Last of the falling blossom.'

'Blink and it's gone.'

'Exactly. Shall we sack this off, get an ice cream each and two deckchairs and sit on Cromer beach?'

'You're the boss.'

'Talking of bosses. How did you deal with Ally being arrested?'

Morgan shrugged. He and his old sergeant had been close until the man was discovered to be passing on inside information.

'I've tried to be forgiving about it. We all veer from the righteous path from time to time, and he was a lonely person. He never said as much, but I could tell, and it's easier to make mistakes when you're alone.'

Ashley nodded. Wasn't that the truth?

47

Morgan paused before an unassuming house on a quiet street. An ageing Nissan Micra occupied the driveway. The lawn was overgrown, yet the bins stood neatly, and the windows and door gleamed with recent attention. A grey-haired guy in a cloth cap waved his trowel at Ashley from the next garden.

She waved back. 'Afternoon, is Jolanta in?'

'Jo? Yes. Couple of hours. I thought one of your lot came earlier.'

Ashley frowned, knowing nobody had. 'I'll check.'

She wandered over to him and introduced herself. He beamed at her.

'Dave Hipkin.'

He took off a gardening glove and merrily pumped her hand. The air smelled sweet. Ashley stared over his fence in awe. Blooms blossomed from all four corners of his garden. Purple roses smothered a wooden arch at the entrance to an immaculate lush lawn. It was a place where a fairy tale could be set.

'So beautiful,' she whispered.

He glowed with the praise. 'Well, it all started—'

Ashley raised a finger, smiled, then cut him off. 'I'll come and hear all about it after I've spoken to Jolanta.'

'I'll get the lemonade out.'

Ashley strolled along the Wozniaks' path to the front door where Morgan was waiting. 'Amazing, eh?'

'What is?'

'The flowers.'

Morgan glanced up from his phone, peeked over her shoulder, then looked back at the screen.

'Sorry, I've been bidding on some tyres on eBay.'

'I might as well have brought Barry.'

Ashley took a moment before knocking on the door to mentally prepare herself for tearing the walls of a woman's life down.

'Just take notes for me, please, Morgan. She's a similar age to me, so hopefully she'll open up. Keep any questions to when I give you a nod and be ready to shift tack. It's possible she knew all about her husband's trade and has been living the existence of a gangster's moll.'

Ashley rapped on the door and Morgan's tyre purchase was forgotten when it opened. The woman who appeared was built like an athlete. She also had on the tightest running gear known to humankind. It was lucky Ashley hadn't brought Barry after all, or she'd have been reeling his tongue back in like putting away a retractable hose.

'Jolanta?'

'Yes.'

'I'm Detective Inspector Ashley Knight. This is DC Morgan Golding.'

'Yes?'

'It's about your husband.'

'Maksim?'

'Yes. Can we come in?'

'Of course.'

They followed her in through an uncluttered hall to a kitchen that was basic but spotless. Jolanta stood next to a chair. She opened her mouth, then clamped it shut. Ashley took two paces towards her, knowing it might unnerve her if she was guilty of anything. Jolanta had thick make-up on, which Ashley could tell was hiding plenty. There were lines on her face and puffy skin around her eyes.

Jolanta slumped into the seat but looked up. Her mouth pouted as she fought back tears.

'Is he dead?' she asked, her voice thick with worry.

'No, he's not. Maksim's at the police station.'

Jolanta broke eye contact. 'What happened?'

Ashley understood immediately that, if not complicit, she was aware Maksim had been up to no good. There was also the question of who had been to visit her earlier. Dave next door had seen someone. He wouldn't miss much being out the front all the time. She kept that information to herself for the moment.

'He's in a lot of trouble. So might you be.'

Jolanta's gaze returned to Ashley. Her face tensed, and she spoke slowly.

'Why would I be in trouble?'

Her foreign accent came through with her anger. Ashley knew this was her chance to get the truth.

'Criminal behaviour in your home. Sharing in illicit revenue. Maybe it was a joint operation.'

Jolanta's teeth bared.

'Skurwysyn!'

Ashley didn't require a translation, but Jolanta hissed it.

'Bastard!'

'I think you need to tell me everything.' Ashley gestured around the kitchen, which was full of photographs of her with Maksim and a captivating young girl who must be their daughter. 'You seemed to have it all.'

Jolanta pulled her ponytail free and ran her hands through her thick black hair.

'If I'm honest, he kind of slipped away.' She blew out a long breath. Then looked around the kitchen. 'I met my husband when I studied at college in Krakow. He was originally from Slovakia, but he moved when he was young. My parents didn't like him because he was just a mechanic, but we fell in love and got married after six months. I convinced him to move to England when Poland joined the EU.'

Ashley and Morgan took seats on the opposite side of the table and he began taking notes.

'It was so easy here. Great money in comparison to home. It felt really modern. We were living our dream. Maksim got decent work. I found a job at the school our daughter attended. She grew up bilingual. Holidays home were so cheap. We bought this house, made friends, English and Polish. I love to live near the sea. Life was perfect.'

Ashley smiled at her as tears welled up.

'Maksim didn't get on with a new boss, so he was forced to find a different job. Then the recession came, and he had to change garage many times. Eventually, he took factory roles. He's a strong man. Reliable. There's always work for men like that, but he doesn't write English well, makes mistakes when talking, and isn't good on computers, so he never got promoted.'

Another tear fell.

'I became full time to make more money. There are twins

with special educational needs in a class who I work with. It's extremely rewarding, and I adore them. Maksim wanted to go back to Poland like some of our friends had after Brexit. My daughter and I didn't want to, so we didn't move, but he was subdued. Two years ticked by, then he was offered a driving job one weekend.'

Jolanta shook her head.

'That's where it went wrong. You know what they say about easy money?'

Ashley nodded. 'There's no such thing.'

'Exactly. He got in with this crowd. Drinkers. He didn't come home some nights but always texted. We'd been together for twenty-five years, so I was quite happy to have him out of the house because he'd gotten so grumpy. They asked him to do some driving jobs, for good money. He was happier providing nice things for us again. There were more delivery jobs for these people, so he quit the factory. He went all over Europe. The pay was brilliant, but it was too much, you understand?'

'How much?'

'Thousands per week. Bundles of cash. I said to him, it must be illegal, but he shrugged.' Jolanta sniffed. 'Maybe I am guilty because I turned the blind eye. His trips got longer. He was gone for two weeks, then a month. He never rang and his text messages slowed. I haven't seen or heard from him for nearly a month. This was the end for me. I went to see my daughter in Nottingham yesterday to tell her I am asking for a divorce.'

'I'm sorry to hear that. What did she say?'

'She knew we'd been arguing. She was sad, but she accepted my decision.'

'So, who were these people he was working with?'

'I've no idea. Some men who said they were from the Polish club started to visit him here. I'd never seen them there before and we used to go fairly regularly. He went drinking with them a lot. He slowly got sucked in.'

'Did you talk to them?'

'Yes, one of them. A dirty man called Bosko. I told Maksim to keep him out of the house. The other guy's name I never knew. I came home from work a few times and he would be in the kitchen and leave as soon as I returned.'

'Maksim never introduced you?'

'No. The relationship was unequal. Do you understand that?'

'No.'

'I believe Maksim was scared of him. He stank of violence. Even his face was a little scary.'

Ashley took her phone out and found a photo of Vladimir.

'Is this him?'

'Yes. Definitely.' Jolanta's fists clenched. 'Now, please explain what Maksim did. I still love him, even though I lost him to this gang or to this one person at least.'

'What do you mean?'

'There was someone he often spoke of. A man he was fascinated by. Bewitched maybe is the right word. He made this new life seem incredibly attractive to Maksim. We were boring in comparison.'

'Who was he?'

'I never saw him and heard no name.'

Ashley paused as Morgan scribbled beside her.

'We're not sure exactly what your husband has done, but he's clearly in over his head. He needs to tell us everything, or he'll end up with a significant jail sentence.'

'May I see him?'

'I can arrange for you to meet him in prison next week.'

'Why would he be in prison? Surely a man is innocent until his day in court.'

Ashley knew the information would be in the public eye soon enough, so she told Jolanta the truth.

'Your husband was found with a girl in the boot of his car.'

Jolanta's face paled. The words hit her like a physical blow. Her hand flew to her mouth, stifling a gasp. A tremor ran through her body as she whispered, 'In the boot?'

48

Ashley nodded solemnly, the weight of the words lingering in the room.

Jolanta's eyes filled with tears, the last vestiges of control crumbling. She clutched the edge of the table, her knuckles turning white.

'No... no, that's not possible,' she choked out. 'He wouldn't... he couldn't...' She violently shook her head.

Ashley reached across the table, her hand gently covering Jolanta's. 'I know this is difficult to hear,' she said softly, her voice laced with empathy, 'but it's important that you understand the gravity of the situation.'

'No. I won't believe it.'

'I'm sorry,' replied Ashley. 'It's the truth. I was there.'

Jolanta's gullet heaved up and down. She rushed to the sink and vomited noisily. Ashley followed and pulled her hair out of the way, then rubbed her back. If Jolanta was acting, she was bloody good at it.

Yet, she'd had a visitor prior to them arriving and not mentioned it.

Morgan poured her a glass of water while she slumped into her seat. Ashley didn't want to press Jolanta too hard. She'd clearly received a terrible shock.

'Is there somebody you can be with? Perhaps to talk to.'

Jolanta's gaze locked onto Ashley's, a mixture of disbelief and desperation in her eyes. 'I have a friend nearby. But what does this mean? What will happen to him?'

'He'll be kept in prison while he awaits trial.'

'Look. I've no idea what my husband has been doing, but it won't be to do with children or young girls.' Again, she shook her head, face full of horror. 'The news came on while I was driving home. Was that Maksim, at Winterton beach?'

'That's right.'

Jolanta's eyes widened as denial returned.

'There must be some kind of mistake. Perhaps he was tricked. I have to speak to him. Face to face. I will know.'

'I'll arrange a visit for you.'

'Please do. I can get time off on Thursday.'

'Will you come to the police station afterwards?'

Jolanta swallowed. 'Do I have to?'

Ashley let a silence fill the air, which seemed to crush the shocked woman before her. She nodded once.

'Yes.'

'Okay, I will.'

'You had someone stop by earlier.'

Jolanta recoiled. 'Who told you that?'

'Who was the man?'

'A stranger.'

'Did he threaten you?'

'Not directly. He said you would come but didn't say why. He insisted I should not worry and must tell you everything.'

Ashley frowned. 'That's unusual.'

'I don't know anything apart from what I told you.'

That seemed true on the surface but criminals made good liars. Jolanta hadn't implicated anyone except the man they already had in prison. They didn't need Jolanta's testimony to prosecute Maksim, seeing as he'd been caught in the act.

'What did your visitor look like?'

'Brown hair. Average build. He kept his sunglasses on.'

Morgan abruptly looked up. 'Did he give a name?'

'No.'

He had to be the one Akari and Mercedes had seen.

'Do you think this was the person Maksim was obsessed with?'

'Maybe. He had a presence, but the glasses were like a mask.'

'Okay. I'll run up a statement when we get back to confirm what you've told us. Do you have a phone number we can easily contact you on?'

Jolanta abruptly got up and wrote her phone number on a notepad, ripped the piece off, but remained quiet. Her shoulders had slumped. Ashley stood up. She considered asking for an email to send the statement, but her gut told her a return visit would be needed.

'We'll head off now. Make sure you go and see your friend. Will you be okay?'

Jolanta didn't acknowledge Ashley's question. She spoke through tears.

'Please, just leave.'

Outside, Morgan blew out a deep breath.

'That was intense.'

'Yes, but I'm inclined to believe her.'

They found Dave Hipkin lurking in his garden. Next to his bench, he'd set up a small table, complete with three glasses and a plastic bottle filled with a cloudy liquid. He waved and began pouring their drinks. Ashley and Morgan both sat opposite him and had a sip. She imagined her tooth enamel burning away. Morgan coughed. His teeth protruded, giving him the appearance of a beaver.

Dave cringed.

'Sorry, I didn't have any ice, but I did make the lemonade myself.'

'Lovely,' said Ashley, trying not to grimace. 'Now tell me about this garden.'

Twenty minutes later, Dave paused for breath.

'Hmm, it's charming,' said Ashley. 'I bet your neighbours appreciate you making the place look so lovely.'

'Jolanta's always saying that.'

'What about Maksim?'

'Once or twice.'

'Don't you talk as much with him?'

'Nah, just neighbourly stuff. I offered to watch a game together a few times over the years, but he was always busy. Young family and all that.'

'Did his behaviour change recently?'

Dave's forehead wrinkled.

'Kind of. His daughter finished school. I suppose life changes. He didn't seem to be about much. I saw him fall over his garden gate one morning at four.'

'Were you only getting back from a nightclub yourself?'

The old guy cracked up. 'Two a.m.'s my limit nowadays. Nah, his singing woke me up. There were other changes. He was often driving different cars.'

'Flash cars?'

Dave cocked his head.

'Not particularly expensive. Different.'

'When did all this start?'

Dave shut one eye while he thought.

'Few months before Christmas. Maybe before that.'

Ashley paused while she considered what else she might ask him.

'Can you describe the guy who was here earlier?' asked Morgan.

'Leather jacket. Jeans. Serious-looking. Short brown hair. Sunglasses. Tall.'

'Car?'

'No, he walked up. I shouted hello, but he ignored me.' Dave rubbed his chin. 'Or perhaps he nodded.'

Ashley handed her business card over.

'Be discreet,' she said with a wink. 'But can you keep an eye out for me?'

'Will do. Jolanta's a nice lady. Who would risk losing her?'

Ashley declined to answer. What possessed people to gamble everything on money, power or glamour was the age-old puzzle. Those temptations had drawn individuals in for years, but the good times were usually fleeting.

By the time it was over, the wager lost, their past lives had gone forever.

'Last question and I'll let you return to your pruning,' said Ashley. 'Would you say Maksim is the type of guy who'd get involved in serious criminal activity?'

Dave shook his head.

'Nope. I'm a good judge of character. He seemed a nice fella. Maybe even a little vulnerable. Not simple, but not the smartest, you know?'

'Yeah, I do.'

Ashley rose from the bench, but Morgan had another question.

'Was his English good?'

'I'd say so.'

Ashley gave Morgan a nod. The gardener got a beaming smile.

'Thank you, Dave. We'll be in touch.'

When they'd returned to the car, Ashley cursed under her breath.

'Did we miss something?' asked Morgan.

'It's not that. What's the worst thing about what we've just heard?'

Morgan scratched his head. 'That the wives are the last to know?'

'No. We thought we had this organisation cooked, but Jolanta had a visitor. He may or may not be an important guy, but it does mean there are still men out there.'

Morgan's face fell as he grasped the fact their investigation was far from over.

49

They returned to OCC and Ashley briefed Kettle on the conclusions she and Morgan had reached on the way back. Kettle's face remained blank, but he grabbed his phone, dialled, listened, then simply said, 'My office, please.'

Five minutes later, Irwin Beckett and Hector arrived. Hector seemed brimming with energy and youth, as if the challenge was invigorating him. Beckett's rounded shoulders indicated the opposite. They straightened when he felt her gaze upon him.

Ashley recalled when Hector first spoke of Beckett. She'd imagined him to be some kind of hard-nosed, brash, overbearing type. Instead, he was simply a committed man doing an immensely challenging role with little complaint, despite the inevitable toll it would be taking.

Hector and Kettle listened impassively while they were brought up to speed.

'That makes our operation at HMP Peterborough imperative,' said Beckett. 'We have to know how much of their structure is left intact. This guy with the sunglasses is clearly a person of utmost interest.'

'Hydra,' said Hector, 'or perhaps we should call him Vladimir, implied there was little of the organisation remaining. We suspected it could be a ploy. The bloke with the shades might be someone he's trying to shield from attention.'

Beckett sucked his teeth. 'Talking to the wife of a low-level driver is hardly a job for someone important. Would their leader really be trotting around Mile Cross on his own?'

'Perhaps it's proof of our success,' said Ashley.

'Great point,' said Kettle. 'Maybe the big cheeses are forced to do menial tasks because they have so few people left.'

Ashley huffed. 'But is the sunglasses bloke trying to protect himself or someone else by putting the frighteners on Maksim via his wife?'

'Ashley, did you get a sense of Vladimir being deceitful when you spoke to him?' asked Hector.

'Not really. He seemed accepting of his situation, but their enterprise has persisted for decades in a business known for its treachery and disloyalty, with many countries' top enforcement agencies pursuing them, and they've survived. Play-acting, manipulation, subterfuge, distraction, smoke and mirrors, and good old-fashioned lies are all going to be part of their rule book. I don't think Vladimir was deceiving me about understanding it's over for him now. Unless someone's planning to spring him from prison.'

Beckett rested his palms on the table and took a deep breath.

'We considered that when we were contemplating using a jail to discover more about the network. The nick at Peterborough is still a B-Cat remand prison, which makes it high security, but my boss is getting twitchy. He's given me a week before Vladimir is moved to an A-cat. I'm not too worried. Peterborough is used to handling a wide range of prisoners awaiting trial, from corrupt accountants to child killers. Nobody's wandering out of there.'

'How about a helicopter hovering over the exercise yard?' asked Ashley. 'Didn't two men escape like that years ago?'

'Yes,' said Hector. 'Late eighties from HMP Gartree, but it's never been done since.'

'They have wires above the yards to stop anything landing nowadays,' said Beckett. 'Peterborough has eight exercise areas. The cons don't find out which one they're on that morning until they're leaving the wing, and, apart from the weekends, they're only on them for thirty minutes. I doubt we need to worry about that.'

'That's an interesting point about Vladimir or the sunglasses guy protecting someone,' said Hector. 'The most likely person has to be Typhon himself, or herself, but I've still not uncovered any direct reference to that man or woman existing. It's most likely to be a male, so either he has an iron grip on his underlings, probably through fear of death, or he doesn't exist.'

'If he is real, he'd need to be reasonably old,' said Kettle.

'Yes. The crimes I'm looking into go back well over twenty years.'

'Unless he's like the Dread Pirate Roberts,' said Ashley.

The others in the room frowned at her.

'Come on. It's from *The Princess Bride*. The current Dread Pirate Roberts makes millions of doubloons, then wants to retire with his ill-gotten wealth, so he serves as first mate under the new Roberts, who then takes over. Just sensible succession planning. Old school.'

'Wouldn't the minions be aware of what the old leader looked like?' asked Hector.

Ashley curled a lip. 'Oh yeah. I guess he could choose a man with a similar appearance to take over, or does he rule from a lofty perch somewhere, and nobody but a few actually get to meet him in person? What I'm saying is, perhaps the Typhon role is passed on.'

'I suppose that's possible,' said Beckett. 'Or do Typhon's children take it in turns?'

Hector smiled.

'Maybe Typhon is one of those real nutters who talks about themselves in the third person.'

'Regardless,' said Kettle, 'it would still be a guy of reasonable age who's been involved for a long time, or the respect wouldn't be there.'

'If we think rationally,' said Beckett, 'we've trawled through an awful lot of data not to have found any direct evidence of an individual. It's troubling not knowing if he exists, never mind if he's fat or has big ears.'

'I reckon it's one man pulling the strings in each country,' said Kettle. 'For each to have escaped justice for so long, they'd need to be extremely intelligent, careful, and ruthless. Vladimir fits the bill. I'd be immensely concerned if there was an overarching boss, because he would be even more intelligent, sharper, more disciplined, and possibly crueller.'

Hector whistled. 'Yeah, that's not an encouraging thought.'

'Perhaps that's the reason Vladimir is being helpful to the organisation, even though his own cause is lost,' said Beckett. 'If Typhon has incredible clout, he'd soon get to him in jail.'

'I was thinking about the Bacton Wood case,' said Ashley. 'That Montenegrin detective said the wars in his area back in the nineties created no end of demons. Maybe that was the melting pot that formed these twisted creatures, and it's the bond which holds them together.'

'That's not a bad supposition,' said Hector. 'We have no idea of this Vladimir character's previous because he gave us a false name. Fingerprints and descriptions are verifiable on Europol, but he's not on there. I might have more joy digging at a national level, and the Balkans is as good a place as any to begin.'

'What about Maksim and this Bosko?' asked Ashley.

'Maksim has lived here for twenty years. It's not like he's been off the grid. I checked with Warsaw if he had any previous and he didn't.'

'His partner has been married to him since they were twenty-one so she'd know about a criminal record, although she said he'd changed recently.'

'Bosko certainly isn't the lynchpin,' said Kettle. 'He's got a sheet as long as your arm for all manner of idiotic stuff since he arrived here from Hungary. This is by far the most serious crime he's been involved in. He's just muscle, and pretty dim muscle at that. Nightclub bouncer was his game. Even Sal remembers him being on the doors when he was out on the town. Barry says the word is a drink problem finished that career, so I suppose he took a job as the heavy at brothels for lack of many other options. I reckon if there is a Typhon, he's still out there.'

'On that note, I'm going to have another chat with Maksim,' said Ashley. 'I'd like to see what he thinks about Jolanta visiting him in prison. I suspect she'll give him a right tongue-lashing, so he might be nervous. If he agrees to see her, she's the brighter of the two, so hopefully he'll take her advice.'

'Let's hope so.'

'The neighbour, Dave, mentioned he had decent English, too, but it was less than perfect when we arrested him.'

Kettle rolled his eyes good-naturedly. Feigning ignorance due to a language barrier was a defence they'd all heard many times.

'Have you had any joy with the sunglasses guy on our system?' asked Kettle to Hector.

'No, the parameters are too large. Tall and brown hair doesn't cut it. There were thousands of matches.'

Beckett turned to Ashley and smiled. 'Let's see if Maksim wants to talk.'

Half an hour later, Ashley and Sal were sitting in front of Maksim, who stared into the distance and stroked his beard. Sal cautioned him, then asked if his predicament had sunk in yet.

'How can it not?' replied Maksim. 'My solicitor has spoken to me and possibly it's not so bad.'

'Don't you want him in here with you?'

'No, I understand now. The future will be bad, but not too terrible.'

'You don't mind years in jail?' asked Ashley.

'He said maximum offence for trafficking was ten years, but he doubts you have enough for that.'

'Does he? There was a kidnapped girl in your boot. Recent draft guidelines for a straightforward kidnap give a sentencing range of six months to sixteen years.'

Maksim raised his hands. 'Six months is fair. I accept.'

Ashley wasn't in the mood for jokes. She prodded a finger at him.

'Your victim was taken with violence, and she was underage. There's no way on earth you'd serve six months. The maximum sentence is on the table. Life imprisonment.'

'I told you. Wasn't me. You must have asked her if I was the one who took her. She'd have remembered my beard.'

'Even if the judge was relatively lenient, you'd be away for years. Would your wife wait? Imagine missing out on your daughter's life.'

'Let us be honest with each other. I have what my solicitor called previous good character. Never been arrested. Just some speeding stuff. He says my culpability is low. A reasonable starting point is six years. I go guilty straight away, one third off, so I get four years. Nonviolent offence for me because I didn't take her, so I would only serve half. Maybe I'm out in two years. Is still ridiculous for being the driver.'

'That's a lot of speculation,' said Sal. 'These men you've been working with are committing horrific offences. You have a daughter yourself. Don't you want to help?'

'By telling you everything?'

Ashley considered her next words.

'Yes. If you're only a driver, your partners exploited you, remember? Put a young girl in the boot of a car you were driving. They didn't care you could serve a decade in prison.'

Maksim threw his hands in the air.

'I know all this and I am angry, but this way I see my daughter in two or three years. I talk to you, I never meet her again.'

Ashley paused. So, he well understood there'd be consequences for betraying those above him. Sal and she persisted with offers of protection, but Maksim was a lost cause.

She decided to change tack.

'Your wife wants to visit next week. I can arrange for her to come in.'

Maksim chuckled. 'Very good. I see you've met her. She might save you having to prosecute me because my head will be missing.' Maksim made a chopping action, then held eye contact with Ashley. 'Ah, you believe she'll tell me to cooperate and sort everything out? That we'll deal with this together as a family. Trust me. I doubt it. She's an honest, fair woman, but she will not be forgiving about this.'

'Your English seems to have improved,' said Ashley.

'I was nervous before.'

Ashley nodded, but his reply had been too quick. She suspected his wife was fundamentally honest, but she was far from sure about Maksim.

50

A subdued air hung over MIT the following week. There were no abductions and no more brothels discovered. The phone lines that had been busy quietened considerably as the days passed. Even so, they knew the Typhon organisation was only down, not out. Ashley welcomed the opportunity to escape the office and drive to HMP Peterborough for a meeting regarding Maksim and Vladimir, who had both refused further interviews and had been remanded in custody after bail was denied at court on Monday.

Today was the day Jolanta had a visit booked with Maksim. Ashley had offered to pick her up, which would have then given Ashley the two-hour journey back for probing questions afterwards, but she'd declined. Ashley couldn't blame her for that.

It was a warm morning and Ashley drove with an elbow out of the window. She made surprisingly good progress and, having allowed plenty of time, found herself sitting in the prison car park with half an hour to spare. She checked her phone, finding an email from Michelle with the toxicology and post-mortem report on the woman found in the container.

Ashley rang Michelle's work number.

'Mortuary, Michelle speaking.'

'Hi, it's Ashley. I read your email.'

'That's efficient. I only emailed it five minutes ago.'

'When you're hot, you're hot. So, it wasn't an overdose that killed her?'

'No, not in my opinion. Heroin is present in her system but not in a deadly amount. She's probably been using for a while and will have built up some tolerance, so it's unlikely that was the sole cause of death.'

'And you mentioned there were no broken bones or heavy bruising and no evidence of other intoxication.'

'That's right. Structurally, she's in reasonable condition, which is rare for people in her occupation, forced or otherwise. Most prostitutes I examine have been poorly treated. Badly knitted bone breaks are common, for example.'

'No serious bruising is very unusual. I wonder whether the customers were freaked out by the situation or just scared of the menacing bloke who ran the operation. He might have warned them damaging his merchandise would not go unpunished.'

'I guess, although men who use prostitutes aren't known for their control. She is malnourished to the point of a few teeth being slightly loose. Judging by the lack of plaque or tartar, that's not through poor dental hygiene, which would mean she was likely in her predicament for a while, but not years.'

'So the death is a mystery.'

'As you know, post-mortems are inconclusive in around five per cent of cases.'

'Maybe she gave up. Died of a broken heart, not from losing a loved one, but at what she'd been forced to do. She lost all hope.'

'As a medical professional, I'm not keen on that as a finding. She was in a significantly weakened state. Her muscles had atrophied, and there was hair loss, which didn't appear to have been pulled out. Lying in a cold container, tired and in ill health, her heart rate could drop, blood pressure fall, then perhaps the relatively small amount of heroin suppressed her nervous system enough, and she simply stopped breathing.'

'Poor girl.'

'We seem to be saying that a lot.'

'The CPS charged the man arrested at the scene with murder. Even though her death was caused by the circumstances she found herself in, I suspect they'll have to downgrade the charge to manslaughter.'

'That doesn't seem appropriate.'

'No, but that's the law. There'll still be enough for a life sentence with all the aggravating factors.'

'It's hard to imagine a bleaker end.'

'I know.'

'How's the rest of the case going?'

'We've captured most of the gang members, but not all of them. Everyone's trawling CCTV, checking mugshots, dealing with overseas forces. It's time-consuming work. Sadly, the two men in charge of the warehouse were shot in the rescue of the girls.'

'Why is that sad? Sounds like they deserved worse.'

'Sad as in that means we don't have the opportunity to grill them. Ipswich MIT is canvassing all of their business parks. There's more CCTV to check in those locations as well. The rescued women were all Romanian, so we had to get a translator. They came to the country for work. Most had thought they were heading to a farm. Apart from the customers, they only regularly saw the two men who died, but a mysterious male with sunglasses showed up a couple of times.'

'Okay, well, good luck. Sorry I haven't been more help.'

'No problem. Hopefully, I won't need to speak to you for a while.'

'Until we go out for a meal again. I'll send you some dates.'

'Excellent.'

Ashley still had twenty minutes until her meeting, but it was sometimes slow getting inside the nick. There was no point in taking her handbag and phone. The former would get searched, and who knew what they might find in it, and the latter would have to go in a locker. No laptops were permitted, either, so she grabbed a notepad and pen.

As she left the car, a blue Land Rover pulled into the space next to hers. She knew the big guy who got out quite well.

'Inspector Barton. Long time no see.'

'I'm actually a temporary chief.' He gave her a bashful grin. 'I hear you've been climbing the ladder, too.'

'Yes. The lure of power and glory eventually sucks the best of us in. Are you here for the meeting with Beckett and the prison director?'

'Yes. They said you'd be attending. I keep an eye on who gets sent down in the county, and I know some of the residents on the remand wing. Any new guys are likely frequent flyers. Between us, we should be able to spot any outliers.'

Ashley hadn't considered that angle. It used to be fairly common for certain types of criminals to deliberately commit an offence with a relatively short tariff. They'd then arrive in prison with drugs plugged up their arses, or having swallowed them in cling film, to sell on the wings, where the price could be tenfold what it was on the street. HMP Peterborough's latest body scanners had put an end to that particular scam because the drugs were seen in Reception and never reached the prisoners.

Barton was thinking ahead, though. Ashley smiled at him.

'Clever. If Vladimir is Hydra, you reckon he might have got

some of his men arrested on other matters and have them in the jail to assist or protect him.'

'If you could afford it and had people who'd do it, why wouldn't you?'

'They'd need to be extremely loyal.'

'Yes,' replied Barton. 'Or very scared.'

51

They strolled in together. Barton naturally adjusted his long stride like Hector did, so she could keep up.

'You look well,' she said.

'Cheers. I've lost a couple of stone being so busy again. I'm back to my fighting weight, which I say is fine, but the doctors would prefer me to lose more.'

'Not that I'm enabling you, but it would be odd and more than a little unsettling if you were rake thin.'

'That's what my wife said. Who am I to disagree?'

'I'd heard you returned to Major Crimes to cover Cox's secondment. What did your missus think of that?'

'I thought Holly would be annoyed, but she barely disguised her joy, which was hurtful. Apparently, having me bored and unmotivated in the house was like living with a twenty-stone locust.'

Ashley laughed with him as they signed in at the gatehouse. Barton was one of the good guys. He'd been in nearly thirty years, and they'd bumped into each other every now and again. She'd picked up a few new tricks on a course he'd run eighteen months ago.

Ashley went through the scanner and had a rub-down search. She and Barton were then taken into the admin building. Ashley usually enjoyed prison visits. They were interesting places, but it was odd to imagine Ally being locked inside this one. She followed their escort into an office and then towards a closed door next to ceiling-to-floor glass windows. The blinds had been drawn, so she couldn't see in.

The officer knocked, and Ashley and Barton were let into the room. The door was shut behind them.

Ashley half expected to find just Beckett and Kettle waiting, but there were four other people quietly going about their business, and a tall man staring intently at them.

'Morning, John, Ashley,' said Beckett. 'Have you met the director here, Nigel Reader?'

Reader was almost as tall as Barton and had a noble presence. His dark-blue jacket and trousers suited his tall, broad frame, and his shoes shone.

Ashley and Barton strode over and shook his hand.

Barton remained next to him. 'No, I was in a different department when Mr Reader took over. Hope you're settling in.'

Reader gave him half a smile.

'I was. This whole situation is untoward and there's certainly been an atmosphere on that wing.'

'In what way?' asked Barton.

'We'll come to that shortly.' He turned to Ashley. 'I've obviously heard of Inspector Barton, but Irwin here said you're excellent at your job too.'

Ashley smiled at him, then nodded at Beckett. 'I try.'

Reader beckoned to a woman in the corner.

'My assistant will take notes of the meeting. Please, have a seat. We've been using this as the command centre, but we've seen nothing obvious so far. The wings, corridors, stairwells, hub area, everywhere in fact in a new establishment like this, is covered by decent CCTV.'

Ashley suspected decent meant not HD. The jail had opened nineteen years ago, but she supposed that was recent when many of the prisons were from Victorian times. HMP Dartmoor started life with prisoners from the Napoleonic war.

Ashley stared at the large TV hanging on the wall. The screen was split into separate images of various parts of the prison, but the biggest image was from a camera looking down a wing. Ashley assumed it was the wing where the men they were interested in were housed.

Reader gestured to the screen.

'The footage is also being watched in the security office. We've brought you inspectors in because you know some of the prisoners and are aware of the case. You've had a chance to see who has been sent here in the last week. John, most of the cons have obviously come from your station.'

Barton nodded but didn't comment.

Beckett finally spoke.

'Our assets have reported in over the last few days, and we are making progress.'

Ashley noted him checking something on a laptop. It seemed he was allowed to bring his in.

'As you know, we've only been given authorisation for this operation to continue until the weekend. I'll get you both fully informed after you've had the opportunity to peruse the new men currently housed on the wing. There were five arrivals yesterday. They are at the front of the folder.'

He handed each of them a file. There would be around eighty inmates in total, which was the maximum on each wing at

Peterborough. Ashley leafed through the profiles, noting the diverse faces but few noticeably Slavic ones.

She suspected Beckett would still protect the identity of some of his sources, even from them. He'd know Ashley was aware that Ally had been undercover. Barton probably would have guessed if he hadn't been told. As for the other 'assets', they could be prison officers, nurses, or other prisoners.

Beckett waited until both Barton and she looked back up. 'Any alarms ringing, Ashley?'

'No, sorry, but I'll check again with my team.'

'Fair enough. Intel points to the atmosphere having changed since Vladimir and Maksim arrived. It's an induction wing, so people tend to be on it for less than a week while the regime is explained to them, then they're moved elsewhere. The induction landing is generally a safe place. There isn't usually time for gangs to form or the men to upset each other too much, but it seems trouble is in the air.'

Prison officers developed jail craft after many years in the role, but so did prisoners. Both would detect a change in the atmosphere in the same way the police could sense who was going to blow at a domestic and who was all mouth and no trousers in a confrontation. Behind bars, there was danger when it went quiet.

'John,' said Beckett. 'Tell us about the men you recognise on the wing, and if you've noticed anyone unusual.'

'Some of these five are from Norfolk, so I won't comment on them. We've remanded about twenty in the last few weeks, which includes the Romanians we found at the whorehouse in Millfield. I assume you're already watching them. The others I know are mostly wing workers. They're all career criminals, but not for anything like trafficking.'

'Anyone we should run a fine-tooth comb over, even if it's just a hunch?' asked Kettle.

'I already looked into a few. Those sentenced to jail directly from their first court appearance are more likely than other inmates to have committed offences with the intention of being imprisoned. They all check out except one. A two-time drink-driver called Veselý who arrived just now with a driving whilst disqualified. Him I don't know. I'm surprised he's been jailed for that, considering how full the prisons are.'

Ashley noticed Reader's eyes narrow.

Barton hadn't identified one of Hydra's men, but he had unknowingly pointed out one of theirs.

52

If Beckett and Kettle were annoyed at having their insider spotted so easily, they hid it well.

'Anyone else?' asked Kettle.

Barton shook his head.

'Okay,' said Beckett. 'When Vladimir arrived, he was classified as a high-risk inmate due to his murder charge, which means he gets his own cell. Maksim was assessed as standard risk, meaning he could share. There were only two shared spaces available. One with a man called Ally Williamson, a former police officer who was jailed for passing on information to criminals, and that drink driver, who is from the Czech Republic. Wing staff gave Maksim the choice. He chose Ally, which was a surprise. Usually the Eastern Europeans opt for their compatriots. Mr Reader?'

'My observers tell me the Romanians arrested in Peterborough have kept an extremely low profile. They haven't spoken to Vladimir or Maksim once. In fact, they avoid even being near Vladimir. Bosko has conversed with them. He seems to speak their language, which is possible with Hungary and Romania being neighbours.'

'Do Maksim and Bosko talk?' asked Ashley.

'Not at length, which backs up both their claims of being small fry. Vladimir talks to both. He seems fluent in many languages. Bosko and Maksim are strong men, but they are completely subservient to Vladimir, who has the stormiest temperament of the three.'

'What about Maksim's general behaviour? If he's to be believed, he's not been inside before.'

'Apart from the staff, Maksim has only chatted at length to Vladimir and the drink driver, Veselý. That's typical of first-timers in jail who don't yet know how it works. The wing officers are experienced. They will have told him to keep his head down.'

'We have had some successes,' said Beckett. 'Vladimir has been overheard telling Maksim it's all gone to hell, but they've also had an argument.'

'What type?' asked Barton.

'Verbal. Maksim pushed back about something. Vladimir shouted at him in a language or dialect we couldn't pick up, so we don't know the details. Maksim's visit is this afternoon. He seems nervous about that but definitely wants to see his wife.'

Reader and Beckett stayed quiet and looked from Ashley to Barton.

'So, something's brewing,' said Barton.

'Yes, but what is it?' said Beckett.

'That is what's unsettling me,' said Reader. 'Given the choice, I'd have that man, Vladimir, off the wing right now. If he was in the block, he couldn't associate with anyone else. There would be no chance to spread lies or manipulate.'

'Are you allowed to move them if they haven't done anything

wrong?' asked Ashley, who then felt daft considering some of the other rules they'd been bending.

Reader smiled.

'We usually say it's for their own protection. Then it's fine for a few days. Vladimir's provisional category A prisoner status came through late yesterday, anyway, and therefore we can't hold him for more than a few days. He's being transferred to HMP Belmarsh tomorrow afternoon.'

Ashley told them about Michelle's post-mortem findings and Kettle frowned.

'You're right. The CPS will drop the charge to manslaughter, but he didn't have to be in for murder for A-cat status. It's about risk to the public.'

Reader was clearly unhappy about the prospect of having an inmate like that still on the induction wing, but he'd accepted having his hand forced. He shrugged.

'It's true we have no evidence or intel of Vladimir planning to escape, and the man's danger is mostly to young women on the street, not to other cons in a jail. Regardless, I'll be relieved when he's gone.'

'What did the wing officers say about their interactions with Maksim?' asked Ashley to Reader.

'He seems a decent guy. He's solid. One of our guys bumped into him, reckoned it was like hitting a parked car, but he apologised profusely afterwards.'

'Sal looked into his background. It all checks out. The factory described him as a diligent worker who was always keen for extra shifts. I don't think he'd have had time for a secret life until he left that role, which fits in with what his wife told us.'

'Bosko is on Peterborough magistrates' court list tomorrow,' said Kettle. 'He might as well head to HMP Norwich afterwards, as can Maksim next week, now Vladimir's leaving. The Romanians' solicitor has requested bail. We've found no firm evidence linking the Peterborough brothel with the Norfolk and Suffolk operations. The woman who was in their pop-up brothel has vanished. The magistrates should do their hearing via video link this afternoon or first thing in the morning. Without the coercion angle, we might even struggle with a charge of inciting prostitution. With no previous in this country for them, any punishment is likely to be suspended at worst, and if they probably aren't going to be sentenced behind bars, bail will be awarded.'

Ashley was listening but also watching the wing camera. It was nine fifteen.

'So, by tomorrow evening, the Romanians are likely to be free and could disappear.'

'Yes.'

'Bosko will have gone to Norwich jail, and Vladimir will be at Belmarsh.'

'Correct.'

'Which leaves Ally in a cell here with Maksim until Maksim departs next week.'

'No,' said Reader. 'I'm obviously aware Ally used to be a police officer. Even the induction wing inmates will soon suss that out, so he'll be moved to the vulnerable prisoners' unit on Saturday.'

'Will he be safe until then?'

'We believe so. The wing workers are often hardened cons, but they won't want to jeopardise their cushy positions. If they realise what he was, they'll just take the mickey. The other prisoners are mostly foreigners, who won't care, or low-level acquisitive offenders reeling from withdrawal. Admittedly, Bosko is a slight concern, but he's been inside many times, and he's never offended behind bars. He'll be gone in the morning anyway.'

'Ally should be fine on the induction wing,' said Beckett. 'He's not a nonce.'

'What about Vladimir?' asked Ashley.

Kettle crossed his arms. 'I suppose his past is mostly a mystery, so we don't know what he's capable of at this point, but the officers are on high alert.'

Something tugged at Ashley's mind.

'Why would Maksim not choose to go in with another Eastern European?'

'It might be he preferred to share with another mature man,' said Reader. 'He and Ally are close in age. They'll probably prefer similar films, music and TV shows.'

'Maksim is forty-five, so he's a bit younger,' said Beckett.

'You don't say? That beard makes him look older,' said Barton. 'Did he always have it?'

'Yes, it's on a lot of his photographs.'

'I've got that feeling,' said Ashley. 'Something's not right.'

'Me, too,' said Barton. 'And we haven't been on the wing.'

Beckett cleared his throat.

'I agree, it would have been safer with Maksim sharing with Veselý, with him being a younger man, but it's only for one more day.'

Reader wrung his hands.

'As I said, we've received no intel nor heard any rumours of trouble, but the staff are nervy and so are the cons. We have eyes on Vladimir at all times and Ally, Bosko and Maksim are being watched too. There are extra officers in the hub area when Vladimir leaves the wing to receive his prescription at the med hatch.' Reader directed his next comment at Beckett. 'I'm looking forward to tomorrow. It'll be a huge relief to get Vladimir out of here.'

Ashley caught Reader frowning at the screen, but the wing

appeared calm. A prisoner was casually mopping the floor, but he didn't have the demeanour of a man who had nothing to do, nowhere to go, and time to burn.

Instead Ashley had the impression of a rodent sniffing the air and checking his surroundings for predators. As though he was forced to be there, but knew there was a snake nearby.

An old guy hurried to the hot-water urn. He glanced over his shoulder as he filled his cup and was swiftly back in his cell.

Reader grimaced and turned to face them.

'I've worked in the prison system for a long time. Standing here, even watching through a screen, I can sense the impending violence in the air.'

53

The four of them continued the meeting with the assistant taking notes. It was a lot more formal than the previous meeting at OCC. How many of those conversations would end up in any official report? Even so, the others in the room continued working but were never introduced.

After two hours, Reader took a phone call. Further intel had come through from an unnamed source that Bosko had an iPhone in his possession. The question was, who had given it to him? Mobile phones were a significant issue for prison security. In effect, criminals could run their enterprises from behind bars. Some would use them to harass and threaten witnesses and ask others to hide any incriminating evidence or come up with false statements to help their causes.

Barton stretched. It had been a long morning.

'Two things about that strike me,' he said. 'One, I thought you had signal-jamming tech, and two, those nano phones are one thing, but a smartphone? Surely it's too bulky to smuggle. They'd all be walking funny.'

Reader had loosened his tie, as it had grown stuffy with all the people present in the room.

'It's the age-old problem of crooked, busy, or lazy staff. Technology has moved on, so now we're getting drones dropping packages in exercise yards and on walkways. We find much more than they collect, but it's like whack-a-mole. Sometimes we miss them. We have hundreds of officers on shift, it only takes one to be dishonest, and we're playing catch-up.'

'Aren't phones useless if the signals are blocked?' asked Ashley.

'The technology works for the smaller phones but isn't as successful with much bigger handsets. If we're not careful, the jammer messes with the officers' radios and even the public's mobiles near the jail. Like everything, it's not perfect. We'll search Bosko's cell tonight, but the phone could be anywhere on the wing by now, or even off it.'

At lunch, sandwiches and cakes arrived, which had been made on the female side of the prison. Barton tucked in, then announced he was leaving. He gave Ashley a big smile as he left and Ashley wished him well. She was staying to observe Maksim's meeting with his wife. A bugging device in the visits room would have been nice, but even Beckett couldn't step that far over the grey line.

Ashley and Reader headed to Security to watch the visit footage as the live screen in the command centre remained fixed on the induction wing. Ashley said hello to the security staff and took a seat in front of the TV in their office. The afternoon session started at two, so the room was empty except for a staff member adjusting some of the chairs.

At five to two, a phone rang. A female officer answered it, then spoke to the room.

'The first set of visitors are coming up from the gatehouse.'

Ashley turned back to the screen. The door for the inmates to enter the visits hall opened and the first prisoners headed to the officers' desk. They handed over their ID cards and were directed to one of the forty-odd tables in four rows of ten.

Maksim was in a chair next to the wall in the middle of his row. The prisoners were spaced about the large room so those present would at least have some privacy. He was still dressed in the ill-fitting grey prison tracksuit he wore earlier. His T-shirt was too big for him and his trousers too short. He fiddled with his beard as he waited.

'There she is,' said Ashley as a group of mostly women were brought in at the other side of the room from where the cons arrived.

Jolanta was at the back. She peered around the people in front of her. When she got to the front and passed through the barrier, Maksim rose from his seat and slowly lifted an arm. Her head went back slightly, then she strode towards him. There was no greeting. She sat in the chair opposite, the low table between them, one leg firmly crossed over the other, arms folded.

There were numerous camera angles that showed them with their faces clearly in view. Maksim had his palms open and did most of the talking. That carried on for three minutes. Then she uncrossed her arms. She pointed at him as she spoke. Maksim nodded glumly.

He replied and she shook her head, with disgust etched over her face. He looked away. Ashley watched as Jolanta's shoulders shuddered. She wiped her eyes and took a succession of deep breaths.

She leaned forward and hissed something at him, then stood and marched back to the barrier. The officer near it pressed the talk button for his radio.

'She'll have to wait for the escort to return from the gate-house to collect her,' said Reader.

Ashley tutted. 'She won't even look at him.'

'That's an angry wife. Okay, I'll take you out the officers' exit now. She'll be leaving in around five minutes. That's your opportunity.'

Ashley was outside waiting by the time Jolanta appeared. When Ashley came into view, Jolanta stumbled, despite wearing flat shoes.

'Are you okay, Jolanta?'

The woman, eyes brimming with tears, hurried past.

'I'll call you tomorrow,' shouted Ashley.

Jolanta lifted her pace and disappeared into the car park. Before following, Ashley glanced back at the stark white building behind her.

Over it hung a large black cloud.

54

Ally Williamson emerged from a deep sleep, as though yanked by an unseen force. Someone seemed to be shouting into his and Maksim's cell. He lay facing the wall and tried to place the voice. The language was guttural, probably Eastern European, but with a rapid tempo. Keys jangled outside. A younger-sounding voice spoke in English.

'Get a move on. They're waiting for you at Reception.'

'Guv, I'm saying goodbye to my mate. Have a heart.'

The deep voice had the accent of someone who'd lived in England for a long time, but never bothered to try to be perfect. It belonged to Bosko. Ally knew Bosko was at court that morning because he'd been telling people. Prisoners due in court were collected with the kitchen workers before anyone else was unlocked, so this must be him leaving the wing.

The officer's tone changed.

'You've done that, Bosko. Move.'

'Okay, okay.'

Ally glanced over his shoulder.

Maksim was standing at the door with his ear pressed

against the crack. He barked a response through the gap, then spun around so fast Ally didn't have a chance to look away. Maksim's eyes bored into his. He smiled.

'Bit of an idiot, that guy, uh?'

'I've only spoken to him in passing.'

Maksim stood next to the head of their bunk bed and stared out of the window. The early sun caught his profile. With his chin stuck forward, prominent nose, and thick beard, Maksim wouldn't have looked out of place on the face of a Roman coin.

'Do you like prison?' he asked without turning to Ally.

'As opposed to other places I've taken a vacation?'

Maksim smiled. Strong white teeth glinted in the morning light. He faced Ally, who had rested his elbow on the thin, strange-smelling pillow he'd been sleeping on.

'Even behind bars, the dawn is beautiful. The beams glancing off the whitewashed walls, sparkling on the barbed wire. The shadows of the night are beaten back. Warms every one of us, whatever our deeds.'

Ally sensed Maksim had something on his mind.

'I suppose so. If there's a God, we're all his children.'

Maksim's gaze bored down on Ally. It seemed as if the imposing man was reading his thoughts as simply as flicking through the cards in a Rolodex, but Maksim had been respectful since he arrived. In effect, they were two people locked in a box bedroom. When you shared such a small space, consideration became important. If you needed to take a number two, decent men tried to wait until the cell doors were open, so the other could leave the room. At night, that option was stolen from them. Maksim had only done it once, blaming that evening's vegetable risotto.

Maksim kept his eyes on Ally.

'What are you in for, my friend?'

Ally had been telling anyone who asked he was in for embezzlement. He decided not to lie. Perhaps Maksim already knew.

'Corruption.'

'Ah. You are corrupt. Like us all, eh?'

'I guess so.'

'They told me what you did.'

Ally's blood cooled as fast as his mouth dried. He licked his lips. 'Who are they?'

'Vladimir.'

'Which one is he?'

Ally detected a slight smile on Maksim, but with the beard, it was hard to be sure.

'They call him the Hydra. Did you know that?'

'No, I didn't.'

'A bad man, apparently. Although Bosko said I should be careful of you.'

Ally swallowed deeply. 'Did he say why?'

'Should I be wary of you?'

Ally's voice was a whisper. 'No.'

Maksim's head tilted to one side. He looked back out of the window.

'Good. I'm going to do my exercises, then I want to tell you something. A confession. Will you listen?'

Ally gave him a single nod and turned to face the wall again. Despite the clunks of metal and the shouts of men as the prison came to life, he heard Maksim's towel drop onto the floor. Ally had observed his rituals most mornings that week. Hundreds of press-ups and sit-ups. Lunges and stretches and other moves. It might have been yoga or tai chi. That morning, Ally imagined he could hear Maksim's muscles creaking like a huge wooden ship at sea.

When Maksim had finished his routine, Ally heard him

splash the lukewarm, metallic-tasting water from their small sink on his face. Ally turned around and saw a rippling back and veiny shoulders. He had no idea about fitness, but he suspected his cellmate possessed incredible strength. Ally finally lost his bottle.

He thought of his family. Tears leaked from his eyes as he remembered the look on his beautiful wife's face moments after she'd delivered their child. He often remembered his daughter as an infant or a toddler. Working so much, he felt as though she went from that age to a teenager who was uninterested in him almost overnight. His distraction with work being one of the many mistakes he'd made along life's path.

Sadly, the image he most recalled when he thought of his wife was her face at the end. A mask of pain. An expression of someone who felt wronged. A person robbed by cancer.

They'd discussed him going undercover. It was her idea to say yes.

'Ally,' she had said, gripping his hand with a strength that hadn't been present for days. 'Do it for me. It makes all this easier.'

At the time, he'd hoped the hollow feeling in his stomach was nerves, not a premonition of his own premature end.

After the Bacton Wood case finished, Ally took a holiday in Australia. It had been a surreal experience, finding himself a ghost among the other happy tourists. His heart too full of sadness to interact with them. After one too many meals alone, he returned to the UK and, when Beckett asked, he agreed to go to HMP Peterborough.

Well, Ally had attempted to get intel for Beckett, but he hadn't learned much. Had it been a waste of time? The only thing he'd really found out was that his cellmate frightened him.

When the doors opened in ten minutes' time, Ally would

head towards the camera in the far corner of the landing and make the sign. The one that said he'd had enough. He could take no more. There was no point in speaking to the prison officers. He didn't know which, if any, was a plant. They'd assume he was taking the piss, or perhaps had gone mad. Maybe he had.

He heard the clang of the wing gates, like steel jaws shutting for the final time, followed by the ominous, rhythmic beat of thick-soled work boots. His heartbeat pounded in his chest to the same pace. Sweat collected in his hair. A desperate urge to scream for help welled up within him, but it would take time for assistance to arrive.

The wing workers would be released first to give them time to prepare the milk and cereal for the others, as well as the depressingly small plastic bag containing four teabags and four sugar sachets for the never-ending day ahead. Heavy keys, clunking in chunky locks, echoed in the high ceiling of the long corridors as those prisoners began to be let out.

Maksim leaned against the radiator and cleared his throat and started to speak. Even though his voice sounded quiet, it filled the room. Ally listened nervously. Why was he being told all this? It didn't make sense.

When Maksim finished talking, Ally realised with horror he had been told too much.

His skin contracted. His pulse, already running, broke into a sprint. What could he do? Their cell was on the top landing and would be one of the last doors opened.

Maksim turned again to the window. Bare-chested, the rising sun shining gold onto his muscled chest. He spoke his final words firmly.

'I'm sorry, Ally. You seem like a decent man, but the Hydra demands a sacrifice.'

55

The prison director got out of his Mercedes-Benz GLS a little before 7 a.m. He strode towards the gatehouse, taking one look back, as he often did. Such a superb four-by-four. Inside, he felt a sense of control that often eluded him within the prison walls. Most days, there was a sensation of relief when he climbed into the vehicle to go home. He'd often wondered if that was why he'd purchased it.

The jail didn't scare him any more, but it used to. He'd joined the service nearly thirty years ago as a dare to himself. It was also a snub to his parents after he'd failed to get good enough A-level grades for the course they'd been keen for him to take at university. There had been some excitement before he'd started, and through training, but his first day on the wings had been a severe shock.

His upper-crust accent riled many of the inmates, and Wormwood Scrubs had been a desperate place back then. Luckily, Reader had been a fit young man, and few challenged him physically, despite him not possessing a fighting bone. He'd kept up the pretence of confidence for a full year. Only once did he falter. A pair of armed robbers got in his face, and he crumpled. His body shut down, tears forming, as they closed in on him in the laundry.

Luckily, the man he'd been working with that day noticed what was going on and entered the room. He was a time-served officer who calmly told Reader to go and lock himself in the office and gather himself. Reader had rushed out of the room, then turned, expecting the other officer to leave, but the door quietly closed leaving his saviour inside with the two inmates.

Funnily enough, neither the cons nor the officer ever mentioned the incident afterwards. They were different days, of course. Back then, damaged men abandoned by the armed services prowled the landings. Control was maintained simply by the fact that they, the custodians, were more violent than their charges.

Shortly after that, Reader was transferred into the team that supervised the workshops and never had to return to the wings. He quietly progressed through the ranks. He wasn't entirely sure what made him stay, but his parents became proud of his progress. They beamed when he became governor. Peterborough was a privately operated jail, so, in this place, he was known as the director.

So as he queued behind the officers arriving for their shifts, he recognised their pinched expressions. Men and women who worked on unstable wings had an air about them in the morning. As they filtered through the locks and security gates, they made a transition. Their guards went up, and their game faces came down.

Reader knew his own struggles on the job were the main reason he was a great boss. He tolerated lapses and mistakes, and the inevitable breakdowns and eruptions, because he'd been there himself. There was a deep-rooted respect within him for the people who carried out such a tough role. His people were important to him. Calm, experienced, valued staff made the prison run smoothly for those on both sides of the doors.

'Morning, sir,' said a group of four officers when he reached the entrance.

'Morning.'

His voice came out croakily. He cleared his throat, but it wasn't his allergies. Since Vladimir arrived, he hadn't been sleeping. When Reader typed Vladimir Nikolayev into Wikipedia and saw what he'd done, he almost fainted. Today was the culmination of all those nerves. The day he got rid of him. He pressed his fingerprint against the scanner and went to collect his keys and radio.

The NCA had assured him the man they held was not the real Vladimir Nikolayev. The Russians had confirmed he was safe and sound in prison. They'd sent photos. Reader should be more relaxed, seeing as the governor in that Siberian hellhole had informed them Vladimir almost lost an eye in a fight two years ago, which left him heavily scarred.

Reader took the stairs to the admin block and found himself hurrying to Security. There were three officers in there. Two of whom were staring at the big television.

'Anything overnight?'

'Nope,' replied the officer closest to him. 'Bosko's gone to Reception for his appearance at court. He shouted through Maksim's cell before he left the wing.'

'What did he say?'

'The guy collecting him said it wasn't English.'

'So, we're all quiet on the Eastern front.'

'Yep. Servery workers are out, and they're releasing the others now.'

Moisture built on Reader's forehead. 'Put Vladimir's cell on.'

The officer brought that camera view up on the big screen. Vladimir was on the lower landing at the end of the wing in a single cell. Reader watched as PCO Naylor slid back his bolt, unlocked the door, lifted the handle, pushed the door open four or five inches, but didn't go in. Do-gooders had wanted the officers to refer to the prisoners as residents and wish them good morning when they opened their doors. The idea was utter bollocks and Reader had done no more than pay it lip service.

Naylor was two cells away by the time Vladimir appeared, but he still glanced back warily. Vladimir ambled under the metal stairwell as though heading towards the servery, then paused. He watched PCO Mbanu, the officer doing the upper landing, finish unlocking the inmates on the left-hand side. When Naylor had cracked the doors of half of the lower right-hand side, Vladimir circled and casually climbed the stairs. One of his arms swung as he moved, the other remained in his pocket. He disappeared from their camera shot.

'Follow him and keep him as the main image,' said Reader, managing not to shout.

The top landing came into view. Vladimir marched through the prisoners leaving their cells. They parted for him. Maksim was standing blocking the entrance to his cell. Reader wished again for more microphones as Vladimir stood talking to him. Maksim looked away and shook his head. Vladimir still had one hand in his pocket. The other arm rose, and he grabbed Maksim's shoulder and prised him out of the doorway. Maksim stayed nearby as Vladimir wandered into the cell.

When Vladimir was out of sight, Maksim stared wildly around him. He shook his head again, then ran his hands through his hair. After a glance over the balcony, he trudged along the wing.

'Split the screen. Keep a visual on the door and follow Maksim with the other.'

Reader stared wide-eyed as Maksim walked down the stairs at the other end of the landing. When he reached the bottom, he stopped and held his face, then strained his neck upwards to look at his cell. Reader glanced at the other side of the TV screen where the door to Maksim's room had been pushed shut.

Maksim rushed to the officer supervising the servery queue. Reader recognised him as the well-respected PCO Bates. After listening for a few seconds, Bates scowled. Reader could almost hear him say, *What?* Maksim repeated himself. Bates shouted across to Naylor, who raced up to Maksim's cell, where Vladimir now filled the doorway. Vladimir barged past the officer and strolled away. Naylor briefly seemed to wage an internal dilemma about following, then rushed inside.

All five radios in the security office sprang to life. The controller's words blared out.

'Personal alarm! Personal alarm!'

56

The brief silence was shattered again by the controller's voice, now urgent and sharp.

'Personal Alarm. Officer Naylor. Last known location Whisky One wing. First Response to attend. I repeat, First Response to attend. Oscar One to attend.'

Reader bit his lip as he stared at the screen. Naylor reappeared out of Maksim's cell. He leaned over the balcony and shouted to his buddy, Bates, who was peering upwards. Bates raced to the stairs, veered under them, and headed to Vladimir's cell. The door was pushed to. Instead of opening it, Bates yanked the door shut and locked it, then peered through the observation flap. After a moment of staring, he shoved the bolt across. Upstairs, Mbanu had joined Naylor. They entered Maksim's cell. The radio crackled into life again.

'All outstations. We have a code red on Whisky One. First Response to attend. Second Response to attend. Hotel One and Hotel Two to attend. Oscar One en route.'

Reader pulled his radio from his pouch.

'QV, this is DGi receiving.'

'Go ahead DG1.'

He was about to shout out a raft of instructions, but the screen told him a flood of officers had already arrived on the wing. Of course, the situation was being handled. His staff knew what to do. Inmates were unceremoniously shoved into cells. A nurse in a blue uniform, lugging a large green bag with a white cross on it, edged cautiously through the wing gates.

Bates ran towards the nurse. He spoke to her, then turned around. She raced after him along the landing, up the stairs. They both disappeared into Ally and Maksim's cell.

Reader felt he had to say something. 'Is an ambulance on the way?'

'Yes, sir.'

57

Ashley had been considering returning to OCC the previous night, but the traffic back from Peterborough had been terrible, with gridlock at King's Lynn's Hardwick roundabout. She'd turned off for Cromer and gone straight home. The next morning, she forced herself to rise at six and headed out for a jog. The first fifteen minutes were hard going, but eventually she got into the swing of it.

By the time she reached the pier, the clouds had beaten back the sun, although a chill wind bullied her when she stood at the end. Ashley often paused for a minute or two at the pier if her run took her there. Even now, with white-capped waves tumbling below and the promise of rain, a sense of peace enveloped her.

That rapidly vanished as she hurried home through the damp streets, hard rain hitting with a vengeance as she arrived drenched. After a cool shower and a quick bowl of porridge, she emerged for the drive to work fully prepared for whatever the day ahead threw at her, but when Ashley walked into the office, she sensed something was wrong.

'Kettle wants to see you immediately,' said Sal.

'What is it?'

Sal grimaced. 'You know how Kettle's never fazed? Today he is.'

Ashley's mind was whirring with possibilities when she sat opposite her boss. He rose from his seat and closed the door.

'I've got some terrible news.'

Kettle dropped back into his chair. A range of emotions swept across his face. He was rarely this animated, which meant that whatever had happened, it was personal. She only had to rack her brains for a few moments.

'Ally?'

'Yes.'

Ashley braced herself. 'Is he dead?'

Kettle pressed his hands together.

'I don't know. The prison director, Reader, called me to say he'd been stabbed multiple times. Once in the neck.'

Ashley put a hand to her mouth. She focused, then shoved Ally's fate and her feelings into a separate box in her head and considered the implications.

'Who did it?'

'Reader has headed to the wing to talk to the staff involved. He's got security checking all the CCTV, but he's pretty certain Vladimir was responsible.'

Ashley glanced at her watch. It had just gone half eight.

'When did it happen?'

'Must have been after they were unlocked for breakfast.'

'What about Vladimir's cellmate, Maksim?'

'He didn't say whether he was involved or not.'

Kettle's mobile phone rang on his desk. He answered as quick as a gunfighter on the draw.

'Kettle.'

He listened for a good five minutes, only saying 'Right' three times.

'I'll let Beckett know,' was how he finished the call. He placed the handset slowly back on the table. Ashley stopped pacing the room.

'They've studied the CCTV. Vladimir went to Ally and Maksim's cell first thing. Maksim argued with him at the doorway. Then Vladimir shoved him out of the way and entered. Maksim had some kind of dilemma. He obviously didn't agree with what Vladimir was about to do because he rushed along the landing, down the stairs, and talked to the officer supervising the servery. I assume he said his pad-mate has been assaulted.'

Kettle took a deep breath.

'An officer raced to check what had happened, probably not expecting to find an attempted murder. Ally was on the bed. Claret everywhere. Two wounds to his abdomen and one to his neck. Pressed his alarm and the responders managed the incident as normal by securing the wing. Vladimir had already returned to his cell. CCTV showed him throwing a small kitchen knife into the bin under the stairs as he walked past. His door was locked. They'll keep him there until DCI Barton arrives to take charge of the crime scene, but the officer who locked the door saw blood on Vladimir's hands and tracksuit.'

'It was an attempted assassination. Did Reader say any more about Ally?'

'Not much. The nurse arrived in minutes. She stopped him from bleeding out. Ambulance was there in fifteen minutes.'

'Fifteen? That's a long time to wait with a knife wound.'

'Prison medical staff are well used to keeping stab victims alive. The vehicle still has to be searched, inside and under, and IDs checked. There are a lot of gates to open before the ambulance can reach the houseblocks.'

'I guess they had the risk of a rogue ambulance waiting around the corner with Vladimir's friends dressed as paramedics.'

'Yep.'

'Shit. Let's hope Ally's okay.'

'Fingers crossed.'

Ashley wasn't sure whether to raise how it would look with Ally being undercover, but Kettle preferred her to say what was on her mind. 'The shit's gonna hit the fan.'

Kettle pursed his lips. 'Beckett will take most of the flak. It was his idea. There was a risk assessment done, so he might survive.'

'Should we have pulled Ally out before?'

'Why do you ask that?'

'Reader implied the wing was a pressure cooker.'

Kettle rubbed his temples.

'The prize was too big. We have to finish Typhon off, or it could easily reform. Ally accepted the risks when he agreed to go undercover.'

'But what did he learn? I should have said more. Maksim asking to share a cell with him. I didn't like it. When something seems off, it's usually because something is off.'

'Maksim had no previous. There could be any number of explanations for him choosing to be with Ally. Perhaps he made a snap decision. It was his first time in jail.'

Ashley finally took a seat.

'I suppose he'd been let down by other Eastern Europeans, but his decision placed Ally right in the middle of events. Maksim might have told Vladimir he suspected Ally was police, or that he was asking too many questions.'

Kettle's expression was one of disgust. 'What the hell did

Vladimir have to gain by attempting to murder Ally? It's an irrational move.'

'Vladimir isn't a young man. What's he going to get for trafficking and forced prostitution with kidnap, aggravated by the victims' ages? Thirty years? Maybe he thought he'd take out a cop as revenge for catching him. It's possible he enjoys killing and took the opportunity when it presented itself.'

'He wouldn't be the first villain to harbour a hatred for police and the authorities.'

'If that's the case, it's frustrating we don't know how Ally's cover was blown. His sentencing was kept off the news.'

'Sometimes it's no more than gut instinct. Vladimir is clearly intelligent. He survived all these years acting on his wits. If the man is capable of strategic thinking, he might reasonably assume we'd put ringers on the wing.'

Ashley's brain had clicked into investigation mode.

'It's interesting Maksim told an officer when he was so subservient to Vladimir.'

'Perhaps he got to like Ally, or this was a step too far. Maksim's defence is that he was just the driver. A nobody in the grand scheme of things. There's no chance he'd want to be involved in a prison killing.'

'You know what? As it stands, whichever way the rest of this pans out, if Ally survives, Maksim saved his life.'

58

Hector knocked on Kettle's door and walked in. Ashley listened while Kettle revealed to him what the morning had brought.

Hector cursed. 'Poor Ally. Fate dealt him a poor hand.'

'Why do you say that?'

'Well, we've finally found out how dangerous Vladimir was, but too late for Ally. We sent Vladimir's DNA to the other European countries where there have been similar murders and received some replies first thing today.'

Kettle bared his teeth. 'You're kidding me? He's wanted for a killing spree over there?'

'Not a spree, but he's probably responsible for an unsolved murder twenty-five years ago in Serbia. A young woman had been raped and killed in a field. Their prime suspect was a man called Vladimir Davidović, but he vanished shortly after the body was found, was never questioned, and they lost all trace of him. He was later wanted for war crimes relating to his involvement in a rogue squad who murdered at will. They tested various pieces of clothing for DNA a few years ago when they reopened the cold file. Our DNA sample matched theirs.'

'So, Vladimir was his real name.'

'It seems so.'

Beckett knocked on the door. He lumbered in and closed it slowly.

'I'm sorry. I never thought something like this would happen.'

Ashley supposed not, but there were so many unknown risks to undercover work it was always a possibility. She briefly wondered how often this type of operation went wrong and concluded this probably wasn't the first time for Beckett. He looked each of them in the eye.

'Don't worry. Any investigation will end with me. I've heard from the hospital. They had to restart Ally's heart, most likely respiratory depression from the blood loss. He's in surgery now.'

'Has Vladimir said anything?' asked Ashley.

'No. Barton tried to speak to him in the cell, but he was abusive and aggressive. A control and restraint team had to go in. Vladimir fought tooth and nail, which gave the prison officers a chance for some payback. I heard Barton fancied going in himself. Vladimir's in the block now, threatening to smash anyone's face in who tries to enter his cell. He'll be moved to the category A prison as planned this afternoon under armed escort. Barton will charge him with attempted murder before he leaves. Vladimir will clearly never be a danger to the public again.'

Ashley decided to ask the obvious. 'Where does that leave us?'

'I've been called back to London. HMP Peterborough will be cleared of our assets. Maksim is at court on Wednesday, and he'll head to Norwich as well. We'll keep looking for the brown-haired guy who always wears sunglasses, but without them, and perhaps wearing a wig, he could drink a pint at the next table and nobody would know. He'll likely go to ground. If there's anyone from Typhon left, they would be fools to show themselves now. It's not a perfect end, if indeed it is the end. What are your thoughts?'

Ashley raised a finger.

'I want to talk to Maksim's wife. Her prison visit did not go well. She appeared furious, and angry people often talk. She didn't answer her phone yesterday evening when I tried after getting home, so I'll visit her house if she doesn't pick up today.'

'Good idea,' said Kettle. 'Should we send two of our team to interview Maksim about what happened?'

'No,' said Beckett. 'It's Barton's investigation now. He knows what he's doing, and it's better for a different force to handle the Ally side of things. You didn't get Maksim to come clean before, so let Barton have a crack. Vladimir won't break, but Maksim might after today. There's clearly some good in him, whereas the rest of them have to be dead inside.'

'What and when do I tell my team about Ally?' asked Ashley.

'Nothing yet,' said Beckett. 'The incident will be released to the news later this afternoon, so I'll email you what you can say by 2 p.m.'

Ashley returned to her desk. Sal raised an eyebrow, but she shook her head.

'Meeting at two thirty. Pass that on to the others.'

She tried Jolanta's phone, but it was turned off. Focusing on her reports wasn't easy. At midday, she got a call from Barton.

'Hi, John. I'll bet you've had a difficult morning.'

'Yeah. Days like these are tough. Have you heard anything about Ally?'

'They're operating on him now.'

'Perhaps that's good news. At least he's still with us. I thought I'd give you a quick update, and we've also tied up a few loose ends. Maksim has clammed up. Won't say a word to me. He's highly stressed, so I probed a little, but didn't push it. You'll have him near you next week. Try again then.'

'Kettle said best to let you guys handle him.'

'Fair enough. I'll have another go. Maksim did ask why you weren't handling the case, so he might respond to you. Let's see how I get on.'

'Sure.'

'Vladimir wouldn't leave his cell.'

'Yeah, I heard that.'

'Prison officers went in with a shield and riot uniforms to drop him. He fought like mad. Strong man. They had to carry him to the block afterwards because he refused to stand up.'

'I hope he was bleeding.'

'Profusely. Maybe he couldn't walk. I'm ringing from the block. I tried one final time to see if he had anything to say, but he refused health care and lay on his bed, staring at the ceiling. Probably conserving his strength for another scrap when they come to take him to the transport vehicle.'

'Thanks for giving me the details.'

'No worries. I've got an update for you on Bosko, too. One of our guys was at court this morning. Bosko gave a guilty plea to facilitating the commission of a child sex offence. The judge accepted he didn't know anything about the women under his care, but that doesn't absolve him of guilt, seeing as one was underage. He stated Bosko's previous offending history guaranteed him a significant custodial stay, and, with the chance of further charges and a risk of absconding, he would be remanded until sentencing in two weeks. There was a van dropping off transfers from Norwich jail, so they've already taken him back.'

'That went as expected.'

'Yes. We've also got a name and background for our deceased from Sacrewell who was found with the carrier bag over his head. His marriage had broken down a few months beforehand. I don't reckon it's related to Typhon.'

Ashley huffed out a breath. 'Okay. Keep me posted if you get any breakthroughs.'

'Ditto.'

At two o'clock, Ashley received an email from Beckett. Ally was out of the operating room and in an induced coma in Intensive Care. Not only had he been stabbed, but his neck and most of his ribs were broken. Luckily, the spinal cord hadn't been severed, but there had been significant compression. His condition was critical.

Ashley led a meeting with the team and explained what had happened to Ally at HMP Peterborough. Zelda and Morgan were the most upset, having spent years supervised by Ally and not knowing of his undercover work. Ashley said they could go home, but both wanted to stay in case there were further developments, as she'd known they would.

At four, after another call going straight to voicemail, Ashley asked Hector if he fancied a drive to Mile Cross to find out if Jolanta was in.

Ashley booked out a car and took the wheel. Hector eyed her suspiciously.

'Why did you ask me instead of taking one of your motley crew?'

'You smell the nicest.'

'That's not the stiffest competition I've entered.'

'I wanted to quiz you about your latest stats.'

'Ah, not to spend quality time with me.'

'That's a lovely bonus.'

'Great recovery.'

'I assume you'll be leaving like Beckett. Any final conclusions for us?'

'I'll submit a report on Monday, but there's more than enough data to say the Typhon organisation was operating efficiently and ruthlessly across the whole of Europe since the late nineties. But, like all great civilisations, it fell apart. The crackdown on people smuggling meant their operation began to leak intelligence. Advances in DNA evidence and cross-border communication helped, but it was the Dutch cracking the messaging service that tolled their final bell.'

'So, you believe it's over?'

'As an international trafficking operation, yes. There appears to be one man left who we definitely need to catch.'

'Typhon?'

'I'm thinking the guy with the sunglasses. Perhaps he's Typhon. I'm really hoping there's not another creature who we haven't come across yet.'

'Beckett said that, but we have so little to go on.'

'Yes, I'm aware that, without leads, it's likely we won't find the sunglasses fellow. But he's clearly in a position of authority and still has access to resources.'

'What do you mean by resources?'

'Money and manpower. People are helping him. That manpower could still commit individual crimes in the future, but probably not for a while. We believe if the sunglasses guy is caught, the rest will melt away.'

Ashley drummed her fingers on the steering wheel.

'What about the motivation for the deaths of the innocent young girls?'

'You're referring to the ones who died swiftly and without visibly being abused?'

'Yes.'

'I've concluded that someone was killing people for two

reasons. The first, they enjoyed murdering pure, beautiful women. They gained pleasure from it.'

'Blonde women?'

'I don't think that was a deciding factor after all. Akari dyed her hair and there were a few brunette victims. Perhaps their angelic looks got the girls noticed.'

'And the second reason?'

'The man responsible didn't commit these crimes by choice. He was compelled to kill them.'

59

Ashley stared at Hector for a moment.

'You reckon the girls were taken to satisfy an uncontrollable urge.'

'Yes.'

'As part of an important ceremony or ritual?'

'Maybe.'

'Not to be sold to sick men who like killing virgins?'

'It's possible there's a bunch of people involved, but my team and teams in other countries have trawled through decades of data. There is nothing to suggest a satanic cult has been operating. Over such a substantial length of time, mistakes would have been made. Individuals get dementia, fall out, go too far. I doubt a group would have evaded detection for that long. So, yes, I think we're dealing with one person, perhaps two. If they were smart and loyal.'

'Best friends.'

'Or family.'

Ashley thought of Jolanta and Maksim. Surely not them, with a daughter of their own.

'So it might still be a human sacrifice thing?'

'Yes. The victims were taken to locations of natural beauty. It's the most unusual and original aspect of the whole investigation.'

'The lighthouses and windmills.'

'They're a serious foible.'

'Only you could bring foible into the conversation. Does that mean a personality quirk?'

'That's right. It shouldn't fit when we're dealing with a person who kills with impunity, but this man is in control most of the time. He doesn't make mistakes even though he has a significant eccentricity: a genetic flaw that compels him to commit these heinous crimes.'

'This flaw might be something we haven't seen before. He may not be worshipping the devil or begging for gifts from the gods.'

'Right, but I suspect in his head what he's doing is perfectly reasonable.'

'Which allows him to remain level-headed.'

'Yes.'

Ashley glanced across at Hector. 'Which means he probably doesn't kill the poor used-up women or people like Esra.'

'No, I don't think he'd want to. It would be beneath him and an unnecessary risk. Assuming Vladimir isn't Typhon, it's possible he was the one who took the lives of the people who had no further use to them, or others like him did. Perhaps that was how it worked with Cerberus and the rest of the operatives in each country, and that's what kept them all loyal to each other.'

'That's a reasonable assumption in light of what Vladimir did this morning.'

'Yes. Whether Vladimir is psychotic or not, he's probably someone who derives pleasure from killing and has been doing so unhindered for decades. There is one final conclusion that fits in with my theory.'

Ashley had stopped at some lights. She turned to Hector.

'What?'

'From my stats, which aren't concrete because some of the bodies were found heavily decomposed, these events are occurring every six months or so.'

'Like an itch that becomes unbearable to ignore.'

'Correct. That's quite a common theme for a serial killer.'

'Don't most escalate and take too many risks?'

'Yes, but I don't believe this person is like that. He can feel his urge coming and is cool enough to plan accordingly. I can't be sure about that though. If you think about it, he's been operating throughout Europe where his organisation isn't the only one in operation. Many ruthless groups are involved in this mass migration. Trafficking is a part of it, but there'll be gangs simply robbing the migrants at gunpoint. Incidents that will end in death. Those murders have muddied the water, stopping anyone from noticing a pattern.'

Ashley accelerated away from the traffic lights.

'Which suggests if we don't catch this guy, he's liable to perform another ritualistic killing in about five months, if, as we suspect, he killed Camille.'

'Yes. They're probably not exactly six months apart, but close. The moon could be an angle. That or the sun, because the incidents seem to occur just before dawn, but I haven't found any significance for Camille's passing in the lunar calendar.'

Ashley drove, deep in thought. If there were no more related events, and no leads in the hunt for the sunglasses man in the next few weeks, the case would be mothballed. They could revisit it in five months' time, but by then the majority of their resources would have been allocated elsewhere.

She still had that feeling they were missing something. It made her more determined to get Jolanta to talk about her visit.

'What about Akari? Wasn't she to be killed?'

'Probably. Maybe he knew the organisation was failing and decided to take the opportunity that had presented itself. That meant he took extra risks and we almost caught him arriving at the beach to meet Maksim.'

As they arrived at Mile Cross, Ashley noticed Hector fidgeting next to her.

'What is it?'

'I was thinking about what you said about falling in love being the last true adventure.'

Ashley grinned. 'Don't worry about focusing on our investigation.'

'It keeps popping into my mind.'

'Ah, you're plucking up the courage to tell me, as usual, that I'm on the money.'

'Not at all, although there is a small amount of merit in your words.'

'Too kind.'

'I was pondering why Ally and the undercover officers would place themselves in peril at the prison.'

'Okay.'

'What's the overriding reason?'

'A sense of duty? Doing the right thing? Being the best person for the job?'

'Maybe those motivations seal the deal, but I reckon the main driver is the thrill of taking a risk.'

Ashley grinned.

'Which is what makes it genuinely exciting in relationships, especially at the beginning. The fact things often go wrong and there's no safety net.'

'Agreed. The stakes are high. If you genuinely love someone, then your heart is exposed.'

'Then Gabriella can slice it to pieces at will.'

Hector's eyes narrowed. 'I believe now she's free of her responsibilities, she'll start dating.'

Ashley reached over and squeezed his hand.

'And you hope to be in with a chance.'

Hector stared down. 'Are we at the hand-squeezing point in our friendship?'

'I think so.'

Hector curled his lip. 'Luckily for me, we've arrived.'

Jolanta and Maksim's house appeared deserted. The car had gone. They left their vehicle and knocked without getting any response. Ashley looked through the window and could see the TV was off. She frowned at Hector.

'Maybe she's in hiding.'

Ashley noticed the avid gardener from next door was weeding.

'Hi, Dave. Do you know where she went?'

'No, she came back yesterday afternoon. Seemed terribly upset. Didn't even say hello to me, which is unusual. Then she reappeared with a small suitcase and left.'

Ashley wished he'd let her know. She forced a smile onto her face.

'Will you ring me immediately as soon as she returns? It's important.'

'Sure.'

'Don't tell her I was here.'

Dave held her gaze, then nodded.

'In fact, let me know if anybody turns up.'

After thanking him and returning to her car, she tried Jolanta's mobile number again. The phone was still off.

A knot of concern tightened in her stomach.

60

Ashley and most of the team had the weekend off. They agreed they'd all come in if necessary, but, apart from the usual range of low-level crimes, there was nothing to interest them. She spent Saturday on edge, concerned for Ally, who was having an operation on his neck. Sunday morning was ruined fretting about how it had gone, and, finding herself at a loose end, she drove to Peterborough to visit him in the ICU.

When she arrived, Barton had put a uniformed officer at the door. Ashley showed her warrant card and was allowed in. A nurse greeted Ashley, passed her a medical mask to wear, and asked her to wash her hands with antibacterial gel.

'Has he had any visitors?'

'No, not yet. His next of kin is a daughter. She rang yesterday, but she might not make it here until next week.'

Ashley strolled into the large ward where eight beds were spaced out. The nurse directed her to the far corner, then strode back to a bed on the other side, which she began to efficiently strip. The place reminded Ashley of the coma victim during the Paradise Park case. A quiet symphony was occurring. The continuous hum and beep of ventilators, heart-rate monitors, IV pumps, and infusion machines filled the air, like the medical version of a rainforest.

Another nurse was talking on a phone at the desk, eyes scanning the ward, no doubt ready for the next inevitable alarm to sound, but, other than the staff, Ashley was the only other person awake. She took a seat beside Ally. He appeared peaceful, but the bone-white skin on his arms and chest was patterned with a mix of blues, reds and purples. She used to feel silly talking in places like this, but age and experience had taught her to ignore those daft concerns.

'Hi, Ally. Ashley here. All things considered, you don't look too bad. Not quite ready for dating but give it a week. I wanted you to know we've charged the man who did this. He'll never walk the streets again. It looks as though the case is over, so you can stop worrying about that. Focus on getting better. The doctors say you're going to be fine.'

Ashley hoped a little white lie was okay in such circumstances. She noted the thick bandage on his neck, and the brace around that. A few inches either way, and he wouldn't have made it, or he'd never have walked again. She carried on talking to him and was surprised to run out of decent material so fast, so new topics ranged far and wide. She even found herself mentioning Sebastian, Hector, and Gabriella.

After fifteen minutes, a young woman arrived and stood beside the bed.

'Hello,' she said. 'Sorry, I don't know who you are.'

'Hi, I'm Ashley Knight. Ally and I worked together for a long time. Are you his daughter?'

She nodded. 'Sally.'

'I'd heard you couldn't make it until next week.'

'I managed to swap my shift. When they listed his injuries, I was worried he'd die before I got here.'

Ashley suspected there was more to it than that. Surely any company would allow compassionate leave.

'He's hanging in there.'

Sally held his hand for a moment, then kissed him on the forehead. They sat in silence for a few minutes.

Ashley glanced over at Sally, who seemed more confused than upset.

'Are you close?'

Sally shook her head. 'No, not really. I wasn't sure I'd come at all. He's a typical detective, I guess. Bit of a drinker. Bit of a gambler. Adored my mum.'

'I'm sure he loves you, too.'

Sally nodded.

'He tried to reconnect with me in my teens, but what sixteen-year-old girl wants to go to a football match with her mullet-headed father?'

'Not many.'

'And yet I'd give anything to do that now.'

'Things like this make us see what's important. He'll pull through and you'll have what most people never get.'

'What's that?'

'Another chance.'

Sally took some tissues out of her handbag and dabbed her eyes.

'I can't believe he ended up in prison.'

Ashley nodded but didn't comment.

'It's as if I never knew who he was.'

'We all have secrets.'

'Not Dad. I still think it was some kind of undercover thing. He was convincing when I spoke to him about it, but I reckon he'd have been really ashamed about prison. Is there anything I should know?'

Ashley waged an internal war as tears dripped from Sally's chin.

'I couldn't tell you, even if I wanted to. If he was, it would undo everything he hoped to achieve.'

'Do you mean he might have been protecting me by not telling me?'

'Something like that.'

Ashley performed an obvious wink and Sally replied with a small smile.

'Thank you,' she whispered.

Ashley suspected she'd have made the same gesture even if Ally had been dishonest.

Ashley left Sally to be with her father and strolled over to the nurses' desk. She explained she was one of the investigating officers on the case and was interested in the extent of his injuries. The nurse checked her computer.

'DCI Barton is the point of contact. A report was sent to him by the operating surgeon.'

'Fair enough. It just seems odd to me. It looks like he's been beaten to a pulp, then attacked with a knife.'

The middle-aged nurse shrugged and gave her a sad smile. There would be little she hadn't seen.

Ashley frowned. Had Vladimir stabbed *then* battered him, or had he wanted Ally to suffer and beaten him up first?

Bosko spent Saturday on the induction wing at HMP Norwich before being moved to a remand wing. He was banged up in a cell with a young man who had the dead eyes of someone who'd been waiting a long time for his day in court. Bosko knew the feeling. It was like having your life in the deep freeze. The youth said his name was Tee, but only smiled when Bosko asked what it was short for.

Bosko made an effort to talk to him, but he only got single-word responses in reply, so he gave up. The lad, who wore small glasses, read the Bible. Bosko found that questionable behaviour.

Bosko knew from many previous spells of incarceration that any conversation was better than none for passing the time. He had a lot on his mind that he preferred not to focus on. The nights were crawling by, and he was grinding his teeth.

He'd somehow got himself involved in something way out of his league. It seemed Maksim had been in the same boat. Bosko had tried to quiz him about it earlier on the wing and again before he went to court, but Maksim had ignored him. Perhaps he hadn't known much more than Bosko.

The atmosphere was wrong in Norwich jail, too. He knew many of the other inmates. Some by name, others by sight. It should have been a relaxed place for him. Easy time. Yet he sensed people were avoiding him. The tension in the air at Peterborough had followed him. By Monday morning, Bosko realised he was in extreme danger.

It had been a strange life he'd led, and much of it a struggle, but he didn't want to die, which surprised him a little. After pondering over that fact while he ate his breakfast, he concluded that while dying wasn't a huge concern, being killed was, especially by a sly knife in the back.

Bosko could only guess whoever he had worked for was now clearing the board. Dead men couldn't talk. Bosko was a fighter, though. In another life, he'd have been a success. Maybe he could have run his own personal protection business. Bouncing at nightclubs had suited him down to the ground because he enjoyed getting stuck in. In fact, he'd looked forward to things kicking off, even though he'd taken a few severe beatings over the years.

While they waited to be unlocked after the officers had their meeting, Bosko slipped from the top bunk and sat on the seat so he could look at his padmate. Early twenties at a guess, but he wasn't wary of Bosko, despite the dramatic difference in their size.

Bosko waited until the youngster was looking at him. 'I want your weapon.'

'What makes you think I have one?'

'You aren't as scared of me as you should be.'

'Maybe I can handle myself.'

Bosko pressed his hands together, which caused his impressive arm muscles to flex. 'Hand over now.'

Tee remained cool. 'Why should I give it to you?'

'I need to protect myself. Or am I worrying about nothing?'

The lad's lifeless eyes stared into his for a few seconds, then he shrugged.

'There's a decent price on your head. The word was out before you got here. Quite a few people would have been anticipating your arrival.'

'I suspected as much.'

'It's a lot of money.'

Bosko jabbed a thick finger at him. 'You speak plenty all of sudden. Maybe you want reward?'

His cellmate smirked.

'They've already charged me with manslaughter. My defence is that my record is clean of any violence, so that would be a no.'

Tee reached down the side of his leg and removed a blue toothbrush. The handle had been filed to a sharp point.

'Of course, a deterrent is needed here. You can have it on one condition.'

'What?'

'Sort out your problem away from this cell.'

'Is deal.'

There were some dangerous-looking guys on the wing, but few would be murderers. Going to HMP Peterborough first had been to Bosco's benefit. Many prisoners' ears would have pricked up at the prospect of a decent reward, but common sense would have prevailed over the following nights. Getting away with it wouldn't be easy. There was no point in having a big wedge of cash if a judge slapped forty years on your tariff.

Bosko took the toothbrush. It was as simple a weapon as they came, but it would serve a purpose. A slashing tool would be of little use against more than one attacker. He needed to put a man down enough that he wouldn't get up. Plunging the sharp end into the soft part of his foes would work, as long as he did it before they inflicted the same punishment on him.

Bosko took off his T-shirt and grabbed his towel. Tee had a pair of green Crocs, which was a further testament to how long he'd been inside. When the door was unlocked, Bosko slipped his feet into them, took Tee's shampoo out of the cupboard, and stepped onto the landing. Too few people had come out of their cells. The wing workers weren't about.

Bosko headed along the line of doors with his head lowered. When he reached the showers, he casually glanced around. Nobody was following him. He waited. No one came. He growled and returned to his room. Living with the threat of being knifed at any moment was no way to exist. He'd seen men driven mad by it.

Bosko had guessed who the most likely candidates were to fulfil the contract. Of those, two guys stood out above the rest. Career criminals from Albania, known for their ruthless debt collecting. It was their cell he walked to.

Bosko wrapped the towel around his left forearm, then unscrewed the top of the shampoo bottle. He pushed their door open when the officers' backs were turned and strode in. The two men were in a standard cell, which was a tight space for fighting. They were both standing against the window. Bosko squirted the shampoo over the floor in front of them, hoping his footwear coped with it best.

One of the men's faces twisted up. He hurled a curse at Bosko, who threw the shampoo container at his head. Bosko withdrew the toothbrush from his underwear and brandished it. The enraged man took out an object from his pocket. It glinted when a ray of morning sun caught its edge.

Bosko smiled and charged towards him.

62

Monday and Tuesday were long and busy days for Ashley as her team investigated the incident at HMP Norwich. Three men had been rushed to hospital. One was blinded in the right eye and had lost an ear, another leaked four pints of blood from a horrendous bite wound to his left triceps, had six broken bones, and needed surgery to remove half a toothbrush from his abdomen, and then there was Bosko. He sustained over twenty separate injuries. Many were slashes and deep bruises, but the most serious was a punctured liver. He had emerged from the cell on his feet but collapsed further down the landing.

Ashley directed operations from OCC, but Jan, Emma, Morgan and Zelda spent both days at the jail. On Tuesday, they made a trip to the hospital to speak to those involved, but, as expected, nobody was in the mood to talk. One of the Albanians' jaws had to be wired shut, so he at least had an excuse.

Sal had carried on looking into the warehouse where the lad with the nunchucks died. The business had definitely been operating for a decade and was probably a front for forced prostitution all that time. It was a sobering thought.

At seven thirty on Wednesday morning, Ashley was leaving the house when her mobile rang.

'DI Knight.'

'Hello, is that the detective who's been visiting my neighbour?'

'Is that you, Dave?'

'Yes. You sound different on the phone, but I guess that's not uncommon. My wife used to talk like the queen.'

'How can I help?'

'She's here. Jolanta.'

'Thank you, Dave. I really appreciate you calling me. When did she get back?'

'Literally a few minutes ago. Some numbskulls threw some fast-food packaging and beer cans in my garden last night, so I was collecting them when she arrived. Jolanta ignored me again, although she seemed in an awful rush. I suppose she might not have seen me, but in the past we've always exchanged a few words.'

'Okay, let me know if she goes out or if anyone else arrives.'

'Will do.'

Ashley wasn't certain what she'd do in that event. She hadn't had enough to put out a BOLO for Jolanta, but why was the woman avoiding her calls? It was reasonable to want to get away from home for a bit, but Ashley suspected Jolanta knew more than she was letting on. Was she running scared? Her husband, Maksim, was in jail, so he couldn't be an imminent threat. Was her involvement the concern, or was it more likely the visit from the sunglasses guy? Maybe he'd told her to leave, or, more probably, she was planning to flee with her daughter.

Ashley knew she had to drive straight there, but it didn't make sense going on her own. Jolanta could be up to her ears in it and therefore dangerous.

Barry lived a couple of villages away. He answered quickly when she rang him.

'This is harassment,' he said by way of answering.

'I assume by that you haven't left for work yet.'

'You assume correctly.'

'I'll be at yours in five minutes. Jolanta's returned to her house, and she's behaving unusually.'

'I said we should have kept her under surveillance.'

'And I told you we didn't have the evidence to do so. There's been enough bending of the rules lately.'

Ashley cut the call and set off. Barry lived with his grandmother in Sidestrand. A fact he didn't advertise, but Ashley thought it was sweet. Although it was probably because she did everything for him, right down to making his packed lunch.

The weather had deteriorated, and it was a chilly morning. The sky, forged from steel, stretched endlessly out of sight. Rhythmic heavy raindrops beat the windscreen like a war drum marshalling courage for the coming battle.

Barry, looking dapper in a suit Ashley hadn't seen before, was peering nervously upward as she approached his house. He leapt breathlessly into the car and rubbed his hands together.

'Morning,' he said. 'Feels as if the clouds are about to touch the ground out there.'

Ashley grinned at his clothes.

'Nice threads. If your tie had been gold, I'd have assumed you were getting married later.'

'There's nothing wrong with looking smart.'

'Bullshit. More like you've got your eye on some poor unsuspecting victim at OCC. Who is it this time? That new cleaner with the purple hair? If she's been around your desk before, you're going to be out of luck.'

'Very funny.'

'Please don't tell me it's the new girl on Reception?'

He looked out of the window at his side of the vehicle.

'Barry! She's about twelve.'

'She's nineteen, and, no, it's not her. She already has a boyfriend.'

'Jeez, and not Gabriella. I hear Mark's crept into prime position.'

A beaming Barry turned back to her.

'Nope. Apparently, he love bombed her, so she dumped him on Friday night.'

'What the hell does that mean?'

'I wasn't sure. Google says it's to do with psychological and emotional control featuring over-the-top shows of affection and flattery.'

Ashley chuckled.

'Sounds to me like the poor guy was just keen. Swift work by you, though. He's probably not taken his slippers home yet.'

Barry crossed his arms. 'It didn't get that far.'

'How do you know all this?'

'Mark confided in Gill, who let it slip to Francis, who told me.'

'The police grapevine at its finest.'

Ashley explained her concerns about Jolanta to Barry.

He frowned.

'So, you think this mystery guy threatened to hurt their child, and she was furious with Maksim for putting her at risk?'

'Correct. When I went to see Ally, his daughter was there. She knew nothing about his police life, and it made me consider how parents protect their children, or, in Jolanta's case, how angry and unforgiving they are when people place them in danger.'

'Husband or not?'

'Exactly.'

'Okay, what part do you want me to play if she's still at home?'

'You're the punchbag if some heavies turn up.'

Barry shot her a dirty look. 'Hey, what about my new suit?'

63

Ashley spent the remainder of the journey worried that Dave would ring to say Jolanta had left, but her phone remained silent. When they arrived, Jolanta was loading a suitcase into the boot of her car. Ashley parked and leapt out.

'Hi, Jolanta. I've been trying to reach you.'

Ashley didn't need to be a detective to recognise the alarm in the woman's face. She retreated from Ashley as if she were a potential mugger.

'We'd like a word in the house, please.'

Jolanta turned and strode back to her front door, opened it and walked inside, leaving the way clear. Ashley and Barry followed her into a small lounge, where Maksim's wife perched on the edge of an armchair.

Ashley took the seat beside her. Barry sat opposite on the sofa and got his notebook out.

'What do you have to tell us?' asked Ashley.

'Nothing,' replied Jolanta without looking up. Her hair was pulled back in a messy ponytail, which she went to adjust, then thought better of it. Crumpled clothes and jeans with mud on the bottom of them completed her look. Whereas before she'd worn thick make-up, now she had none. Appearances mattered little when lives were at stake.

'How did the visit with Maksim go?'

'Bad. It was very bad.'

'Can you tell me why?'

Jolanta cringed. 'No.'

Ashley wondered whether to play soft or hard. She found people who weren't normally criminals didn't know the rules.

'You could always come to the station. We need to understand what's going on. You'll be home by teatime.'

Jolanta shook her head. A sob escaped from deep within her chest. Eastern Europeans were also used to much more forceful police. Kindness often disarmed them.

'Shall I make us a cup of tea?' asked Ashley.

Jolanta rose from her seat. 'I'll do it.'

She moved swiftly out of the room. Ashley shifted along the sofa to check she wasn't escaping out of the back door, but Jolanta went straight to the kettle and filled it from the tap.

The lounge was full of pictures of the family. How quickly things could change. Ashley scanned the photographs. Some were from years ago. A little girl on what looked like her first bike. Smiling at a Disney park. Another one outside what was probably a university. Maksim's bushy facial hair only featured in the more recent ones.

Ashley shouted out to Jolanta, who was smelling the milk bottle.

'How often did Maksim grow a beard?'

'Never while he was a mechanic. It was cold in the factory.'

She returned carrying a tray holding three mugs and a little jug of milk. There was a silver jar with sugar in and an empty porcelain one for the teabags. Anyone with anything serious to hide would likely have refused Ashley's request, which meant Ashley was convinced Jolanta hadn't been involved in the criminal operation.

'You look like a tight family,' said Ashley, gesturing to the photos.

'We were.'

Jolanta sat, sniffed, then bowed her head again. She rocked slightly in her chair and seemed in no shape to withstand direct questioning.

'What kind of threats did they make?'

Jolanta froze.

'Did they threaten to hurt your daughter?'

The woman's fingers trembled.

'You can tell us. We'll make sure she's safe.'

Jolanta's head came up. Her bloodshot eyes stared at Ashley. 'What about my husband?'

'Did they say they'd hurt him, too?'

Ashley couldn't hear the response. 'Pardon?'

The frightened woman spoke louder.

'Kill. They promised to kill them both.'

Ashley took a moment to consider what she needed to know.

'Did the man with the sunglasses make the threats?'

'I can't tell you. He said he'd know.'

Barry had managed to keep quiet until that point.

'His words mean nothing. They've murdered before.'

Jolanta flinched.

'It's true,' said Ashley. 'We must hear every word he told you, then we can protect your daughter and Maksim.'

Tears poured from Jolanta's eyes.

Ashley thought back to the last time she'd been in this house. Jolanta had been concerned, but not terrified.

'He came to see you again, didn't he?'

There was an almost imperceptible nod of the head.

'Before your visit?'

'Yes.'

'Did Maksim say anything to you?'

Another slight shake of her head.

'Did he apologise?'

A stronger shake of the head. How could Ashley get this lady to talk? She thought of Bosko.

'There was a man arrested around the same time as Maksim. A bit player like him. He got badly assaulted in jail a few days ago and was close to dying.'

Ashley waited for Jolanta to respond, but the words didn't seem to register. Ashley glanced again at the photographs. The couple were so much in love. She pictured the woman staring impassively at Maksim in the visits room. No emotion except anger, but she'd looked nervous when she arrived. Or was she petrified?

Ashley's stomach flipped as a terrible possibility dawned on her.

'Jolanta. Was the man you visited in Peterborough prison your husband?'

64

Jolanta's head rose. Her lips in a grim, tight line.

'No, he was not.'

Barry exploded. 'Who the hell was he?'

Jolanta cringed. Ashley gave him a warning glance.

'Had you seen him before?'

'He looked like Maksim. Same size, same beard. Similar hair, but not my husband, no.'

Ashley took a deep breath.

'Did you know before the visit you weren't meeting Maksim?'

'Yes. The man in the sunglasses arrived just before I left. I think he waited until I went to my car.'

'Why didn't you say something?'

'I couldn't.'

'Because they would hurt your family.'

A sob wracked Jolanta's body. 'They had videos.'

'Of what?'

Jolanta covered her face for a few seconds, then steeled herself, but spoke through her fingers.

'My daughter's flat. They filmed her going inside. That's

where I've been. I took her to an old friend's place in Nottingham. Someone I can rely on. I only returned to fetch my things.'

Ashley marvelled at how she'd held it together to protect her daughter in such a pressurised situation.

'What did the man tell you to do in the prison?'

'Pretend I was angry. To sit there and say little. Then I must sit tight and tell nobody. They would return Maksim to me, and we would all be fine.'

Barry frowned. 'I don't get it.'

Neither did Ashley, at first, but the synapses in her brain were firing. The person they'd arrested at Winterton had been impersonating Maksim.

'Shit,' she said quietly, staring at Barry. 'At the beach with the girl in the boot, he told us he was only a driver. He clearly wasn't.'

Barry caught up fast.

'He was there to—' He stopped mid-sentence, aware of Jolanta, who had placed her hands over her face, then mouthed 'sacrifice' to Ashley.

'Yes.'

Her mind was racing. 'That car which arrived but we couldn't trace. It wasn't there to meet him.'

Barry shook his head. 'They were picking him up.'

Jolanta uncovered her face. The stunning lady they'd met a few days prior was gone. Exhaustion had etched itself onto her face, accentuated by dark circles under sore eyes.

'He's dead, isn't he?'

'We don't know that.'

'I'm not stupid. The criminal in the visit hall has been impersonating my husband. They sucked Maksim in. Fooled him, so they could pretend to be him.' Jolanta's voice rose into a screech as she finished the sentence. 'But why? I don't understand.'

'I still don't get it,' said Barry.

'Get what?' asked Ashley.

'Why have her go to the prison and act like he's Maksim?'

'So we don't suspect we captured someone rich and powerful.'

'Yes, but he already had us fooled. Whatever, he's in prison. There's no way he'll beat the charge when he was driving a car with a snatched child inside it. We'd have probably found out it wasn't him at some point, anyway. Ring the jail and tell them to keep him in his cell until we arrive.'

Ashley got up and walked into the kitchen. Barry followed and closed the door.

'You're right. That's a lot of effort, for what reason?' Ashley grabbed her phone from her pocket, then almost dropped it. 'Oh, no.'

Barry's eyes widened. 'What is it?'

'He's at court this morning.'

65

Barry shrugged.

'That's okay. We'll ring Peterborough Crown and tell them to keep him locked in the cells.'

Ashley's eyes darted to the time on her phone. It was five past nine.

'No, it's too early. The first case isn't heard until ten, and the jail is fifteen minutes away, if that.'

Barry swallowed hard. 'He might already be in transit.'

'Yes.'

'Bloody hell, although won't he be cuffed in the van?'

'No, there's no need. The prison transport enters the nick to load them onboard. There's nowhere for them to run because the jail is secure. They'd only cuff him if he was kicking off. The handcuffs only go on when they arrive for them to be escorted off the van to the cells at the court.'

Barry raised his hands. 'Who do we contact first?'

'Call Control. Give them a full update. Once the van leaves the prison, it's a police issue. They'll know the exact number to contact. We need to provide as much information as possible.'

She had the director's details in her phone, so she found him and pressed dial. It began to ring. The kitchen door opened. Jolanta stared at them with a horrified expression. Ashley's call was answered. Passing the message on was too important to worry about Jolanta listening.

'HMP Peterborough. Nigel Reader.'

'It's DI Ashley Knight. We have a big problem. Maksim Wozniak is not who we think he is. He's someone far more dangerous. Did he go to court today?'

'I'll have to check to be certain. Hang on. My office isn't far from the gatehouse. They'll know exactly where he is, but they don't always pick up the phone. Thirty seconds.'

Ashley heard a door open, then heavy steps as Reader left his office. His footsteps echoed as he went down some stairs. Keys jangled. Locks clanged. She followed Barry's conversation behind her.

Reader had kept his mobile to his mouth. *'Morning, David. Has the court transport left?'*

'Yes, sir. A few minutes ago.'

'Thank you.'

Ashley's blood ran cold. She heard a phone handset being picked up. There was a pause. She could just make out the other end.

'Reception. Officer Saxon.'

'Bill, it's Nigel Reader. Maksim Wozniak was on the court list today. Did he go?'

'Yes. Full bus of six. Took some loading.'

'Did he cause trouble?'

'No, he was sweet as a baby. A couple of the YOs kicked off, but Maksim was nice as pie. Almost too nice.'

'Okay, thanks.'

'Ashley. He was on the vehicle, and they've left the jail.'

'Understood. Local police are being informed. I'll be in touch.'

Ashley cut the line before he had a chance to realise what she was implying, but there was nothing Reader could do. She looked at Barry, who had his call on hold.

'Well?' she asked.

'Cambridgeshire police are told in advance of the route taken each day. Every available unit is heading to various points along it. They're contacting the logistics company that transports the prisoners. They'll tell the driver to turn around and return to the jail.'

'Okay. Inform Control the van left a couple of minutes ago. There are five other inmates onboard with the man we thought was Maksim, and that includes two young offenders.'

Ashley nibbled a finger while Barry repeated her words to Control. Perhaps they were worrying over nothing. He finished his call and looked at his watch grimly.

Tension tightened its grip on Ashley. Had they warned Peterborough police in time?

They'd know soon enough.

66

Prisoner Custody Officer Hywel Jones waited for the barrier to be lifted, then slipped the engine into gear. He looked over at his partner for the day.

'Hay fever again?'

Shehman stared back through rheumy eyes and spoke with a croak.

'Yes. I get it bad this time of year.'

'You can crack the window if you want.'

'Actually, that makes it worse. The pollen gets in.'

Hywel drove straight through the next roundabout, having checked the day's route beforehand. They varied the journey, but he couldn't see the point of it. There was only one way out of the prison, and for the first five hundred metres a car could easily follow them, but Hywel had never experienced any trouble. It wasn't as if they were transporting Al Capone.

The previous Friday, Hywel had driven the vehicle that transferred the man who stabbed a prison officer at HMP Peterborough to HMP Belmarsh. He hadn't been concerned then either, although that time they'd been given two armed escorts. The guys today were nothing special.

They'd told them during training that anyone trying to escape from a van was an idiot. One, it wasn't easy – police officers would be on the scene in minutes – and two, the chances of them vanishing and staying that way were negligible. You needed a wedge of cash and a lot of support to evade justice, and 99.9 per cent of all prisoners didn't have either. That was probably why they ended up in their predicament in the first place.

Not only that, but, upon capture, it was back to court for a further extension of your sentence. Sneaking home and shagging your girlfriend a couple of times, or, worse, finding her in bed with your best mate, was hardly worth another year inside.

Hywel went through a green light past the hospital, took a left at the roundabout, and accelerated down a slip road to merge onto the parkway. The traffic was reasonable, but a little Renault in front was driving slowly. He had to brake sharply, which caused a chorus of complaints from the men being bounced around in the small booths.

In his driver's side mirror, Hywel saw a white Ford panel van pull out sharply, so he wasn't the only one who'd taken evasive action. At the Thomas Cook roundabout, his route took him to another slip road, which had a steep decline. The panel van pulled in behind him, cutting up a red vehicle. There was only one lane to turn left and Hywel hoped the driver was aware of the sharp bend at the bottom of the slip road or he ran the risk of driving into the back of him.

'Base to PT44, are you receiving?'

Shehman grabbed the radio. 'PT44 receiving.'

'You've been requested to return to the prison immediately.'

Shehman frowned at Hywel. 'We're on the parkway approaching the Holiday Inn roundabout.'

'Understood. At that roundabout, turn around and return the way you came. A police escort will be with you shortly.'

'Confirmed. Returning to base. PT44 out.'

Hywel noticed a flash of movement in his wing mirror. The white van was accelerating hard on the outside lane. The hairs on his arms and neck stood to attention. Behind the van, a red estate car swerved and stopped across both lanes. Brakes screeched. Horns blared out.

'Bugger,' he said.

'What is it?' asked Shehman.

'Press the alarm.'

The Ford passed them, then veered into their path. Impact was unavoidable.

'Shit!' shouted Shehman.

Hywel rammed his foot on the brake pedal. Howls of protest came from the prisoners behind him. The van braked with them, and they touched. Metal ground on metal. Hywel had no option but to stop or he would have driven into the muddy bank at the edge of the road. His knees had turned to jelly, and he stalled the engine. One youngster in the back bellowed out they were fucking pricks.

Time slowed. Hywel thought of his baby boy and tired wife as he'd kissed them goodbye that morning while they'd both slept. His lad had moved a little, but Gail had been out for the count. Their scent came to him, then was gone.

A guy with brown hair and sunglasses appeared from the Ford van. Hywel's bladder tightened when he recognised what the man held.

Protocol was to cooperate. The van's alarm was linked to the police station, which was beyond some trees on the other side of the dual carriageway. They would be here soon. Control had told them that, too. Hywel remembered the red estate. He could see the snarled-up traffic behind it. Help would be delayed.

The end of the shotgun was pressed against the glass a few inches from Hywel's head now. The glass was supposed to be reinforced, but he doubted that would stop the contents of a shell blasted from a few millimetres away. Without overtime, Hywel earned twenty-two thousand pounds a year. He opened his door.

The man calmly stepped back, but kept the weapon trained on him.

'You have ten seconds to live. Get out, open the side door. Let the prisoner with the beard out first, Maksim Wozniak, then the rest of them. One mistake, and it's boom in the face for both of you. Now move!'

Hywel staggered as he got out but managed not to fall, his legs oddly leaden as he lurched around the vehicle. He dropped his keys, but they were on a chain. He grabbed them up, opened the door, and stepped into the enclosed space of the van interior. The bearded guy had been the last to load. He was crouched and staring through the observation panel. Hywel unlocked his door, and Maksim slipped straight past him and outside. Then Hywel released the others one by one.

'What the fuck?' asked one of the youths.

'You can get out.'

'Is this a fucking joke? We're on a dual carriageway.'

Two of the other prisoners were old. They appeared confused and scared. Hywel left them in their seats and stepped from the van. A suited man in his mid-thirties followed him out, then the two young offenders. The foul-mouthed youth stared at the white van parked in front of them, then at the traffic jam a hundred metres away. Some cars had started using the hard shoulder to go around the sideways red car, which was also moving again.

The lad laughed at his mate. 'Damn, man, it's an ambush. Let's bounce.'

They took off on their toes along the hard shoulder. The guy holding the shotgun and Maksim were scrambling up the mud under a pedestrian bridge. Hywel spotted the fence at the top had been cut. He zoned back in. Multiple sirens sounded in the distance. The red car, driven by a man wearing a mask, roared past him.

The suited fellow looked aghast. He shook his head. 'This had nothing to do with me. I'm only in for a commercial burglary.'

Shehman got out of his seat and projectile-vomited onto the tarmac. Ahead, the boys were sprinting along the next slip road and would soon be out of sight. There was nobody in view at the top of the bank.

Thirty seconds later, a marked police car screeched to a halt, lights flashing, sirens howling, in the fast lane on the opposite side of them. A uniformed woman leapt out from behind the wheel and stepped over the crash barrier.

'Where are they?' she hollered.

Hywel tried to speak, but no sound came out.

'Have they gone?' she shouted.

'Yes,' he finally managed. 'They went that way.'

She followed his pointed finger up the bank to the gap in the wire fence. A police van braked sharply next to the female officer, having weaved its way through the melee, and two men leapt out.

'Come on, follow me,' said the woman.

The three coppers strode towards the bridge.

'Wait!' shouted Hywel. 'They have a shotgun.'

The officers came to an abrupt stop. It appeared the police weren't paid enough for certain things, either, but then they began to edge up the bank.

67

Ashley didn't have time to obsess over what their investigation might have missed, because Jolanta had pulled a coat on.

'I'm not staying here.'

'Wait, Jolanta,' said Ashley. 'I'll ask Notts police to meet you where your daughter is. They'll give you a number to ring if you feel unsafe.'

Jolanta sneered.

'Right. At this moment, the only people who know her location are me and my friend. You can email me when you've got your act together. My phone will be off.'

She strode past them, slid the bolt on the back door, then returned to the lounge, where two carrier bags of clothes sat on the bottom of the stairs. She grabbed them with one hand, opened the front door, and stepped outside.

Ashley and Barry had little choice but to follow.

'I haven't got your email, Jolanta,' said Ashley.

Barry recorded it as she spat out the words, then they both watched as Jolanta locked the door, jumped in her car, and rushed away.

Barry puffed out his cheeks.

'We've had better mornings.'

They drove back to OCC expecting a call from Control, but nothing came until they were parking, when they were told there had been an ambush and an escape. Ashley sent Barry to enter his notes into the system while she headed to Kettle's office. He was slamming the phone down when she entered. In all the years she'd known him, she'd never seen him do that.

'This case is really affecting you.'

Kettle massaged his forehead. He glanced up at her. Heavy circles had formed under his eyes.

'My first murder, a neighbour took a kid. We interviewed the entire cul-de-sac, but didn't pin it on the guy responsible until it was too late. I've never forgotten how I felt afterwards.'

Ashley understood. Successes faded. It was the failures that remained vivid. There was something so awful about children going about their lives, unaware that evil lurked in their neighbourhoods. If you were the detective who'd missed an opportunity to save a child, or if you were just too late, the memories were never far away.

She dropped into a seat opposite him.

'It's no wonder the police never caught this guy. His planning is off the scale. I take it he escaped.'

'Yes, he did, and you're right. Bosko and the Romanians went to court and there were no issues. Vladimir got escorted under armed guard to Belmarsh. No problems. Maksim had been the one to warn the officer that Ally had been assaulted. He fooled us all.'

'Remember when we had him in custody, and how he behaved on the wing? He acted subservient to Vladimir the whole time.'

'While Vladimir was prepared to murder to give him the

chance to escape, even if it meant spending the rest of his life in jail.'

'Who the hell is he?'

Kettle inhaled deeply and exhaled slowly.

'I feel sick to the stomach you almost found out in time. Brilliant work, by the way. You had a feeling back at the jail. What else did Jolanta tell you?'

Ashley repeated what they'd uncovered.

'Jeez,' was all Kettle could say.

'Reading between the lines, Maksim was approached because his appearance closely matched the man who's just absconded.'

'God, I hope it wasn't Typhon.'

'It has to be someone of extreme importance for them to go to these lengths. I don't think they'd do it for a rich customer. It's too risky. There's been some incredible forethought in all of this. From the manipulation of Maksim to this morning's escape. What happened with the prison transport?'

Kettle huffed with disgust.

'There was only one man in a van and one in an estate, if you can believe it. There might have been other vehicles nearby as backup, but the red estate car blocked the carriageway while the van shunted the prison vehicle into the side of the road. That bloody guy with the sunglasses appeared with a shotgun and gets Maksim off the bus. They raced up a bank under a pedestrian bridge. There are four directions in which they could disappear. A housing estate, Bluebell Wood, Thorpe Meadows, or through Ferry Meadows. All of which have plenty of exit routes.'

'Has nobody seen anything? Two grown men running, one in prison grey, must have caught someone's attention. I know the area. There are loads of retired people living there. They'll be out cycling, walking dogs, jogging.'

Kettle shook his head.

'All available officers are at the scene talking to residents. But if he had a car waiting on Holywell Way, he could have slipped out of the city in no time. They're desperately scanning the nearby cameras, but every minute they take doing that means he could be a mile further away.'

'What about the red estate?'

'Already on fire in a car park at Orton Mere. Again, there are multiple routes away from that location, too. We can't get the helicopter until this afternoon. They could be hiding somewhere nearby, but they've been so clinical. A clever man would have swapped vehicles by now. Peterborough's parkway network is so efficient, local police lack the officers to close off more than a few roads, but they'd likely be closing the gate after the nag has bolted anyway.'

Ashley tried to think of a solution, but they'd been played for novices.

Kettle rolled his neck.

'Let's try to get our heads around this. If it was Typhon who impersonated Maksim, it seems a complicated way of covering himself if he got caught.'

Ashley gave him half a smile because she'd worked it out.

'This escape plan was a bonus. The Typhon operation has been dismantled and is finished in Europe. They were on the run. England was their last stronghold, so they fled here. What would be the easiest way to come and go, and, if we're honest, the method we'd least expect?'

Kettle closed his eyes. 'Oh, God.'

'As they pulled Maksim into their circle, he was travelling back and forth using his passport without concern. I suspect he was ferrying people who could legally travel to give him a false sense of security. On his last trip, he finds his new pals have become unfriendly. His passport is taken, and Typhon, if that's who he is, can journey to the UK with ease.'

'At least he's going to be stuck here. I bet if he's using other people's IDs, then his birth name is on the police's wanted list in his home country.'

'Yeah, I'll get Sal onto Border Force to do the necessary. The cheeky bastard probably flew into Norwich airport.' Ashley shook her head. 'What else can we do?'

'The manhunt is under way. We have to hope we catch him somewhere. I'm on the news at lunch.'

'Won't Barton do the press conference from Peterborough?'

'No, it's our case, and I reckon our escapee will return to Norfolk. He clearly had a safe place here until we caught him in Winterton.'

Ashley chuckled.

'I can see it now. If anyone's seen a bearded man and one with sunglasses, please ring...'

Kettle laughed. 'That's the spirit.'

A dejected Ashley returned to her desk. She gathered her team and broke the news. A sea of depressed faces stared back at her. They'd all suspected this would be a career-defining case for them.

Those suspicions had been confirmed, but for all the wrong reasons.

68

Ashley was clearing her desk to leave on Friday afternoon when Hector came and stood beside her, a cryptic message in his eyes.

'Got a minute?'

'Sure.'

She followed him to the conference room, where his team was packing up. There was only the other male officer present, but Ashley detected an atmosphere.

'Is it more intel too late?'

'In a way, but I'm not certain if it would have helped us. Do you remember what you said to me at the end of the Paradise Park case?'

'That I'm always right and don't you forget it.'

'You regularly say that, so it's possible, but I was referring to your comment that sometimes we don't so much solve cases, as chase them to their conclusion.'

'Yes.'

'Well, this is similar.'

'Apart from the fact the two men we're searching for have

vanished off the face of the earth, and we don't even know their names.'

Hector gave her a hint of a smile.

'We sent the DNA of Bosko and the man we thought was Maksim to be checked in Europe after the success we had with Vladimir's profile. Bosko had no matches, so he probably wasn't involved over there. I suspect he was unfortunate to get involved with them when he was looking for work.'

'Or DNA capture wasn't up to much back then.'

'Well, maybe, but our data suggests he's spent nearly his whole adult life in the UK. He came to England with a Hungarian passport, but they haven't issued him with another one, and he's never had a UK passport.'

'So Bosko was little more than a security guard.'

'Yes, but we have a match with the other profile. You remember the girl who was strangled in Giethoorn?'

Ashley nodded, her interest piqued. 'Yep.'

'The DNA found on her clothes belonged to the man we thought was Maksim.'

'Did the Dutch have a name?'

'No, but it confirms he was in contact with the victim. It's not a coincidence.'

'I suppose that's a help for when we find him, but not exactly cast-iron proof he was responsible for her demise.'

The other member of Hector's team rose from his seat, picked up the box he'd been putting things in, and stuck it under his arm.

'I'm heading off, Hector. I'll see you in London on Monday.'

'Of course, Vince. Thanks for your efforts this week.'

Vince didn't reply.

Ashley watched him yank his coat off the back of a chair and disappear.

'Is all the disappointment getting to your people, Hector?'

'I guess it has been a brutal and unsatisfying couple of weeks, but no, it's not just that.'

She frowned at him when he didn't volunteer any more. 'Go on, you chump. Spit it out?'

'I'd left to attend a meeting with Beckett but forgot my folder, so I came back after about fifteen minutes. Vince was chatting animatedly with Gabriella. They both stopped talking when I returned, and she left shortly afterwards. At the door, Vince said he'd see her on Saturday night.'

Ashley pulled a face.

'Oh dear. Shall I hug you again?'

'Very funny. He knew I liked her, and I've struggled to be civil with him since.' Hector's eyes blazed. 'Wait a minute! Did you know when we were in the car she was seeing other people?'

'Erm, no.'

'How about you spit it out?'

'She's simply letting her hair down now she has fewer responsibilities. I doubt she's sleeping with them.'

Hector's face fell. 'Them?'

'We can talk about it tonight. What time are you finishing?'

'I'll be here until late and all day tomorrow with what I've uncovered.'

'Is it that important you can't finish whatever it is in the morning?'

'I want to make sure the right departments are ready to go on Monday, but I also need to feed the news to the team hunting for the escapees. It probably won't help, but I should do it anyway. We've still got data trickling in from all over. I'm free on Sunday and definitely in the mood for some drinks.'

'Stay over at mine. I heard there's a band on at The Fishing Boat, and they do a decent bar menu.'

'Deal. Now, stop distracting me. You're going to want to hear this. We asked all the countries if they had any similar cases to ours in living memory. Strangulation deaths are pretty rare. Some of the countries had poor record-keeping in the past, but a few gave us a variety of incidents. One is very promising.'

Hector walked over to the map on the wall. He'd somehow fitted even more pins in it. He pointed to a bunch of them.

'This is Slovenia. There's a place called Piran, which has a few lighthouses. It's an area where they speak Italian and Slovene. Over thirty years ago, a young woman was murdered near one of the lighthouses.'

'Strangled?'

'Yes, and raped. Actually, they weren't sure of that. The intercourse may have been consensual.'

'That's not the same as what we're dealing with here.'

'Hold your horses. The authorities didn't solve the case, and the file was left open. There were two brothers spotted behaving shiftily in the area the previous week. The majority of Slovenia is landlocked, except for a tiny sliver of land reaching out into the Adriatic Sea. The Slovene police traced the men to a farm further inland, where they'd both worked for a few months.'

'So, you have their names?'

'Yes. The brothers very much kept themselves to themselves, but the supervisor had taken their details for tax purposes. The younger brother was tall with brown hair and in thrall to the older one, who was shorter and stockier. They had returned for their things and left the night before the girl was discovered. There was a sighting of both of them in Trieste a week later, which is a few hours across the Italian border. The younger one's name was Ratimir Chernoff.'

'Sounds like our man with the sunglasses.'

'Yes,' replied Hector. 'And the older brother was named Trifon.'

69

Ashley still had the weekend off. Knowing the names didn't help much, unless the European police looked into them further and found a trail. She spent Saturday doing the past fortnight's undone housework, which was nearly all of it. She washed clothes, changed the bedding, shopped for food, had a half-arsed attempt at gardening, then fell asleep in front of some old episodes of *Friends* after drinking a bottle of red and eating a tub of chicken noodles from the Chinese at Suffield Park. When she woke, there was a chunk of Dairy Milk stuck to her cheek.

Sunday morning passed swiftly with hoovering, dusting and tidying before the judgemental weasel was due to appear. At midday, Ashley knew Hector had arrived. Not that she heard his fancy, silent electric car. It was Arthur next door wishing him a good afternoon before he knocked.

Hector stepped inside the house and gave her a quick peck on the cheek. He glanced around suspiciously at her pristine lounge.

'Did I drive through a portal to another dimension on the way here?'

'Ha ha. No, I've changed.'

'Rubbish. You just didn't want me realising you're more of a messy piglet than you actually are.'

Ashley noticed his little suitcase on wheels.

'It is one night you're staying, isn't it?'

They set off in high spirits on the thirty-minute stroll to East Runton. Hector came to a halt when they reached the point on the clifftop where the white steps went down to the promenade. He pulled in the sea air.

'Shall we walk on the sand?'

'Not in these shoes.'

Hector raised an eyebrow at her latest purchase from Next. A pair of zip-up, navy-blue, leather, ankle-high cowboy boots.

'Should I be concerned? I'm leaving if there's line dancing.'

Ashley leaned on the railings beside him. 'Why have we stopped?'

Hector spread his arms wide.

'This view,' he said. 'The pier. People walking on the beach. Splashing kids. Running dogs. The huge blue sky. Cloud trails stretching to the horizon. This is what Cromer means to me. I'm not sure I truly got it before, but just looking at this view makes my muscles untense and my breathing slow.'

Ashley hooked her arm through his and dragged him up the path.

'Okay, you've persuaded me. You can live with me when you come back after your little project finishes.'

She felt him tense.

'Is that a no?'

Hector stopped and stared ahead.

'Part of me would love that, but it would be a backward step. What I need is mentoring in a big busy city environment with different problems from London and Cromer. Somewhere like

Manchester, Bradford or Newcastle. Sorry, but I don't believe I'll be returning. There are sad memories here, too.'

'Gabriella?'

'Yes. I get I'm being daft. We were only friends and probably not even that.' Hector's gaze dropped to the pavement. 'I suppose I've been a fool.'

'True love always encounters difficulties.'

'Are you quoting Shakespeare at me?'

'Barry said it to me, but he was talking about supporting Norwich City Football Club.'

'Idiot.'

'Well, from one fool to another, let's get leathered and forget all our woes for a while.'

'I've got work tomorrow.'

Ashley dragged him onwards. 'Don't worry, Grandpa, I'll have you home and tucked in by nine. The band come on at three. We can have a pie containing unspecified animal meat first to line our stomachs.'

'Sounds disgusting.'

'Rubbish. You'll wake in the morning with a hairy chest, your voice two octaves deeper, and immediately insist, from then on, that everyone calls you Bernard.'

'I really will have gone to a different dimension.'

Ashley entered the pub to a cheer. It wasn't rammed, but most of the tables were taken and the customers present sounded as if they'd been there since opening time. The applause was for a man who'd slipped off his stool at the bar. The landlady, Sue, helped him back onto it and slapped him playfully on the shoulder.

'That's your first warning!'

Ashley waved at the other staff as they waited to be served. Rob and Glen were preparing the stage for the band. Jane and

Regan scurried around with large plates of steaming food. The barmaid, Lucy, grinned at Hector, then winked at Ashley.

'Ooh, the girls will be pleased you've brought your friend. I'll prepare the guest bedroom.' She leaned forward conspiratorially and spoke loud enough for everyone nearby to hear. 'Which is actually the dungeon.'

Ashley chuckled. Hector not so much.

They took their drinks to a table. A pint of Stella for her and a whisky for him.

Ashley gulped a mouthful of lager. 'Scott's daughter's having a baby.'

Hector sipped his drink and considered what she'd said for a few moments.

'Which, if you'd got with him, in some ways would have made you a granny.'

'Yes.' She curled her lip. 'I know it's stupid to think like that.'

Hector nudged her with his elbow.

'You have Bhavini and her son. Evil Godmother is a much more suitable label for you.'

'Funny you should mention that. I've got Bee's baby for a few hours on my own next Saturday, which is a bit scary. I'm going to push him around Cromer so she and her mum can have afternoon tea at The Cliftonville.'

'Fabulous, I love that place. I could sit there and nibble at sandwiches, drink Earl Grey, eat cake, and enjoy their sea view all day long.'

'Said no man ever, well, certainly no copper.'

'Afternoon tea is a civilised experience.'

'Go on, pick a coronary-clogging pastry product from the menu. I'm starving.'

Fifteen minutes later, Hector ordered their food and got

another round in. He appeared shifty afterwards and she chuckled at him.

'What did you ask for?'

'Spinach and ricotta cannelloni for me, and roadkill pie for you.'

'Fabulous, my favourite.'

Ashley picked up her fresh pint.

'I was wondering, now you've been promoted, how did you get on giving instructions to the guys who used to be the same rank as you?'

'Most of the staff in London only knew me as a sergeant and nearly everyone was helpful and polite.'

'I meant since you returned to OCC.'

'No problems. Everyone's pretty professional here.'

'Even Barry?'

'No, not Barry. I only asked him to do one thing. It was to find me a file. He told me to piss off and do it myself.'

Ashley's drink dribbled down her chin as she laughed.

Hector shook his head.

'I could make Chief Constable and he'd still call me Fast Track.'

They enjoyed their meals and each other's company. When the band came on at three, the pub got even busier. The singer was a guy called Vic Salter, who did a great Chuck Berry. Ashley found herself clapping along enthusiastically as more pints went down. Hector was quiet.

'What's up?'

'Just feeling gloomy. I thought I'd be given a slight stay of execution with us knowing who Typhon really is, even though that intel is ancient, but the files have gone to NCA headquarters in London. My team and I are definitely leaving with them, and I'll return to my old role. I feel a touch jaded.'

'I'm glad you've enjoyed being here, even though the case was horrific.'

'I had been looking forward to learning under an experienced inspector.' Hector knocked his whisky back. 'It's a shame there wasn't one about.'

Ashley laughed.

'Yes, if there was, we'd have probably done better. I don't reckon the shit has hit the fan yet over the prison debacle. By the time your current role is finished at the end of the year, I'll be wearing white cotton gloves on the A47, and you'll find Kettle peeling carrots in the staff canteen. Beckett will be swinging from a gibbet under Jarrold Bridge.'

Hector grinned. 'I'm not so sure.'

'You think he'll evade scrutiny?'

'Nice phrase.'

'Thanks.'

'Consider this. The newspapers knew nothing about the operation. Any news about what really goes on in our prisons is highly restricted. Ally is in a coma in hospital. Yes, that's bad, but the Typhon organisation is crushed. We suspect the brothers to be from Slovenia and have their names. We have a reasonable idea of their appearances, so they'd struggle to operate here now, and they're banished from Europe.'

'Yet they remain on the loose.'

'Many would consider the ends to justify the means, even if they wouldn't admit to it in public. Everything will lead to us apprehending them one day.'

'Said like a Chief Constable. You know, I researched Typhon in Greek mythology, but I'm still not sure exactly what he was.'

Hector pursed his lips. 'Sometimes it's hard to tell the difference between gods and monsters.'

Ashley focused on the tunes, laughter and happy faces, but

when they left the pub, she couldn't help thinking about their case.

'Even after everything I've seen over the years, it's hard to believe people can become so deviant.'

Hector's eyes were glassy, but his speech was fine.

'During this case, I had terrible dreams where I pictured a beautiful girl on a beach. Long blonde hair flowing. Evil personified leaning over her. Hands grasped around her neck.'

'Angels and demons.'

He nodded. 'Exactly that.'

'So why do you think we'll catch them? Their lackeys are probably skint, but after operating undetected for so long, the head honchos will have millions in crypto accounts and bundles of cash in Swiss banks.'

'Perhaps, but maybe all this started with that girl they killed in Prina. I don't think money is their primary motivation. Being rich merely facilitates their offending. Killing is an irresistible urge, perhaps a familial one, hard-wired into both their psyches.'

There were too many long words for Ashley's beer-sodden brain.

'What are you saying?'

'It will only be a matter of time before they're caught, because they will never stop.'

70

A week passed without a trace of the fugitives. Hector departed, and the case swiftly became a lower priority. It was strange to go into the conference room and find it reclaimed for its original purpose.

Ashley spoke to the mothers of Akari and Mercedes, the surviving victims. Akari remained at her secret location in the country but continued to struggle. She'd refused to even see her boyfriend, so there was no chance of another meeting with Ashley.

Mercedes agreed to chat to Ashley over the phone, but she simply said she was coping and would be fine. Ashley tried to encourage her to consider professional help, but Mercedes was adamant. Emma had heard Sebastian had written about Mercedes' experience and sold it on her behalf to the highest bidding newspaper.

Ashley bought a copy of *The Sunday Telegraph* when the piece came out. There was nothing in it the girl hadn't told the police, but the article was haunting. Sebastian had obviously got a professional photographer to take the photographs of

Mercedes. Her natural beauty had been brought out in abundance, but the main image of her staring directly at the camera took some forgetting. After reading the horrific details again, Ashley struggled to tear herself away from that melancholic stare.

Sebastian went to South America. Ashley had received two emails from him since he'd gone, which were friendly and funny, but not in any way romantic. Perhaps she'd misread him.

A week later, on a blustery Monday afternoon, Ashley got some welcome news. Ally had come out of his coma. A nurse rang her saying he wanted to meet her as soon as possible so she drove straight there after work.

The woman recognised her when she arrived, and let her in.

'Don't exhaust him. He has another important operation tomorrow morning on his spine. I told him to leave the conversation until afterwards, but he believes it's so serious that he really needs to have a chat with you first.'

The nurse looked as if she was about to say more but then just said to follow her.

Ashley stood at Ally's bedside, where he lay flat and unmoving. He didn't appear much improved, with the bruising still evident, although perhaps in lighter shades of purple and yellow. His eyes popped open.

'About time,' he whispered. 'I stopped the morphine earlier, so my head was clear. Feels as though I've been rogered by a bull elephant and not in an enjoyable way.'

He chuckled, then grimaced. Ashley pressed her hand against his.

'Take it easy. We can do this at a later date. Focus on getting better.'

'No, it has to be before the operation. They've scanned my body and most of the wounds will heal, although my bowels are damaged. I'll need to keep the stoma. My neck is troublesome, though. The bones are badly broken. It's a miracle my spinal cord didn't get severed. They inserted steel pins to support the area in the hope the bones knit together again. I got the feeling they weren't overconfident that would happen.'

'I'm so sorry. They can perform miracles nowadays, so fingers crossed.'

'I have a tiny bleed on my brain as well. They noticed it in the scan. There's a risk I might not survive the attempt to fix it, or, if I do, that my memory won't be the same. So, first, a question. What do you think happened at the prison?'

'There were cameras tracking you. Vladimir was seen entering your cell and leaving covered in blood. He's been transferred to Belmarsh and will be charged with attempted murder.'

'What about Maksim?'

Ashley had debated whether to tell Ally that Maksim escaped from the transport vehicle, or about their concerns about Maksim being Typhon. He might have heard bits from visitors or the staff.

She decided to see how their chat went.

'Maksim notified the officers that Vladimir had attacked you.'

Ally strained in the bed, then winced with pain. His right eye watered, and he bared his teeth in a grimace.

'Bastard.'

'Yes, I could place the noose over Vladimir's head myself.'

'No, that's why I have to explain now, in case I don't make it. It wasn't Vladimir who broke my neck that morning. It was Typhon.'

Ashley's breath caught in her throat.

'Let me write out a statement.'

She leaned closer as Ally closed his eyes and began to speak.

71

DS ALLY WILLIAMSON'S STATEMENT

Maksim had been staring out of the window as they unlocked everyone that morning. The look he gave me was unsettling. Even though he spoke softly, his words hit me hard.

'I have a short story for you, Ally. It's a boast about how I fooled the police. Yes, my organisation is finished, but you are going to help me escape from here.'

I recoiled in the bed. 'How the hell can I do that?'

'I've heard rumours about you. Selling information to the underworld? I judge people, especially those who sleep below me in the same room. You don't seem the type. Which leads me to believe you were planted here, just in case I ended up on this wing. Like that drunk they tried to put me in with.'

My mouth dried and my heartbeat began to gallop. I tried to play for time. 'What gave him away?'

'I don't know for sure, but I've only survived this long by playing the odds.'

It was obvious Maksim was a big shot. I wondered whether I should shout out, but I needed to gather information, so I listened to what he had to say.

'Many years ago, when I was a young man, I took a woman into the countryside and, during sex, I began to strangle her. It released something in me I didn't know existed. A sense of incredible power. It was a warm day, blue sky, in a charming place. Afterwards, I was at peace, but a dark urge grew inside me, even if I tried to resist it.'

Maksim crossed his arms and grinned. His muscles bulged as they flexed.

'I had to recreate that first occasion. To murder in nature.'

'Windmills and lighthouses?'

'Yes. Not for the sea, not for the cliffs, but the sky. I had to be among the clouds with the gods watching. I soon stopped with the sexual part. It felt... dirty, like it spoiled something pure. I wanted to find beauty, and innocence.'

Maksim's eyes closed in rapture at the recollection.

'Even with my superb English, it's hard to describe the strength it gives me. The sheer euphoria.'

I recoiled in absolute panic.

'You've been doing this for thirty years? You're Typhon?'

His smile widened. 'Trifon was my given name. My brother and I built a trafficking empire, which provided me with the women I craved, the network to move them, the funds to make it all happen. I became Typhon, and I enlisted my children – Sphinx, Cerberus, Gorgon... They carried out my bidding. You'd be surprised how easy it is to find kindred spirits.'

He released a mirthless chuckle.

'My brother had a different mother, but the same father. His urges were less pure, but equally lethal. He has worked in the shadows. Men such as Vladimir, Hydra, stepped up to be figureheads. Montenegrins, Romanians, Italians, Dutch, they came from all over. Cruel savages who would run a country for me. Men who erased evidence without thought or consideration.

Respect to you. They are all gone, captured, and those that aren't yet will be soon. It is over.'

I struggled to catch my breath. 'Why are you telling me this? What can I possibly do?'

Typhon stared out of the window. A wistful look in his eyes.

'I lived under the radar in Holland for years, but the walls were closing in. We had few trustworthy men left in Europe. Only England still had a functioning network. I had to come, but the Dutch authorities were everywhere. Boats were stopped, planes grounded. Vladimir suggested using Maksim. He'd heard of my doppelgänger at a Polish club. We recruited him as a courier. On his final run, I became him, and he... well, he was disposed of.'

I closed my eyes. 'This is a high security jail. You'll never get out.'

'You know, Norfolk is a unique location. I have never seen such dawns and dusks. The beaches, your rivers. My favourite spot here is a lighthouse on a cliff.' Typhon's eyes glinted in the morning light. He grinned. 'I sometimes sit there with Lydia among the heavens and take my rightful place.'

'I still don't understand. How am I going to be of any use?'

'You can assist me, Mr Police Officer,' Typhon said, with a voice bereft of emotion, 'by doing nothing.'

For a moment, I was confused, and then he said his final words.

'I'm sorry, Ally. You seem like a decent man, but the Hydra demands a sacrifice.'

Before I could react, Typhon twisted to the side, crouched, then nonchalantly smashed a huge fist into my ribs with a sickening crunch. The next blow nearly broke my jaw. I tried to cry out then, but only a gurgle escaped my throat. He landed more blows.

Typhon reached into the bunk, seized the collar of my T-shirt and drew me close. His thick forearm closed around my windpipe, while his other hand twisted a big hank of hair, yanking until he heard a crack. He casually tossed me back onto the bed like a broken toy.

Then he smiled. I was virtually unconscious when Vladimir arrived, but I still felt the blade go in.

72

Akari often found herself walking around the lake during the early hours. There was a wooden arbour where she liked to sit. Her mother had panicked the first few times she'd noticed her bed was empty and had searched everywhere. Once she'd discovered Akari's secret spot, she'd go and sit beside her and talk. They would gaze across the tranquil water together, but Akari suspected her mother's fatigue mirrored her own because the last few weeks they'd sat in silence.

Night after night, Akari was haunted by her mother's tormented cries. With her daughter unable to revisit what had been done to her, perhaps imagined horrors were worse for Victoria than the reality.

Akari presumed her mum thought she was gradually healing. It had been two months now, but she couldn't sleep either. Exhaustion filled her bones. It felt as if she were crumbling from within.

Her father visited every weekend. He needed to return to work during the week, but each Friday night, their family would eat in a silence broken only by banal snatches of conversation, punctuated by forced smiles and nods. The minutes crawled by, while the pressure built.

Tonight, the lake lay still as glass. A lone bird hung above her in the still air. Its plaintive cry as it swooped away pierced Akari's heart. The memory of seagulls circling as the car boot opened at the beach, knowing she would soon die.

Every time she thought of her fortune at having lived, she remembered her friend Camille, who'd hadn't been as lucky. Akari saw her now, suspended above the lake, then slowly descending, their eyes locking before Camille slipped beneath the surface.

A sad smile touched Akari's lips as she stood, discarding her slippers. Clad only in an old cotton nightgown, she walked towards the water's edge. The oppressive tension within her seemed to ease with each step. She tiptoed into the shallows, the gravelly bottom firm beneath her feet. Wading deeper, the water reached her chest. With a gentle push, she dived forward, then rolled onto her back, floating effortlessly. A stray stick brushed against her head, but she barely registered it. Here, in this liquid embrace, she was safe.

A crescent moon watched her as she drifted towards the misty centre of the lake. The water should have been cold but it felt like a warm blanket. If she stopped using her arms, stopped struggling, blew out her breath, the torture would be over. She would finally rest.

As she exhaled and liquid trickled into her ears, she heard a distant voice, like hearing a radio in another room. She tried to blot it out, but the voice grew more insistent. Akari flipped over and trod water, suddenly aware of the lake's unknown depths.

She'd lost her sense of direction, and, within the mist, had no idea where the closest bank was. The same shout filtered through the night. It was a male voice, and it was yelling her name.

A shiver ran through her. The once comforting water now felt menacing, sapping her strength. Her limbs grew heavy, her movements sluggish.

'Akari! Where are you? Answer me!'

Akari struck out at the imaginary hands pulling her down, her arms and legs flailing desperately. The lake was round. If she kept going, solid ground would appear at some point, but her energy was almost gone.

The mist parted, revealing a man in a tailored suit, standing ankle-deep in the water. He scanned the lake frantically, his eyes widening as they landed on Akari. Her father shed his jacket, lunged forward, and plunged into the lake.

Akari summoned her last reserves of strength to stay afloat as he swam towards her. Her legs kicked feebly, her arms dipped lower, her head slipping beneath the surface.

In that final moment, a single, heartbreaking thought consumed her: Why had she forgotten their love?

73

Vladimir walked onto the wing and waited for the officer to close the gate behind him. Two months in solitary had taken a toll. Forced solitude, meals alone, silence – it had chipped away at his sanity. Never had he been trapped with his own thoughts for so long. The prospect of decades of self-reflection was unsettling, yet he knew that, in time, drugs and their blissful oblivion would be within reach.

Vladimir had read in one of the old newspapers they'd given him that HMP Peterborough's escapee was still at large. That was positive. Typhon would look after him inside. He'd want to keep Vladimir sweet, so his secrets stayed that way.

The relative freedom for the men on standard wings surprised him, but trouble was a regular visitor. Vladimir understood hard and violent people. He was one himself, but some inmates concerned him. Young guys with no realistic prospect of ever getting out until they reached their dotage had little to lose. He'd already seen throwaway comments about something as innocuous as a football team, or a wrong look, incite bizarrely vicious overreactions. A furious, desperate, savage fight erupted every few days. Those brawls would be quelled in an equally aggressive way by officers who then dragged the bloodied men away.

Vladimir grabbed his laundry bag and wandered down the landing. He pushed open the laundry door with his foot. Empty. He stuffed his one spare set of prison clothes into the big washing machine, inserted his token into the slot, then heard the door creak shut behind him.

Vladimir had no time to twist or cry out. A rubber hose came over his head and his throat was squeezed shut; the person responsible so strong they could lean back and lift him off his feet. As his air ran out, he understood that Typhon did want his silence. He was guaranteeing it.

Vladimir didn't struggle. He accepted his fate because he deserved it. As much as any man ever had.

74

Four months had slipped by since Typhon's escape, and the pace at MIT had returned to a semblance of normality. Ashley's team assisted with one murder case in Norfolk and two in Suffolk, but none of them required enormous amounts of detecting. Barry had commented it was nice to get back to basics.

More importantly, no more youngsters had been snatched and no more bodies turned up near beauty spots. The newspapers featured the occasional update about trafficking, and Seb's article about Mercedes was read all over the world, but as the months passed, and without further fuel for the fire, interest waned. Vladimir's death in custody garnered significant attention with headlines about killing the Hydra, but the world swiftly moved on. Such was the nature of the news cycle.

Occasionally, someone would mention the investigation in the office, but even that was rare now. Nobody liked to be reminded of what they all considered a failure on their part, and no one wanted to dwell on the fact the Chernoff brothers were free. Even so, the team bore a silent weight.

The summer holiday season was over, and the dark nights of

October were drawing in. A slight depression sank over Ashley. It would be another winter alone. She had started to build up her social life and made The Fishing Boat her local, which helped. Arthur and Joan, who had returned to work, often went with her for rowdy Sunday afternoons listening to live music.

Bhavini, Emma and Ashley met regularly out of work, and they'd even visited Hector in London for a curry at Brick Lane. She'd been out with Michelle a couple of times, but kept them as girly outings, so Scott wasn't there. She wondered if Michelle had figured that out but was pleasant enough not to mention it.

The lighter workload allowed Ashley to resume her commitment to keeping fit. With the tide out that morning, she'd run along the beach to Sheringham and met Bhavini and baby Jagat for a coffee, although she was forced to walk home to begin with after eating a brick-sized chunk of American cheesecake.

Ashley had resumed a slow jog by the time she reached Cromer. She adjusted her speed as she went down the hill next to Warren Wood and noticed a familiar-looking dog waddling around. She recognised the animal and glanced around for who was walking him, but the only other person in view was an old man in a flat cap with a walking stick.

The Labrador bounded towards her as she ran past, so she stopped. He had a few more grey hairs and a few less pounds, but it was definitely Buster.

'Who are you with?' she asked as his brown eyes pleaded with her for more fuss.

'That you, Ashley?'

She glanced up at the hunched-over guy who was carefully making his way through the grass.

'Ally?'

He didn't reply until he'd reached her. 'Feels like about half of me, but yep.'

She hid her shock at how frail he appeared.

'It's good to see you out and about.'

'Yeah, been a month now.'

'I rang the hospital, but they said you'd been moved.'

'Yes, I went to a spinal unit.'

'If you'll excuse my bluntness, I read in the news when Vladimir died you were in a vegetative state and unlikely to recover after that operation.'

'Even courgettes need some fresh air.'

Ashley smiled. It seemed retired police kept their gallows humour. She squatted and gave Buster a kiss on the head so Ally couldn't see her face. Then she realised Beckett had deceived the world once more. Ally's recovery had been kept a secret. Beckett wanted Typhon to assume Ally never had a chance to repeat what Typhon told him.

Now MIT had the truth, they had a watertight case around the two brothers. They just needed to find them. The real Maksim Wozniak's body had been discovered by some kids messing around in a disused warehouse on the outskirts of Amsterdam. His wife, Jolanta, had moved to Nottingham and refused any police contact.

Ashley wasn't going to comment on the case, until she stood from petting Buster and caught sight of the lighthouse behind the wood.

'Do you think Typhon plans to return?'

Ally nodded grimly. 'You didn't see the look on his face when he spoke about this place. I'm sure of it, and remember it was you who recalled Lydia's bench on the clifftop. He'll come again. It'll be dawn or dusk, and I'll be waiting.'

Ashley stared at the stooped fellow in front of her. His once vibrant mullet now limp and thinning grey hair.

'Then what are you planning to do? Give him a few backhanders and cuff him?'

Ally chuckled. 'Call for reserves.'

Ashley shook her head, but she supposed Ally's plan made sense. It would give his life purpose. Hope could help someone in his predicament, even if it was a hope for revenge. There were also Hector's findings. He was convinced Typhon would be compelled to act again, and the pattern suggested it would be six months since his last kill. In about three weeks, it would be exactly that.

Ashley watched Ally gently throw a ball underarm to Buster. He winced.

'Does it hurt a lot?'

'If I'm honest, it's constant. The pain medication only works if I raise it to a level where I'm zombified. Out here, with the dog, I can cope. My daughter's gone back to the north. She rings once a week, but I have nobody else except my mum, and she's had a mini stroke. We hold each other up. I'll carry on until one of us falls.'

75

Two days later, Ashley received a pleasant surprise. A phone call from Sebastian at Schiphol Airport inviting her to dinner the following weekend. She pretended to check her diary, then confidently suggested the new bistro in town.

'Okay, I can do Saturday. How about I book a table at Gibson's for eight o'clock?'

'Is it good there?'

She thought of the subdued lighting and friendly service.

'Yes, it is.'

'Great. I'll pick you up.'

'No, that's fine. It's only a ten-minute stroll for me. Don't be late.'

'Never.'

At quarter to eight on Saturday, she left her house. There was a cool wind, but walking would warm her up. Oliver from next door was riding his bike in the street with a pal. His friend whistled, which made her laugh. Oliver choked when Ashley's perfume swamped them.

Ashley tapped her foot on the pavement.

'Shouldn't you kids be in bed?'

'I'm nearly thirteen, lady,' said Oliver. 'The night is young.'

Ashley laughed at the cheeky scamp. 'How's your mum doing?'

Oliver's lip pouted. 'A bit sad. She misses my nanna. Maybe she could go where you're going and have some cocktails.'

Ashley stared down at her red midi-dress and two-inch red heels. Flattering but not revealing, and hopefully elegant. She'd been tempted to pin her hair up, but didn't want to appear too keen, although she had worn gold drop-earrings. Maybe she was keen. She had to admit, even with her short black jacket, there was a hint of cocktail about it all. The thick M&S paper carrier bag in her hand ruined the look a little.

'Are you heading to a ball or something?'

'I'm hoping to have a ball.'

Oliver leaned back on his seat with a confused expression on his face. She chuckled.

'Get inside, you two, before you catch your death.'

Ashley was about fifty metres from the house when she had to take her trainers from the bag. It would have been midnight before she arrived otherwise.

She was five minutes early, but her date had arrived. Gibson's was a small family-run business that ran as a café during the day and restaurant at night. The experienced chef used the best Norfolk produce to create fresh tasty dishes whilst staying true to a traditional bistro.

Sebastian had a dark-blue suit and white shirt on, but no tie. He was making the young waitress at the bar blush. His face lit up when Ashley opened the door.

'Here she is,' he said.

Ashley smiled as he kissed her on the cheek.

The young woman showed them to a corner table. Every seat

was taken in the restaurant. Hushed chatter and the clink of cutlery and crockery filled the air. She passed them the menus.

'Can I get you any drinks, or would you like a few minutes?'

'Share a bottle of red?' asked Sebastian.

'Took the words right out of my mouth.'

He scanned the wine list. 'Is the house red good?'

'Of course.'

He nodded, and the waitress left them to choose their food.

Ashley raised an eyebrow. 'House red, eh?'

'Us writers do their jobs for love, not money.'

'You should have said times were hard. I'd have suggested Spicy Bob's Kebab Shack.'

Sebastian pulled a face. 'You can tell a lot about a place by the quality of its house wines.'

'I'm only pulling your leg.'

'I know. Is your bag full of stolen cash from the evidence room to pay for tonight?'

Ashley took her trainers off and slipped on her heels. She gave him a quick show of ankle, then kicked the M&S bag under the table. She had to hunt in her handbag for her glasses so she could read the menu.

'What can I say? I'm a practical girl.'

They perused the choices for a moment and Ashley sensed him staring at her.

'You look stunning, but you do remind me of someone.'

Ashley let his eyes run over her face. 'Is it Velma from *Scooby-Doo*?'

Sebastian clicked his fingers. 'That's it.'

'Yes, I know. People often shout "where's Scooby?" as I walk by in the street.'

'It's a compliment. She's hot.'

'It's funny how a strange subsection of the male population

gets off on animated hotties. There's a popular list of the best cartoon shags. Sadly, I'm well down it, after Jessica Rabbit and Lola Bunny, and even Betty Rubble.'

'You're top of my list.'

'Hmm, should I focus on that, or the fact you have one?'

Sebastian laughed his head off. 'What do you recommend here?'

'I had smoked haddock and leek risotto last time, but that's because I was with Hector and I didn't dare order the calves liver. He'd suggest the beetroot Wellington.'

He curled his lip. 'I'm struggling to picture that.'

Ashley giggled. 'They don't just whack one in the top of a plastic boot.'

'Not tempting. Anything else?'

'A friend came and said the Gressingham duck was amazing. That's what I'm having.'

'Done.'

The waitress poured the wine and took their order. Sebastian raised his glass.

'It's nice to go out with a lady with an appetite. My last girl-friend liked to push salad around her plate.'

She chinked his glass with hers.

'I prefer to push my salad off my plate.'

76

The verbal jousting continued throughout dinner, punctuated by laughter and the occasional stolen bite of Eton mess, after Ashley had resisted dessert.

As their coffees arrived, the conversation inevitably turned to the Typhon investigation. Sebastian's demeanour shifted, the playful banter replaced by a sombre expression.

'I've been in contact with Mercedes,' he said, running a hand through his now longer hair.

Ashley tipped her head to one side. 'How is she?'

'Strong,' he replied, pausing to collect his thoughts. 'Perhaps too strong. Although money won't be a problem.'

'No?'

'I got a phone call from Storm Model Management. They loved the article I wrote. The world's her oyster.'

'I'm pleased for her. Akari's father called me. She's much better. I asked to speak to her, but she's gone to Australia with her boyfriend.'

'Someone else moving country to escape you.'

'Hilarious.'

'You know, Mercedes asked me exactly what the details were, but I wasn't involved in the end of the case. Were the women being sacrificed to some heathen god or killed for fun?'

Ashley blew out a breath. She didn't particularly want to revisit the gruesome details.

'Some of this is conjecture, but our theory is that a man killed a girl and enjoyed it. His brother was of the same ilk. They went on to set up a trafficking network all across Eastern and Central Europe, which then filtered towards the west. They got away with it for decades.'

'Bloody hell.'

'Yes. The authorities finally began to close in on them, and Norfolk was their last outpost. Trifon, who for some time had become Typhon, developed a sickness for killing females with his own hands, but they needed to be pure. Virgins. His brother wasn't so selective. Originally, we believe they took the best of the crop from the girls they fooled into thinking they were heading for a better life. Near the end, as the organisation fell apart, they simply grabbed the women off the streets.'

Ashley raised her coffee cup to hide the grimace that had formed on her face.

'We thought they were only interested in blondes, but it seemed any pretty girl would do. If they were virgins, Typhon had them. If they were not, Ratimir sold them. They were murdered if they were surplus to requirements or when their use was over.'

Sebastian swallowed and was lost for words for a moment.

'And these guys are still on the loose?'

'They are.'

One of the owners appeared at their table.

'Cheers for coming, Ashley. Anything else for you?'

'No, thanks, Emilie. Pass the message on to Matt it was wonderful. Just the bill, please.'

'I'll tell him it was okay, or he'll be after a raise.'

Ashley laughed as Emilie left to give her husband the compliment. The waitress returned and Sebastian whipped his wallet out and paid before Ashley could comment.

When they stepped outside, they both stood awkwardly.

'Sorry,' said Sebastian. 'Note for next time. If you plan to mention serial killers, do it at the start of the meal. Come on, I'll give you a lift home.'

'It's ten minutes, remember? I want to walk. Clear my head a bit.'

Sebastian let out a huff. 'Can I escort you back?'

'I'll be fine, Seb. I've had a great evening. Let's do it again.'

'Is that a promise?'

Ashley resisted a playful retort and instead leaned up to kiss him softly on the cheek.

'It is.'

77

A strange vibrating sound awoke Ashley. She realised the noise was her phone on the bedside cabinet, which she'd turned to silent. She picked it up. The first thing she saw was the time: 5 a.m. The second that Ally was the caller.

'This better be good,' she said without thinking.

'Shush and listen. Ashley, he's here.'

'Who is he, and where is that?' she asked, instantly alert.

'I'm almost certain Typhon is near the lighthouse at the edge of the golf course.'

'What makes you think that?'

'Because I'm at the field near to the swings. I saw torchlight dancing along the top path. Someone's there, with a smaller person.'

'It's unlikely to be him.'

'Ashley, listen. We might not have much time. When I climbed out of bed before dawn, I turned on the early news, as I always do. There are reports of a girl missing in Thursford. She was supposed to have left a friend's house at eleven last night, but never made it home.'

Ashley was now fully awake. The local police would have connected the dots to the Typhon case. There was probably a sizeable presence at Thursford, but that was twenty-five minutes away. Even with lights and sirens, a driver couldn't push too hard on those winding country roads.

'It still doesn't mean it's definitely Typhon up there.'

'In the past, he didn't kill the victim until a few days later, but that was probably because other people were taking the women and delivering them for him. The brothers are on their own. Listen, I'm sure it's him. I walked the dog by a white Škoda Octavia estate car at the bottom of the steps leading to Happy Valley. I reckon Ratimir was in the driver's seat. He even had his sunglasses on.'

'Registration?' Ashley asked, reached for pen and paper.

'It's the only vehicle there!'

'Have you rung it in?'

'No, I called you. I'm going up to check. There won't be any help close enough. He might do what he planned to before Uniform get here.'

'No, Ally. You're in no fit state to tackle him on your own.'

Silence lingered for a few seconds.

'I need to try.'

Ashley's mind was galloping. What type of person would be wearing sunglasses at this time of day? She leapt out of bed. 'Okay, okay. I'll call it in. They'll be about twenty minutes. No sirens.' She put Ally on speaker, then pulled on her jogging kit.

'Ashley?'

'Yes.'

'Are you coming?'

'Of course I am.'

'Good. Bring something.'

Ashley grabbed her mobile and clattered downstairs. She

took hold of the baton she kept behind the sofa at the front door. 'Wait for me!'

'Turn the ringer off on your phone. Beware of the vibrate, too. It might be quiet on the clifftop. Text me when you're close.'

'I will do.' She stopped herself from cutting the call. 'Ally, you must wait for me.'

The line was already dead.

78

Ashley was tempted to charge out of the house, but she needed to focus. First, she had to speak to Control.

'Good morning, DI Knight. Go ahead.'

'Regarding the missing girl in Thursford. We believe she's in Cromer with the ringleaders of the Typhon trafficking organisation. I have a location.'

Control was usually cool as ice when dealing with incidents, but there was a noticeable pause.

'Understood. What's the address?'

'The top of the cliffs at Happy Valley next to the golf course and opposite the lighthouse. There's a man there with the girl, and the other brother is waiting in a white Škoda Octavia estate on Overstrand Road, just after Cromer Country Club.'

Ashley waited for a reply for five seconds.

Control responded, 'Closest unit is sixteen miles out. Multiple vehicles dispatched, ETA twenty minutes.'

'Suspects are liable to be armed and dangerous. Approach without lights and sirens. There are numerous exits. DS Ally Williamson, retired, may be at the scene. I'm heading there now.

My mobile will be on but silent. Ask the nearest officer to contact me when they reach the outskirts of Cromer.'

'Understood. Who else should I send or call?'

Ashley would ring the other most important person, but she didn't hesitate in her reply.

'Send everyone.'

79

Ally took a deep breath and tried to gather his strength. Torchlight flickered again near the cliff edge. The beam vanished, then the lighthouse's sweeping light briefly illuminated two figures on the path before plunging them back into darkness. The field was a sea of damp, overgrown grass, and the short walk had left Ally winded. But Buster, his mother's loyal old Labrador, was a steady presence at his side. Ally clipped the lead onto Buster's collar.

'Go on, boy,' he whispered.

Buster knew the way. They'd been doing the same route for months. Age had slowed Buster, but he was still a strong dog. Ally lurched after him using the hound almost like a husky. The path was steep and ran along a gully between where Lydia's bench sat and where the lighthouse shone. With Buster's help, by the time he'd reached the top, he wasn't as exhausted as he'd feared. He rolled his shoulders and flexed his fingers. Adrenaline flowed through him.

Thick gorse had encroached on either side of the track. It showered his jeans with cold moisture as he brushed through.

Buster's nose twitched, his nostrils flaring as he tugged Ally forward. Their laboured breaths were like ragged claws, scraping against their throats. Ally briefly worried the sound might alert Typhon, if he was there, but the crashing waves and a screeching seabird masked their approach.

When they were almost at the spot, Ally unclipped the lead, and Buster bounded ahead. On the bench, backs towards them, sat a broad bald man in a grey coat and a blonde woman in a blue parka. The dog waddled past, tail spinning, as Labradors were wont to do, before he twisted around and made his way towards them.

The man glanced at Buster sniffing at his legs, then looked over his shoulder at Ally. His face was initially blank, then a flicker of recognition, followed by confusion.

'You?'

'Yes, Maksim. Or should I say Typhon?'

A thin smile touched Typhon's clean-shaven face before he turned away again, clearly calculating his next move. But the sound of Ally cocking his revolver made him tilt his head back. 'The newspapers said you were a vegetable, Ally.'

'That's what you were led to believe. Now, stay where you are, or I *will* shoot.'

80

Just before reaching Overstrand Road, Ashley discreetly pressed the baton against her thigh, concealing it in case the Škoda had moved. At the kerb edge, she paused. The sunglasses guy, Ratimir, would be parked around the next bend. There was no time to check his position, and she couldn't risk being seen.

As she resumed running in the opposite direction, Ashley pulled out her phone and called Barry.

'Pick up, pick up,' she muttered under her breath.

He answered, his voice gruff. 'What the hell do you want?'

Ashley explained breathlessly, the words tumbling out, as she sprinted along Old Coach Road.

Credit where it was due, Barry understood immediately. 'What's the plan?'

'Ratimir is parked on Overstrand Road. The cavalry are coming from Thursford, so they'll enter Cromer from the south and east and head through town. You need to make sure he doesn't escape the other way through Overstrand.'

'Right. Shall I block the street with some bad language?'

'Use your fucking car.'

'My new car?'

Ashley was about to swear again, but he had gone. She could rely on Barry. He would know what he had to do, so she focused her attention on the task at hand. She deliberately bypassed The Warren and instead took Cliff Lane. At the seafront, she hurried along the top path, past Warren Wood towards Happy Valley and the lighthouse.

Over the sea, the first hint of sunrise edged into the sky with an ominous orange glow. She thought of Typhon, gritted her teeth, moved the baton to her right hand, and picked up the pace.

In the dim light, she detected movement ahead, followed by a bloodcurdling scream.

81

As his exertions took their toll, Ally couldn't prevent himself from wheezing.

Typhon smiled.

'You sound tired, my friend.'

Ally ignored him. He shifted his focus to the blue-coated blonde, who still hadn't turned around.

'Are you Josie? The girl from Thursford?'

She didn't move. A muffled sob was her only reply. He suspected Typhon had his hand on her leg or arm.

'Can you stand for me, please?'

Josie wobbled but stayed seated. A brief glance over her shoulder revealed her eyes, which were as wide as saucers. She looked back.

'Let her go, Typhon,' snarled Ally.

Slowly, Josie rose from the bench.

'Walk forwards a few paces, please.'

Ally was fearful she would fall.

'Make your way down the slope in front of you. Careful now, it's slippery. Stick to the right through the ferns, then stay right, and jog along the path. Keep going. You'll see the pier. It will lead you into town. Don't stop running until you find one of the fishermen and ask them for help. Now go.'

She peeked across at Typhon, as if for permission.

'Go!' roared Ally.

Josie stumbled and tripped down the track, but kept her feet. He listened to her slipping, sliding, gasping. Then a high-pitched shriek tore through the night. Had someone caught her? She made the sound again. The howl of the petrified. She screamed again, a long, terrified wail. The screams continued, growing fainter as if receding into the twilight.

Typhon twisted around to glance at Ally. The killer appeared completely different with no hair. Perhaps it was the fading moonlight, but even his eyes looked a strange yellow-green instead of blue.

He rested his arm on the back of the bench. 'What now, Sergeant?'

'I said stay still. Do not give me an excuse to squeeze the trigger.'

'UK police don't shoot unarmed men. You're not a killer.'

'You're right on one count, but I've retired.'

Typhon held eye contact. 'I remember telling you why I love it here.'

'Yes, that was a big mistake.'

'The bright lighthouse beam, around and around, the incredible pier, the booming waves, the sea breeze, the salty air, and the sky. Always the endless sky. Can't you feel the power here?'

'You're more twisted than you look. You said you felt close to the heavens. To the gods. Do you really think you can converse with them?'

'Oh, no, Ally. You fail to understand. When I am here, I don't believe I can talk to them.' He gave him a wide grin. 'I know I *am* one.'

Ally's jaw dropped open just as Typhon launched himself from the bench, a flicker of steel in his hand. But Ally was ready. He fired. A deafening roar echoed through the valley, the recoil jolting his weakened arm. He knew he'd missed, the bullet flying high. Baring his teeth, Ally aimed for Typhon's stomach. He tried to tense his feeble core muscles, then pulled the trigger again.

The end of Typhon's weapon spewed fire at the same time. Multiple shots rendered the air. Blasts ricocheted in the valley.

Gulls cried and fled. The wind hesitated, and the sea paused.

Silence reigned.

82

A figure in a blue jacket came hurtling down the path, and before Ashley could react, the woman was upon her, struggling and screaming in her face. The girl shrieked again, so loud and piercing that Ashley instinctively recoiled, then she was gone, her howls fading as she fled along the cliff path.

Ashley ran the other way for another hundred metres before stopping to seek cover amongst the gorse. She had the beginnings of a stitch, but she was almost there. Lydia's bench was just above, overlooking the spot where Ashley now crouched. She would have to break cover, make a dash for the gully, and approach the bench from behind.

The beam from the lighthouse lit up the valley with each turn. She cursed as she lost her night vision, but it didn't matter. The sun was rising, and it was no longer dark.

Extending her baton, Ashley prepared to rush forward as the strobe light circled again, then a single bang filled the air. Then gunfire erupted. There were two distinct sounds. Two different weapons. She froze. Then there was a cacophony of what sounded like explosions as the valley magnified the noise.

She waited for more shots, but now there was only a deathly still.

Throwing caution to the wind, she kept to the left and made her way along the steep track directly to where she'd seen the flashes of muzzle fire, knowing if she met an armed Typhon making his escape, her life would be over.

Near the summit, she heard laboured breathing, then a gurgling sound. Gripping her baton, she crept forward. A man in a grey jacket lay on his side, a clump of grass preventing him from rolling further down the slope. His eyes met hers.

'Help me,' he whispered.

Ashley stared at his neck, which he clasped with both hands. Blood oozed between his fingers. She jogged past him to the clifftop. Ally was sitting on the bench. He offered a weak smile, then tilted sideways.

Ashley rushed over and sat beside him. She wrapped an arm around his shoulders to keep him upright.

'Are you okay?'

'Is he dead?'

'Not quite, but it won't be long.'

'That's...' he paused, then sighed '...justice.'

'Are you just exhausted? You haven't been hit, have you?'

Ally closed his eyes. In the gloom, Ashley hadn't seen the damp hole in his coat, but the lighthouse highlighted the growing red stain. She undid his buttons with numb fingers, then lifted one side of the material. She gasped. A bullet had entered his body below the solar plexus.

'Oh, Ally.'

Ashley remembered her mobile. She yanked it out of her pocket and saw Control had called. Ally needed an ambulance, although she suspected one would be on the way.

With a grunt, Ally knocked the phone out of her hand.

'No,' he gasped. 'No, I don't want that.' He tried to swallow. Blood trickled from the side of his mouth. He groaned, then tried to smile through red teeth. 'This is fine.'

'No, Ally,' she insisted. 'I'll stop the bleeding. Hang on.'

Ally shook his head. 'Just hold my hand.'

Ashley grasped his fingers, his response surprisingly strong. His head fell back against the bench, the roaring waves seeming to grow louder as the sun climbed higher. Dawn had broken. A new day.

Ashley pulled Ally towards her. His head lolled onto her shoulder. She clenched her teeth to stop herself from sobbing as Buster emerged from the bushes and lay at Ally's feet, whimpering softly.

The lighthouse beam seemed to linger on Ally's peaceful face as the tension left his body.

His grip weakened, his eyes fluttered closed, and he quietly slipped away.

83

Barry cursed as he searched for his keys, finally finding them under his nan's crossword puzzle book on the kitchen table. He threw on a pair of trainers and got in his car wearing the clothes he'd had on. A T-shirt and boxer shorts. He pressed the ignition, spun his Honda Civic off the drive, and raced out of the cul-de-sac.

Sidestrand was only a few miles from Cromer. He barrelled through the quiet village of Overstrand, accelerated up the hill, then dropped to the speed limit. Royal Cromer Golf Club lay ahead. Then it was only a couple of hundred metres to where Ashley said the Škoda was waiting.

Barry glanced at the pristine interior of his beloved, but small, motor. He'd been on various driving courses, so he knew what he was doing, but it was different from when you were driving a marked, high-powered BMW X5. Since he wasn't in uniform, Barry wondered if what he was about to do was even legal. He pushed the thought aside.

By the time he drove past the golf course, he was doing twenty-nine miles an hour. The Škoda was parked on the right where he expected it to be; in between two streetlights at the bottom of the steps to Happy Valley. Even though he couldn't see the exhaust yet, the wisps of steam rising in the cool air confirmed the engine was running.

Barry licked his lips. At fifty metres, he made out the driver, a figure in sunglasses. Barry's phone, resting on the seat beside him, remained silent. He signalled left, as if turning into one of the bungalows across the street. At just under ten miles an hour, Barry approached the Škoda. He allowed himself a grim smile on realising it was an older model. The driver steadfastly looked away from him.

'Bollocks,' said Barry. Instead of pulling into a drive, he yanked the steering wheel hard to the right. His tyres screeched in complaint. The front of his vehicle crunched straight into the driver's door of the estate car, in the hope of making it unopenable. At that speed, his airbag wouldn't activate, but Ratimir's side one did.

Barry quickly unbuckled his seat belt and scrambled out through his passenger door. He edged around his car to approach the Škoda. Raising his baton, he slid onto his bonnet and smashed the driver's window, then punched the startled Ratimir in the face, shattering his sunglasses.

Fearing a gun, Barry unleashed a flurry of blows, his fist a piston, stopping only after the tenth strike when his hand began to throb.

84

It had been a long, gruelling day by the time Ashley finally got in her car to leave OCC. She could barely raise her feet to drive.

It had been roughly a minute after Ally's passing that she had called Control. Within minutes, two officers had arrived, rushing past Typhon's dead body on their way up the hill.

Upon regaining consciousness, Ratimir had promptly been arrested, placed in a van, and transported to OCC. Ashley had washed her hands in one of the ambulances, then insisted on walking Buster home.

As expected, Ratimir sat in his cell and refused to cooperate. They would charge him the following morning with murder and a whole raft of other offences. He would die in prison. Barry remained upset about his car, despite Kettle telling him repairs would be covered.

Beckett had returned, looking a man much relieved and thankful for the efforts of MIT. Ashley had spent most of her time making and double-checking statements about what had happened. She was almost delirious with tiredness but strangely wired when she got home at 9 p.m.

She'd been in only a few minutes when there was a knock at her door. It opened to reveal Sebastian.

'Evening.'

'That was good timing, or have you been lurking in the street?'

He held his wrists together.

'Guilty, ma'am. Perhaps the punishment could be another attempt at a meal. Maybe one with a more upbeat ending.'

'It's a bit late for dinner bookings.'

He gave her an impish grin. 'I didn't mean tonight.'

She smiled back. 'You are not boyfriend material.'

'I know, but that's the life we lead. People in general aren't on the lookout for a partner who sometimes doesn't come home, works weekends, is prone to snappiness from stress, and lives an existence of highs and lows. Not to mention the discussions over breakfast where minds are elsewhere, and conversations are forgotten.'

'I'm still hopeful of finding someone like that out there.'

'That special guy could take a while to come along.'

'So what?'

'You might get run over tomorrow.'

'I might run you over tonight.'

Sebastian laughed. 'Perhaps all we get are stolen moments.'

'Like these?'

'Like these.'

She stepped back to let him in the house, then reached up and kissed him. This time it was softly on the lips. He rested his fingers on her hips.

'You know what,' he whispered. 'I hoped this would happen when I first shook your hand.'

Ashley didn't say anything, but so had she.

* * *

MORE FROM ROSS GREENWOOD

Another book from Ross Greenwood, *The Village Killer*, is available to order now here:

https://mybook.to/VillageKillerBackAd

ACKNOWLEDGEMENTS

When I wrote my first book, it seemed there were only a few people involved, which probably explains the hundreds of typos, which most of you were too kind to point out. This is somehow the seventeenth and the people who assist in numerous ways nowadays is vast. I was Boldwood's twenty-first author, and they now have over two-hundred. Their team has grown rapidly, but they still manage to maintain a collaborative approach, so a big thank you to them.

I need to mention my beta readers, many of whom have been with me from the start. Jane Howarth, Richard Burke, Kath Middleton, Diane Saxon and Trish Halstead give me great feedback when the novels are in their early drafts. Paul Lautman's ability to untangle my complicated plots is second to none, and Alex Williams' skills with the written word mean that when the company's editors finally get eyes on my work, their job is usually a polishing one.

I hope you'll be pleased to hear I'm contracted to twenty books. I'm in the enviable position of having written the next in the Norfolk series already. You won't have to wait long for *Death at Fakenham Races*, which should be up for pre-order or sale now. I've got one more of those to write, but there will also be another DI Barton first.

I've tried to write three books this year which, if I'm honest, has beaten me. Trying to begin a Barton thriller whilst editing two Norfolk novels, at various stages in the process, has sent my head spinning at times. A few family health scares along the way has also taught me not to spend too much time hunched over my keyboard.

Somehow, with your help, I've sold over six-hundred thousand copies now. A million seems a sensible but testing target. Hopefully you'll be along for the challenge.

As you can imagine with two young children still at school, most of the burden has fallen on my wife. Thank you, Amanda, you deserve that heated throw I bought you on Black Friday. As for the kids, I'm not sure they noticed.

Best wishes, Ross.

ABOUT THE AUTHOR

Ross Greenwood is the author of crime thrillers. Before becoming a full-time writer he was most recently a prison officer and so worked everyday with murderers, rapists and thieves for four years. He lives in Peterborough.

Sign up to Ross Greenwood's mailing list for news, competitions and updates on future books.

Follow Ross on social media:

 instagram.com/rossg555

 x.com/greenwoodross

 facebook.com/RossGreenwoodAuthor

 bookbub.com/authors/ross-greenwood

ALSO BY ROSS GREENWOOD

The DI Barton Series

The Snow Killer

The Soul Killer

The Ice Killer

The Cold Killer

The Fire Killer

The Santa Killer

The Village Killer

DS Knight Series

Death on Cromer Beach

Dear at Paradise Park

Death in Bacton Wood

Death at Horsey Mere

Standalones

Prisoner

Jail Break

Survivor

Lifer

Chancer

Hunter

THE

Murder

LIST

THE MURDER LIST IS A NEWSLETTER DEDICATED TO ALL THINGS CRIME AND THRILLER FICTION!

SIGN UP TO MAKE SURE YOU'RE ON OUR HIT LIST FOR GRIPPING PAGE-TURNERS AND HEARTSTOPPING READS.

SIGN UP TO OUR NEWSLETTER

BIT.LY/THEMURDERLISTNEWS

Printed in Great Britain
by Amazon